DEADLY COUNTDOWN

Yakunin swung Govskaya around and slapped his face hard. "Get hold of yourself!" the captain shouted. "We are not here to start World War Three!"

Balling his fingers into a fist, Govskaya swung his hand around in an arc and caught Yakunin on the side of the head, knocking him back against the periscope pedestal. The captain's head struck the flange bolts with a loud, sickening thud and he fell to the floor unconscious. Felix Stelest leapt up from his chair and flung himself at the political officer. Swinging wildly, the *zampolit* knocked Stelest aside and yanked a service pistol from the holster nestled in his armpit. He aimed the weapon at the stunned weapons officer. "Fire," he ordered, "or I will kill you!"

"We are not correctly lined up with the American sub," the weapons officer protested. "The torpedo would . . ."

"Do it!" Govskaya screamed, ramming the gun into the side of the officer's head.

He glanced at his unconscious captain, then at the dazed *michman*. Swallowing hard, the officer pressed the firing button.

TORPEDO ALLEY

DEL DOW DELL

PINNACLE BOOKS
WINDSOR PUBLISHING CORP.

PINNACLE BOOKS

are published by

Windsor Publishing Corp.
475 Park Avenue South
New York, NY 10016

First printing: October, 1988

Printed in the United States of America

To Helen
An Eternal Companion

CHAPTER ONE

August 27—5:05 p.m.

Dark, foreboding clouds gathered over Diamond Head and blew north toward Honolulu. Their shadow crossed over the turquoise waters at Waikiki beach, across the narrow white strip of sand, then inland over the Kalahaua highway, threatening the golfers along the Ala Wai course. Tourists shopping at the Ala Moana Mall, the largest center in the Hawaiian Islands, ducked for cover, but island natives, knowing they still had time before the daily downpour, sauntered between the numerous hotels and office buildings that made up the concrete jungle inland from the famed beach.

Traffic was beginning to pick up along the roads that fed the two main east-to-west freeways, as the late afternoon sun moved west across the Pacific. In the shadow of the passing clouds, a white, bob-tail truck with the words *Military Restaurant Supply* stenciled on the side, pulled out from Fort De Russy and onto the main road, working its way across the lanes toward the Ala Moana Freeway ramp.

Inside, two men wearing light gray uniforms, chatted amiably as they sped north, trying to beat the impending deluge.

"I don't think we'll get out of Kapalama before the rains hit," said the tall, skinny driver with the hawk-like nose, as he glanced in the large sideview mirror. "It's already over Waikiki."

His companion, a short, chubby redhead with freckles sprinkled liberally across his cherubic face, frowned. "Better at Kapalama than up in the hills at Fort Shafter," he replied. "The last time it took us three hours to get through the pass. Boy, was Anne mad when I got home."

The tall man chuckled good-naturedly. "Face it, Manny. You're henpecked."

"Anne and the kids were expecting me, Jack," Manny said defensively. "It was Peggy Sue's birthday party."

"You're still Casper Milquetoast in your own home!" The driver, Jack, roared with laughter as his partner stared at the floor, his pudgy cheeks flushing a deep crimson. Neither man noticed the dark Lincoln towncar pulling out suddenly from the side of the road.

The Lincoln darted quickly in front of the truck. Looking up, Jack gasped, jerking the wheel hard over and slamming on the brakes simultaneously. As the truck skidded across the shoulder, Manny was thrown heavily into the dashboard. The bob-tail bounced over the curb and into a reed-covered sand bank several yards off the highway.

Thunder rocked the skies as the long-awaited cloudburst hit. The Lincoln pulled up beside the disabled truck. A police car, its roof light flashing, pulled off the road directly behind the Lincoln. A yellow-slickered officer leapt out of the car and immediately started to put out flares.

Traffic along the highway was now slowing to a crawl as the road became slick and treacherous.

Several passing motorists stared out of their windows to get a better look at the commotion at the side of the road, but the heavy rain effectively blocked out any good view.

In the cab, Jack dazedly lifted his head off the wheel. Manny lay moaning on the floor under the dash.

"Manny?" Jack asked, his voice tight with concern. "You all right, Manny?"

"I think so," Manny replied, shaking his head clear. He moved slightly, and immediately regretted it. "My shoulder!" he gasped.

Suddenly the door on the driver's side was flung open. Jack turned to see a man in a dark suit and tie holding a machine pistol just inches from his face.

"Out!" the man ordered.

Before Jack could protest, the black-suited man grabbed him by the shoulder and yanked him from the cab. He could see the policeman setting out flares just a few yards away.

"Hey!" Jack yelled, waving at the officer frantically. "Hey!"

The policeman turned in his direction and stared impassively. After several seconds he nodded grimly and returned to his work.

"You are wasting your breath," Jack's captor whispered in his ear.

The passenger-side door of the truck flew open. A second armed man grabbed a handful of Manny's shirt and dragged him roughly out into the rain. Manny screamed in agony as he rolled onto the wet sand, clutching at his right shoulder.

"He's hurt!" Jack yelled. "Can't you see that?"

A third man, considerably shorter and stockier than the first two, stepped from the Lincoln and walked up to Jack. Without a word, he slapped the protesting driver hard across the face. "You speak when you are spoken to," the man growled. His voice was heavily accented.

Anger was quickly replaced by fear as Jack noticed the stocky man pull a gun from inside his suit coat. Jamming the weapon into the truck driver's face, the man spoke to one of the other hijackers. "Get them in the back," he ordered.

"Yes, Colonel," the other replied obediently.

"Colonel?" Jack looked up in surprise. "We deliver food to the bases, not weapons."

The man who had been called "Colonel" brought his free arm back and slapped Jack violently once again, knocking him to the ground. One of the others grabbed Jack's arm, dragged him to the rear of the truck and tossed him roughly into the back. Quaking with fear, Jack watched helplessly as Manny received similar treatment, the torrential rain drowning out the wounded man's agonized shrieks. The hijackers unceremoniously dumped Manny beside his terrified partner.

The short, stocky man with the narrow eyes walked slowly over to the Lincoln. The driver lowered the power window and stuck his head out. "Everything is under control?" the driver asked.

The stocky man nodded. The driver handed a dark briefcase out the open window which the colonel accepted without a word.

"We will be meeting you at the airport?" the driver asked. The colonel nodded, placing the briefcase at his feet as he removed a silencer from the inside of his coat and screwed it onto the barrel of his gun. He picked up the briefcase and glared at the driver. "Have the plane fueled and warmed up for when we arrive."

"*Da*, Comrade Colonel. It will be ready."

The colonel nodded, lowering his military-issue *Tokarev* to his side. The Lincoln moved off, rounding a sand dune and bouncing back onto the highway just beyond the police car. The colonel's face tightened as he walked toward the back of the truck.

Manny and Jack were huddled on the floor in the rear of the truck, sandwiched between boxes of foodstuffs stacked along the walls. They looked up as the stocky man climbed into the bob-tail and made his way back along the narrow, central path between the boxes.

"Get out of your uniforms!" he snapped, setting the briefcase on the floor and waving his gun at the captives. "Now!"

Both Jack and Manny unzipped the uniforms and stripped down to their shorts. They shivered in the sudden change of temperature. "It's cold," Jack complained.

"Not where you're going," the colonel said. He raised the gun and shot Jack directly between the eyes. Before he had a chance to react, a second shot caught Manny in the chest, throwing him back against the wall, blood spurting like a geyser from the wound. He slid slowly down the wall, falling dead on top of his dead partner.

The two men in black suits looked at the lifeless truckers without emotion.

"Get into those uniforms!" the colonel ordered.

"*Da*, Comrade Colonel," the taller man answered.

The hijackers quickly climbed into the gray uniforms as the colonel pulled boxes over on the two bodies, effectively burying them. "It is past five," he said. "It is time we were on the road."

"We'll be at Kapalama by six, Colonel."

"See that we are!"

The two hijackers, now dressed in the gray uniforms, jumped out of the truck and hurried around to the cab. "Did you see that?" the first asked his companion. "Turbin killed them both and didn't even bat an eye."

The other glanced nervously over his shoulder. "He's an officer. They're all like that. But I think Turbin's the worst!"

In moments the truck engine cranked into life, and the vehicle bounced over the sand and back onto the road. Blending with the slow-moving traffic, it began heading north. Standing on the side, the bogus policeman watched impassively.

The Kapalama Military Reservation, nestled unobtrusively across from Sand Island between the Keehi Lagoon, the north harbor basin, and the Nimitz Freeway, is a base seemingly without distinction. Overshadowed by the more visible and famous Pearl Harbor, Hickam Air Force Base, Pacific Command and ComSubPac headquarters, little Kapalama is often lost to the casual tourist.

Yet deep within the bowels of its top secret underground levels, Kapalama is the Pacific headquarters of WWMCCS—World Wide Military Command and Control System—and provides security information to National Command Authorities. Connected by direct cable to the Cobra Dane surveillance network at Shemya Air Force Base in the Aleutians, and through them to Cobra Judy aboard the U.S.S. *Observation Island*, which roams the Pacific, Kapalama is the seat of intelligence gathering across tens of thousands of square miles.

Here, in subterranean levels, protected from high-impact nuclear strike, the men and women of the

5540th Electronic Security Group labor around the clock to decipher coded Soviet messages. Their source information is obtained from such far-flung stations as the secret intelligence corps at Cape Lisburn across from Russia's Chukchi Sea, the monitoring station at Babel Thuap on the Paulu Islands, and the radar station at Wakkanai on the northern tip of Hokkaido Island in Japan.

At the center of the hub is the Deciphering Section, situated just outside Kapalama's huge secret files entombed in temperature-controlled vaults a half flight down. This section breaks down everything received through the Cobra system, sends the information to Fort Meade in Maryland, and from there to the National Security Advisor in Washington for the president's regular 9:30 morning briefing.

It was in this section that Air Force Major Mariano Guerrero sat at his desk fidgeting, pretending to oversee the seventy-five stations where analysts were monitoring consoles throughout the huge room. But in actuality he had other concerns on his mind. Concerns that dealt with the KGB.

It had been over six months since Maria had entered the Roundtable Bar where Guerrero spent most of his evenings. It was not a typical hangout for military personnel, and it was for that very reason he frequented it.

"Buy a girl a drink?" she had asked.

Guerrero looked up. Standing beside him had been a woman so startlingly beautiful that he found himself struck speechless. As he gaped at her, she had laughed, tossing her head back so that her long black hair flipped casually over one shoulder.

"No?" she had asked, seductively batting her long lashes. "Then maybe I can buy *you* one."

Had he not been so completely overcome by her

dark, sensual elegance, Guerrero might have asked himself how anyone so young and appealing could possibly find him attractive. Fifty-five years old, the major was short, with a large, misshapen nose that had been brutally redesigned by repeated beatings during his five-year stay in a Hanoi prison. His face was red and puffy, with deep sockets housing two dark, beady, rat-like eyes. All in all, Maj. Mariano Guerrero was far from a beautiful young lady's ultimate fantasy.

But Maria was a professional. She had been trained at the American Center outside Moscow, and was one of the Kremlin's Department V superstars. She had wormed her way into the hearts and beds of many heads of state around the world to further the KGB's subversive international goals.

"You look like your wife doesn't understand you," she had said pointedly.

Guerrero stared down at his glass.

"I'm . . . a widower," he quietly replied.

"Really?" she asked. Her voice was velvety soft, almost a purr. "How sad for you." She linked her arm through his, drawing his bare flesh against her breast. "You must be very lonely."

She had kept him off balance the entire evening. And it hadn't ended there. She showed up at the Roundtable almost every night. Soon she was sharing his bed, driving him to work, picking him up at Kapalama, and easily worming her way into his confidence. It was not long before he was telling her his entire life's story.

Guerrero had been shot down as a back-seat flyer over Vietnam and wasted away in the Hanoi Hilton for five years. During that time, his wife had been diagnosed with cancer, forcing the base hospital doctors to perform a double mastectomy. They

14

believed they had arrested the problem. But despite constant observation, she had died two years later. When Guerrero finally returned home, it was to an empty house and a lot of unanswered questions.

Little by little he became dissatisfied with higher command, blaming the Air Force for his wife's death. His behavior was considered irrational at times, and he was frequently ordered to appear for psychiatric evaluations. But because of his hitherto unwavering loyalty, he was kept on at Honolulu, where his wife had died, and given a desk job at Kapalama.

He was immediately at odds with command at the super-secret base. Within a month, he had figured out how documents could be stolen and smuggled out of the complex. But no one would listen to his ideas for improving security. One night, trying to appear important to Maria, he told her how top-secret plans could be stolen. She feigned disinterest and disbelief, until Guerrero decided to prove to her how easily it could be done.

"Look at this," he bragged the following night, brandishing a top secret document, complete with chemically impregnated papers meant to trigger electronic detection gear at all exit points.

"What is it?" she had asked, knowing immediately what it was she was being shown. And she could hardly control her excitement.

"ComSubPac communication codes," Guerrero boasted. "Some of the most heavily guarded secret documents at Kapalama."

She had fawned over him all night, had worn him out in bed, slipped him a sleeping pill, and then leisurely spent the night copying the documents with a special hand-held duplicating roller. When pictures of the documents sitting on a desk in front of a large, red, hammer and sickle-adorned flag were handed to him, Guerrero knew he was trapped. And that is when Maria bowed out and Col. Vladimir Turbin entered Guerrero's life.

At a restaurant one night Maria had introduced Turbin as a business associate, then went to powder her nose and never returned. Where Maria's approach had been soft and seductive, the colonel's had been hard, demanding, overbearing. "You are working for me, now!" he informed Guerrero. "And you will get for me exactly what I want, when I want it!"

Guerrero had felt his blood heating up, turning his face an even more fiery red than usual.

"And if I don't?" he replied.

"Then I will kill you!"

At first Guerrero had laughed. But the sound died in his throat when he looked deep in Turbin's dark, soulless eyes. The Air Force major had seen the same expressions in the eyes of his captors in Hanoi. Turbin could and would snuff out his life without a second thought. And the death would not be painless. A chill ran down Guerrero's spine, turning his legs to jelly. He could probably deal with the shame and imprisonment that would accompany his exposure as a traitor. But pain and death were something else entirely. There was nothing to do but obey.

Now, as he stared out across the section at the decoding stations, Guerrero faced the most difficult task of all. The Kremlin wanted certain highly controlled documents and the colonel himself would be at Kapalama to pick them up by six o'clock.

Guerrero thought about the base personnel. They were all lazy and disinterested, he believed. Getting the documents would be no real challenge, nor would secreting them out of the building cause him any concern. He had done this several times before, though this time he had to go into the back vault where time delays and cameras were constantly in operation.

"Serves them right!" Guerrero muttered. He was going to get even for all the wasted years, for his wife's death, for being abandoned, left to rot in Hanoi. The colonel had agreed to pay him two hundred thousand dollars for the theft. Enough, Guerrero believed, to leave the country and live out his life in style somewhere people did not ask questions.

He looked at his watch. It was time. As he started to rise, a man in a dark suit appeared beside Guerrero's desk. "Major Guerrero?" the stranger asked.

"Yes," Guerrero responded, startled.

"I would like to talk to you, sir."

Guerrero glanced at the clock on the wall behind his desk. He had no time for idle chatter. "I'm sorry, but I'm in a hurry."

"Maybe you had best take the time, Major," the man insisted. He opened a leather case and flashed an identification card bearing his picture, the name Millard Haus and the title FBI Station Chief.

Guerrero's heart jumped into his throat. He slumped back into his chair.

"That's better," the stranger said, taking a seat next to the desk. "Is there somewhere around here we can talk in privacy?"

Guerrero nodded. "There's a conference room," he muttered weakly.

"Splendid," the FBI man replied. "Shall we go?"

CHAPTER TWO

5:33 p.m.

The white bob-tail truck darted in and out of traffic along Ala Moana highway. The downpour and the resultant vehicular snarl had jammed the roads, putting those in the truck well behind schedule.

"I surely do not want to be late," the driver whispered to his companion. "Not with *him* in the back."

The second hijacker turned to look at his partner and scowled. "We're not going to be late. Stop worrying."

A thousand feet over the highway, hovering in the cloudburst, Traffic Helicopter One for station KQUA in Honolulu was being buffeted by the heavy winds. Johnnie Lahanna, the station's senior traffic announcer, hung onto his seat, clicking his tongue repeatedly against the roof of his mouth in annoyance. "Can't you get above this?" he asked impatiently.

The pilot, Jerry Williams, sighed, keeping his eyes locked on the windscreen. *Three years in this bird,* he thought to himself, *and this clown still pretends not to know which way the wind is blowing.* "This soup will clear in less than ten minutes," he shouted over the engine noise. "You know that as well as I do."

"Meantime we get our insides turned every which way but loose!" Johnnie grumbled, digging his fingers even tighter into the sides of the narrow passenger seat.

The pilot shook his head. "For the dandy of the airwaves up here, you sure don't like flying much."

Lahanna tightened his seat belt. "Hell, I'll put up with anything that's a path to a d.j.'s job."

Williams took the helicopter into a sharp one-eighty-degree turn, dropping abruptly below a dark gray storm cloud. Johnnie tensed, sat up rigidly, and cursed under his breath. As they swept back over the highway, Williams noticed some erratic movement below out of the corner of his eye. "Say," he asked, "isn't that your friend down there? That hack for restaurant supply?"

Lahanna squinted out of the side window onto the congestion beneath them. The white bob-tail truck was easily discernible through the gray mist, cutting dangerously in and out of the snarled traffic.

"Yeah, that's Jack," Lahanna replied, sitting up with interest. "He's sure driving wildly. Never known Jack to drive fast."

"Maybe he's got a hot date tonight," the pilot suggested.

Johnnie grinned broadly. "Boy, have *you* got the wrong cowpoke!" he said.

Both men laughed uproariously. Eight hundred feet below, the bob-tail continued weaving erratically through the midday congestion.

Six miles to the north, base personnel at Kampalama watched the approaching clouds with trepidation. Many scurried across the compound, trying to complete their business and get indoors before the rains hit.

In a third level conference room, Mariano Guerrero sat across a table from Millard Haus. The FBI man's black suit was badly wrinkled, looking as if he had slept in it. His tie was askew under an open collar. All the way down the stairs and into the room he had talked garrulously about sports, the weather, television. Once seated, though, his mood changed abruptly. "We know what you've been up to," he said, his voice hard-edged and penetrating. His eyes were narrowed into slits under heavy brows. Had Guerrero not known what the FBI man was about to say, he would have been shocked at the sudden transformation.

"You're facing both a court-martial," Haus went on, "and a civilian life sentence for handing secrets over to the Russians."

Guerrero said nothing. He hung his head low, his eyes focused on the tabletop, his hands folded tightly in his lap. How could anyone have found out about his passing stolen secrets to Turbin? It had been so well planned out. He never took the same approach twice, had never used the same exit. And his drop sites had always been chosen at random. Except for that first meeting, he had never once been seen with Turbin, nor had he ever seen Maria again. How had they pieced it together?

Once again the FBI man's mood shifted drastically. A broad, cheerful grin lit up his features. "But we can keep you out of prison," he said, his voice condescending, patronizing. Removing a pen from his shirt pocket, Haus began twirling it absentmindedly on the table. Staring at the spinning object Guerrero had trouble concentrating on what the agent was saying to him. Haus's voice seemed to be coming from somewhere else. ". . . pass along the type of information we want." The FBI man continued twirling the pen. "Nothing will change. Not outwardly at least."

The small, windowless room was stuffy and Guerrero was having trouble breathing. The room was seldom used except for high-level discussions so the air-conditioning had been turned down. As beads of sweat began to roll down his forehead, Guerrero found himself wishing he had made the adjustment when they first entered. But now it was too late. Guerrero's thoughts raced through his head madly. There had to be some way out of this. The years in Hanoi had taught him to concentrate on a single issue to the exclusion of all others. Ignoring the agent's spinning pen and blocking out his droning monologue on how they would pass off unimportant data to the Soviets, Guerrero forced himself to think only of escape. But mere escape would not be enough. He had to carry off the intended theft and make the sale. Without the money, he had no future.

Only Haus stood in the way of his success.

"I have to go to the john," Guerrero said.

Haus stared at him for a moment. He rubbed his face roughly, considering the request. Seconds ticked by in silence.

"Sure, Major," Haus said finally. "You don't mind if I just tag along and keep you company, do you?"

They walked out of the conference room, down a narrow corridor, and into the men's room. As Guerrero passed through the doorway, he glanced at the flight of stairs leading down to the file vaults.

"You go ahead," Haus said, walking over to the mirror. He removed a long comb from his pocket and began preening his curly black hair.

Entering an open stall, Guerrero noticed a mop and bucket standing by the commode. He grabbed the bucket by the handle and turned back, taking three quick steps toward the sink where Haus stood. The agent saw him coming in the mirror and spun around, reaching for his gun. Guerrero swung the bucket forward with all his might. It caught Haus in the face, knocking him backward against the sink. The agent's head smashed into the mirror, shattering the glass into hundreds of tiny shards.

As Haus slumped to the floor, Guerrero hit him again with the bucket, and then again, splitting the agent's head open like a ripe melon. Haus rolled over lifeless.

Breathing heavily, Guerrero glanced at the closed door of the restroom. He hurried over to the body and dragged it inside an empty stall. Huffing from the exertion, Guerrero lifted the limp corpse onto the toilet, propping it back against the wall. He reached under the stall and grabbed the mop. Guerrero proceeded to wedge one end against the stall door and the other into Haus's chest. He then crawled out under the door.

He quickly wiped up the blood from the tile floor with paper towels and washed telltale signs from the sink and mirror, careful to avoid cutting himself on the broken glass. Within seconds he was out the door and heading down the flight of stairs to the vault.

The bob-tail truck swerved across two lanes and onto the Nimitz Freeway. The rain had begun to abate as the storm moved farther north, leaving the road wet and slippery. Off to the east was State Capitol, and to the west was the Aloha Tower. But neither of the hijackers was concerned with the tourist sights.

Guerrero stepped inside the vault. Airman First Class Christopher Michaels looked up from his desk inside a wire cage and smiled. "Hi, Major."

"Hi, Chris," Guerrero mumbled. He signed the register and waited while scanners registered his profile, matching it against those authorized to be in the area.

"What're you looking for this time?"

"Just some sub data. Pearl seems to have lost one of their boats and thinks we might know where it is."

The young airman chuckled. "Just like the brass to lose a submarine."

Guerrero nodded distractedly. "Who's on duty back there this afternoon?"

"Hamilton and Finklestein. They came on at two."

The sensor light blinked and a soft bell sounded briefly. The cage door popped open and Guerrero stepped inside. Thanking the airman, he hurried down the long rows of locked files to a rear cage, similar to the one he had just passed through.

"Major Guerrero," he said, flashing his priority security badge to the tall, grim-faced black airman standing guard.

"Sign in, Major," the guard, whose name was Hamilton, replied, pushing a log book and pen toward Guerrero. When the signature was completed, Hamilton pulled a card from the register and took his time comparing the handwriting. Guerrero stood waiting, his eyes darting nervously around the cage, shifting his weight from one foot to the other. At any moment he expected every security buzzer in the complex to sound, signaling the discovery of the murdered agent.

"Okay, Major. You check out."

Guerrero stepped toward the gate. The light overhead turned back to green and Guerrero smiled, mumbled a goodbye, then hurried on through.

A young airman named Finklestein accompanied Guerrero into the locked red section. After securing one of the documents he needed, Guerrero asked the airman to open another file for him. As the airman bent to unlock a bottom drawer, Guerrero yanked open his shirt, pulled out several sheets of specially prepared paper and spread them along the counter. He then took the documents in his hand and stuffed them inside the shirt, quickly buttoning it up again before the airman stood up.

Guerrero scooped the papers on the counter up into a stack and dropped them back into the empty folder. He handed it back to the airman.

"I made a mistake. This isn't the file I need." Finklestein looked up at him.

"I forgot," Guerrero apologized. "The McPeek file has been dropped in classification. It's in the blue drawers."

The young airman shrugged, and dropped the folder into a drawer, closing and locking both files.

Three minutes later Guerrero was back at the front desk, signing for a blue file folder he had specially asked for the day before. As Hamilton recorded the extraction, Guerrero stole a quick look at the overhead clock.

It was five minutes to six.

"Okay, Major. This is logged to you for twenty-four hours. If you need it longer, you'll have to bring it back for renewal."

Guerrero nodded. He took the file, nodded to both airmen, and started through the gate. The air was

24

suddenly split by the jarring clang of alarm bells. The gate slammed shut with a loud, metallic crash. Everyone froze.

A look of complete surprise crossed Guerrero's feature. He glanced down at the folder in his hands.

Hamilton grabbed the folder and looked it over carefully. He punched information into his computer and studied the display. "Hmmm, it was just downgraded two days ago. Must not have gone through the chemical analyzer yet."

"I'll escort him out the other side," Finklestein offered.

"And I'll log it through for Chris's register."

As the young airman walked with Guerrero, the major grinned inwardly. His ruse had worked, just as he knew it would. He had chosen this document because of its recent change in status, had sprayed it a day earlier with a chemical to cover the alarms triggered by the documents under his shirt, and now was using it to cover his theft. By the time the computer checks analyzed the documents, verified they had already been chemically restored, and pieced the theft together, he would be long gone and out of the country.

Once on the stairs, after Finklestein had returned to his station, Guerrero ran up two steps at a time until he reached a back corridor. He followed the corridor to the supply lift, rode up to ground level and started down the hall. Approaching the exit gate, Guerrero saw the three-tiered security check with its half dozen Air Police monitoring chemical, electronic, and x-ray equipment. Arranging his features into a neutral expression, Guerrero calmly continued down the corridor.

The bob-tail pulled off the Sand Island access road

and around to a side entrance to the Kapalama Military Reservation. Though only an entrance for loading and unloading commissary goods, a double-gated, heavily guarded fence blocked their path.

The truck pulled to a stop and honked. Two armed Air Police looked out through the bullet-proof glass of their guard shack. They checked the license, called it in over the computer line to Five-O, waited for clearance, then pressed the buzzer that opened the first gate.

The driver stepped on the gas and edged into the narrow space between the gates. The outside gate closed behind them, sealing them in.

"Entrance code," a voice asked over a loudspeaker.

The driver took the card from his jumper pocket and inserted it into an electronic reader situated to the side of the truck.

After a pause, the inner gate opened. The driver gunned the engine and drove into the small yard. He turned the truck around and backed into the loading dock.

The two hijackers got out of the cab and walked around to the back. They opened the tailgate. Colonel Turbin glared at them from behind a row of crates.

"Start unloading," he hissed. "And don't be in a hurry!"

The two hijackers glanced up at the Air Police watching them from a distance. They looked back at each other, then began unloading boxes of food-stuffs.

CHAPTER THREE

5:52 p.m.

"Hey! Guerrero!"

Guerrero froze. He turned to see Col. Thomas Moore approaching him from down the hall.

"I want you to come with me," Moore said, clapping Guerrero on the shoulder. "Something's gone wrong down below."

Beads of perspiration broke out across Guerrero's forehead. If he went below with his station boss, he would surely be found out. The body of the FBI agent could not go undiscovered much longer. Yet, if he ran, the alarms would be activated and the entire base would be shut down. There would be no escape.

Before Guerrero could respond, one of the Air Police stepped up to Moore to ask him a question. With Moore's back turned, Guerrero slipped into the hall and hurried toward the commissary.

Without looking back, he ran through the swinging doors to the commissary kitchen and crossed unobserved to the back portion of the pantry which opened directly onto the loading dock.

Outside, he edged along the cement wall. He could see the two hijackers unloading the bob-tail. Grabbing a white dock coat and quickly putting it on,

Guerrero lifted a box off a shelf, and headed for the truck. He walked right past the two men unloading the truck and stepped up into the open back.

"Let's get out of here!" he hissed frantically.

The two hijackers pulled down the tailgate, locked it and hurried around to the cab.

Inside, Guerrero grabbed for support as the truck lumbered up out of the loading dock and across the yard.

Turbin's voice came out of the darkness. "Did you get it?" he asked.

Guerrero spun around. A small flame lit up the inside of the truck. The cigarette lighter only partially illuminated Turbin's face as he eyed Guerrero suspiciously. "I asked if you got it?"

Guerrero stared apprehensively into the cold, black eyes of the KGB man. He felt his insides knotting up as he handed over the blue folder. The colonel opened it eagerly and glanced at the contents. After a few moments he frowned and tossed it aside. "This is nothing," he growled. "Where is it?"

Guerrero swallowed nervously. "Where's my two hundred thousand?" he asked.

The two men eyed each other in silence as the truck passed through the two gates and out onto the access road. It was Turbin who finally relented. He picked up the briefcase he had carried inside with him, opened it, and withdrew two large, bulging manila envelopes.

"Two hundred thousand in American dollars," Turbin said flatly, handing the packages to Guerrero.

Guerrero pried open the clasp on one of the envelopes, looked inside and gasped. He poured the contents out onto his lap. Ten stacks of crisp one hundred dollar bills, one hundred bills to a stack, came tumbling out. Guerrero figured the second envelope must contain the same.

"The documents," Turbin said, his voice threateningly low.

Guerrero unbuttoned his shirt and extracted the stolen documents. "It's everything you wanted," he said, handing them to the KGB man.

Turbin grabbed the papers from Guerrero and held them up to the lighter. As the colonel perused the documents, Guerrero counted the money. Finally satisfied, Turbin dropped the papers into the briefcase and sealed it closed.

Guerrero looked up from his counting. "Now what?" he asked.

"Now we go to the airport."

The U.S.S. *Batfish*, a hunter submarine of the *Sturgeon* class, slid quietly through the Pacific, four hundred feet beneath the surface. Amidships, in her dimly lit, climate-controlled sonar room, flashing lights and banks of monitoring screens were ablaze with activity. Two men sat watching and waiting as the boat's passive sonar arrays listened for a target.

"Mr. Vogt, make sure that mask is properly seated," the sonar supervisor said. "We don't want to telegraph our position prematurely."

A civilian engineer, leaning against the racks of electronic gear along the aft bulkhead, wiped his face with the back of his sleeve and stepped forward. He was part of the design team from the Marine Division of Rockwell whose equipment was being tested by *Batfish*. A former Navy commander himself, he moved with catlike grace. He checked the temporary console where his equipment was housed, and nodded with satisfaction. "Everything's in place," he said calmly, masking the excitement he felt. "They won't even know we're in the same ocean with them."

"Let's hope not," his supervisor replied. "But keep in mind that Bertanelli's no fool." He turned to one of the operators. "Anything, Reeves?"

"Recommend the captain slow to twelve knots, Mr. Sessions," the operator said, hunched over his screen.

The supervisor nodded and radioed the message into the control room.

Vogt gripped his legs above the knee, forcing himself to relax. Two years of sweat and blood rested on these trials. *Batfish* was one of three submarines using his company's new technology of acoustic masks and counterfeit signatures. It was designed to fool enemy sonar, and was now covering *Batfish* as she attempted to get in close to sink a target boat.

"I think we've got her," a second operator snapped nervously. He turned up the gains on his terminal. "Right about . . . *there!*"

All eyes followed the fuzzy isobars on the detection screen as they flowed downward in waterfalls through the three level measurements.

"Filter out biologics," Sessions ordered.

The first operator worked on the keys of his terminal.

"Wash out ambient noises."

The clutter on the screen from marine life and natural sea noises slowly disappeared. The blip that showed up on the BQQ5 sonar arrays in the first level solidified into a target on the third waterfall.

"I do believe you are correct, Harper," the supervisor said, studying the blip intently. "Put a tracker on her and run it through the BC-10." The four men in the small, red-lit room stared excitedly as the image on the computer identification screen materialized.

"It's her!" Ramsey grinned. "By damn, we've got Bertanelli in our sights!"

"I can't believe how quiet that six-eighty-eight is!" Reeves whispered in awe.

"She's running with one of those new Japanese silent propellers."

"Even so, we've got her!"

The officer flipped the switch on his intercom mike. "Sonar to control. Target sub bearing one niner two. Range, seventeen thousand yards. Depth, four zero zero feet. Elevation-depression angle, minus three degrees."

In the control room, Cmdr. Aubrey Parkin was overjoyed. He was about to give "Crazy Tony" Bertanelli his first hard contact. "Control to weapons. I want a firing solution on the target, *now!*"

"Aye."

Parkin turned to his executive officer, Lt. Cmdr. Peter McFerson. "Tony isn't going to like this."

The XO smiled. "Maybe it'll knock some of that cockiness out of him."

"I doubt it."

"Captain, we have a firing solution on *Pocatello*."

Parkin turned to Cmdre. Anthony Gustovson, the umpire on board for exercise PLAYFUL. The commodore nodded.

"Control to sonar. Hit him with a hard one! And don't make it brief."

An operator powered up the BQS-13 active sonar suite and pressed the impulse button. In the bow of *Batfish*, an active transducer shot a bolt of high-frequency sound toward the target sub.

Ping, ping, ping, ping.

The hard contact slammed off the hull of *Pocatello*.

Pong!

In the control room of the Los Angeles class attack submarine U.S.S. *Pocatello*, Adm. Galen Sward smiled gleefully. A square-jawed, crisp-voiced man in his fifties, Sward, the umpire on board, believed in going by the book—one of the many reasons he disliked the boat's impetuous skipper. "Captain, you've just been sunk!" he boomed gleefully.

Cmdr. Anthony Bertanelli, sometimes called "Crazy Tony"—though never to his face—scowled and shot Sward a look that could kill if looks, in fact, could.

Willard Jamison, the curly-haired executive officer, spoke up. "Without those special electronics," he said, "he wouldn't have gotten close, let alone fired a shot." A tall, skinny man with a hatchet face resembling Ichabod Crane, Jamison had sailed with the captain before, and knew how hard it was on Bertanelli to be at such a disadvantage.

"That's what this is all about, Commander," Sward announced, making no attempt to keep the elation out of his voice. "We're here to test whether or not Miss O'Brien's acoustic masks and counterfeit signatures will work against our best detection equipment." He shot Bertanelli a joy-filled glance. "And so far they certainly have!"

"So the first one goes to them," Bertanelli muttered. He leveled his pale blue eyes at the admiral, giving no quarter whatsoever. "There are two more attempts. Don't count *Poco* out yet."

Sward chuckled hollowly. "I counted you out before I ever came on board, Captain."

High over Highway 64 and the Nimitz Freeway, Johnnie Lahanna in Traffic Helicopter One had just completed his quarter-hour update. As Jerry Williams swung the chopper around and started north to pick up Highway One, Lahanna intently watched the traffic below through his binoculars.

"That's strange," he mumbled, half to himself.

Williams turned to look at him. "What is?"

"Jack's truck. He should be enroute to Fort Shafter and then on to Tripler Army hospital."

"Funny way to get there," Williams replied, swinging the helicopter around for a better view. "He's heading north on Ninety-two."

"He should have taken Sixty-three east."

"Maybe he's going to drop off some food at the airport."

Lahanna shook his head, focusing the high-powered lenses. "They only supply military reservations. There's no reason for him to be going where he's going."

"There could be a thousand reasons, Johnnie," Williams offered, pointing the helicopter back to the north. "You've just got a suspicious mind."

"You bet I do. I'm going to call Five-O!"

The *Pocatello*'s Petty Officer First Class, Jason Caldwell, slouched over his sonar control panel just outside the control room, in the same position he had been in since *Batfish* had sunk them earlier.

"Is he asleep, or dead?" Maggie O'Brien asked. One of Rockwell's top engineers and the inventor of the special mask and counterfeit signature technology being tested, she was only the second woman to ever be on board an attack submarine during an exercise at sea. Her authority had come all the way from the Joint Chiefs of Staff.

Sonarman Second Class Dwight Zimmer glanced

over at the seemingly comatose Caldwell. "Neither," he replied. Zimmer had been Caldwell's watch partner since they came aboard *Pocatello* right after the boat had first been launched at Newport News along the James River in Virginia.

"Well, what's he doing?"

"Detecting."

Maggie snorted derisively. She had expected a somewhat more professional trial of her equipment conducted by someone more adept at locating enemy submarines. She figured Caldwell would have trouble finding himself in a mirrored room.

"I assure you, Miss O'Brien," sonar officer Thomas P. Ralston said from across the room, "that *Pocatello* is the best boat in the fleet."

"So I've heard."

Pocatello was at sea in a special exercise with the *Lexington* carrier battle group. Part of the submarine picket line, they were to detect the three "enemy" boats and keep them from breaking through to the carrier. Normally a simple assignment, it had become a herculean task because of Maggie O'Brien's special electronics. Caldwell's earlier failure to detect the "enemy" had been the first of his career.

"Control to sonar," Bertanelli's voice blared over the p.a. speaker. "Hear anything?"

"Not yet, skipper," Caldwell replied, causing Maggie to jump. She really had thought he was asleep.

"Need I remind you that we're oh for one?"

"They got lucky."

"Let's not let it happen again."

"Aye, aye."

When given commission of *Pocatello*, Bertanelli had brought Caldwell with him from the old *Drum*.

The two had been together for nearly six years. In all that time, they had been 25-0 in exercise kills. Until now.

Caldwell lifted his hand slightly. Almost imperceptibly, he bent a finger and touched a key. Zimmer immediately leapt to work at the keyboard of his own terminal.

"What's he doing?" Maggie asked.

Ralston shrugged. This was his first voyage with the crew and neither his training at Annapolis, nor at the officers' submarine school at Orlando had prepared him for the likes of Jason Caldwell. In a service where sonar operators are a breed unto themselves—usually wacky, always loners, and seldom friendly—Caldwell was a dichotomy. Possessing the typical tendencies of the sonar technician toward analytical brilliance, Caldwell was a throwback to an earlier, less disciplined day. He was a zany prankster who loved a practical joke. Ralston's first day aboard *Pocatello* had been a nightmare. Caldwell had asked him to get the key to the sonar equipment from the captain. When Ralson asked Bertanelli for the key, the entire control room crew had broken up. He had also found his bed short-sheeted, a water snake in his shower, and his toilet case filled with shaving cream. It had been a hard initiation for Thomas Ralston.

"Recommend to the captain we come right five degrees," Caldwell said.

Ralston passed along the request to the control room, where Bertanelli nodded absently and replaced the mike. Turning to the diving officer, the captain said, "Come right to course zero four zero."

"Zero four zero, aye."

Pocatello was Bertanelli's most important command. He had skippered the *Sturgeon* class *Drum*, and earlier, *Dace*, a *Permit* class boat. His outstanding record, and the fact that he was liked by Adm. Bryan Cummings, Commander in Chief of the Pacific Fleet, got him command of the *Los Angeles* class boat. Designated SSN 756, *Pocatello*'s keel was laid down in April of 1986, and finished a record twenty-three months later. The vice president, secretary of the navy, and governor of Idaho all addressed the gathered dignitaries, spectators, builders, and their families. Pocatello's mayor had christened the namesake boat with the proverbial bottle of champagne.

"What do you hear, Jason?"

Caldwell stared at the isobars on his CRT screen. Something was out there all right. "Stand by," he replied, working the terminal with lightning-quick movements unnoticed by those sitting behind him. Caldwell was a virtuoso who performed solely for himself, not for his adoring fans.

In the control room, Bertanelli tried his best to hide his impatience. He had never liked picket duty. He considered himself a hunter, not a gate keeper. "All ahead slow," he ordered.

In the reactor room, coolant slowed, heat exchangers were dampened, and steam to the turbo-alternators dissipated. The boat slowed until momentum on the diving planes could barely keep steerage. The hull creaked and popped noisily.

Lt. Cmdr. Barker Higgins, the navigation officer and third member of the boat's management team, looked up from his TV-imaged chart table. "They're sure taking their sweet time."

Lt. (j.g.) Marvin Ashton, the boat's weapons officer, shook his head. "I sure don't like being a sitting duck," he said, stating what were probably the sentiments of the entire crew. *Pocatello* was an attack boat. Sitting and waiting only frayed the nerves.

"Not the role for *Poco*," Bertanelli agreed. "Helm, drop us into the thermocline."

"Three degrees down bubble."

"Three degrees down bubble, aye."

The boat dropped fifty feet, passing through a paper-thin barrier between hot and cold bodies of water. Around *Pocatello*, the water was now sixteen degrees colder. Enough difference for sonar suites to be deflected upward.

"That won't help you, Captain," Sward declared loudly, thoroughly enjoying Bertanelli's discomfort. He had love for neither the man nor the misfits who populated his boat.

In the maneuvering room, Lt. Paul Hargrove turned away from the battery of instruments monitoring the nuclear reactor just beyond the bulkhead. He could not keep this depth unless more power was used. He picked up the telephone and dialed the control room. "How 'bout some more juice, Skip? Without it, we're going to become a balloon."

Bertanelli smiled. Despite being "sunk," the crew had not yet lost their sense of humor. He glanced at Sward, then turned to the diving officer. "Bring us up to six knots," he ordered.

"Increase speed to six knots, aye."

"Ash, I want quick firing solutions the minute we spot a target."

"Aye, aye," Ashton replied, his thin mouth tightening into a slit. At the rate they were going, he would only have a brief moment to lock on and fire. If he had any time at all. As weapons officer, it was his job to target in enemy submarines, preparatory to firing a torpedo or missile. In the case of the exercise, he would have to target in the "enemy" before the active sonar could be used to telegraph a hit.

37

"Captain, you better have a look at this," Higgins said, watching the BSY-2 command center. He had called up the sonar images on the 25-inch ancillary TV screen that gave the command center immediate information on any section of the boat.

Solid blips appeared on the screen, representing the *Spruance* class guided missile destroyers, *Fletcher* and *Ingersoll*. Several other surface combatants of the battle group were also there, though their distances were difficult to determine. Three other picket subs could be readily identified.

"What is it, Barker?"

Higgins pointed to a streak that had suddenly appeared on the outer distance range of the sonar. "That," he said.

CHAPTER FOUR

6:15 p.m.

The white bob-tail truck pulled into a side entrance to the Honolulu International Airport. Roaring across a parking apron it shot through a gate and skidded to a stop a short distance from a private Lear jet warming up on the tarmac.

The hijackers hurried to the back and swung the twin doors open. The light flooding into the truck's interior illuminated a hand sticking out from beneath boxes near Guerrero's foot. He jumped back involuntarily, emitting a thin, strangled shriek.

Turbin shot a disgusted glance in his direction, then moved toward the open gate. "Come on, we are in a hurry."

Guerrero stared intently at the two dead drivers. For the first time he realized the implications of his theft. Two men were dead. Three, counting the FBI agent back at Kapalama. How many more would die? "Was that necessary?" he asked.

"Death is always necessary," Turbin said without bothering to turn around. He leapt to the pavement with the briefcase in his hand and headed across the tarmac toward the waiting plane. "Bring him," he ordered over his shoulder to the others.

The two hijackers reached up and pulled Guerrero from the truck bed.

Guerrero's eyes widened when he saw the waiting Lear. "I'm not going with you," he insisted. "I have my own flight arranged."

The two men picked Guerrero up under the arms and carried him toward the Lear. The steps of the plane were lowered and Turbin climbed in. Guerrero was set down roughly and herded into the plane after him.

"What's going on?" Guerrero demanded. "Where is this plane headed?"

"Kamchatka."

"But I have a flight to Rio!"

"Your reservations have just been changed."

Turbin headed up to the front.

"But—"

"Sit down," Turbin called over his shoulder, "and enjoy the flight."

Guerrero turned toward the door. It was quickly closed from the outside and locked. The turbines built up power and the plane began moving across the tarmac and onto a taxi lane. Guerrero looked out the window to see the two hijackers climb back into the bob-tail and drive away.

With a sinking feeling, Guerrero slumped into a seat. *How the hell am I going to get out of this?* he asked himself.

In the Honolulu district office of the Federal Bureau of Investigaton, resident agent Conwell McIntosh picked up his ringing telephone. McIntosh, a big, affable Irishman with a bulbous nose and flabby cheeks, and a friendly, easy-going nature, was not known for the type of dedication that usually

40

marked agents within the Bureau, which was the chief reason he had not risen higher during his twenty-seven years of service.

"McIntosh," he said into the mouthpiece. He listened for a moment, then straightened. "Yes, sir. I'll be right there." He dropped the phone onto its cradle and grabbed his coat. The speed of the agent's movements would have pleased his boss had he been around to see them. But the station chief was sitting in a bathroom stall at Kapalama, never to see anything again.

Aboard *Pocatello*, Jason Caldwell flipped the switch on his intercom. "Sonar to control," he called. "Possible contact bearing three four eight degrees. Distance fifteen miles. Speed about three to four knots."

The streak solidified into a blip, then separated into several indistinct registers on the ancillary screen in the control room.

"It's just biologics," Ralston radioed.

"Looks like whales to me," Ashton agreed.

"Pipe in the sound," Bertanelli ordered.

The underwater sound of whales was distinct. Their hoots, beeps and whistles could be heard through the sea noises surrounding them. Suddenly Caldwell began beeping and hooting in time with the whales, causing those in the control room to look around with a smile. It was common knowledge that Caldwell loved his whales.

"Sounds like whales, too," Ashton said with a grin.

"Sometimes it's hard to tell them apart," Bertanelli agreed. He turned away from the monitoring station and moved to the rail surrounding the periscope pedestal, surveying the many mechanical, hydraulic and electrical indicators out of habit.

"Hell of a time to be playing around," Sward mumbled.

"Breaks up the tension," Bertanelli replied.

"An independent cuss."

"But one mean sonarman."

Sward glared at the captain, then shrugged. Just another note to put in the scathing report he intended to turn in to Fleet Command when PLAYFUL was completed.

In the sonar room, Caldwell turned up the whale sounds. He mimicked them as Zimmer shot him a surprised glance. This was certainly no time to be goofing off. Behind them, Maggie O'Brien sighed heavily, certain the umpire in the control room would disqualify the exercise. She was not impressed by the wacky Caldwell. The man, she thought, was blowing the validity of the exercise that could determine her future career in the aerospace industry.

Ralston leaned forward and reached for Caldwell's shoulder. His pimply face was beet red. "We're at risk, sailor!" he bellowed. "Wash out that sound!"

Caldwell hooted and beeped louder in response.

"Dammit, Caldwell! Filter it out!" Ralston reached for the buttons on the console that would eliminate the whale noises.

Caldwell knocked Ralston's arm aside roughly. "With all due respect, sir," he said, "those are not whales!"

McIntosh stood looking at his boss's body propped on the toilet seat. It had not been moved until the FBI agent could arrive. Five-O had not yet been notified.

"Holy shit!" McIntosh bellowed. "Who could

42

have done such a thing!"

"We were hoping you could tell us," Colonel Moore replied sternly. "That's why we called you. We'd like to know why he was here."

"He . . ." McIntosh began, then clamped down on the words. He had been ordered not to reveal the fact that his boss had been checking up on the suspected treasonous activities of one Major Guerrero. "I don't know, exactly," he muttered.

Moore looked at the big agent with distaste. "This is no time to be coy," the colonel said flatly. "What was going on here?"

"I'm afraid you'll have to take that up with Washington, Colonel."

Irritated, Moore turned away to an aide. "Get me General Mayland on a secure line."

With Caldwell's announcement, Zimmer sat bolt upright in his seat. His face was mottled rose and gray from excitement and strain. He stared at his three-stage repeater screen. The top section, monitoring at two-minute intervals, showed the clutter of several whales. The second level, an accumulation on each line of the first level data, registered the heartbeats of the sperm cetaceans. The third level, an accumulation of the second, showed eight seventy-foot male *mysticreti* bearing southeast, cutting across *Pocatello*'s bow fifteen thousand yards distant.

Ralston looked at his own ID computer and saw the diagram of the whales registered. "What are you talking about?" he thundered. "Of course those are whales!"

Caldwell shook his head.

Maggie O'Brien smiled knowingly. She was surprised the flaky Caldwell had even noticed. The counterfeit signature the adversary was using had obviously been accurately made.

"What d'ya mean they're not whales?" Ralston repeated, his face turning beet red.

Caldwell ignored the young officer. His hands flew across the keyboard, filtering, adjusting, enhancing. Slowly the whale sounds faded, then disappeared completely. In their place was a soft, barely discernible *whirring* noise.

"Coolant pumps," Zimmer exclaimed.

"Damned if we don't have us a *Sturgeon*," Caldwell said.

Ralston strained his ears while Zimmer fed the input into the computer.

"Sonar to Control," Caldwell radioed. "Confirming aggressor sub at fifteen thousand yards. Bearing two one zero. Speed five—"

Ping!

The high pitch of a target-seeking sonar erupted through the overhead speaker. Zimmer tried to yank his earphones off his head, but he wasn't fast enough. Despite the unit's automatic surge depressant mechanism, the sound exploded in his ears and he yelped in pain. Maggie winced in sympathy for the young sonarman, but smiled happily when she saw the computer identify *Silversides* several moments later. *Pocatello* had been "sunk" a second time.

In the control room, Bertanelli swore violently, smashing his fist down onto the pedestal railing. He couldn't bring himself to look at the gloating Sward.

"That's two," the admiral announced gleefully. "Put a fish up your butt before you even knew they were around." His laughter echoed throughout the room.

The electricity in the control room was almost visible. The crew wanted their officers to react, angry

44

that *Pocatello* had taken yet another beating. Bertanelli turned on his heels and strode across the control room toward sonar.

"You have the conn, Willie."

"The captain's left the control room," the diving officer called.

Bertanelli's anger had not abated by the time he reached the sonar station. He pushed roughly past Maggie O'Brien and marched over to Caldwell. "What the hell happened this time?" he demanded.

"Another mask," Caldwell said, his voice almost a whisper.

"That's oh for two," Maggie O'Brien announced and immediately regretted it as Bertanelli turned sharply around and glared at her. His tall, muscular, well-tanned bulk towered over her. Any other woman might have been intimidated, but Maggie was determined to stand her ground. She had not achieved her present lofty position in a man's world by allowing herself to be browbeaten.

Bertanelli regarded Maggie for several seconds. He was impressed with her spunk. This pretty, flame-haired engineer with the serious expression was the cause of his present frustrations. He had not wanted her on his boat to begin with, nor had he wanted to play the patsy in these trials. "You're obviously very good," he said evenly. He continued to regard her and she continued to meet his intense stare unflinchingly. Interesting, Bertanelli thought. Very interesting. Then out loud he added, "But against a stacked deck, even a diesel could reign supreme."

Maggie was confused. The captain certainly had a right to be angry, but he apparently showed no sign of it. "The purpose of this exercise," she said, her tone solicitous, "was to demonstrate that the masks of my SUBDACS would allow an enemy submarine

45

to penetrate the picket defenses of a battle group and sink the task carrier." Her face was flushed with excitement. A tiny strand of reddish hair fell across her face and she absent-mindedly brushed it aside. "It seems to me, Captain, that we have proven such is the case. Twice!"

The atmosphere was thick with tension. Bertanelli found himself suddenly aware of Maggie's pert, turned-up nose, and her fiery green eyes flashing in the red light. A faint trace of perfume wafting up to him brought Bertanelli back to reality, reminding him that this was no place for a woman. "Russian *Alfas* can already get to our carriers without acoustic tricks, if they've a mind to," he informed the engineer, his voice mellifluous, resonant, and convincing. "Despite the fact they're so noisy we can hear them for miles, they are so fast they can get past any picket sub and loose a barrage of torpedoes." His eyes narrowed. "They wouldn't need acoustic masks even if they had them."

Maggie stared at the captain, her hard eyes biting into him. After many spirited hours spent with high-level management personnel, she had learned not to be afraid to state her opinions. "Our new *Seawolf* class boats will be in operation soon," she said, "and Ivan knows they'll negate the speed of his *Alfas*, *Mikes*, and *Akulas*. And since the Japanese firm saw fit to sell the computer designs for our top-secret silent propellers to the Soviets, we no longer have silence solely on our side. Soon the Russians will be operating with as sophisticated passive sonar suites as we do, and then all of our advantage will be gone." Her chin jutted forward with authority. "All that's left will be my electronics to give us an edge."

Bertanelli nodded, genuinely impressed. The

woman was right. But at the moment he was more concerned about the morale on his boat than the future of the Navy. "My fight's not with you, Miss O'Brien," he replied. "But your device has made this boat a patsy. That is neither good for the officers, nor for the Navy." He paused briefly before continuing. "I need something to fight back with. Do you have one of your boys aboard that we can use?"

Maggie cocked her head mischievously, a smile crossing her attractive face. A thought that had been building up in the back of her mind began working its way forward. "How would you like to test out the complete SUBDACS system?" she asked.

Bertanelli said nothing, watching her intently.

"No matter what acoustic nature the *Sturgeons* employ," Maggie continued, "I could tell you exactly how to find them."

Still Bertanelli was silent, but a spark seemed to come alive deep within his eyes.

Maggie went on. "These trials were not intended to demonstrate the SUBDACS-2 system, but it is aboard. With a little mechanical know-how, I could get it working for you."

Bertanelli hesitated. He was supposed to be on picket duty, yet his orders were fairly general and somewhat vague.

"Admiral Sward won't like it," Ralston interjected.

Bertanelli turned abruptly, silencing the officer with a sharp look. Then he turned back to Maggie. "Let's do it!"

Maggie eyed him speculatively. If her system proved effective, it would cut down the turn-around time to production by more than a year, not to mention how it would improve her career status.

"It'll take me about two and a half hours to interface it with your system," she said, a slight quiver in her voice betraying her excitement.

"You've got two hours," Bertanelli replied sharply. He turned to Caldwell. "Give her anything she wants." Starting for the door, he stopped beside Ralston, then turned back. "I want this room sealed off," he said as an afterthought. "Sward is not to step foot in here until after the third engagement."

"What do I tell him if he wants in?" Ralston asked.

"Tell him you've got crazy radiation readings on everyone's dosimeter," Bertanelli said, stepping through the door. "Or say you've been hit with the plague. Just keep him out of here!"

"Aye, aye."

Bertanelli stormed out. Zimmer turned to Caldwell. "How did you know?"

"About the whales?" Zimmer nodded. "It's easy when you know whales. I've recorded dozens of tapes of them, and listen to them whenever I want to relax."

"So?"

"The sound we picked up was a recording."

"But how did you know?"

"Because whoever recorded it used one sound repeatedly. Here, listen for yourself." Caldwell reloaded the tape and rewound it. "It'd be like listening to a person repeating the same word over and over again."

As Caldwell played the tape, Zimmer listened intently. Even Ralston found himself cocking his ear and trying to pick out the similar sounds.

"Don't sound the same to me," Zimmer confessed after several minutes.

"Me neither," Ralston added.

"If you knew whales, you could tell."

Maggie made a mental note to check the whale tapes when she got back to her office. She wanted to know why the full sounds were not employed on the counterfeit signature disc. But for now, she had more pressing concerns. She put the thought aside and bent over her SUBDACS control panel.

CHAPTER FIVE

6:31 p.m.

"General Mayland, sir?"

Gen. Marcus H. Mayland, commander of Tactical Rapid Deployment forces, including Hickam Air Force Base, as well as the 5540th Intelligence Group at Kapalama, looked up from the dinner table and turned to see his aide standing uncomfortably in the doorway. Though he was considered a notoriously rigid commander, nicknamed *Steel Britches* by those who served under him, Mayland was a devoted family man whose practice it was to make sure he had dinner at home whenever possible—a practice he hated having disturbed, which was what Lieutenant First Class Anderson Appleby was doing at that very moment.

"What is it, Andy?" the general inquired gruffly.

"Telephone call, sir."

"Tell 'em I'll call back."

Appleby cleared his throat nervously. "Uh, sir? It's General Morrison."

Mayland glanced around the table at his family. His five remaining children—his eldest, Brad, was away on the mainland at Stanford—as well as

Lorayne, his wife of twenty-three years, stared at him inquisitively.

Mayland sighed. "Put it through to the study, Andy."

"Yes sir." Appleby turned and disappeared down the hall, glad to be out of the line of fire.

Mayland wiped a spot of gravy from his chin, carefully folded the napkin, placing it beside his half-filled plate, and stood up from his chair.

"What about my story, Daddy?" his five-year-old Joann piped up. "What about Horten?"

Mayland leaned down and gently kissed his daughter on the forehead. "Don't worry, honey," he promised. "Tonight you'll get Horten." He winked at his wife, then strode from the room.

Once in his study, he picked up the special square telephone sitting atop a black box. "This is Mayland."

Gen. Robert F. Morrison, Air Force Commander at Pearl, spoke curtly. "Switch to scramble," he ordered.

Mayland manipulated switches on the black box. An echoing tone sounded in his ear as, along the line, special transducers switched on, making it almost impossible to eavesdrop on the conversation. Mayland studied the lights on the panel before answering. "I'm clear here, sir."

"Marc," Morrison said, his voice more friendly, though no less concerned, "we've got an FBI agent dead in a washroom at Kapalama."

Mayland was startled. "How did it happen?"

"Bludgeoned over the head, it appears."

"Murdered?"

"Looks that way."

"What the hell . . . ?"

51

"The washroom is fifty feet from the file vaults."
For a moment Mayland was too stunned to speak.
"You don't think . . . ?"

"We're checking it out now," Morrison said. "Better get right over there. We can't stand another Walker fiasco like the loss of those cipher codes."

"I'm on my way."

Hanging up the phone, Mayland grabbed his uniform cap from the desk top, leapt to his feet and headed for the door, nodding to Appleby who stood a few meters away.

"Let's go, Andy," he said. "Something big is up at Kapalama."

The *Pocatello* rocked gently side to side from the wave action of the rough sea. "Periscope depth, Captain," the helm officer announced, turning away from his station.

"Raise the forward periscope and the EMS," Bertanelli ordered.

"Periscope up, aye. EMS up, aye."

Bertanelli stared into the forward periscope while Jamison checked the readings from the EMS, a broad-band receiver meant to pick up radar transmissions.

Sward stood watching curiously a few feet away. Inwardly he was hoping for a quick third kill. He couldn't wait to get back to Pearl to report to Admiral Cummings of *Poco*'s humiliation.

"I have *Fletcher* bearing one seven five degrees," Bertanelli said.

"EMS shows *Ingersoll* at about three miles." Jamison squinted at the blips on his screen. "We have a faint reading just over five miles, probably

Lexington. No planes near us."

"Raise the antennas."

"Antennas up, aye."

Two more masts broke the surface of the North Pacific. One was a UHF receiving antenna, and the other, a laser transmitter used for transmitting over satellite to Pearl. It could also be used, when directed, to any nearby high-density receiver, like the one on the nearby aircraft carrier.

Aboard *Lexington,* Rear Admiral Pedro Rafill was handed down a message. He read it over quickly, then glanced at his XO, Capt. Thom Perkins.

"*Pocatello* is requesting permission to follow up on a lead. Says they know where the wolf pack is forming."

Perkins smiled. "I'm surprised Bertanelli didn't ask to break picket duty before this."

"Being a target must have been pretty hard on old Tony," the admiral replied. "I wonder what old Sward is thinking right now."

Pocatello's communications officer, Lt. Francis Lamonica, turned away from his equipment. He hurried out of the radio room and into the control room to hand Bertanelli the message he had just received.

The captain read the message quickly. A sly smile crept across his features. "Retract periscope and antennas," he ordered.

"Periscope down, aye. Antennas down, aye."

"Flood forward tanks."

"Take us down to five hundred feet."

"Diving to five hundred feet."

Aah-ooh-gah, aah-ooh-gah, the klaxon sounded.

"Dive the boat."

The planesman pushed forward on the yoke and *Pocatello* began a sudden descent. Ballast and trim tanks located between the outer and inner hull of the boat opened up to the sea. With the inrushing water, *Poco* went from six thousand tons to her maximum displacement of 6927 tons.

Bertanelli looked across the control room to the sonar station beyond the far bulkhead. He hoped Maggie O'Brien knew what she was doing. He was really sticking his neck way out.

Guerrero sat in the Lear looking nervously out the window. He could see the island of Kauai off to his right, and Niihau was just barely visible ahead. By now he figured Honolulu Air Traffic would know the Lear was not on any acceptable flight pattern. As they continued out over the Pacific, someone at HAT would get curious, then concerned. But by then it would be too late. The Lear would be well on its way to Russia.

He took the second envelope from under his coat. Opening the clasp, he looked in at the money and reached in to touch it. He found the feel of the stiff green paper somewhat reassuring. He wondered idly if he could exchange it for rubles once they reached Kamchatka. Perhaps they'd let him get a flight to Japan.

"Comfortable?" Turbin asked, walking back into the cabin from up front where he had been talking with the pilot and copilot.

"When we arrive, am I free to leave?"

"Of course, of course," Turbin replied impatiently. "What do you take us for, uncivilized barbarians?"

Guerrero chose not to answer. Turbin sat in a side-facing seat and placed the briefcase on his lap. He wrapped both arms around it and sat back to doze. Guerrero reached into the envelope again for more reassuring contact with his new-found fortune.

The atmosphere in *Pocatello*'s control room was charged with excitement. The whole crew realized they were going hunting. Admiral Sward, however, was the only one not impressed. "The Russians are already experimenting with stealth arrays and acoustic masks," he said flatly.

"So I've been told," Bertanelli replied.

"Perhaps you should talk to Rawlings from *Seattle*," Sward added. "He had an experience with Soviet masks."

"He still identified the boat and chased it home."

"If it had been war, Captain, that *Alfa* would have made kindling of *Seattle*!"

Bertanelli knew Sward was right. He had talked to Rawlings after *Seattle* returned to Pearl. The man had still been shaking from the experience. Somehow the *Alfa* had been duplicating the signature of a fleet sub, and if *Seattle*'s sonar operator had not known of a change in fleet operations concerning that particular boat, they never would have stumbled on the Russian's duplicity.

Bertanelli stubbornly shook his head. "That was *Seattle*. *Poco* is a better boat."

"You're oh for two, Captain."

"We're about to change all that."

Sward frowned. His dislike for Bertanelli had begun eight years ago. Sward had been instructing at Annapolis in Bertanelli's senior year, and had developed a limited opportunity scenario for a naval encounter. It was a test meant to try the creative ability of the young naval graduates in a most difficult situation. But Bertanelli had made an end run around the problem, solved the difficulty without ever confronting it head on, making Sward's Scenario, as it became known, totally meaningless. Sward was not about to forgive and forget. If there was one thing the admiral hated more than anything else, it was being made to look foolish.

"Change course to one seven eight degrees," Bertanelli ordered.

"One seven eight degrees, aye."

Sward watched Bertanelli handling his boat. He was a capable officer, the admiral knew, but far too cocky and much too reliant on luck. Certainly not the kind of man Sward felt should be entrusted with the lives of a hundred men and a billion dollar submarine. Because of this firm conviction, Sward had even tried to block Bertanelli's appointment to *Poco*. It had been Admiral Cummings who overrode his objections. The captain was Cummings's fair-haired boy.

Of course, Sward knew, part of the reason for the promotion was Bertanelli's excellent record in fleet exercise games. Still, commanding an attack submarine was no game. Sward had commanded the *Tiger Shark*, a World War Two diesel boat, during MacArthur's invasion of North Korea in 1952. It was there he had learned that nothing previously experienced in Navy trials and tests could prepare a commander for wartime's actual moment of truth. Sward's had come when he heard the sonar pinging of a Korean picket sub outside Inchon harbor. He had been ordered to clear the area, and it took him nearly two hours to work up the courage to go after the sub. Two hours then seemed like an eternity.

"You really think you're lucky enough to pull this off, don't you?" Sward asked sharply.

"Haven't you heard, Admiral?" Bertanelli chuckled. "I have legions of guardian angels watching over me."

"I've long suspected as much."

It had always riled the admiral that Bertanelli had never been disciplined for his legendary disregard for orders. When "Crazy Tony" had pinned that first Soviet submarine against the continental shelf in the Bering Sea near Cape Rodney, north of Nome, forcing the Russian to surface, Sward had expected the roof to fall in on Bertanelli. But the Soviet sub turned out to be an *Alfa*, the titanium-hulled speedster no American had seen up close before. And when Bertanelli had taken Polaroid pictures of it, Fleet Command put him in for the Legion of Merit, and his crew up for a Unit Citation. A year later, when he again forced a Soviet sub to the surface after constraining him against the northern ridge of the Attu Island at the western edge of the Aleutians, it had been close enough to Soviet waters that Sward had silently hoped for an international incident. It would, he believed, force the Navy to punish Bertanelli severely to satisfy the Russians. But it turned out to be a new *Akula* class Soviet submarine, loaded down with tons of special camera and electronic eavesdropping gear. The Russians claimed they did not have such a spy boat in the Pacific and denied the entire incident. Bertanelli had again been awarded a Legion of Merit and his crew given a second Unit Citation.

"This time, Captain," Sward taunted, "pictures won't do you any good."

Bertanelli shook his head. Though there was a partial smile on his lips, his eyes betrayed only a trace of humor. "It's not pictures I'm after," he said. "We're going to "sink" three *Sturgeons*!"

When this exercise had first been discussed by Fleet Command at Pearl, Sward had eagerly volunteered himself as umpire. This time there was no way Bertanelli was going to win, and Sward wanted to be present when the great captain met his Waterloo.

"You're still oh for two."

"All ahead full," the captain ordered.

"All ahead full, aye."

Pocatello shuddered slightly, its reactor heating up, sending steam through the heat exchangers to feed the turbogenerators. Within seconds two geared turbines were up to full power. The single shaft whipped up to two thousand revolutions per minute and spun the large Japanese-designed propeller, especially developed to keep water from creating oxygen bubbles that would implode back into the propeller wash, creating cavitation that would be picked up on enemy sonar. *Pocatello* was under way.

"Reel in the TBS," Bertanelli ordered.

In *Poco*'s sonar room, Zimmer swore at the clutter suddenly appearing on his screen. They were deliberately making enough noise to leave a signature on the *Sturgeon* sonars even a blind man could follow. "Shit, everyone for twenty miles is going to know where we are," he muttered, "including the Russians."

"Don't sweat it," Caldwell replied happily. "We're going fishing."

"Wearing a big red sign saying, 'Here We Are'!" Zimmer pushed a button, reeling in the towed array, a thousand foot cable that looked much like a garden hose with 144 hydrophones implanted on it. Without this passive sonar array, *Pocatello* could run nearly blind at high speed since water passing over the boat rendered the radome in the bow and the hydrophones along the hull nearly useless. They could not see, but could easily be seen by others.

CHAPTER SIX

7:50 p.m.

General Mayland's black limousine was turning off the Nimitz Freeway onto Sand Island access road when his car phone buzzed. His aide, Appleby, answered it, then handed it to the general.

"Marc?" It was General Morrison. "There's been a Level One theft at Kapalama."

Mayland had been preparing himself for the worst. But a Level One theft! It seemed impossible. That was Eyes Only documents for top-level command. "Shit! What happened?"

"It seems a Major Guerrero walked off with some pretty top stuff. Luckily for us, a KQUA helicopter reported that Guerrero boarded a Lear jet at Honolulu International. The pilot filed a flight plan for Anchorage, but radar has them headed toward Petropavlovsk."

"Why aren't they flying under the radar nets?"

"Good question. Maybe they're expecting company." The general paused briefly to let the connotations of his observation sink in, then continued. "ComNafPac has alerted the *Lexington*, but she's just a training carrier and has limited attack capability."

Mayland did not hesitate. "You want me to scramble something?"

"Yes. Get a Section up immediately. Honolulu radar can give you the approximate location to vector them in on. I want that Lear turned around and brought back to Hickam. We cannot allow it to reach the Soviet Union."

"What the hell did they steal?"

"I can't tell you, even over a secured line. All I can say is that it could change the balance of power in the Pacific!"

Maggie O'Brien worked furiously at the printed circuitry of the SUBDACS innards aboard *Pocatello*. She broke out several connectors, plugging them into different configurations alongside the sonar control console. By utilizing the combat system of the ACS-2 and reversing the SUBDACS controls to the radome in the bow of the boat, she could enhance hydrophone transducers strung along the hull. Instead of only listening, *Pocatello* could utilize its own masks and send counterfeit signature broadcasts to eavesdropping submarines. All she had to do was match the decibel cycle of sound to the pulses of the mask.

"That thing about ready?" Bertanelli asked, sticking his head through the door of the sonar station.

Maggie jumped. She wiped the perspiration from her forehead. "Almost, Captain," she said, trying to mask her annoyance.

"We're running out of time, Miss O'Brien."

She shook her head in exasperation. "We agreed on two and a half hours."

"We agreed on two," Bertanelli said, pointing to

his watch. "And that's fifteen minutes away."

Maggie sniffed and turned to Caldwell to ask for the soldering wand. The air was thick with the smell of burnt flux. Bertanelli turned away and motioned to Ralston. "We should be picking up something soon. We dug big holes in the ocean back there and the *Sturgeons* will know exactly where we are."

"It'll take them a few minutes to catch us, sir." The young officer's throat was suddenly dry. He knew the captain was planning something, but for the life of him, he could not figure out what.

"I calculate about fifteen."

Caldwell glanced at the bulkhead clock. "That'll give you a three-minute leeway, Miss O'Brien."

"I heard you the first time," she snapped, soldering connectors onto the cables that would allow them to fit the sonar inputs.

"A little testy, aren't we?" Bertanelli asked.

She glowered at him. "We both know you didn't want me on your ship."

"Boat, Miss O'Brien. A submarine is called a boat."

"I had to get JCS approval to be here just to monitor my own equipment." A thin chill hung on the edge of her words. "If I were a man, there would have been no question about my right to be on board!"

"This is a man's world down here, Miss O'Brien. We play by hard and dangerous rules. It's no place for a woman."

"You have something against women?" she asked, looking up into his eyes, her own eyes blazing with indignation.

"Not on the beach."

"But on *Pocatello*?"

Bertanelli's nostrils flared slightly. "This may be

62

the last bastion of male supremacy, Miss O'Brien, but it's a bastion nonetheless."

"You sound like a perfect role model for a male chauvinist."

"I have nothing against women. You, no doubt, are a genius at what you do. I admire your accomplishments. I could not do what you have done. Nor can you do what I do. I just believe we should stay in our own environments and do what we do best."

"I see."

"I doubt it, Miss O'Brien. Women seem to have this unfathomable belief that they belong everywhere. I, for one, do not believe they belong down here." He looked at his watch. "You now have eleven minutes." He turned toward the door. "Don't screw it up."

"I wouldn't dream of it!" she yelled.

Bertanelli paused in the doorway. "There has never been a mutiny on an American ship, Miss O'Brien."

"It's a boat, Captain."

The sudden lively twinkle in Bertanelli's eyes only helped to incense her more.

Bertanelli chuckled as he stepped out into the corridor. Maggie glared after him for a moment, then returned to her equipment, seething with rage. "Who the hell does he think he is," she shouted. "God?"

"Sometimes," Caldwell replied. "Definitely sometimes."

A Vought F-8 Crusader catapulted into the afternoon sun from the aircraft carrier *Lexington*'s launch deck. The day fighter pulled into a vertical twenty-one thousand foot-per-minute climb to achieve mission altitude of thirty-five thousand feet, then leveled off, swung to port and headed south. A second Crusader lifted off the deck almost immediately and rose to join the first.

The F-8s were holdovers from the Vietnam War, now used primarily as training planes. In those days, the Crusaders were the scourge of the Tonkin Gulf, responsible for fifty-three percent of all MiGs shot down during the war. They had participated in the first reprisals in 1964, were used as both photoreconnaissance and escort planes, and often led bombing strikes against North Vietnam as lead decoys. But the Voughts had fallen into disuse of late and, except for their four cannon and two wing-mounted sidewinders, they were ill-equipped for modern-day combat.

Lt. Gray Davis, a thirty-seven-year-old Alabamian, commanded the present "Hunter" mission. He was one of the flight instructors aboard *Lexington*, and the most experienced pilot available to fly. His wingman, Lt. (j.g.) Wayne Holme, pulled in alongside him at just over five hundred miles per hour.

"Hunter One to Home Plate," Davis radioed *Lexington*. "At thirty-five angels, on course to intercept. Vector us in."

"Home Plate to Hunter One. Turn to two zero three degrees. Last identification, target at thirty-four angels."

"Roger, Home Plate." Davis glanced through the curved plexiglass canopy at his wingman. "Let's go get him now, Wayne ol' buddy," he drawled.

Going to full throttle, within minutes both planes were screaming west at just over one thousand miles per hour.

*   *   *

Six hundred miles west of Honolulu, and two hundred miles south of the *Lexington*, the *Mike* class Soviet attack submarine *Suslov* glided silently through the water, running at periscope depth. An urgent radio message from Eastern Naval Force at Petropavlovsk in southeastern Kamchatka had gotten the *Suslov* moving from the position it had been maintaining just over the most western point of the Kinmei Seamount.

The newest and most advanced of the Soviet killer submarines, the *Suslov* had been launched from Severodvinsk in August of the previous year. At nine thousand tons, it was longer than a football field and boasted a single liquid metal cooled nuclear reactor and could hit a top speed of thirty-seven knots submerged. The bull-nosed boat was coated with cluster guard anechoic tiles, and its titanium hull made it impossible to detect by magnetic disturbance from the air.

With silicon impacted shafts, trailing sound-absorbing baffles, and hydraulic suspended reactor and engine mounts, *Suslov* was the quietest boat in the Soviet fleet. It also had the new Japanese silent propellers which had been sold to the Russians despite a threatened embargo by the Americans for whom the design had first been created. The controversial sale had resulted in mass marches on Washington and the smashing of Japanese-made radios and electronic equipment by irate citizens along Pennsylvania Avenue. But the demonstrations had been to no avail. Business was, after all, business.

Captain First Rank Emelyan Yukunivich Yakunin, a thirteen-year veteran of submarine command, was ignorant of all of this history. As far as he knew, the special equipment on his boat had been designed and manufactured in Leningrad. Nor did he really care. All that mattered to Yakunin was the fact that the super silent boat had allowed him to slip in beside unsuspecting American surface ships without their sensing his presence—an achievement no other Russian captain had ever accomplished, twice earning him the Order of Lenin, one of which had been bestowed on him by Premier Ognev himself.

Now Yakunin stood in the control room of *Suslov*, surveying his boat and crew, the eerie glow from the fluorescent lighting and monitoring screens casting a greenish glitter on the black-uniformed men who served him. Mostly conscripts from *kollectiv* farms with limited experience in electronics, the crew of the *Suslov* were young men embarking on a new and exciting adventure—one where they had already seen their captain outsmart the American imperialists on two separate occasions.

His own harshest critic, Yakunin himself was not impressed. There had been no SOSUS or ASW—Anti-Submarine Warfare—monitoring stations looking for him. They simply had not been looking for him. Had Yakunin fully comprehended the sophistication of American sonar, which could monitor Soviet submarines from a thousand miles away using their TBS towed arrays systems, he might have given himself considerably more credit.

As it was, Yakunin's impressive achievements did give him a certain status over the *zampolit* Mikola Govskaya, the Kremlin's eyes and ears aboard his boat. It was always difficult on these first voyages with a new crew. The men usually had more knowledge of the Party than they did of fighting machinery, and little interest in either. But Yakunin had no political ideologies. All he cared about was the sea. He had gone to sea in the first place to avoid the squalor and day-to-day deprivation of Soviet life. While a patriot, enobling everything good and honorable in Russian men, Yakunin was neither a Soviet, nor a Party member. He accepted Communism as inevitable, discussed it intellectually and promoted it within the Service as he was expected to do, yet never did he consider himself a *Komsomol*. He was a *red bourgeois*—a member of the "new class"—and a *Menshevik*, one of the small but growing number of intellectual leaders within the Soviet Union. He knew it was inevitable that such groups would control the country in time. Until then, he was more than content to remain at sea.

Turning to his sonar operator, Yakunin asked the man what he saw.

"Nothing, Comrade Captain," came the reply. "All screens are clear."

Yakunin nodded. *"Michman,* how much water under the keel?"

"We have just cleared the ridge, Comrade Captain," the warrant officer, Felix Stelest, replied. "We have two thousand five hundred meters beneath us."

Yakunin looked down at the paper he held in his hand, a recently received and newly decoded top-secret message from Submarine Command at Polyarnny. The captain frowned. He was not excited about the prospects of these new orders. The simplest missions always seemed to have an element of difficulty to them that no one ever anticipated. And to surface in the middle of the Pacific in the daytime would certainly divulge *Suslov*'s location to the entire United States Navy.

"Why are we changing course?" Mikola Govskaya, the boat's political officer, demanded. Though junior to Yakunin in rank, the boat's *zampolit* always had unrestricted authority whenever he should choose to use it.

The captain handed Govskaya the message. The

political officer read it over twice, then looked up at Yakunin inquisitively. "Strange errand for *Suslov*."

"They must be expecting trouble."

Govskaya nodded. He handed the note back to Yakunin, then turned and walked over to the chart table. The executive officer, Captain Third Rank Lev Savitsky, edged over next to Yakunin, glancing over his long-time friend's shoulder. "What's going on?" he asked.

"High Command wants us to proceed to certain coordinates in case we are needed."

"Needed?" Savitsky glanced back at Govskaya. "Needed for what?"

"Who knows the mind of Moscow?" Yakunin replied softly. "I have a bad feeling about this, Lev."

The smaller, kindly-faced Savitsky nodded knowingly but said nothing.

Crumpling the note up in his hand, Yakunin turned back to his crew. "*Michman,* prepare to dive," he ordered.

"Very well, Comrade Captain."

"Flood forward ballast tanks."

"Forward ballast tanks flooded, Comrade Captain."

"Bow planes down eight degrees. Stern plates up." Yakunin turned to his warrant officer. "All right, Felix, take us down."

Stelest nodded and relayed the order. The hull shuddered as the turbine started to revolve. *Suslov* angled over and rocketed down into the ocean's depths.

President Colin Freeman had been the dark horse candidate, coming out of nowhere to surprise the nation and win the recent election with a substantial majority of the popular vote. The Iowa senator had been a virtual unknown until the campaigning began. But during his party's bitterly fought primary battle, Freeman had displayed a sharp mind and a quick wit coupled with a rock-solid grasp of the important issues of the day. All this, plus his youth— being a mere forty-one years old—and a rugged, all-American handsomeness that seemed to be accentuated by the television cameras, added up to a November shoo-in. But up until this moment, President Colin Freeman had been an untested commodity whose most difficult decision had been which tuxedo to wear to the inaugural ball.

All that was about to change, however, as the new president sat behind his desk in the Oval Office staring at four-star Gen. Harris Shriner seated directly across from him. Deep worry lines seemed permanently etched into Freeman's forehead as the general outlined the situation.

"Guerrero got everything, Mr. President," the general said. Marion T. Olsen, seated to Shriner's left, shifted uncomfortably in his chair.

The frown on the president's face seemed to intensify. "And just what exactly do you mean by everything, General?" he asked.

"Battle logs, station points, communication frequencies, and the Priority Red Codes, sir."

The president sat back in his chair, momentarily stunned.

Admiral Olsen cleared his throat. "The station points will allow the Soviets to pinpoint every boomer and attack sub in the Pacific, sir," he said. "Our boats will be sitting ducks out there."

Shriner and Olsen, the two ranking members of the Joint Chiefs of Staff, had been summoned by the president as soon as he had been informed of the

Kapalama theft. The intensity of their expressions revealed the enormity of the present crisis.

"The Priority Red Codes were just issued," Shriner went on. "It'd take us three or four months to recoup."

"And just what is being done about all this, gentlemen?" the president asked, his tone level and firm.

"We have launched two fighters from the *Lexington*, sir," the admiral replied.

"And two more from Hickam," Shriner added. "We'll simply turn the Lear back to Honolulu, or . . ." His voice trailed off. Had the previous occupant of the Oval Office been sitting across the desk, Shriner would not have hesitated to recommend force. Now he was uncertain.

"Or what, General?"

Shriner glanced at Olsen. "We certainly can't let the Lear reach Russia, sir."

"Definitely not!" Freeman boomed. "What is your recommendation?"

There was a slight pause. Then Shriner answered. "If we can't turn the Lear around, then we shoot it down."

"You damn well better!" the president shouted. He leaned back in his chair and eyed the two men suspiciously. "Now, just how did this occur?" he asked, his hands folded across his chest.

"A foul-up between the FBI and our people at Pearl, sir," Olsen said quickly.

"Mostly the Bureau," Shriner added. "They had this Guerrero under surveillance, but let him get away."

"The thing is, sir," Olsen continued, "that nobody told our security that Guerrero was under investigation. Or even that he was suspected of selling secrets

70

to the Soviets."

"Had the military known," the general interjected, "we could have limited or controlled his access to such sensitive documents."

"So you're saying it's all the Bureau's fault?" Freeman asked.

"Of course not, sir," Shriner said. "But this could have been avoided had we known of Guerrero's questionable activities."

"Perhaps you also ought to consider beefing up the security at Kapalama. These stolen secrets could set us back years, maybe even give the Soviets control of the Pacific. We must not, under any circumstances, allow this to happen!"

The two officers squirmed uncomfortably in their chairs. This president was considerably tougher than either had originally thought. "We'll stop them from getting to Russia!" Olsen promised emphatically.

"See that you do!"

Two General Dynamic F-16E fighter planes started down the runway at Hickam Air Force base and ascended majestically into the early evening sky. Banking south, they lined up on the Diamond Head beacon and rose rapidly to thirty thousand feet.

Capt. Travis Romney, in Intercept One, glanced over at his trailing wingman, Lieutenant First Class Alex Marshall. Travis jerked his thumb up in an age-old salute, then switched on his radio and dialed in Hickam Command. "Halbred, this is Intercept One at three-four angels," he radioed, "heading one niner five degrees, approximately one zero miles southwest of beacon three."

"Intercept One," the radio crackled in response, "come right to course two six five degrees. You are looking for a civilian Lear jet on course two four seven, at two-eight angels, approximately four five zero miles west of you."

"Roger, Halbred." Travis switched the control to his wingman. "Got that, Alex?"

"Roger."

"Turning right to course two six five."

The two Fighting Falcons turned over on their starboard wing and came on course.

"Intercept One, this is Halbred. Switch on your nav/attack system."

Travis froze. Unconsciously he touched the ear section of his helmet. "Say again, Halbred?"

"Switch on your attack system."

"Did you say we're looking for a civilian Lear?"

"Affirmative, Intercept One," the radio buzzed back. "Is your attack system on?"

Travis obediently reached forward and switched on the beyond-visual-range Lantirn system. Despite his great misgivings, Travis Romney's decade of dedicated service in the U.S.A.F. had taught him to obey orders quickly and without questions. Heads-up displays jumped to life on the plexiglass before him, and screens began sweeping over the horizon for possible targets. "Attack system on, Halbred."

"Do not lock on target until ordered to do so, Intercept One. Repeat, do not lock on, until ordered to do so."

"That's a roge, Halbred." Travis switched his radio transmitter off. Pushing all nagging doubts from his mind, he raced his F-16E toward its destination.

CHAPTER SEVEN

8:15 p.m. (Honolulu)/0615 Hours Zulu (Pocatello)

Pocatello slid gracefully through the subthermals toward the Milwaukee seamount, about fifty miles southeast of the battle group. With his noisy departure, Bertanelli had successfully lured the three *Sturgeons* after him.

"Navigation, where are we?" the captain asked.

Higgins checked his instruments. "One mile from Milwaukee," he replied.

"Diving Officer, take us down to one thousand feet."

"One thousand feet, aye."

"Helm, circle us around the seamount. Maintain all ahead full."

In sonar, Maggie grumbled as she worked frantically to complete the SUBDACS conversion. "Fifteen minutes, Miss O'Brien," she muttered, mimicking Bertanelli's voice. "Don't screw it up, Miss O'Brien." She switched leads from her terminal to that of the boat's sonar. "Six more minutes, Miss O'Brien. Are you going to be ready, Miss O'Brien?"

Caldwell, dividing his attention between his CRT screen and Maggie's soliloquy, grinned broadly. He had been with the captain a long time and understood her frustration all too well. Bertanelli could be a hard man to work for, he thought. But all in all, the captain was fair, and Caldwell had no complaints.

Maggie yelped in pain as she smashed her finger trying to tighten one of the cables. "Damn nice of him to give me three more minutes," she snapped. "As though all I'm doing here is switching a light bulb!"

Caldwell and Zimmer exchanged amused glances.

As if right on cue, Bertanelli's voice came booming over the p.a. speakers.

"Control to sonar. Is that damned thing ready yet?"

Maggie did not bother looking up. "Tell him the damned thing is *almost* ready!"

Ralston relayed the information through the intercom.

"I believe you have one minute left, Miss O'Brien."

"One minute left, Miss O'Brien," Maggie mimicked, shaking her head in exasperation as she plugged in the last connector. "What does he think this is, a test?" Deftly she typed in a command and watched as it came up on the sonar CRT screen. "Bingo!"

"Sonar to control," Ralston transmitted. "We're up and ready."

"About time," Bertanelli said. "Stand by."

Maggie glanced up at the speaker and frowned. Caldwell turned in his chair and regarded her inquisitively.

"Just what'll that thing do, Miss O'Brien?" he asked.

"Something your sonar cannot do, Jason." Maggie smiled. The excitement and pride in her words was clearly evident. "It'll see through marine disturbance too great for your BC-10 to wash away.

74

It'll pick up an emission trail of a nuclear reactor after the boat is long gone." Maggie's grin widened. "It'll even tell you of a presence when your hydrophones are being screened out."

Caldwell's face tightened, taking on a dark, concerned expression. "That'll make sonar obsolete."

"I think not. SUBDACS has limited range. It is merely an additional tool to work along with your sonar."

Caldwell looked doubtful. He was visualizing his beloved sonar being sent into mothballs.

"I'm switching on," Maggie said. She pushed a button and instantly the clutter on the CRT screen quadrupled.

"Holy shit!" Zimmer hollered in pain, yanking his earphones from his head.

Caldwell scrambled for the gain controls and gave the knob a spin. "Geeze, you might have warned us!"

Ralston sat back in his chair and smiled. Any discomfort the sonar operators experienced was fine with him. They were both too smug and self-centered to suit his tastes.

"I'm sorry," Maggie said. "We use crystal conductors that moves sound at six thousand meters per second while enhancing the ratio four point five."

"That's twelve thousand miles an hour!" Zimmer exclaimed.

"And over four times louder." Caldwell chuckled. "We can now hear porkfish making love."

"Can't you ever be serious?" Ralston demanded.

Caldwell frowned. "That's a serious matter to porkfish," he replied.

Zimmer studied his terminal intently. "We're picking up something."

Caldwell began spinning conrols to filter out ambient noises. Three blips appeared, then solidified

75

in the waterfalls until target registrations occurred. "The *Sturgeons*," he said, matter-of-factly.

Ralston stared at the blips on the screen in disbelief. "The blips," he said, "they just . . . appeared!"

"They were there all the time," Maggie replied. "But the masks they're running made them invisible to your sonar."

"Then how?"

"SUBDACS picks up their neutron emission. Once it is registered as a submarine, sound is magnified and the speed is increased until the revolutions of the mask are exceeded. When that happens, the hydrophone suites zero in on the exposed sound." Maggie grinned proudly. "It's all very simple."

Caldwell shook his head in amazement. "I'm just glad you're on our side."

"Is that plugged into the BSY-2 system?" Ralston asked.

Maggie nodded. Quickly he called the information in to the control room.

In one of the most ruthless and bloody coups in modern history, Oleg Dmitrevich Ognev had wrested control of the Soviet Union from the vaunted youth movement, effectively burying *glasnost* while closing the doors to Western interference. A short, pig-faced man with bushy eyebrows, Ognev, at 74, was one of the last of the Russian "Old Line." Now, with his substantial girth nearly overflowing from his creaking chair, the Soviet Party Chairman glared suspiciously over the top of his desk at his chief military advisor, Field Marshall Nikolai Istomin. "You are certain everything is going like clockwork?"

the Russian leader asked.

"*Da,* Comrade Chairman," the officer replied. A bloodied veteran of both the Second World War and the Afghanistan debacle, Istomin was the most decorated uniformed officer in the Soviet Union. "The plane has taken off. We have an escort on the way and, just in case, we have dispatched three submarines along its flight path."

Ognev cleared his throat noisily. Removing a handkerchief, the chairman spat into it, folded it over and returned it to his pocket. "The documents are aboard?" he asked.

"So I have been told."

Ognev shot the officer an accusing look. "You do not know for certain?"

"Comrade Chairman," Istomin said, choosing his words carefully, "the KGB was placed in charge of this operation. They have reported that Colonel Turbin has radioed in, confirming that the documents are in his possession."

The hard lines in Ognev's face relaxed as he sat back. "Then we can now move," he said, building a steeple of his hands across his ample stomach. "This new American president will have no taste for the hard decisions he will have to make," he added, smiling smugly. "Mark my words, General, he will be slow to act. Too slow to make any difference."

The field marshall nodded, keeping his features stern and his body erect. "Admiral Gugin awaits only your orders to loose his entire eastern fleet into the Pacific."

"When I have the plans in my hands, Nikolai. Not before."

"Of course, Comrade Chairman," Istomin agreed. "Of course."

Ognev felt himself tingling with excitement. He

77

had the Americans right where he wanted them. A few more hours and the stolen documents would open the door for the Soviets to gain control of the Pacific—a goal many of his predecessors had shared, but none had been able to accomplish. The chairman chuckled softly. Once Freeman, an unknown without the strength of hard-line Washington support behind him, had been elected, Ognev knew the time was ripe.

"I want to know the instant those documents are in our hands," the premier said. "And put Admiral Gugin on standby alert."

"Yes, Comrade Chairman. I will attend to it immediately."

Istomin saluted, turned sharply and left the office. Ognev sat quietly behind his desk for several moments. Then a boisterous laugh exploded from deep within his massive body. "The Pacific is mine!" he crowed to the empty room.

Bertanelli glanced around the control room. In moments he would strike, but not until the boat was ready.

"Control to sonar. Any change?"

"Sonar to control. None."

Bertanelli smiled. He liked being privy to information his adversaries did not have. Though the other subs thought they were running invisible behind their masks, "Crazy Tony" had them in his sights.

"Passing Milwaukee, Captain."

Bertanelli nodded. It was time. "Left full rudder."

"Left full rudder, aye."

"All ahead full."

"All ahead full, aye."

The boat moved abruptly forward and Bertanelli

found himself holding on to the pedestal rail for support.

"Sonar to control. Seamount blockage. We've lost sonar contact with the *Sturgeons*."

Bertanelli smiled. *And they've lost contact with us,* he thought. "And Miss O'Brien?"

"Registering neutron emissions."

Jamison's eyes narrowed. "Neutron emissions?" he asked quizzically. "What the hell is that?"

"Beats me," Bertanelli replied.

"You think she knows what she's doing?"

"The JCS must. They put her on this boat."

Jamison shook his head gravely. But Bertanelli smiled. "All ahead flank," he ordered. "I want thirty-five knots."

"All ahead flank, aye."

The captain's smile widened, splitting his face from ear to ear.

In the reactor, poppet valves clicked, vents opened, steam in the exchanger rose and spilled over into the turbines, adding more revolutions to the shaft that turned the propeller. *Pocatello* knifed through the ocean at flank speed.

Aboard the U.S.S. *Batfish*, Cmdr. Aubrey Parkin stood watching the drama unfold before him with wry amusement. He had never met Bertanelli, but he knew of his reputation, as did nearly every seaman aboard. Their first "sinking" of the *Pocatello* had been met with raucous cheers throughout the boat. A second sinking, Parkin knew, would not only bring bedlam to *Batfish*, but likely get him the command of a *Los Angeles* class submarine. Maybe even the 758 which was due to be launched early in January.

"Steady as she goes," he muttered.

"Aye."

"Sonar to control. *Pocatello* is turning to port. She's gone to flank speed, digging big holes in the water."

"Helm, all ahead flank speed."

"All ahead flank, aye."

"Sonar to control. She's gone behind Milwaukee. We've lost her."

Parkin hurried to the chart table. He ordered up a view from the UKY-5 nav/computer. Within seconds the entire sea bottom was displayed. "Plug in the BQQ2."

Transducers in the fifteen foot sonar sphere in the nose of *Batfish* fed information from hydrophones in a conformal array on the sides of the forward hull to the BQS13 array system. This, in turn, was fed to the UYK-5 nav/computer, and then onto the chart table viewing screen. Parkin traced the route of *Pocatello* around the jutting seamount that topped out at 1,050 feet.

Suddenly the captain straightened. "By damn, he knows we're on his tail!" Despite himself, Parkin felt the corners of his mouth begin turning up in a smile.

"How could he know that?" Lt. Ted Hallen, the navigation officer, asked in astonishment. "We're running one of those masks."

"It doesn't matter," Parkin replied. "This time he's outsmarted himself."

"How's that?"

"Just watch a master at work." Turning to the helm officer, Parkin ordered, "Left full rudder. Come to course one seven five degrees."

"Left full rudder, aye. Course one seven five degrees, aye."

Parkin looked at Hallen. "Get ready," he said.

"We're about to bag Crazy Tony once again."

Gen. Marcus H. Mayland raced in through the doors of Hickam command center. His vice-commander, Col. Justin Mallory, looked up as his superior whizzed by. "We have a shoot order, General!"

Mayland stopped short. "On the Lear?" he asked. Mallory nodded.

"Admiral Blanchard called it in a few minutes ago."

Mayland looked down at the situation board. "Shooting down a civilian plane. This is crazy."

"We made a voice print for you, Marc. I knew you'd want to hear it yourself."

Mallory pushed a button on the desk recorder and played the message back. "If the Lear cannot be turned around," the distinctive voice of Adm. William T. Blanchard, Chief of Pacific Command, ordered, "the JCS has approved that you shoot it down. The plane must not be allowed to reach its Soviet destination."

Mayland looked back to the situation board. He had little doubt the Lear would turn around when approached by two armed fighter planes. "Where is the target now?"

Mallory ordered the tracking be called up. "It skirted Midway airspace and is now turning northwest toward Kamchatka."

A light appeared on the board.

"And the *Lexington* flight?" Mayland asked.

Another light materialized, far to the northeast.

"I doubt the Crusaders will have enough range to rendezvous with them," Mallory said. He ordered another overlay, and two more lights appeared crossing over Midway Island. "The F-16s will intercept in twenty minutes."

Mayland surveyed the board. "Just in case, ready a section at Shemya."

Three red lights suddenly appeared on the board four hundred miles west of the Lear jet. Monitors across the board began to light up and buzzers sounded noisily.

"Incoming bogeys!" a floor supervisor called out.

"MiGs, by the look of them," another reported.

"They're traveling near Mach Two!" yelled a third.

Mallory looked at Mayland. "What the hell?"

"That's why the Lear has been flying up there!" Mayland exclaimed. "He hasn't been concerned about being picked up on radar! He's counting on an escort!"

CHAPTER EIGHT

8:35 p.m. Honolulu/0635 Hours Zulu

The two F-8 Crusaders flew into the setting sun, nearing the limit of their six hundred mile flight radius.

"Spot anything, Wayne?" Gray Davis asked of his wingman.

"Negative."

Davis looked out his canopy, then back on the radar screen. He checked his fuel, tapping the instrument glass out of habit. "Shoot," the Southerner mumbled, "we'd better spot something pretty damn fast."

"I've got five minutes fuel to mid-point," Wayne Holme said.

Davis checked his radar again. No blips were showing. He dialed in the carrier on the radio band. "Hunter One to Home Plate. We-all have a negative."

"Home Plate to Hunter One, continue on course. Your target dead ahead."

Davis tapped the fuel gauge once again. Present conditions had not allowed for a refueling so they were flying dry.

"Five minutes fuel remaining before we-all gotta

turn around," he radioed the carrier.

"A tanker is now in the air, Hunter One."

Too little, too damn late, Davis thought, shaking his head. He called over to Wayne Holme. "That there's another fifteen minutes air time."

"We're cutting it pretty thin. They better be fast on that tanker when we turn back."

Davis nodded. With a trainee on the hose, they could burn up a lot of gas while being refueled. "We'll give it fifteen minutes."

"You're needed over the target," the carrier radioed. "We just identified three MiGs heading for intercept."

Davis's jaw dropped. "Hell's fire! You-all expect us to face three MiGs with dry tanks?"

"This is not a shooting exercise," the carrier responded. "You are under rules of engagement only."

Who makes up these damn stupid rules? Davis asked himself.

Field Marshall Nikolai Istomin stood watching the situation board at Moscow Central. Cadres of uniformed monitors watched individual screens throughout a large war room.

A young aide ran up to him and saluted. "Comrade Field Marshall," he said, "our flight will make contact with the Lear seventy-five seconds after the American fighters."

"That's too late!" Istomin bellowed. "Have them go to their after-burners. They must arrive sooner!"

"But, Comrade Field Marshall. If they do that, they will not have enough fuel to make it back."

"The devil with that! We must stop the Americans from capturing or shooting down Colonel Turbin!"

The aide turned and passed the order along. Then he turned back to Istomin. "And when our planes reach the Americans?"

"Have them open fire. I want no witnesses!"

Bertanelli swung away from the monitoring station. "All ahead stop. Right full rudder. Maintain this depth." He turned to weapons control. "Marv, load up the target sonar. We're going to have company pretty quick."

Ashton activated the Mark 117 Mod 6 fire control system. He switched on the sonar targeting sensors and waited.

"Sonar to control." Ralston's voice squawked over the intercom. "We are tracking two targets. One bearing three one six degrees, the second at three one niner. Range fifteen thousand yards. Elevation/depression angle ten degrees positive." The two *Sturgeons* were still several hundred feet above them.

Two targets! Bertanelli grabbed the intercom telephone. "Control to sonar. What do you mean, two targets? There should be three!"

"Two, sir."

Bertanelli whirled to face Jamison. 'It's got to be *Batfish*. Parkin didn't take the bait."

"We have computer ID on *Silversides* and *Bluefish*." It was Caldwell's voice on the intercom this time. "No sign of the *Batfish*, sir."

"Renick and Armstrong always were a mite anxious," Jamison offered.

Bertanelli nodded. He knew Renick and Armstrong personally. He did not know Parkin, who had transferred from the Atlantic Fleet less than six months earlier. But word had it the commander was a fine officer.

"I have firing solutions, Captain," Ashton said calmly.

"Control to sonar. Is *Batfish* still screened out by the seamount?"

"Aye, sir."

"Then Caldwell, hard ping 'em both! And don't hold back the juice."

Caldwell gleefully powered up the active transducers and punched the impulse control, sending out a wave front of sound energy.

Ping, ping, ping, ping!

Pong!

Pong!

Bertanelli smiled and glanced back at Admiral Sward. "That's two!" he said, proudly. *But where's the third?* he asked himself.

"I have a bogey at two o'clock, twenty miles out," Alex Marshall called. "But it sure as hell isn't a Lear jet. It's making almost a thousand knots."

In the lead F-16, Capt. Travis Romney moved the knobs on his radar controls. He was getting the same indication as Alex. "Maybe that's the flight from *Lexington*."

"Wait! I have another blip at eleven o'clock. Two-eight angels. Speed, four hundred thirty knots."

Travis shuddered involuntarily. "I have him, too," he confirmed. "Halbred," he radioed, "we have sight of the bogey. We're slowing to five five zero knots."

"Do you have visual contact?" Hickam asked.

"No."

"Must have positive identification. Fuselage ID number Tango, Echo, Whiskey, three, one, seven, niner. Repeat, must have positive identification."

"I see the target!" Romney called out.

President Freeman shook his head in disbelief. "Are you certain, General?" he said into the telephone receiver.

On the other end of the line, Shriner inhaled deeply. "Sir," he reported, "the MiGs are confirmed."

"Who'll reach the Lear first?"

"It'll be close, sir. The MiGs went to after-burners a minute ago. It might be a tie."

Freeman swore quietly under his breath. Shooting down spies escaping with state secrets was one thing, even if they were in a civilian plane. But shooting at Soviet aircraft, no matter what their intentions, might be another. "What do you suggest, General?"

"We can't tie our pilot's hands, sir."

"And we can't act prematurely. Is that clear?"

"Rules of engagement?"

"That's the best I can do."

"I want to be clear, sir. If the MiGs show any hostile act, our pilots have permission to protect themselves? They can open fire on the Soviet planes?"

Freeman paused briefly. "That's how I understand the rules of engagement, General."

"Thank you, sir."

"Keep me posted."

Breaking the connection, Shriner slowly set the instrument back in its cradle and picked up a direct line to Hickam. Hearing a familiar voice on the other end, Shriner spoke, dispensing with the formality of an introduction. "General Mayland, you can tell your pilots they are free to protect themselves under the rules of engagement."

"What about the Lear?" Mayland asked.

"Shoot it down!" Shriner replied, emphatically. "And do it before the MiGs can make a difference!"

Bertanelli was furious. He had seriously misjudged another commander, in this case Aubrey Parkin in the *Batfish*, which was something he was not prone to do. Such mistakes often resulted in sunk submarines.

"Sonar to Control," Caldwell said over the intercom, "Miss O—." He caught himself, stopping before he mentioned her name over the speaker. "We're, uh, we're picking up a reading bearing zero niner zero degrees."

"*Batfish?*"

"I, uh, don't know, Captain. It's behind the seamount."

"Then how can you get a reading on it?"

"It's, uh—"

"From neutron emissions, Captain." Maggie's voice broke in over the intercom. Everyone in the control room looked up in surprise. A woman's voice on the loudspeaker was something not often—in fact never—heard.

Bertanelli stormed out of the control room and made a beeline to sonar. "And just what is that?" he asked, bursting into the station.

"SUBDACS can identify the presence of a nuclear power plant up to twenty five thousand yards," Maggie replied calmly.

"But the seamount."

"The source must be coming over the seamount, Captain. The water is heating up."

Bertanelli grabbed the intercom telephone. "Willie, this is Tony. Turn us around quietly to bearing zero niner zero. And rig for ultra quiet." He turned to Maggie. "So Parkin is coming over the seamount, is he? Well, we'll give him a warm welcome." He started to turn away but stopped in mid-rotation. He eyed Maggie intently. "I sure hope you know what you're talking about, Miss O'Brien," he said. Then he turned and walked out of the room.

"I have three more blips fifteen miles west of us," Alex called. "And, hot diggity damn, they're coming *fast!*"

"Three bogeys heading at us from the west," Travis radioed Hickam. "Speed approximately Mach two."

"Halbred to Intercept One. You are ordered to splash the target Lear. Now!"

Travis felt his blood freeze. "Shoot him down? What the hell for? He's a civilian!"

"This is General Mayland," the deep voice buzzed in Travis's ears. "You have three Russian MiGs coming at you, and we believe them to be hostile. They are probably escorts for the Lear, which contains vital information that cannot be allowed out of our hands. Shoot the Lear down, and the MiGs will turn away."

Travis stared at the Marconi Avionics holographic HUD displays, registering the Lear, the F-8 Crusaders, and the approaching MiGs. Suddenly, the two blips to the north turned away. Maybe the retreating aircraft were the MiGs and the ones approaching were from the *Lexington*. He offered the theory to Mayland.

"Dammit, Captain," the General shouted impatiently, "shoot down the Lear! *Now!*"

Travis took a deep breath. Suddenly cast in the roles of cop, judge, jury and executioner, his thoughts flew back to the previous weekend. A good buddy had taken Travis and his six-year-old son Tyson for a ride in his private Lear jet—one frighteningly similar to the aircraft Romney was now ordered to shoot out of the sky.

Travis shook the memories from his mind and got back to the pressing business at hand. He glanced at the blips on his radar screen. If they were Russian, he would not stand a chance. Not at this speed. He looked across to his wingman. "I'm diving on the target now," he radioed.

The F-16s dropped four thousand feet, slowed to four hundred thirty knots, and pulled alongside the Lear jet.

"Lear jet Tango, Echo, Whiskey, three, one, seven, niner," Travis radioed. "You are ordered to return to Honolulu and land at Hickam Air Force Base."

There was no response. Travis looked across at the pilot who was stubbornly refusing to acknowledge his presence. The man's face was grim as he stared unblinking out the windscreen.

Travis swallowed hard. "I say again, Tango, Echo, Whiskey, three, one, seven, niner. Return to Honolulu or we have orders to shoot you down!"

Across the fifty yards in the Lear jet, squatting behind and between the two pilots, Colonel Turbin craned his neck to look out the side window at the F-16.

"He wants us to turn back to Honolulu," the pilot reported.

"Ignore him!"

"But he has *guns!*"

"Our planes will be along any moment!"

"I hope you are right, Colonel!" The pilot

nervously glanced across at his co-pilot. He worked his throttles, nosing over on the wheel. The Lear dropped several thousand feet. But the Falcons stayed right on its tail.

"Maybe we can stall them out," the co-pilot suggested.

The pilot nodded, dropping the Lear down below four hundred knots. The Falcons stayed right with it, using their flaps to slow their speed even further. At three hundred and fifty knots, the F-16s were in danger of stalling.

"Bogeys now at five miles," Alex shouted into his radio. He glanced across at the Lear. He could not see Travis beyond the commercial plane. "Speed, one thousand knots. Baby, they're coming right for us."

Travis moved in closer to the Lear and fired a short burst from his 20mm M61 cannon. "You are ordered to turn back," he transmitted, barely able to control the shaking in his voice. "Steer course zero eight five degrees."

"Captain Romney," Mayland yelled over the threat radio. "Shoot him down!"

They were at ten thousand feet, and still dropping.

"I have a visual on them!" Alex called excitedly. "Three MiG 31s. Positive ID. They're Foxhounds, and they look lean and mean."

Travis glanced up and saw the approaching MiGs. They were so close he could see the six Acrid and Apex missiles mounted under their wings. The F-15 Eagle look-alike with stolen F-18 Hornet lookdown/shootdown and multiple target engagements technology, headed straight for the F-16s. Each dropped its external fuel tanks.

In the Lear, Turbin saw the MiGs and laughed

gleefully. "See? I told you we'd have company soon."

"He says he's going to shoot us down unless we turn, *now!*" the pilot said nervously. He was on the verge of breaking, Turbin knew. The colonel snorted. He had little use for such gutless cowards. The Motherland employed far too many of them for his taste. "Just hang on. Our planes will make mincemeat of these flyboys."

Through the window, Turbin could see the MiGs fly straight at the two Falcons, then swerve slightly at the last moment, screaming on past them at supersonic speed. The F-16s were knocked aside by the wash. In the Lear, the pilot had to fight to maintain control.

Travis stabilized his fighter and peeled off to the left. "Break right, Alex," he yelled. "And engage."

"Hot diggity damn!" Alex hooted. "They shuffled the deck and sure dealt us one helluva hand." He turned to starboard and climbed, kicking in his afterburner. Raw fuel was dumped into the afterburning turbofan and out through the tailpipe as the twenty-four thousand pound thrust Pratt and Whitney engines pushed the Falcon forward like a startled cat. "They're turning!" Alex called. "They're coming back! Yeah! We're going to splash us some MiGs!"

CHAPTER NINE

8:43 p.m. Honolulu/0643 Hours Zulu

Everything was powered down on the *Pocatello.* The reactor was at three percent, barely enough to turn the generators and supply power to the essential machinery.

"Sonar to control," Caldwell whispered. "Neutron emissions increasing. We should have passive contact within a couple of minutes."

Bertanelli grinned despite himself. Caldwell obviously did not have the slightest idea what he was talking about. He was merely repeating information the woman was giving him. *Hell,* the captain thought, *I don't even know what she's talking about.*

"Weapons, be ready to lock on the second we have a contact."

"Aye."

"Parkin is in for a big surprise," Jamison said, loud enough for Sward to hear. "Looks like we're going to be three-for-five in a loaded contest."

"Stand by," Caldwell whispered.

"Standing by," the weapons officer responded.

Bertanelli glanced at Jamison. They both grinned broadly. After all, winning, they knew, was what it was all about. There was no second place.

Aubrey Parkin leaned over the repeater screen checking the information on the sonar clutter from the seamount. "Control to sonar. Do you hear anything?"

"Sonar to control. Not yet, sir."

"When we clear that seamount," Lt. Cmdr. Peter McFerson, *Batfish*'s executive officer, said, "we'll have him."

Parkin smiled. "I'd like to see the expression on Crazy Tony's face when we hit him again."

"Clearing seamount in forty-five seconds," sonar reported.

Banking his F-16 Falcon into a wide loop to the left, Travis turned in on the Lear. The civilian jet was still dropping, trying to get down out of sight and clear of the battle that was about to erupt between the fighters.

Travis locked on his nav/attack system.

"The MiGs are running hot!" Alex called.

Waiting until the lines connected on his screen, Travis then fingered the button on the AIM-9J wing-mounted Sidewinder missile. For an instant, he thought of his wife and son. What would Jan say about him firing on an unarmed civilian plane?

Turbin saw the Falcon turning in for the kill. "Bank!" he yelled. "Bank, you bastard!"

The pilot pulled hard over to starboard. But it was too late. The missile on the Falcon's left wing dropped, ignited, then came screaming toward them.

"He's fired!" the co-pilot shouted frantically.

Turbin backed away from the front and into the cabin, still clutching the briefcase tightly. As he started toward the door, a terrified Mariano Guerrero jumped up in front of him.

"What's happening?" the American cried.

Turbin raised his gun and shot Guerrero in the chest. The American went flying backward, his body spinning around in mid-air and landing in a crumpled heap on top of a packing crate, smashing it to splinters. The blood from his chest wound seeped out, staining the stacks of one hundred dollar bills he still clutched tightly to himself, even in death. His lifeless eyes stared at the floor, and at the scattered bills lying beneath his head.

As Turbin reached for the door handle, the missile hit.

Ramming into the rear-mounted engine, the AIM missile exploded into a brilliant ball of fire. The tail section was ripped off cleanly and the Lear went plummeting down to earth nose first.

Travis's Falcon was flying at eight hundred feet, a sitting duck for the MiGs.

"I have a lock on," Alex reported, his voice straining with excitement.

"Fire!" Travis yelled, pulling up his stick and kicking in his afterburner. But at the same time the light and warning buzzer on his control panel went on simultaneously. A MiG's weapon system was locked on to his plane.

Travis pulled back on the throttles and banked left, nosing down his Falcon. On the screen, two missiles streaked across the three mile distance. He knew he had no maneuvering room whatsoever. "Make sure the Lear is dead, Alex," he radioed to his wingman, "then make a run for it!"

With the enemy missiles screaming toward their target, Travis decided to attempt the impossible. At the last second before impact he banked sharply to the right, standing his plane on its wing, fifty feet off the water. The radar controls inside the warhead of the AA-7 Apex missile wavered, lost the connection, then re-established, swerving too late to compensate. Angling down over the port wing, it missed by ten feet. Travis leveled and banked to the left, dipping his port wing dangerously close to the water. The infrared homing of the AA-6 Acrid missile became fouled by Travis's tight turn, and struck the water, exploding on impact.

The concussion knocked the Falcon forward. Travis tried to level off but his wing struck a wave, somersaulting his plane into a tight turn. He yanked back on the stick and kicked the aileron to starboard in an attempt to straighten out. The Falcon turned into a negative G spin, bouncing across the water at thirty feet like a flat skimming rock thrown across the surface of a pond.

Half a mile away, the Lear jet hit the water and bounced. Settling on its wings, it sank quickly. The side door was flung open and one man, with a briefcase in his hand, leapt out. Then the plane was dragged under, carrying the two Russian pilots and the corpse of Mariano Guerrero to their last resting place.

Twenty-one thousand feet above the surface of the water, Alex's air-to-air Sidewinder missile struck the Mikoyan MiG in the welded stainless steel fuselage fuel cells forward of the tail section. With a tremendous BOOM, the Foxhound blew apart. Without missing a beat, Alex lined up on another MiG. Below, Travis reached up against the weight of gravity and yanked the canvas canopy down over his head, firing his ejection seat. He shot fifty feet into the air as the F-16 hit the water for the last time and broke apart, the wings and tail section spinning out across the sea like broken propeller blades.

Travis was flung high into the air, then dropped straight down like a rock.

Field Marshall Nikolai Istomin spun around on his heel to face his aide. "Three MiGs and still the Americans shot down the Lear! Where does the Motherland get these inept pilots?"

The aide held his tongue. Anything said now would only serve to further enrage the field marshall, an officer well known for his violent temper and unreasonable punishments.

"Get me Admiral Gugin on the phone!" Istomin ordered.

The aide whirled around, hurrying to comply. In seconds the admiral was on the line. "What can I do for you, Nikolai?" he asked.

"Get that submarine of yours into position!"

"The *Suslov*?"

"What the devil other submarine have you got out there? Of course the *Suslov*!"

"Then Turbin's plane went down?"

"Yes! Let's hope your submariners are not as inept as Boris's pilots!"

The wind buffeted Travis as he tumbled through the air. His parachute had popped open, but he knew he was far too low for it to do any good. He rolled into a tight ball as the water rushed up to greet him.

He hit hard. Sharp pain shot through his right leg as his body spun around from the impact. He screamed in agony. Then he was under the water, gulping in great mouthfuls of ocean. For a brief moment his training deserted him and he nearly panicked. But hours of underwater escape practice reasserted itself and he broke his downward plummet and began crawling back toward the surface. The pain in his leg was overpowering.

Directly above him, Colonel Turbin clung desperately with one hand to a section of the Falcon's wing that had shorn off on impact. With the other hand, he gripped his gun and the briefcase tightly. If Turbin was to drown, it would be while holding on to the documents he had been sent to obtain.

A few feet away, Travis bobbed to the surface and gasped for air. He knew his right leg was useless, feeling as if someone was poking a thousand needles into it. Turbin swung around to face Travis, a look of intense hatred etched on his face.

"Up yours!" Travis hissed between clenched teeth. His life vest had inflated on contact with the water and now held him afloat. If not for that, his injuries would have pulled him down under the water.

Turbin floated free of the debris, switched the gun to his free hand, and aimed it at Travis. He fired before Travis could think to move. The bullet tore through one of the water wings of Travis's vest, exploding the air from it, and knocking Travis sideways. Turbin tried to fire again, but the hammer fell on unresponsive metal. He pulled the trigger twice more, then gave up.

Travis laughed, more out of nervousness and relief than bravado. Coolly he reached under the vest and pulled a .45 from his shoulder holster. "All right, sucker," he said, "now it's my turn."

An explosion high above them pulled their attention skyward. One of the two remaining MiG

31s began a flaming downward spiral, with one wing shot away. Alex's F-16 streaked past, banked sharply, and tried to line up on the remaining Foxhound. Travis cheered loudly, hooting and hollering as Alex followed the Russian into a series of banking maneuvers. Finally, the faster MiG kicked in his afterburners and shot westward across the sky.

"Run, you sucker!" Travis yelled derisively. "Run on home!"

Alex dove his Falcon toward the two figures treading water below him and waggled his wings. Travis waved as the jet flew past, climbed straight up and then disappeared.

"He's radioing Honolulu right now," Travis said gleefully, ignoring the intense pain shooting through his leg. "In a couple of hours there'll be a rescue unit out here."

"You're in way over your head, flyboy," Turbin spat.

"Look who's talking," Travis laughed. "This ocean belongs to the United States Navy, and these skies to the U.S. Air Force! I'm right at home."

Turbin stared at the pilot through slitted eyes. "Whether we get to Russia or back to America, you're going to pay!" he promised. "No one does this to me and lives!"

"Scratch two MiGs!" the radio operator shouted. "Intercept Two is on the way home."

Those in the room cheered along with the corporal. General Mayland allowed himself a relieved smile. It was hard losing a plane, but to think the slower F-16s had splashed two MiG 31s flown by Russian pilots was worth the loss. "The Lear was clearly destroyed?" he asked.

The operator nodded. "However, Lieutenant Marshall reports a survivor in the water along with Captain Romney, sir."

A survivor!

Mayland swore. He picked up a secure phone and dialed Fleet Command. In a moment he was put through to Admiral Cummings. "We have a little problem, Admiral," he began. "And I'm hoping you have some usable hardware to lend us."

After hanging up with Mayland, Cummings immediately called Vice Adm. Edwin Rowden, Commander, Submarine Forces, Pacific Fleet. "Eddie, we need to divert something to thirty-degrees north, one hundred eighty degrees east," he said. "What d'ya have?"

Within ten minutes a compact high density Red Priority message was shot up to the Pacific Communications Satellite where it was read by photovoltaic cells, then bounced back down by a parabolic dish to ELF Command at Bremerton, Washington. Through a twenty-six mile antenna buried in the ground, ELF Command radioed the message over extra low frequency waves to the submerged *Pocatello.*

Bertanelli stuck his head in the sonar room. "Well?" he asked impatiently.

"Emissions solidifying, Captain." Maggie's voice was calm, efficient and controlled. "In less than a minute you'll have *Batfish* on your sonar targeting system."

"You're absolutely certain this thing knows what it's doing?"

"Of course," she replied, quietly but firmly. "I designed it."

He nodded, apparently satisfied, and stepped back into the control room. He motioned to Ashton. "Any second now," Bertanelli said.

The weapons officer licked his dry lips and nodded.

Bertanelli switched on the intercom. "This is the captain," he announced softly. "Maintain ultra quiet in the boat. We don't want to give away our position."

He replaced the microphone on the desk and glanced at Jamison. All eyes were on the weapons fire board. When the green light switched to red *Pocatello* would have a firing solution on *Batfish*.

Suddenly the bell in the ELF receiver started clanging noisily, the jarring sound shattering the tense stillness in the air.

Aboard the *Batfish*, Parkin was glued to the CRT repeater screen in the control room. His mouth felt as dry as a sand dune. "Come on, Tony, show yourself!"

"Nothing yet, sir," announced sonar over the intercom.

"We're breaching the seamount," the navigational officer reported.

"Any second now, Skipper," the XO said. Like the rest of the crew, he felt victory so close, he could almost taste it.

"Sir? I'm picking up a clatter down there. Bearing two eight four degrees. Elevation/depression about twenty degrees negative. Range, seventeen thousand yards. I don't know what it is, but it's noisy as hell!"

Parkin turned excitedly. "Pipe it in."

The overhead speaker began to crackle with sea noises, then a faint clanging sound was discernible. At first Parkin was puzzled, then a smile broke out

101

across his face. "Control to sonar," the captain said. "Feed that location into the targeting computer and be ready to fire on my command!"

"Turn that damn thing off!" Bertanelli yelled.

Communications officer Francis Lamonica grabbed for the bell on the ELF receiver. Finding no way to silence it, he ripped it off the set. He looked apologetically at the captain, then returned to glare at the feed coming in over the extra low frequency line at one character every thirty seconds. "Hell'uva time for ComSubPac to make contact," he muttered.

In the sudden silence, Bertanelli swung to the diving officer. "Blow all tanks," he ordered. "Take us up, fast!"

"Weapons locked on at two four eight degrees, skipper."

Parkin smiled ruthlessly. "Control to sonar, stand by."

"Aye."

Parkin glanced at Capt. Ronald H. Ferguson, the umpire on board *Batfish* from Fleet Command. He returned Parkin's look without emotion.

"With your permission, sir."

Ferguson nodded.

"Control to sonar," Parkin called. "Hit him with a charge!"

The chief petty officer at the sonar console aboard *Batfish* powered up and pushed the impulse button. A high-frequency energy bolt shot out from the *Sturgeon* class boat on a narrow directional beam toward the location *Pocatello* was believed to be.

Ping!

Everyone in the control room froze, waiting for the returning sound that would telegraph a successful hit.

"Sonar to control. I'm picking up blowing tanks. Creaking and popping noises."

There was no returning sound. The charge passed uninterrupted through the ocean.

Parkin swore. "She's coming up!" He swung around. "Helm, right full rudder. All ahead full!"

The hard sonar bolt was heard aboard *Pocatello* as it passed by some distance below them.

Bertanelli's face split into a wide grin. "Control to sonar. Hit him!"

Caldwell motioned to Maggie and she pushed the impulse button.

Ping!

The hard contact flew out from *Pocatello* across the fourteen thousand yards, slamming into *Batfish*, then bouncing back at equal speed.

Pong!

Maggie smiled proudly. It was she who had located the target, zeroed in on it when normal equipment was useless, and had even fired the shot that "sunk" the *Batfish*. All in all she was quite pleased with herself.

"Captain!" Lieutenant Lamonica shouted, hurrying across the control room to Bertanelli's side. "The ELF . . . it's a Priority Red message!"

"Priority Red?" Bertanelli repeated in disbelief.

All eyes in the control room focused on the captain. Admiral Sward started coughing uncontrollably while the color drained from Jamison's face. Priority Red was a combat warning code in the case of war. The captain took the message from

Lamonica and motioned to Jamison. Together they hurried to Bertanelli's cabin.

Once inside, the *Pocatello*'s skipper shut and locked the door. Then he opened the safe, withdrawing a small code book and the yellow envelope that contained the boat's battle orders. He glanced at Jamison grimly, then opened the code book.

CHAPTER TEN

8:54 p.m. Honolulu/0654 Hours Zulu

Maggie was still trembling with excitement. She had entered a man's world and performed effectively right alongside them. And her equipment had proven flawless. It had detected *Batfish* when no other sonar gear could have found her.

"That was fantastic, Miss O'Brien," Ralston said, beaming.

Maggie's face was flushed a bright scarlet. Perspiration dampened her face and throat and her tan blouse was soaked around the V-neck and down the front. Wisps of hair fell from the tight bun she wore at the back of her head. She looked anything but prim, yet she had never felt better in her life. "That was . . . electrifying!" she said excitedly, gasping for breath.

Zimmer tossed her a towel. "Looks like you could use this."

She grabbed the towel from the air gratefully and dabbed at the perspiration on her forehead.

Caldwell looked her over and grinned. "This boat

carries enough air-conditioning equipment to cool a fair-sized town on July afternoon," he quipped good-naturedly, "and look at you."

She glanced down at herself, then shook her head. The gesture seemed somewhat incongruous for Maggie, almost girl-like and gentle. "Who cares?" she said cheerfully, her grin broadening until it looked as if her face would split in two.

"This calls for a glass of champagne," Ralston suggested.

"I'd rather have a chocolate sundae," Maggie giggled.

"Zimmer, go get Miss O'Brien her sundae. She deserves it."

Maggie's eyes widened. "You have ice cream aboard?" she asked incredulously.

"We have two machines that make our own," Ralson said. "There isn't anything you could want that we don't have."

"Except privacy."

"Well, usually we don't need it."

She laughed. "Is it always like this? All this . . . excitement?"

Caldwell cleared his throat. "Actually, we spend weeks out here in absolute boredom," he said, "interrupted only by a few seconds of sheer terror."

The secure phone rang. Ralston picked up the receiver. "Sonar," he said. Bertanelli's voice came through the earpiece.

"Have Miss O'Brien come to my quarters immediately."

"Aye, aye." Ralston replied and hung up. He turned to Maggie. "Captain wants to see you."

"Really?"

"In his quarters."

"Probably wants to congratulate you on the fine

106

job you did," Zimmer suggested.

Maggie blushed. She swept the wayward wisps of hair back off her forehead and stood up. Suddenly she was very aware of her appearance, her drenched, smelly blouse and her sweat-streaked makeup. She strode purposely from the sonar room, wishing fervently that she had brought a change of clothes aboard.

Seated in his cabin, Bertanelli studied the decoded message from ComSubPac. He sighed deeply, then handed the paper to Jamison. "Well, at least there's no war."

"Then why the hell did they send a Priority Red message?"

"Read it."

Jamison read the message. He shook his head in disbelief and read it again. "This is a simple rescue mission," he said finally. "Why Priority Red?"

"Look at the last paragraph again."

Jamison read it aloud. "Allow no hostile interference. Repeat, no hostile interference." He looked at Bertanelli, puzzled. "You expecting any?"

"It wouldn't be in the message unless there was a reason."

"What about Miss O'Brien?"

"What about her?"

"She's a civilian."

Bertanelli sighed once again. "A woman on a fighting mission."

"Maybe she can be of help. Keeping any Russian boats off our back while we're searching."

"We've got Caldwell. He may be a flake, but he's the best damn flake in the fleet."

"I think Miss O'Brien might be better."

107

Bertanelli weighed that for a moment. "Maybe," he said. "But drills are different from the real thing." He took the message back from Jamison and read it over a final time. "Order the helm to these coordinates and bring us up to flank speed."

Jamison nodded, turned and opened the door just as Maggie was about to knock.

"Come in, Miss O'Brien," Bertanelli said.

As Maggie stepped inside the small cabin, Jamison left, shutting the door behind him.

"You wanted to see me?" Maggie's voice was velvet-edged and strong, with a hint of excitement.

Bertanelli let out a long, audible breath. "Want some coffee?" he asked, gesturing to a chair opposite him.

She shook her head, noting that he had not stood when she entered. Even seated, Bertanelli's size and masculine good looks stood out, making Maggie even more conscious of her own smelly, unkempt condition.

"We've just received possible battle orders from ComSubPac," Bertanelli began. He took a deep breath and plunged ahead. "I wanted to see you in here before we reached our destination."

Maggie tensed. This was no buildup to a compliment.

"I don't know what this is about," Bertanelli went on. "But something serious is taking place and we're going to be right in the middle of it."

"Sounds ominous."

"We're being diverted from the exercise to pick up survivors from a plane crash."

Maggie's eyebrows shot up in surprise. "A strange mission for an attack sub."

"The Russians may also be interested in this. And, for whatever reason, my orders are clear that this cannot be allowed. If they insist on butting in, we're to stop them."

There was a stunned, tense silence. "You mean scare them away?" Maggie asked finally.

"The Russians do not scare easily."

"Oh."

"Let's face it, Miss O'Brien. They have nuclear warheads on their torpedoes just like us. If we shoot, they shoot. No one wins." He paused and looked past her at the picture of his children hanging on the far wall. His wife had died three years ago and his sister, Polly, had practically raised the two little girls ever since. He did not see them very often. And he knew he might never see them again. Bertanelli sighed, then turned back to Maggie. "But ComSubPac expects us to carry out our orders. Frankly, I don't expect any problems, but—"

"Yes, you do, Captain, or I wouldn't be in here."

Bertanelli regarded her intently. "You're very frank, Miss O'Brien," he said.

"I've made a place for myself in a man's world, Captain. I'm the foremost engineer in my field. I didn't get there by being coy."

"I'm sure you didn't."

"I developed this SUBDACS system. Senior management didn't believe I could do it; the Navy didn't believe I could do it; my own team didn't believe I could do it. But I did it. It took twice as long as it should have, but I showed them all." A winsome smile crossed her face. When she spoke again, her voice was softer, almost a whisper. "And today my masks have proven effective, as did my scintillator."

"Is that what it's called?" She nodded. "Your equipment is very impressive."

"I'll take that as a compliment, Captain. The first you've offered, I might add." She stood, and he stood with her, taking a step backward.

"Should we encounter any Soviet subs wherever we're going," she told him, "I'm sure my equipment —and I—will be of great help to you."

Bertanelli was used to dealing with subordinates who obeyed him, or superiors who gave him orders. But fencing with an electronics wizard, and a woman at that, was a totally new experience. One he was not sure he liked. "I was thinking that you could teach Petty Officer Caldwell how to implement the new system should we need it," he suggested.

Maggie stared at him boldly. "How much time do we have?"

"A few hours, perhaps."

She frowned, her eyes intent and serious. "You will notice, Captain, that I am wearing officer tans for this cruise."

Despite himself, Bertanelli found himself staring at the unfamiliar curve filling out the uniform blouse Maggie had on. "I can see that," he said.

"And since I am the most qualified on the new system, and since it couldn't be taught to a *genius* in less than thirty to forty hours, I'd like to suggest that, should the occasion arise, you consider me your new sonar officer."

Bertanelli took another stunned step backward. Suddenly, how Maggie had outmaneuvered those who had been in opposition to her, both in and out of the Navy, became clear. Backing into the desk, he stopped short, quickly regaining his composure. "I have Lieutenant Ralston as my sonar officer."

"No doubt he will be a good officer—some day." She stepped forward to stress her point, pressing Bertanelli further into his desktop. "But right now he is little more than a gung-ho graduate from the Academy with no experience in any conditions, and would be a detriment should you encounter a shooting engagement."

The freckle-faced, twenty-three-year-old Ralston was exactly that, Bertanelli knew. The sixth sonar officer *Pocatello* had received, Ralston was the least qualified to guide sonar operations in a tight spot. "We get the new ones because we have Caldwell. He is a legend in the fleet."

"Jason Caldwell has two hundred and sixty-three hours on the BQQ5." Maggie said sternly. "I looked it up."

"He is the best."

"So I understand. But I have three hundred and fifteen hours on the BQQ5, plus another four hundred hours on SUBDACS, not to mention that I conceived it, gestated it, and gave birth to it almost by myself!" She spun around suddenly and moved toward the door. "And, I expect, Captain, that if the safety of this boat is in question, you would want me on that equipment."

She opened the door, smiled pleasantly, and stepped out into the corridor, closing the door behind her. Bertanelli stared at the space she had just vacated and breathed a heavy sigh. "Must be a holy terror at Rockwell!" he muttered.

There was a brief knock on the door. On Bertanelli's command, Jamison stepped inside.

"What'd she say?" he asked curiously. "Was she scared?"

Bertanelli grinned. "You wouldn't believe me if I told you."

Having been in the water for three hours, Travis was beginning to wonder how much longer he could hold on. The pain had dulled his senses and shock

111

had made him drowsy. The damaged vest kept him at a tilted angle, with half his upper body in the water and half out.

He had no idea what was in the briefcase the Russian carried, though the man's gentle treatment of it suggested that the bag must be the reason for the frantic order to shoot down the Lear. With shock and exposure dulling his senses, Travis began to fantasize about the briefcase. Maybe it contained such vital secrets that the entire world was ready to go to war over it. *Snap out of it, Trav,* he thought to himself. *Get real!*

He knew his leg was broken. There were long periods when he blanked out completely. He always snapped out of these dozes believing the Russian was about to grab him and his gun. But the man was ignoring him, content to hold on to the wing section, clutching his precious briefcase. Travis fervently hoped Pearl would have something sent out to them soon.

Travis heard a bubbling noise off to his right. As it grew louder, he turned to discover the source. Black metal poked up out of the water, displacing white swirling waves all around it. The sail of a submarine came into view. Finally the entire boat rose imperially out of the ocean.

Travis cheered wildly. He had expected a surface ship, but at this point anything that floated would do. Keeping his Russian captive in sight, Travis slowly, and with great difficulty, backpedaled with his one good leg toward the emerging deck.

"We're here, Captain," the navigation officer reported.

Bertanelli nodded. "Helm bring us up to periscope depth."

"Aye."

"Control to sonar. Is that Russian boat still on the surface?"

"Up there all quiet and sitting pretty," Caldwell answered.

Bertanelli swore.

"Now what?" Jamison asked.

Bertanelli shook his head. "Damned if I know. If they've picked up whoever it was we were supposed to find, we've got to get 'em back."

"This is pretty risky, Captain." Sward tossed the words at Bertanelli like stones. "You might end up in a shooting war over this."

Bertanelli spun around and glared at his accuser. "I have my orders, Admiral!"

Black-uniformed seamen appeared along the foredeck of the boat. One carried a pole and hooked Travis, hauling him backward toward the sub. Another tossed a life ring to Turbin.

"Thanks, guys," Travis said with relief. "But you sure took your time." The man nearest him grunted and Travis was pulled up onto the sub's slick surface near an open hatch at the base of the sail. "Don't let that man out of your sight," Travis ordered, pointing at Turbin. " That briefcase contains something extremely important. Pearl will want to take a look at it."

He watched Turbin being pulled toward the sub, then Travis was hauled through the hatchway. He winced in pain as his leg was bounced around roughly.

"Hey, careful!" he yelled. "I think my leg's busted!"

One of the black-clad seamen looked at him bewildered, then turned to the other sailors. *"Sp'eshit'e! Uvodit'e ch'elov'eka,"* he shouted. "Hurry, get this man below!"

Too weak from shock and exposure to realize that those on deck were not speaking English, Travis allowed himself to be handed down the ladder onto the conning station where he came face to face with the sub's captain. He stared into Emelyan Yakunin's narrow black eyes, noting the captain's perpetual scowl and uneven teeth. Travis noticed the red star over the anchor emblem on the rolled down collar of the man's white turtleneck sweater. The pilot glanced quickly around at the black-uniformed men, most of whom wore small black caps with the same star and anchor emblem on them.

"Oh, shit!" Travis swore quietly, realizing he was definitely *not* on an American boat.

"A fitting greeting under the circumstances, Captain," Yakunin replied in excellent English. His weathered face creased into what one would suppose was a smile. "Welcome aboard *M.V. Suslov*, the vanguard boat of the *vozhd* class. It is what I believe your people call the *Mike* submarine."

Being somewhat of a Russian historian, Travis knew the name Suslov well. "Mikhail Vladimirovich Suslov," he said, shaking the cobwebs from his brain, "the chief Party ideologue under three Soviet chiefs of state. Member of the Leningrad Troika, antagonist of Brezhnev and his Dnepropetrovsk Mafia, and participant in the downfall of Nikita Kruschev." Travis lifted his chin, meeting the icy gaze of the Russian. "A fitting name for your boat, Captain."

Astonishment crossed Yakunin's features. "You

114

surprise me. I thought all Americans were uninformed about the Soviet Union." Yakunin flashed his bizarre half-smile once again. "Yes," he said. "It is a fitting name." He turned and started giving the orders to get under way just as two more sailors led a shivering, water-logged Colonel Turbin into the control room, still clutching the coveted briefcase. The KGB officer shook himself from the seamen's grasp and worked his way over to Travis, who was studying the electronics of the control room intently.

"I do not forgive, Captain," Turbin hissed in Travis's ear. "Do not think you will get off this boat alive."

Hearing the sound, Yakunin turned, his eyes locking with those of the KGB man. For several seconds they regarded each other; the captain inquisitively, the colonel challenging, suspicious.

Finally Yakunin motioned to the sailors holding onto Travis. "Take him away," the Russian commander ordered. The sailors turned and quickly hustled the American out of the control room. After eyeing Turbin once again briefly, the captain glanced down at the diving panel, noting that all the hatches were sealed. "*Michman*, dive the boat," he said.

"Very well, Comrade Captain."

"Take her down, Felix."

The warrant officer nodded, then turned to issue orders to the helm. "Flood forward trim tanks."

"Flooding forward trim tanks."

"Ahead, slow speed."

"Very well, slow speed."

"Stern planes down ten degrees."

"Very well, ten degrees."

The *Suslov* began slipping rapidly under the water.

"Sonar, Comrade Captain. Picking up a submarine blowing tanks, surfacing. Five thousand yards, bearing three one seven degrees."

"The devil be damned!" Yakunin swore bitterly. "Caught us on the surface where we couldn't hear him." He swung to the engineering officer. "Flood all tanks! Fast dive!"

Engineering Officer First Grade Stepan Krylov opened all the seawater vents and they dropped like a rock, going straight down.

Just over a mile away, two *Pocatello* spotters climbed out of the hatch and onto the sail. They both saw the *Suslov* at the same instant. White water frothed all about her as she sank beneath the surface.

"Soviet submarine diving," one radioed to the control room. "Five thousand yards! Bearing one three seven degrees! Going down *fast!*"

Jamison gained the bridge just in time to see the water bubbling over the top of the *Suslov's* sail. He yanked a mike from the watertight box under the sail flange. "Bridge to control!" he shouted. "She's down! Dropped like a rock! Hell of a maneuver!"

"Anything on the surface?" Bertanelli radioed back.

"An oil slick and part of a plane's wing. No people."

"Get off the bridge! Quick!"

Jamison turned to the lookouts. "Clear the bridge."

The two spotters jumped from their positions in the racks and climbed through the hatch. Jamison swept the sail, then climbed down after them, triggering the automatic release. Quickly the hatch closed over him.

In the control room, Bertanelli glanced at the "Christmas Tree." All the red lights flashed to green on the diving panel.

"We have water-tight integrity," the officer of the deck announced.

"Dive the boat. Dive the boat," Bertanelli ordered. "Steep angle. Take us down."

"Twenty degree down bubble," the diving officer called.

"Twenty degree down bubble, aye."

"Battle stations, nuclear!" Bertanelli ordered.

"Battle stations, nuclear, aye."

The quartermaster's voice echoed over the speakers throughout the boat. "General Quarters. General Quarters. This is not a drill. All hands man battle stations, nuclear. This is not a drill."

In an organized frenzy, a hundred and forty-two men raced to their assigned posts. In the sonar room, Jason Caldwell turned away from Maggie O'Brien and the SUBDACS panel. He swung back to his own CRT screen and terminal.

"Tanks flooding, hull creaking and popping," Zimmer said excitedly. "He's dropping straight down. Glad I'm not on *his* boat!"

"He beats us down and turns, we're sitting ducks!" Caldwell announced.

All eyes focused on the CRT screen.

CHAPTER ELEVEN

9:10 p.m. Honolulu/0710 Hours Zulu

The identification of another submarine had come so fast and taken Yakunin by such surprise, that the captain had forgotten completely about the KGB officer still present in the control room. Turning to sonar, Yakunin noticed Turbin standing beside the console, the briefcase held tightly in his hand. Though attempting to mask his condition, the effects of his time spent in the water were clearly noticeable. While standing straight, his body wavered from side to side slightly. His stare, though hard and cold, had a discernibly glassy edge. His free hand grasped the back of the sonar operator's chair for balance and support.

Yakunin frowned as he studied the stranger. The captain had seen this man's like far too often over the course of his career to suit him. He knew the breed well—the fanatic.

"You are Colonel Turbin?" Yakunin asked. The KGB man nodded once but said nothing. "You have been through quite an ordeal. Perhaps you would care to change into dry clothing and to lie down?"

Turbin's face darkened. "I would prefer to remain here," he said coldly.

Yakunin continued to stare at the stranger. An uneasy, nagging sensation in the pit of his stomach seemed to be warning him that serious trouble had boarded the *Suslov* along with Col. Vladimir Turbin.

Yakunin fought back the feelings of impending disaster and got back down to the work at hand. "Whatever you wish, Comrade," he said to Turbin, then swung around to face Aleksei Mezhova, the *Suslov*'s sonar officer. "Where is the American boat?"

"I still have too much interference on my screen, Comrade Captain. We made a lot of noise going down."

"Torpedo Room, load tubes two and four with conventional torpedoes; load three and five with nuclear warheads."

Everyone in the control room shot Yakunin a quick glance.

"All ahead slow," the captain said.

The planesman struggled frantically with his controls. The forward momentum gave him some steerage and kept the sub from popping back up to the surface. But it was a tricky maneuver, and a dangerous one. If he made a mistake, they could slide down into the chasm beyond *Suslov*'s tested depth of four thousand four hundred feet.

Aleksei Mezhova looked up, his features etched with concern. "Comrade Captain," he said, "the American is diving. I hear tanks flooding, steam vents popping. He's coming down after us!"

Bertanelli watched his own instruments carefully. He knew the Russian must be slowing his sudden descent by now. In thirty seconds the enemy sub's

119

sonar would be searching for *Pocatello*. And by then Bertanelli knew he had to be ready to shoot!

Jamison scurried down the ladder from the conning station above. "It's no *Alfa* or *Akula*," he said, panting, trying to catch his breath. "There was no bullet-shaped stern fin."

"He have a rounded sail that tapered to a point aft?"

Jamison nodded.

"It's a *Mike*."

The XO whistled. "No wonder it was so quiet. That thing's got everything the Russkies own."

"How do you know what it is?" Sward said accusingly. "Nobody's ever seen one of them."

"Three of our men just did." Bertanelli turned back to the ancillary screen. There was so much action in the water, it was hard to make out an immediate target. Quickly, he picked up the intercom mike. "Miss O'Brien. Do you have him on that gizmo of yours?"

"Neutron emissions dead ahead. Range, five five zero zero yards. Depth, five hundred meters. I believe he's circling, trying to come back on us, Captain."

"All ahead stop," Bertanelli ordered. "Rig for ultra quiet."

"All ahead stop, aye. Ultra silent running, aye."

"Sonar to control." It was Caldwell. "I hear torpedo tubes flooding."

"Control to weapons. Load tubes one and three with standard torpedoes, tube two with an ALWT, and rush a decoy into tube four."

In the torpedo room, Lt. Harmon Crippen turned away from the speaker. "Merriam, get a MOSS into tube four on the double. Rafferty, Billings, cut loose two Mark forty-eights and load 'em in one and three. Ellis and Lopez, put a Mark fifty in tube two."

All hands jumped to the torpedo racks. Two Mark forty-eight Mod four wire-guided torpedoes were unbolted from their restraints, moved along the rails with rachets, and slid into the firing tubes. Crippen closed the doors, set the electronic locks in proper sequence, then ran the circuit tests as the AWLT and MOSS decoy were run into their tubes.

"Torpedo room to control," Crippen reported. "Tubes loaded and ready."

"Control to weapons. Arm the warheads."

At the weapons station in the control room, Lt. Marvin Ashton's face had gone chalk white. He bent forward, barely able to breathe. Though carefully trained in his task, he had hoped never to have to use his training in a true battle situation. Sweating profusely, he encoded the numbers onto his keyboard. "Mark forty-eights and fifty armed and ready, sir," he reported.

"Flood all four tubes," Bertanelli commanded.

"Sonar to control. I hear outer doors opening."

Bertanelli radioed forward. "Weapons, as soon as tubes are fully flooded, open all outer doors."

"You're playing a game of chicken!" Sward yelled, his voice shaking noticeably.

"You're damn right I am," Bertanelli exploded. "He has to know that if he fires, he dies too!"

It had suddenly become very quiet in the control room.

"Marv, hit him with a target beam," Bertanelli ordered. "Let him know we know exactly where he is."

In the sonar room, Maggie turned to Caldwell, her eyes wide with fear. "Is he really going to shoot?" she asked, her voice trembling slightly.

Caldwell shook his head. "It's a game, Miss O'Brien," he said philosophically. "They wave their

121

fist at us, we wave one back. They wave two fists, we wave two back."

"And if they shoot?"

Caldwell paused. "Then it's no longer a game and we shoot back."

"Comrade Captain, I have the *Am'erikanskaya*. Bearing zero two six degrees. Speed six knots. Range fifteen hundred meters."

"Weapons, lock on."

At the sonar console, Mezhova started to program in the bearing for the weapons lock on. He stopped in mid-motion, staring at his dials, puzzled.

Yakunin stared at him impatiently. "Well?" he asked.

Quickly, Mezhova tore the earphones from his head.

A loud *ping* bounced off the *Suslov*.

Yakunin swung around as if staring right through the hull at the *Pocatello*. "The devil be damned!" he swore.

"We are targeted, Comrade Captain," the sonar officer said fearfully.

"And so is the American!"

"What now?" Warrant Officer Felix Stelest waited patiently for orders. He had been on enough runs to have developed complete confidence in Yakunin.

"I believe the Americans call this a Mexican standoff, Felix," the captain replied.

"Do something!" the *zampolit* Mikola Govskaya screamed. "Shoot!"

Suddenly alert, Col. Vladimir Turbin watched the drama unfolding in front of him. Though the submarine was of no concern to him—only the contents of the briefcase he held tightly in his fist—

122

his calculating eyes missed nothing. Measuring the men in the control room, he could see the political officer would be the first one to crack under the pressure.

Yakunin eyed the *zampolit* without emotion. "We shoot, and he will shoot," Yakunin said calmly.

"Fire and he will run away!" Govskaya replied. The sweat was starting to run down his face in rivulets.

Yakunin laughed with unconcealed bitterness. "You are starting to believe your own propaganda," he said. "The Americans are not cowards."

"Careful, Comrade Captain," Govskaya warned, his voice tightening, "or I will quote you in my next communique to the Party Council."

Yakunin grunted in disgust. "Engineering," he said, turning his back on the *apparatchiki*, "switch us over to turbo-electric. And give me an acoustic cover that will fool the Americans. I want to go out of here as quietly as possible."

Govskaya swung the captain around violently. "You can't do that!" he screamed. "We have an American in our sights! He intends to do us harm! I order you to fire!"

Yakunin glared at the *zampolit*. "Take your hand from me, Mikola," he hissed. Reluctantly, Govskaya complied.

The political officer turned on Stelest, the warrant officer. "Shoot!" he ordered.

No one moved to obey. Govskaya reached out for the firing controls on the weapons console. Yakunin grabbed the *zampolit's* hand and jerked it back, just short of the launch button. Swinging Govskaya around, he slapped his face hard. "Get hold of yourself!" Yakunin shouted, shaking the man violently. "We are not here to start World War Three!"

Balling his fingers into a fist, Govskaya swung his hand around in an arc and caught Yakunin on the side of the head, knocking the captain back against the periscope pedestal. Rolling over onto the conning platform, his head struck the flange bolts with a loud, sickening thud, and Yakunin fell to the floor unconscious.

Felix Stelest leapt up from his chair and flung himself at the political officer. Swinging wildly, the *zampolit* knocked Stelest aside, and yanked a service pistol from the holster nestled in his armpit. He aimed the gun at the stunned weapons officer. "Fire," he ordered, "or I will kill you!"

The officer glanced at his unconscious captain, then at the dazed *michman*.

"Do it!" Govskaya screamed.

"We are not correctly lined up!" the officer protested.

"The torpedo is wire-guided!" Govskaya yelled, his face turning beet-red. "Shoot!"

When the officer did not immediately react, the political officer pulled back the hammer. The click echoed loudly through the control room.

"I said shoot!" Govskaya screamed, ramming the gun into the side of the officer's head. "Shoot!"

Swallowing hard, the officer pressed the firing button.

"Torpedo in the water, port side!" Caldwell shouted over the intercom. "I repeat, torpedo in the water! Bearing two zero six degrees! Sixteen hundred yards! It's wire-guided!"

"Control to weapons," Bertanelli ordered. "Fire the MOSS."

The submarine shuddered slightly as compressed

air shot the decoy torpedo into the water from its tube amidships. Automatic trim tanks immediately compensated for the sudden loss of weight.

"Steer the decoy along the torpedo track."

The MOSS, a decoy torpedo with an electronic tape recorder in the nose that sent signals duplicating *Pocatello*'s nuclear signature, quickly reached its maximum speed of sixty-three knots. Once clear of the boat, it arched to the left, and was steered on the track between *Pocatello* and the Soviet boat.

"Slow the MOSS down and start broadcasting."

The decoy slowed to twenty knots. The tape recorder was activated and *Pocatello*'s nuclear noises filtered through the ocean.

"MOSS running true," Caldwell announced.

Zimmer rushed into the sonar room, the remains of a chocolate ice cream sundae smeared down his shirt and pants. "Took everybody by surprise," he mumbled apologetically as he claimed his chair. "The mess hall is in chaos."

Caldwell was not listening as he searched frantically for the Russian boat. "I know where he is, but I've lost him," he muttered. "He must've gone quiet."

Outside the Soviet acoustic homing torpedo heard the MOSS recording, ran it through its tiny onboard computer, and locked on to the signature of its target. Tail fins were realigned as the thirty-four hundred pound, twenty-two-foot-long torpedo knifed through the water at fifty-five knots.

Caldwell reached over and spun down the gain controls on Maggie's console barely a second before the torpedo blast echoed through their sets.

Yakunin shook his head, then wished he hadn't as

pain shot through his jaw. At the same instant, sharpness shot through his temple where he had struck the bolts on the periscope flange. He started to stand, quickly inspecting the control room as the nearby blast of the torpedo reverberated through the hull. *Suslov* rocked violently, sending Yakunin sprawling to the floor a second time.

Govskaya laughed wickedly, the shrill sound reverberating off the bulkheads as he danced wildly up and down.

Yakunin climbed to his feet and grabbed the gun Govskaya was waving in his hand. Spinning the political officer around, Yakunin grabbed a handful of his shirt and tossed the smaller man into the hands of Felix Stelest. "Lock him up somewhere!" Yakunin growled, shoving the gun into his own pocket. He turned to Turbin. "Get off my bridge!" he ordered angrily. "I want no one in here but naval personnel!" The captain turned to a nearby seaman. "Take him out of here!" Yakunin snapped. "Take him anywhere, just get him out of here!"

The KGB officer eyed the captain coldly. Then he spun around and stormed out of the control room, the seaman following on his heels.

When Turbin had left, Yakunin quickly turned to the sonar officer. "Did we hit the American?" he asked.

"I don't know, Comrade Captain. The ensonified zone from the blast is spreading and covering everything in its wake."

"Then he is either dead, or blind."

"That is correct."

Yakunin turned. "Helm, all ahead full," he ordered. "Steer two five zero degrees."

"Very well, all ahead full."

In nuclear engineering, the uranium rods were

lowered, creating an immediate increase in heat, while absorbing a little over one percent of the neutron flux. Nuclear Officer First Rank Veli Ternovsky opened the valves as the liquid, heated to over twelve hundred degrees Celsius, created steam in the top of the generator, turning the turbos at an unbelievably high speed. Within minutes, the *Suslov* had gained its peak speed of thirty-nine knots.

In the control room, Yakunin split his attention between the instruments and sonar. "Load up a decoy signature, Aleksei," he ordered. "Make them think we're feeding turtles or something. And give me a mask to cover our departure just in case they can see through the ensonified zone before we do."

The billions of bubbles created by the torpedo detonation had built a zone between the two submarines that blocked passive sonar detection. The hydrophones were picking up air being forced through the ocean, bursting, and then collapsing in upon itself before forming again. The noise set up such a clatter that, until the zone dissipated and the sea returned to normal, it would be impossible for Caldwell to locate the Soviet submarine.

Still, he worked diligently to try and wash out the encroaching sounds. But with each layer filtered out, another explosion of imploding air bubbles would burst through the speakers.

Ralston stuck his head in the door. "How long, Jason?" he asked.

"Five minutes. Maybe more."

The sonar officer passed this information on to the control room where Bertanelli was torn between firing on his attacker and making a run for it under cover of the zone. The captain looked up at Ralston.

"If you were the Russian, Willie," he asked, "what would you be doing right now?"

Ralston considered the question for a moment. "I'd be shooting again," he answered. "He'd know we couldn't detect the fish until it cleared the zone. And by then it'd be too late."

Bertanelli nodded. "Makes sense. But why fire only one torpedo? If he wanted to finish us off, why not two? Or all four?"

"We were too close for nuclear. Maybe one non-nuke was all he had loaded."

"And maybe he didn't intend to fire at all." Bertanelli glanced speculatively at Sward. "Opinion, sir?"

"I'd get the hell out of here."

Bertanelli nodded. "Another sensible thought."

He picked up the secure phone. "Control to weapons," he said into the receiver. "Load up a nuke, arm it, and put it on automatic." He turned back to his officers who were staring at him in disbelief. "ComSubPac wants whatever that *Mike* is carrying not to reach Soviet shores," he explained. "If he fires through the zone, we're dead. But so is he!"

Sward shook his head in dismay. "Remind me never to play poker with you," he said.

"I could have told you that," Jamison quipped good-naturedly.

Bertanelli picked up the intercom mike. "Control to sonar. Anything?"

"Sonar to control. We're still blind."

Seated next to Caldwell, Maggie O'Brien was working furiously at her controls. Unlike passive sonar, the SUBDACS system was not dependent on sound from arrays of hydrophones situated across the hull. It could actually "see" through the water and pick up emissions left in the wake of a nuclear submarine. The question was, how much distortion was being caused by the zone?

Maggie sat at her console frowning. Caldwell looked up. "What is it, Miss O'Brien?"

"I think I know where the Russian is."

All eyes in the sonar room focused on Maggie. Caldwell fiddled with his gain controls again, trying to pick up the sounds she was apparently hearing but he was not. He shook his head and looked up at her. "Impossible," he said.

"I believe he is heading west. Two five zero degrees. And he is traveling very fast."

Open-mouthed, Caldwell stared at her. There was a brief moment of stunned silence in the sonar room.

"I'll get the captain," Ralston said finally, leaping to his feet and racing out the door.

In an instant, Bertanelli was standing in the doorway. "What's this all about?" he demanded.

"She thinks she knows where he is," Caldwell offered, shrugging his shoulders. "But I don't see how."

Bertanelli turned to Maggie. "Well?"

"He's heading west, Captain. Probably on a course of two five zero degrees. I'd guess he is making near forty knots."

"Can you hear him?"

"No. I can see him."

Bertanelli hesitated. Dare he trust his boat to this woman? What if she was wrong and the Russian was just waiting for *Pocatello* to move? If the sub fired once, he might fire again. Bertanelli turned to Caldwell. "Switch on the speaker."

Sound exploded into the room, air implosions overriding all other sea noises.

"I'd guess he's fifteen thousand yards away by now," Maggie said calmly.

"What is this, woman's intuition?" Bertanelli asked, annoyed.

Maggie glanced up at him defiantly. "I am reading my instruments, Captain," she said, her stare firm and unwavering, "and I'm telling you where he is. What are you going to do about it?"

Bertanelli looked at the SUBDACS console panel. "I hope you're right, Miss O'Brien," he said. "We've got a trigger-happy Ivan on our hands and you're the only one who seems to know where he is or what he's doing."

"Right now, Captain, he's running away. If you want to catch him, I'd suggest you do something pretty fast."

Bertanelli shot another glance at the SUBDACS panel, then glared at Maggie. "If you're wrong, Miss O'Brien, we're all dead!"

Maggie hesitated.

"Well, what is it, Miss O'Brien?" Bertanelli demanded. "Do you know where he is, or not?"

Maggie looked squarely into Bertanelli's eyes. "He's heading west," she replied confidently.

Bertanelli nodded. "All right. You stay on him. I want to know where that bastard is at all times. And anyone else that shows up in these waters!"

"Aye, aye, Captain," she said with a smile.

Bertanelli looked at her queerly for a long moment, then turned to Caldwell. "She's running the show until we find that sub," he said, almost apologetically.

Caldwell's face dropped. "Aye," he replied, his voice less than enthusiastic.

Bertanelli stormed out of the sonar station as abruptly as he had entered. Ralston and Zimmer exchanged startled looks. Maggie's smile broadened.

"They'll cut off my dolphins and laugh me right

out of the service," Caldwell moaned.

"No one will know, Chief," Maggie said sympathetically.

Caldwell shot her an angry look, then glanced at Zimmer and Ralston. "Hell, everyone will know!"

Maggie shrugged. She understood the male competitive spirit better than most women. In fact, Maggie O'Brien gloried in it. She knew no one got anywhere by whining and crying. After all, look where her drive had taken her! "Stow it!" she told Caldwell forcefully.

"We've got us a submarine to find."

CHAPTER TWELVE

9:30 p.m. Honolulu/0730 Hours Zulu

General Mayland hesitated outside the door to the office of Adm. William T. Blanchard, Chief of Pacific Command. From Pearl, the admiral directed the activities of all the services under the unified command directorate. Nicknamed "T-bone," he was known for never deviating from a plan once it had been begun.

A Marine sergeant opened the door and Mayland walked in. Blanchard was behind his command desk, a huge plank of mahogany stretching ten feet across one end of the office, some thirty feet from the door. As Mayland walked across the spacious office, he noted the Naval memorabilia that was scattered along display shelves, the models of ships from all eras in glass cases along the walls, and the rosewood wheel from *Constitution* that sat upon a pedestal in one corner.

"Have a seat, Marc," Admiral Blanchard boomed good-naturedly.

Mayland glanced at his boss, Admiral Cummings, and Maj. Gen. Robert F. Morrison, Deputy Chief of the Pacific Fleet, sitting across from the normally taciturn admiral. Commodore Keith Terry sat to the side of the others, well behind them as was befitting his station. Behind Blanchard, an aide hovered with a coffeepot in his hand, trying to look as inconspicuous as possible. Mayland pulled over a chair and eased into it, careful to remain to Cummings's left and slightly behind him.

"Did you know the FBI had your Guerrero under investigation for the past three months?" Morrison asked.

Mayland was shocked. "Three months?" he cried. "Hell no! Why didn't they say something?"

Blanchard lifted his china cup and sipped his coffee slowly before answering. As he stared at Mayland over the brim, the general felt a knot form in his stomach. "They claim too much secret info is leaked out here at Pearl."

As soon as the admiral lowered his cup, the aide was immediately at Blanchard's side, pouring more coffee. He silently offered some to Mayland who shook his head.

"Leaks?" Mayland sputtered angrily. "What does he think this is, Congress?"

Admiral Cummings nodded. "The admiral," Cummings said, "straightened them out."

"But three months!"

Blanchard stood and moved around to the front of his desk. He sat easily on the edge, looking straight at Mayland. "That's water in the baffles. We have more important things to do now."

"How bad is it, Keith?" General Morrison asked.

Keith Terry, the junior officer present, looked at his superiors uncomfortably, nervously shuffling file folders on his lap. "Guerrero got everything, sir." Terry informed him. "Battle logs, station points, communication frequencies, and the Priority Red codes."

Cummings sat back in his chair heavily. His green eyes flamed with indignation beneath his bushy red eyebrows. "The station points will allow the Soviets to pinpoint every boomer and attack sub in the Pacific."

"Every boat would be a sitting duck," Terry agreed.

Mayland squirmed uncomfortably. Kapalama was his concern and the theft had occurred right under his nose.

"The Priority Red codes were just issued," Cummings added. "It'd take us three or four months to recoup."

Mayland knew the Priority Red code book was issued every six months to ComSubPac. It contained special one-time pads filled with randomly generated transpositions for each letter of a signal. The more he listened, the worse it seemed to become. He wondered if he was going to end up the sacrificial lamb because of this. For a brief moment he thought of Lorayne and the kids. If all this came down on his head, they would be the hardest hit.

"With those codes in the hands of the Soviets, there would be no way to contact our ships at sea in secrecy," Terry continued. "Our underbelly would be exposed from Alaska to Australia!"

"Well," Blanchard drawled, "at least we shot the bastard down and the documents are at the bottom of the Pacific."

Mayland cleared his throat uncomfortably. This was not a moment he had been looking forward to. "Our F-16 pilot reported a survivor in the water," he informed them.

Blanchard looked up in surprise.

"I was just about to tell you, Bill," Cummings added, "an ELF from *Poco* said the Russian sub picked him and our pilot up before they could get on station."

Blanchard leapt to his feet, his eyes narrowing into slits. "We'll have to sink it!" he roared. His voice echoed throughout the large room. He strode back behind his desk and sat heavily. He reached for a letter opener and eyed the point menacingly. "Who've we got on station out there?"

Mayland breathed easier. The discussion was moving away from him and Kapalama. "*Pocatello*, sir."

"And who's commanding *Poco*?" Blanchard shot back.

Cummings hesitated, uncrossing his legs and shifting his weight. "Tony Bertanelli," he said.

Blanchard dropped the letter opener and stood, knocking over his coffee. The aide was immediately beside him, wiping up the steaming black fluid and producing another cup, which he quickly filled.

"Bertanelli?" Blanchard boomed. "You mean 'Crazy Tony' is our man out there?"

Cummings nodded reluctantly. Though an avid Bertanelli supporter for years, he did not know if anyone else shared his enthusiasm for the contro-versial captain.

But Blanchard laughed heartily, his guffaws rattling the glass case housing his models. "Hell, man, we have nothing to worry about!" he roared. "Old Tony'll run 'em aground even if he has to follow him halfway up the Volga!"

Cummings relaxed. Obviously Blanchard was delighted with the captain fate had chosen for the situation.

The aide refilled Cummings's and Terry's cups. Morrison motioned him away. "The question is," he said, "are the documents on that submarine?"

135

"Our pilot said he thought he saw the other man carrying something," Mayland offered. "It might have been a briefcase."

Blanchard had started to lift his cup to drink. Now he slammed it back down in the saucer, slopping coffee over the rim. "We can't take the chance they're not," he said decisively. "Sink it!"

"And our flyer?" Morrison asked, already knowing the answer. "What happens to him?"

"If he's aboard the Russian sub, he's a dead man."

Travis Romney, dressed in Soviet seaman's black pants and blouse, sat on a bunk in a small cabin aboard the *Suslov*. A Russian medical officer had straightened the broken leg and applied a half brace, giving him some medicine to take the edge off the pain. The treatment had surprised Travis considerably. He had not figured the Russians capable of such humane and tender acts.

Nor had Travis been confined, which was another surprise. Obviously, he believed, they considered him no threat. He smiled wryly at their oversight. He did not know what the stocky man carried aboard in the briefcase, but Travis knew it either had to be destroyed or the sub slowed down somehow so ships from Pearl could overtake it. But how?

He eased up onto the broken leg, using the heavy, curved wooden cane the doctor had supplied him with for support. Testing the strength of the partial cast, he grimaced in pain and edged out into the corridor, hobbling toward the sounds of the noisy power plant. He had been given a tour of a nuclear sub at Pearl and remembered the SCRAM button on the engineering panel that could shut down the reactor. He felt certain the Russian boat would have something similar.

"Gdevyie'osa'?" someone called out. Travis turned to see one of *Suslov*'s crew staring at him curiously.

Though he did not know Russian, the tone of the question was unmistakable. Gingerly Travis reached for his crotch, feigning a full bladder.

The Russian hesitated, then nodded. *"Da. To'al'et tam."* He pointed forward.

Travis continued on. But after a dozen steps or so, he heard the man yell again. Turning, Travis saw the Russian pointing to a door. *"Eta tam,"* the man said gruffly.

Travis pretended ignorance.

"Krom'e vas!" The seaman continued to point.

Feigning understanding, Travis put his hand on the latch of the door. The Russian nodded as Travis opened the door and stepped inside the tiny head.

"How primitive," he muttered, looking around. He wrinkled his nose at the putrid smell and wondered if American subs were equally devoid of comfort. He tried to sit on the seatless commode, but found it difficult to crouch so low over the Russian-styled device.

After a few moments, the seaman knocked on the door and stuck his head in.

"Pridit'e sa mnoy." The Russian beckoned with his hand for Travis to follow him.

Travis pretended to button up the ill-fitting pants as he hobbled past the Russian and into the corridor. "I'm thirsty," Travis said when the man pointed back toward the small cabin. "Coffee."

"Cof-fee?" the Russian repeated quizzically.

Travis made a drinking motion and Ivan's eyes lit up suddenly. *"Da, kof'e. Pon-atno."* He nodded his understanding and led Travis toward a small galley. A cook wearing a dirty apron over baggy pants and yellowed shirt looked up. *"Am'erikanskaya,"* the man said. *"Ch'ashku kof'e."*

The cook smiled, revealing two rows of crooked yellow teeth. He picked up a mug and wiped it dry with the grimy towel draped around his neck. He poured steaming hot coffee into the mug and handed it to Travis.

"Thanks," Travis said, looking at the black liquid dubiously. "I think."

"Pozhaluysta." The cook smiled, bending closer and peering at the wings on the flight cap Travis still wore. He said something excitedly, pointing at the wings, then made a gesture with his arms outstretched, as though flying. He stopped and looked at Travis inquiringly.

"Yes, I am a pilot," Travis said. He returned the flying gesture then pointed at himself.

The cook grinned broadly. Pulling a billfold from an inner pocket, he opened it, carefully extracting a picture of a young man, looking very much like an earlier version of himself. "Pi-lot," he said with accented emphasis. *"Moy sin."* He held the picture out to Travis.

The American nodded, squinting at the poor reproduction of the cook's son. "Very nice," he said, smiling back at the proud father. Despite all his prejudices, Travis found himself liking the old boy.

Others came into the small mess next to the galley and the cook was off to see to their needs. Travis tasted the coffee and found it thick and bitter. He sat down, wondering how he could get through the boat to the reactor controls in the maneuvering room.

In the Oval Office, President Colin Freeman met with a somber group of advisors, including his chief of staff and long-time friend, Charlie Carmody, the secretary of state, Bruce Falk, and secretary of defense, Richard Rifkin. Others were in and out of the office, as continuing news was brought to keep the president up-to-date.

"What are the chances we can intercept their submarine?" Freeman asked, sitting with his head back against the high chair cushion, staring up at the ceiling.

Chief of Staff Carmody leaned forward on the couch. "Admiral Olsen feels they're pretty good," he said.

Perched on the edge of a table beside the fireplace, Defense Secretary Rifkin added grimly, "Seems like a long shot to me. It's a big ocean."

"I agree with Dick," Falk added. "How the hell can anyone find a submarine that doesn't want to be found?" He sat with legs and arms crossed, his back stiff and unbending.

"Then we have some hard decisions to make." Freeman leaned forward, glancing around the office at his advisors. He rested his hands palms down on the empty blotter in the middle of the ornate desk. "Let's hear our options," he said.

Rifkin shook his head. "If we don't pull back our submarines, they'd be sitting ducks. The Soviets will know where every last one of them is and there's nothing we can do about it."

"The Soviets could move every submarine they own into the Pacific while we're trying to recover from the loss of those codes," Falk added. He sat across from Carmody on the opposite couch with stacks of files scattered beside him. He reached inside one and produced a sheet of paper. "It'll take three months to issue new ones," he added grimly, handing the paper to Freeman.

The president slammed his fist on the desk suddenly, causing every man in the room to jump. "We pull back, and we lose the Pacific!" he shouted. "Dammit, the cost to get it back again would be enormous! Maybe damned near impossible!" He stood up and crossed to the French doors behind him. In times of stress, staring out onto the rose garden and the swelling green grounds beyond tended to soothe the president, clearing his head. But not this time.

"We have one option, as I see it," Rifkin suggested. All heads turned eagerly in his direction. He glanced around at the men on either side, cleared his throat and continued. "You've got to order the *Pocatello* to sink this Russian sub. And fast. Before it can run away and hide."

"And what excuse do we give the Russians for sinking one of their boats?" Falk asked.

"EXCUSE?" Rifkin exploded. "They'll know damn well why we've done it! We don't need any goddamned excuse!" He turned to the chief executive. "Sorry, Mr. President." Freeman nodded slightly.

Rifkin swung around on Falk. "I say we do it. And to hell with the consequences!"

The others in the Oval Office nodded their heads in agreement.

Falk glared back at Rifkin. "Even if it starts World War Three?" he asked bluntly.

"If we lose those documents, it likely will anyway," Carmody interjected coolly. "The Russians will be able to do anything they want in the Pacific."

"Shit, we'd be lucky if we could still get surface shipping to Hawaii," Rifkin added.

The president turned back to the window and

stared out over the grounds. He would let his people fight it out among themselves for a while before making his decision.

"And they could impede our import-export with Asia," Rifkin continued. He slipped off the table and moved to the center of the room. "Our entire economy could be ruined without their firing a shot."

"We can recover from the loss of the codes," Falk insisted. "But how are we going to recover from World War Three?"

A silence engulfed the room. Freeman turned from the French doors and regarded his advisors solemnly. After what seemed an eternity, he spoke. "Gentlemen, I have made my decision."

The president of the United States crossed to his desk and picked up his phone. "Scott?" he said into the receiver. "Get me Admiral Olsen."

Caldwell stared across the room at Maggie, whose eyes were glued to the instrument panel in front of her. His earlier irritation having been replaced by a wily, mischievous smile, Jason Caldwell was not a man willing to relinquish the upper hand for long. He had waited until Ralston was out of the sonar room. Now it was his chance to strike.

"Miss O'Brien?" he said. Maggie looked up. "Since it appears you'll be in here for some time, you'll need to put this on to save your eyes."

Maggie stared quizzically at the small round tin Caldwell was offering her. Obviously Navy issue, it was labeled FOR SONAR OPERATOR'S PROTECTION. "What is it?" she asked.

"We use special fluorescents while we're at sea," Jason told her. "They give off low-grade gamma rays that can penetrate the face and eyes. If you don't use this protection, you could be seriously injured."

Maggie looked at the tin dubiously. Caldwell opened it and handed it to her. Taking it from him, she peered at the dark substance within. She turned to look at an open-mouthed Zimmer, then turned back to Caldwell. "Why aren't you two using it?" she asked suspiciously.

"We get gamma globulin shots before leaving port," Caldwell explained, "and take pills three times a day. Otherwise . . ." He shrugged to indicate the futility of the alternative course.

Maggie stuck her finger into the soft mixture. "Looks like shoe polish."

"It's a non-toxic electrophoretic albumin. One of these tins costs the Navy over a hundred dollars."

She worked her finger gingerly into the mixture, then scooped out a small glob. She wrinkled her nose at the smell. "Whew!" she exclaimed, grimacing. "What am I supposed to do with this junk?"

Caldwell made a sweeping motion with both hands around his eyes. "Spread it on like this."

Reluctantly Maggie began applying it to her skin. Her nose wrinkled even further. "Geeze, smells like buffalo droppings."

Behind Caldwell, Zimmer was having serious trouble keeping a straight face.

"Couldn't they have added some perfume, or something?" Maggie asked.

Caldwell dipped his finger into the tin and added a few touches around her eyes, and on her eyelids. "Don't want to miss any place. Not with your tender skin."

She nodded.

Caldwell stepped back to observe his handiwork. With the glop spread around her eyes, Maggie seemed to closely resemble the Lone Ranger. Caldwell shook his head seriously. "Oh, oh," he said, feigning concern.

"What is it?" Maggie was alarmed.

"Your eyes."

"What's wrong?"

"They're green."

"Of course they are." She hesitated, then asked guardedly, "Is that bad?"

"You're going to need extra protection." Caldwell turned away from her and reached into a drawer below the console. "You'll have to spread the globulin all over your exposed skin." He straightened. "And wear these," he said, handing her a pair of heavy dark glasses similar to those worn by welders.

Five minutes later, Lieutenant Ralston passed through the door marked *Authorized Persons Only* and entered the sonar room, carrying a tray with four mugs. "Your coffee, Miss O'Brien," he said cheerfully.

Maggie turned from her SUBDACS display and looked at him. With her face completely blackened, she looked like a refugee from a minstrel show. She had the heavy goggles on and a white towel was wrapped over her hair and tucked into her collar. Startled, Ralston nearly dropped the tray.

"What's wrong?" Maggie asked desperately. "Do I have it on wrong?"

Ralston was furious. He glared at Zimmer who looked quickly away. "Caldwell!" he snapped.

"Just a moment, sir." Caldwell leaned over to Maggie. "Miss O'Brien, the captain just called. He wants to see you in the control room, immediately."

"Like that?" Ralston demanded.

Caldwell shrugged helplessly. "An emergency,"

he said.

"But—"

Maggie slid out of her chair. "I'll be right back," she said, hurrying from the room before Ralston could intervene.

She stepped across the corridor and into the control room. Admiral Sward was the first one to see her. His jaw dropped nearly to the floor. "What the hell—?"

Jamison, who had been talking to Bertanelli, stopped in mid-sentence. Chuckles rippled through the control room as the remainder of the watch crew caught sight of her.

"Mr. Caldwell said you wanted to see me, Captain," Maggie said, trying desperately to understand what was so funny.

Bertanelli turned, lifting a coffee mug to his lips. When he saw Maggie, he nearly choked. The chuckles had built into laughter and Maggie was uncomfortably aware that everyone was staring at her. "What's so damn funny?" she demanded angrily.

"Er, nothing, Miss O'Brien," Bertanelli said, just barely managing to keep a straight face. "Someone, uh, just told a joke. Just before you entered."

She looked around at the crew, who quickly busied themselves with their instruments. "I see," she said uncertainly. Were they laughing at her? Being a woman, she had been the brunt of male humor before. "What was it you wanted, Captain?"

"Wanted?"

"Caldwell said you wanted to see me."

"Oh. I, uh, wanted to know, uh . . ." Bertanelli could not take his eyes off her blackened skin and her towel turban.

"Yes?"

144

With much effort, Bertanelli recovered his composure. He regarded Maggie with great seriousness. "Have you, uh, found anything on your equipment?"

"Not exactly. There was a streak across the CRT just before the explosion. Nothing that registered on sonar, but I believe I can pick up an emission trail."

"Well, uh, why don't you get back to it, Miss O'Brien?"

She nodded and started to turn, then glanced back at Bertanelli. "Is something wrong, Captain?"

The captain's eyes widened in mock surprise. "What could possibly be wrong, Miss O'Brien?"

She stared at him, shrugged, then turned and left the control room. A raucous burst of laughter followed her exit. Admiral Sward shook his head. "I'm on a ship of fools," he muttered.

CHAPTER THIRTEEN

10:10 p.m. Honolulu/0810 Hours Zulu

Premier Ognev's outer office was bustling with activity. The paranoid premier, aware that his two predecessors had been violently deposed, had heavily stocked the area directly outside of his door with KGB agents posing as secretaries and clerks. Actual face-to-face contact with the man was as rare as hen's teeth.

As Field Marshall Istomin was ushered through the double doors, across the red carpeted floor, and into the inner sanctum, he shuddered to think that a man could live that way. The marshall much preferred the life of a soldier. At least then, he believed, you knew who your enemies were.

"Ah, Field Marshall," Ognev said, looking up as Istomin entered the poorly lit office. "Any news?"

The premier's large, heavy, Georgian-crafted desk was cluttered with papers and faded maroon folders marked TOP SECRET. Istomin walked up to the desk and saluted smartly. "The documents and Colonel Turbin have been picked up by *Suslov*," he reported. "We will have them within forty-eight hours."

Ognev smiled broadly, causing creases of fat to

almost totally obscure his beady, pig-like eyes. "That news deserves a drink." He stood and walked to a tall, richly polished mahogany cabinet with fluted doors. "Moldavian wine?" he asked, removing a bottle of dark liquid from the upper shelf.

"Thank you, Comrade Chairman," Istomin said. He would have preferred vodka, or at least an American whiskey. But it was never wise to refuse the premier.

"I take it, then, Field Marshall," Ognev said, walking back to his desk carrying two full wine glasses, "that you do not foresee any problem?"

Istomin took the proffered glass. "None at all," he said confidently.

Ognev raised his drink high. "To our conquest of the Pacific, then," he said, his voice booming.

As the premier sipped his wine, the field marshall tilted back his head, downing his own drink in one gulp. Being a serious drinker, Istomin did not believe in wasting time with sniffing or savoring.

"I will alert Feliks to ready the eastern fleet," Ognev said. He took another sip, then closed his eyes euphorically as he rolled the sweet nectar around his tongue. "Within a week, the Pacific will be ours."

As Yakunin stopped in front of Mikola Govskaya's quarters, the guard at the door snapped to attention.

"At ease, Fyodor," the captain said.

The seaman relaxed, feeling somewhat awkward holding the toylike AK-74 at port arms.

"Open the door, if you please," Yakunin ordered softly.

The seaman fumbled with his key but in a moment had the door open. Yakunin entered. The political officer was seated on his bunk, staring at the door

147

solemnly. Seeing the captain entering, he sat up straighter, forcing his features into a scowl.

"I understand you wanted to see me, Mikola."

"I demand to be released," the *zampolit* said, his voice cracking slightly like that of a whining child.

"You disobeyed my orders. You fired on an American submarine without provocation. You hit your superior officer. You threatened the life of a member of my crew. How the devil do you expect me to release you?"

A slow smile spread across Govskaya's face. "First of all, Comrade Captain, you are not my superior officer. As *zampolit*, I have the last word on this boat. Secondly, I struck you when you interfered with my carrying out my duty. Third, the American submarine was threatening to attack. And fourth, I am armed in order to use force, if necessary, to carry out the will of the Party on board this vessel. You have no right to detain me!"

Yakunin eyed the small man with distaste. He realized that the officers at a hearing—which he knew this incident would no doubt spark—would see the situation as Govskaya had just stated it. Yet, if he released the *zampolit*, there would be no basis for a hearing and the Naval High Command would support him for his actions.

"I will release you on one condition, Mikola," the captain began.

Though the political officer tried to feign a superior attitude, it was evident to Yakunin that the man would do almost anything to get back on the bridge.

"I want your word that you will not interfere with my command again."

"I cannot do that!" Govskaya sputtered. "I am the *zampolit* on board!"

"Then you will be a *zampolit* locked in his own quarters." Yakunin turned toward the door.

"Well, perhaps," Govskaya said quickly, stopping the captain in his tracks. "But I have a condition of my own."

Yakunin paused with his hand on the knob. He did not turn around.

"I want my gun back."

Yakunin felt he could afford to be generous. In fact, he realized, giving the man back his gun would be a point in his favor in the eventuality of a hearing. He turned around. "As long as you keep it in your holster," Yakunin stated conditionally.

"Certainly."

"Then you are reinstated for duty." Yakunin turned and stepped through the door. Outside, he relieved the guard, sending him back to his own quarters. Govskaya stood up and straightened his uniform. His face twisted in a crooked smile as he thought of enacting sweet revenge once they reached home. He would file a report so scathing that Yakunin would not even be allowed to pilot a garbage scow along the Mother River.

Maggie's face was beet red and had been ever since Ralston had taken her to the head and told her of Caldwell's prank. At first she had been furious, and the difficulty she had washing the black goo off her face and out of her hair did nothing to improve her disposition.

But by the time she returned to sonar, her anger had passed, and she was actually smiling. Submarine initiations were legend in the Navy. Had she spent less time being critical of those around her, she might even have anticipated such an occurrence.

"How did you get that tin?" she had asked Caldwell, after reclaiming her post.

"I had it made in Osaka. There's a vendor there that claims he can make anything for a price. Cost me nearly twenty bucks. But it's been worth it."

"He got me the first day," Zimmer said.

Maggie had laughed, which easily won over the two sonarmen. Now she sat staring at her displays, trying to find the answer to the streak which had appeared on the screen so briefly, totally unaware of the crewmen and officers who kept finding reasons to poke their heads into the sonar room. They wanted to see for themselves if a woman really was handling the sonar controls of their boat, as rumor had it. Many had walked away shaking their heads in disbelief, while others, in a daze, paid up on previously made bets before returning to their off-duty stations.

After making another in a series of adjustments on her controls, Maggie bolted upright. "That's it!" she shouted. "Mr. Ralston, have the captain come to flank speed and steer two nine five degrees."

Ralston hesitated, not quite ready to relay sonar suggestions to the captain that came from a woman.

"What have you found?" Caldwell asked.

"Remember that streak I saw just before the ensonified zone disrupted your sonar?" When Caldwell nodded, she pushed a key and a scratching sound came over the loudspeaker. "This is what it was," Maggie said.

"Feeding turtles," Zimmer said immediately.

"Can't be," Caldwell replied, shaking his head. "We were too deep for turtles."

"Exactly!" Maggie exclaimed, beaming. "We were at nine hundred and fifty feet when the torpedo exploded. No turtle can dive that far."

"Then what is it?" Zimmer asked.

"The Soviet sub," Maggie replied.

Caldwell ran it through the computer. No ID showed up on the screen, and no indication registered. He looked puzzled.

"It was too far away for your equipment," Maggie explained. "But seeing the neutron emissions told me that it wasn't some kind of deep sea animal."

Caldwell shook his head incredulously.

Maggie laughed. "Trust me," she said.

Caldwell grinned back at her. "Trust you? Sounds like you're trying to sell me a used car. Everyone knows you can't *see* much in the ocean. You can only *hear* things. And I know every sound there is in the Pacific. I heard nothing!"

Undaunted, Maggie enhanced the reading off her compact laser disc, turning it up while filtering out unwanted images. "Run this through your equipment," she said.

Caldwell inserted the plugs and coded the information into the BC-10, the most advanced sonar computer ever designed.

Noises began filtering through the speaker.

"Feed pumps, coolant vents," Zimmer said.

They could hear the distinct sounds of hull pops and creaking, obvious indications of a submarine starting to get under way, changing elevations in the process. Seconds later the ID computer registered a probable Soviet submarine.

"No signature ID," Caldwell muttered. He fed in the sound of the Soviet boat they had discovered on the surface earlier. Lines curved, converged, and stabilized. "Same boat."

"Try the distance rating," Maggie urged.

Caldwell worked at the keyboard. He studied the waterfalls on the CRT screen. Suddenly a blip appeared, then formulated a target on the third level at seventeen miles. "Thirty thousand yards."

"It isn't really that far away," Maggie said.

Again Caldwell looked puzzled.

"He's using an acoustic mask," she elaborated, "along with the counterfeit signature of feeding turtles."

"What ratio?"

Maggie keyed information into her computer. "Five point three to one."

Caldwell did some quick mathematics in his head. "Then he was barely six thousand yards away?"

"Exactly."

"He could have rammed a fish up our butts and we wouldn't have known the difference!"

"Except he couldn't hear us through the zone any more than we could hear him."

"But with that little box of yours," Caldwell mused, his smile widening as the implications became clearer, "we could tell where he was and ram a fish—"

"Exactly."

"Lady," Caldwell exclaimed happily, "I think I'm in love with you! When can we get married?"

Zimmer chuckled. Ralston looked around the room uncomfortably. Maggie laughed.

"Then that's how you knew where *Batfish* was?" Zimmer asked.

Maggie nodded.

"And you've picked up the Russkie's present location from that?"

Again she nodded. "But we've got to get after him quickly, or I'll lose the track. The emissions only have a one-hour life."

Caldwell switched on his intercom mike. "Captain, if you want that Russian boat, suggest we come to course two niner five. Flank speed."

In the control room, Bertanelli stared momentarily

at the speaker, then grabbed the mike. "Is that Miss—uh, your combined opinion?"

"Yes, sir, it is."

"Hurry, Captain," Maggie added, "before we lose them."

When Mikola Govskaya entered the control room, Lev Savitsky turned to Yakunin, raising his eyebrows in surprise. "It is necessary," the captain told his friend quietly.

"I'm not so sure it is wise, Emelyan Yukunovich," the executive officer said, shaking his head. Savitsky was the only crew member who had been with Yakunin on every voyage the captain sailed. In a Navy where High Command deliberately shuffled crews around so no alliances could develop, Savitsky's tenure with Yakunin was a rarity.

"I am thinking ahead, Lev," Yakunin replied. "There will be a hearing." Savitsky slowly nodded.

"Besides," the captain added, "he is a devil. I would rather have him where I can keep an eye on him than off plotting something behind my back." The two friends' eyes met and held. A man who believed personal loyalty to be the greatest of virtues, Savitsky was willing to follow Yakunin anywhere the captain decided to lead him. "I hope you are right." Savitsky sighed.

"So do I."

Across the control room, Govskaya watched the two men chatting with apparent ease and familiarity. Then and there he decided to include the executive officer in his report.

Admiral Feliks Gugin studied the large table

layout of his fleet in the Okhotsk Sea. Seventy flags, representing various surface and submersible combatants, showed the position of every ship in the fleet.

"A formidable force," his aide said. Gugin nodded unconsciously.

More than a dozen uniformed women were busy moving markers across the room-sized table, keeping every location up-to-date.

"Yes," Gugin replied, frowning. He had heard that the Americans used light tables and computerized tracking, but his order for a similar situation board had been turned down by the frugal premier. Ognev was trying to rebuild the nation's economy at the expense of what he called military frills.

"Someday," the aide added, "we will be moving it east."

"*Da.*" Gugin loved nothing more than to stand and watch his Far Eastern fleet in action. He had always known that one day he would be allowed to move them into the Pacific. "Very soon," he said. *Perhaps even today,* he thought, and an electric shiver of excitement coursed through his body. He knew everything depended on the next few hours.

A woman with a microphone clamped around her neck turned toward the admiral. "The *Pravda* is requesting permission to bring his group into port."

Gugin shook his head. "*Nyet!* Permission denied." He looked at the message he had just received from Field Marshall Istomin. "Tell Admiral Stirlitz to take his battle group toward Simusir in preparation for entering the Pacific."

Everyone in the room turned to look at Gugin. "The Pacific?" his aide asked hesitantly.

"The Pacific!" Gugin repeated. It was all he could do to keep from shouting out his enthusiasm. "The time is very close!"

154

Suddenly the room erupted with cheers. Gugin felt the celebration might be a bit premature, but he allowed the demonstration to continue. After all, if worse came to worse, the group could be recalled by High Command before it passed through the channel.

A woman began slowly turning the twelve surface combatant battle group toward the channel between Simuri and Urup Islands in the Kuril chain. Nine escort submarines were also turned, each pointing toward the channel and to the Pacific Ocean beyond.

Bertanelli glanced at the speaker. He knew it would take time before he got used to hearing a woman's voice over the intercom. Perhaps he never would. He shrugged and turned to the helm. "Come to course two niner five," he ordered. "All ahead flank speed."

As the orders were repeated, Sward moved away from his lounging position at the periscope pedestal. "What if she's wrong?" he asked, the natural authority that comes with command evident in his voice. "That Russian could be lying in wait out there for you to make a move."

Bertanelli nodded solemnly. "Now's as good a time as any to test her equipment for the Navy."

Sward frowned. "Captain," he began, "I'm sure you know that I wasn't in favor of your appointment to this command."

"So I've heard, Admiral."

"Well now I think you're making a big mistake."

"Noted."

"Assuming she's right," the admiral went on, "and we survive long enough to catch up with the Russian, what are you going to do then?" He shook his head in disgust. "You have nothing but a bunch of misfits aboard."

Bertanelli's eyes blazed with unconcealed fury. With great difficulty, he managed to hold his anger in check. "When push comes to shove, Admiral, I'll stack this crew up against anything you've got in the fleet!"

They glared at each other in hateful silence.

"Captain?" Jamison said, shattering the tension. "I think you better see this."

Bertanelli turned away from Sward and stepped over to the chart table. Higgins had projected the western Pacific on the screen, and flashing indicators flowed along a track leading to the northern end of the Kuril Island chain.

"On this course," Jamison said, "we're heading right for the home waters of the entire Far Eastern Red Banner Fleet."

Bertanelli nodded. He had decided that following Maggie's readings was the only chance they had of locating the Russian submarine in time. And Pearl had been very explicit about the importance of doing just that. "He's probably heading for the sub pens at Sumsu Island."

"You're going to follow him in there?" Sward exclaimed, his eyes widening.

"I don't see that we have a choice. Blanchard gave us no option."

Jamison and Higgins nodded gravely.

Sward moved over beside *Pocatello*'s Management Team. "How far do you intend trailing him?" he demanded.

"Until we catch him, Admiral."

"They'll have a hundred submarines around Samsu."

"Then we have to catch him before he gets there."

156

"You don't even know where he is."

Bertanelli smiled. "Miss O'Brien does."

"Miss O'Brien," Sward scoffed. "You mean Little Black Sambo?"

Bertanelli pulled the rumpled communication from his pocket and thrust it in Sward's face. "Perhaps you better read this, sir," he said calmly.

Sward took the paper, unfolded it, and read:

> Z145527ZAUG
> TOP SECRET
> FM: CC COMPAC
> TO: USS POCATELLO
> SINK THE BASTARD
> BLANCHARD

Sward read it over twice. "That's T-Bone. Cryptic as ever."

Jamison whistled nervously. "I sure hope they know what they're doing at Pearl," he said, half to himself. "Sounds to me like someone at CINCPAC doesn't have both oars in the water."

Sward glanced at him angrily. "Four-star flag officers know exactly what they're doing, mister."

"I certainly hope so," Jamison added under his breath.

CHAPTER FOURTEEN

August 28-12:45 a.m. Honolulu/1045 Hours Zulu

Listening closely to his boat, Nuclear Officer First Rank Veli Ternovsky—a nineteen-year veteran on board Soviet nuclear submarines—did not like what he heard. He surveyed the instruments on the console in front of the four seamen monitoring the readings. All dials were red-lined, as was the custom in the high-pressured Soviet reactors.

Through the bulkhead, the reactor was running at its full rating, the plant's overall thermal efficiency at forty-eight percent. The revolutionary design, gained from experience in the *Alfa* submarines, put out over sixty thousand ship horsepower to the single shaft turning the propeller. But something was very wrong. Ternovsky scratched at his temple unconsciously as he noted that the reactor was pressurized to twenty-eight kilograms per square centimeter—about thirty-nine hundred pounds per square inch. The rods were absorbing just over one percent of the neutron flux, enough to permit or to prevent the desired chain reaction. Gauges showed that the heat was sent along the inside loop through the steam generator, back through the primary coolant pump, and into the reactor once again in its normal pattern.

The heat-exchanger showed normal, as did the flow of liquid coolant.

What could it be? Veli thought to himself.

He checked the indicators on the outside loop. All gauges showed everything to be normal. But Ternovsky could not shake the impression that he was hearing—or feeling—something that should not be there.

He walked over to the secure line and dialed the control room. "Comrade Captain," he said, "I would like to shut down for thirty minutes. I believe something is wrong and I wish to check it out."

In the control room, Yakunin considered the request carefully. It was about time to cut power anyway and do a sonar search. Perhaps he could kill two birds with one stone. "Thirty minutes, Veli," he agreed. "But not a second longer."

Yakunin turned toward the helm officer. "Bring us down to five percent power," he ordered. "We are going to take a look around." He picked up the intercom mike. "Sonar, be ready to sweep the area. We will be drifting for thirty minutes."

"Very well, Comrade Captain," came the reply.

Govskaya looked up, startled. He had been going over the charts on the plotting table, but now leapt to his feet and hurried across to Yakunin. "You can't do that," he insisted. "Our orders are to make all possible haste to Sumsu!"

Yakunin sighed. "Thirty minutes will not make any difference, Mikola."

"I'm sure Moscow will think otherwise!"

As Yakunin started to respond, sudden pain struck him in his chest and moved across his left shoulder. It was a feeling with which he was only too familiar. The first time he had ever experienced it, Yakunin had been certain he was having a heart attack. But over the years he had learned to rely on that pain. It was an early warning system that usually accompanied danger.

Yakunin turned away from Govskaya, rubbing his chest slightly, and faced the sonar screens. "Is there anything out there, Aleksei?" he inquired.

The sonar officer scanned his screens. "Nothing, Comrade Captain."

Noticing his old friend's distress, Lev Savitsky stepped up to Yakunin. "What is it?" he asked, his voice low and cautious.

Yakunin shook his head. "I feel something, Lev," he said quietly. "And I don't know what it is. I believe something . . . someone is out there."

Savitsky glanced at the screen, then back to Yakunin. "Where? I see nothing."

The captain waved absently. "Behind us. It is . . ." He paused. "I feel it is the American."

"What American?"

"The one we encountered earlier."

Savitsky's eyes widened. "But we sunk him!"

"Perhaps. But I do not think so. I think he is behind us, Lev, closing the distance." Yakunin rubbed his chest. He stared intently into his friend's eyes. "I can feel him."

In maneuvering, Ternovsky traced diagrams along a large plot board. Seeing everything check out, he decided to take a look aft in the engine room. On a hunch, he unpacked a portion of the shaft near the aft bulkhead.

"The devil be damned!" he exclaimed, looking at a small, hairline fracture in the casing about three feet from the first bearing housing.

He started to reach for an intercom mike when a call came over the loudspeaker. "Prepare to get under way."

Ternovsky looked at a bulkhead clock in astonish-

160

ment. "It's only been ten minutes !" he radioed back.

In the control room, Yakunin picked up the secure phone. "I'm sorry, Veli, but we must get under way. The safety of the boat is at stake."

"But we have a crack in the shaft," Ternovsky reported.

There was a stunned silence in the control room. "How did that happen?" Yakunin demanded finally.

"Probably a fault in the casting."

Yakunin grunted. "Vaunted Soviet workmanship."

"I must fix it immediately."

"And if you don't?"

"The rust inside is loosening," Ternovsky replied. "At two thousand revolutions per minute, the crack will expand until it vibrates a bearing loose or begins whipping out of alignment."

Yakunin glanced at the sonar screens. Though they were still clear, the pain in his chest and shoulders was increasing. "How long can we run the way it is?"

"Who knows?" the nuclear officer replied. "For a while, perhaps. But eventually that shaft is going to vibrate so badly we will make enough noise that every ship in the Pacific will hear us."

Yakunin walked over to the plotting table. He pulled a chart of the Kuril island chain and perused it carefully for several moments. Satisfied, he returned to the secure phone. "I will change course to Preznev through the Friza Straits," he said. "That will cut six hundred miles off our course. Can we make it?"

"Perhaps," the officer on the other end replied doubtfully. "I'm not sure."

"Keep me informed."

Bertanelli stuck his head in the sonar room. Seeing

Maggie at work on her terminal, he decided not to enter. As he stood for a moment watching her deft movements, something stirred inside him, a feeling he had thought was long dead.

He saw Mandy's image floating briefly before him. Beautiful, frilly, breakable Mandy. Theirs had been a whirlwind courtship. Bertanelli had been home on extended leave and she had been the belle of the ball at an officer's party in San Diego. Her father was an admiral, had introduced them, and within a week Tony and Mandy were married. In two weeks, he was back at sea. In nine months, Sherri Louise was born. Nine months after another leave, Tina Anne entered their lives. But the long months spent alone had their effect on Mandy. She began to drink. Heavily. It was rumored she spent more than a few evenings away from home. Fearful of getting pregnant again, she became distant, unwilling, and untouchable each time Bertanelli came home on leave. After a while, he found himself choosing to stay at sea for as long as possible. After three years of rocky marriage, when Tina Anne was only a year old, Mandy drank herself into a stupor and drove her car into an onrushing train.

As quickly as it came, the image faded. Bertanelli shook his head to clear his mind and stood in the doorway quietly staring at Maggie. Even in the officer tans, she definitely looked very feminine. Bertanelli shuddered. *Get hold of yourself*, he thought.

Abruptly he turned on his heels and walked quickly back into the control room.

Travis Romney had been sitting in the small mess hall adjacent to the galley of *Suslov* for several minutes. Those drifting in and out seemed to take his presence for granted. Most had nodded to him, some had tried to communicate but had found the experience difficult. In the end, they simply left him alone.

The cook had been quite friendly, bringing Travis a bowl of *lagman*, a beef noodle soup, and a pastry loaf with a savory salmon filling. "*Kulebiaka*," the man said, beaming when Travis looked at it suspiciously. "*Eto och'en' khorosho*." He had poured them both a small amount of *starka*, a dark vodka Travis found quite smooth and pleasant. "*Na zdorovie*," the cook had said, toasting the American. "To your health."

During this exchange, Travis noted a schematic of the Soviet submarine on an oil-splattered wall chart in the cook's station. He had clandestinely memorized it, especially the location of the maneuvering room.

As the cook busied himself preparing the noon meal, Travis stood and, partially supporting his weight with his cane, slipped out of the mess. He made a sharp right and hobbled down the corridor as quickly as he could. Two crewmen entered the corridor from the engineering section, nodded, and passed by. Travis sighed heavily, then hurried on

Colonel Turbin knocked on Yakunin's door. At the captain's invitation, the KGB officer entered. "You wanted to see me?"

Yakunin nodded. He offered Turbin a shot of vodka. They toasted the Politburo and downed their drinks.

"Perhaps you can tell me what this is all about?" the captain began.

"It's about following orders," Turbin replied curtly.

"What does that mean?"

"It means that what I carry is none of your business."

Yakunin glared icily at the KGB man. "Of course it's my business. The lives of everyone on board may depend on my knowing what's in that briefcase."

Turbin grunted and waved his hand in a gesture of dismissal. "It has nothing to do with your ship, Captain. It is a KGB matter."

Yakunin felt his face burning with anger. "Is that why an American submarine is following us clear across the Pacific?" he said, struggling to keep his fury in check. "Because it is a KGB matter?"

"Your concern is the American submarine," Turbin replied matter-of-factly. "Mine is the contents of the briefcase. Why don't you just take care of your responsibility and leave mine to me?"

The colonel turned toward the door. Yakunin grabbed Turbin's shoulder and angrily spun him around. "I want to know what it is that is driving the American commander that follows us!" Yakunin hissed, his face just inches from the KGB man's. "I want to know how far he will go to get back whatever it is you carry!"

The colonel roughly batted Yakunin's hand away from his shoulder. "I have told you all you need to know," he said, turning and reaching for the doorknob. Then he stopped and swung back around to glare at the captain, his voice dangerously low. "And don't ever touch me again!" He spun around, threw the door open, and stormed out.

Ternovsky felt the sweat pouring down his face.

Certain that the shaft was getting worse, he desperately needed time in order to strap and pack it. That, at least, would keep it from deteriorating any more and whipping out of alignment. It would also help keep the noise level down several decibels. But how was he going to get the time needed to complete the repairs?

He walked uneasily through the compartment and into the engine room beyond. As he lifted the secure line and dialed the control room, he wondered what he would do if he could not get the captain to stop the boat.

In the control room, Yakunin noted the call light and lifted the instrument. "Yes, Veli?"

"Captain, I strongly recommend we stop for emergency repair."

Yakunin sighed. "I thought we had been through that, Veli."

"This is different, Comrade Captain. It's the inside high-pressure pump. I must replace it."

"Is it defective?"

"It is making a racket, Comrade Captain. If I don't change it soon, it could lose a clapper, or perhaps be punctured." Veli swallowed hard. He knew such a catastrophe would not only disable the boat, but most likely destroy it. "We have been running at dangerously high temperatures for a long time," he continued, "and I'm afraid the corrosive build-up has reached a point where repairs are of the utmost importance."

"Are you sure it is the pump, Veli?" Yakunin asked, grasping at straws. He *knew* the enemy was trailing him. He did not know how the American had survived a torpedo fired at such close range. But Yakunin not only believed he had, he also believed the American had found some way, impossible as it might seem, to track him across the Pacific.

"I believe it is essential that we change the pump, Comrade Captain."

The American, Yakunin calculated, would be about two hours behind him, maybe farther. Even if it was a *Los Angeles* class boat, it could only turn thirty knots while *Suslov* was running at thirty-nine. He had at least two hours lead, probably more.

Yakunin sighed. "All right, Veli," he agreed. "We'll—"

"Nyet!" hissed Govskaya. "You cannot stop!"

Yakunin swung his head around to see the political officer listening in on his secure extension.

"But Comrade *zampolit,*" Veli replied frantically. "We must! If we don't take care of this, we could be destroyed."

"How long can we run with the pump the way it is?" Gofskaya demanded.

The chief engineer paused. He could envision the vibration of the shaft eventually popping every rivet and bolt in the boat. They would bring *Suslov* into port—if indeed they ever reached port—with enough spaces between her plates to see through. Not a pleasant thought for the nuclear officer. He would be the laughingstock of every engineer in the fleet.

"We must change the pump *now,* Comrade *zampolit.*"

"Request denied!"

Ternovsky blinked in astonishment. How could you deny a request for such a repair job? He swore loudly as the line went dead.

In the control room, Yakunin stared at the political officer in astonishment. Very carefully he replaced his own telephone and strode toward the *zampolit.* Forcing a broad smile onto his face, he put his arm around the shorter man affectionately. "A wise decision!" Yakunin exclaimed, loudly enough for everyone in the room to hear. He leaned in close and whispered in Govskaya's ear, "If you ever do that on my boat again, *zampolit*, I'll hang you by the *m'acha* and emasculate you!"

Startled, Govskaya looked up at Yakunin's smiling face. "What?"

"You heard me, Mikola Govidivich," Yakunin hissed, still grinning broadly. "On my boat, don't ever countermand one of my orders again!"

The blood rushed quickly into the political officer's ordinarily pallid, emaciated face. Yakunin slapped the man heartily on the back and leaned in to kiss both his cheeks. With his lips next to the *zampolit's* ear, Yakunin whispered, "Let me make it perfectly clear. If you want to live through this cruise, don't countermand my orders again."

The political officer was shocked. Though outwardly, Yakunin was being friendly and affable, his words were threatening, insulting and, in Govskaya's mind, treasonous. "I will report your attitude and threats to the Party in my next communique," the political officer raged quietly. Despite his mounting anger, he had kept his voice low to match Yakunin's.

"It would be my word against yours, Mikola," the captain whispered. "And after your earlier indiscretion, you wouldn't have a leg to stand on. Besides, look around you. Does it appear any of my crew would testify that I had threatened you?" To emphasize his point, Yakunin embraced the political officer warmly in a bear hug, then strode back to the chart table.

Govskaya was dumbfounded. He had been tricked and left with no outlet for venting his inner fury. Angrily, he stormed out of the control room.

167

Yakunin looked after him for a moment, then chuckled. He had not been promoted to the Red Banner Fleet's highest ranking sea-going position because of his darkly handsome good looks. He was a shrewd officer, capable of out-thinking and out-guessing anyone he had ever met.

He started to reach for the secure phone, then stopped. The pain in his chest intensified and shot through him like a searing iron. *The American is close!* he thought. Yet sonar showed nothing. Still, he knew the boat stalked him. The American captain, he suddenly realized, might be as shrewd as himself. Maybe even more so.

Veli Ternovsky walked back into the maneuvering room, beside himself. If he did not repair that shaft soon, it would shake apart the entire boat. He shook his head and glanced toward the manned control panel. Suddenly he was aware there was a sixth man in the room. One wearing baggy pants and blouse of a common seaman and supporting his weight on a crude wooden cane.

Veli glanced at the American.

Travis was just about to reach for the SCRAM button on the console when he saw the officer. In a brief instant, both men understood what was about to happen. And both moved at the same time.

CHAPTER FIFTEEN

Maggie stared at her instruments. Somehow she had to reacquire the neutron emission track from the Soviet sub. But where was it? And why had the reactor been shut down?

"It's still beyond our range," Caldwell said, busily studying his own instruments.

"Why would a submarine stop in the middle of the ocean?" Maggie asked.

"He could be sonar searching," Caldwell said. "He can't see much running near forty knots. Sonar, even the most sophisticated, is blind when a submarine is running at high speed. Above twenty knots, there is so much noise from a boat's own machinery, propeller cavitation, and water passing across the hull, that the hydrophones are nearly useless. As a result, submarines will slow every so often to search the area and reacquire position fixes. In a search and destroy mission, submarine captains employ a technique called sprint and drift. Short, calculated high-speed runs to a given spot, slowing to reacquire their target, then another mad dash. He's been slowing every two hours, coming down to about ten knots or so. But this is different."

"Maybe there was a breakdown," Ralston suggested. "Soviet boats are unreliable."

A breakdown! Suddenly, Maggie understood the problem. She ran a track through her machine, compared it to the track they were previously following, then inserted a new one. "Suggest to the captain that we come to course two zero three degrees," she said excitedly.

"You've reacquired the emissions?" Caldwell asked, squinting at her screen. He could see nothing on her monitor.

"No."

"Then?"

"I think the captain called it woman's intuition."

In the control room, Bertanelli received the instruction to change course calmly. "Come to course two zero three." He had cast his lot with Maggie and intended to ride it out.

"Course two zero three, aye."

"Now what's up?" Jamison asked.

Sward bent over the chart table and studied the TV projected image of the western Pacific.

"Damned if I know," Bertanelli replied.

"She's got us heading toward the southern Kurils," Sward said. "I thought we all agreed the Russian was making full steam toward Sumsu."

In the sonar room, Ralston shook his head in confusion. "Why southwest?" he asked. "I thought they were headed northwest."

"They've got, or are going to have, a major breakdown," Maggie announced.

All heads turned in her direction.

"Your equipment tell you that?" Ralston asked.

Maggie shook her head. "It's the only thing that

170

makes sense."

Zimmer exhaled loudly. "She's gazing into a damn crystal ball," he exclaimed, wiping the sweat from his face.

"I think the captain ought to hear this," Ralston said as he picked up the intercom mike.

The four technicians in *Suslov*'s maneuvering room whirled toward the chief engineer as he yelled. Travis leaped past them, reaching the SCRAM switch and wincing from the pain coursing through his damaged leg. Ternovsky made a wild grab for him. With a swiftness the chief engineer could hardly believe, Travis flipped up the plastic cover and jammed the switch down, closing off power to the reactor.

Beyond the bulkhead, control rods dropped into the reactor vessel and the reactor scrammed. The neutron chain reaction came to an abrupt stop. Heat production in the reactor ceased, and a dozen alarms sounded at once on the engineering control board and throughout the boat.

Several thoughts raced through Ternovsky's mind at once. If the reactor fully depressurized too quickly, its many gallons of coolant would explode into steam and seek a release into the surrounding compartment. And on Soviet boats, there was no secondary shield to contain such a break. He let go of Travis and rushed to the board that was now lit up like Times Square with flashing warning lights. "Cut off residual heat!" he yelled. "Close main steam feed!"

With no one paying any attention to him, Travis started dragging himself toward the door.

One engineer was spinning a wheel, cutting off the

steam supply to the engine room. Another dampened the rods so reactor coolant could absorb the heat as the plant reaction came to a sudden stop.

Ternovsky grabbed an intercom mike. "Emergency!" he shouted frantically. "Reactor scram! Reactor scram! Emergency!"

"All hands to damage control stations!" the overhead speakers bellowed. "This is no exercise!"

Without steam to the turbines, the main propulsion shut down. *Suslov*'s prop slowed and stopped.

"Engineering, rig for battery power," Yakunin ordered.

In seconds, *Suslov* was making slight headway under the power of her turbo generators.

"Blow forward trim tanks," Yakunin said.

"Very well, blow forward trim tanks," the warrant officer repeated, slowly recovering from the panic that had totally engulfed him seconds before. He, and each man aboard the *Suslov* had just experienced a nightmare feared by every submariner.

The diving officer watched the fathometer with apprehension. The boat was still falling, but at least the rate of descent was beginning to slow. "Eleven hundred meters, Comrade Captain," he reported, his voice tight.

Yakunin glanced at the fathometer, then dismissed it. His major concern was restarting the reactor, an operation that could take up to two hours after a SCRAM.

"Maneuvering!" he called over the intercom.

"This is Ternovsky, Comrade Captain."

"Everything all right back there?"

"Under control, Comrade Captain."

"How soon can you restart?"

Ternovsky hesitated slightly. "Ninety minutes," he reported.

"What the hell happened?"

"The American."

Yakunin cursed under his breath. He knew he should have locked the pilot up in a cabin somewhere. "Any damage?" he asked.

"Nothing, Comrade Captain. We can be under way in ninety minutes."

Yakunin glanced at Govskaya. "While your crew is working on the reactor, Veli, go ahead and replace the inside valve, or whatever it was you wanted to do."

"Yes, Comrade Captain."

"Report to me in my cabin as soon as you have restarting procedures begun. And bring that American."

Ternovsky replaced the telephone. He glanced at the controls to make sure everything was normal, then glared at the American pilot lying in an exhausted heap near the door. "How did you get in here?" Ternovsky hissed.

Travis smiled. "Through the door," he answered cockily.

The Russian reached down and grabbed Travis by his lapels and jerked the pilot roughly to his feet. Travis grimaced as his body was racked with pain. Ternovsky pulled the flyer close to him, their noses almost touching.

"I ought to have you shot!" the Russian growled evilly.

"Go ahead," Travis replied, gritting his teeth in agony. "I did what I had to do."

Suddenly the chief engineer's face split into a wide grin. "But instead I might give you a medal!" He leaned the startled American up against the door jamb and bent down to retrieve Travis's cane which was lying nearby. "Without knowing it," the

173

Russian continued, handing Travis his walking stick, "you have likely saved our boat from a crazy *zampolit* and eventual destruction!"

Travis blinked in surprise. He looked around at the technicians going calmly through the restarting procedures.

Ternovsky roared with laughter. "I wanted this boat stopped for the past two hours," he explained gleefully. "But our political officer denied me the time to fix our shaft. Without repairs, this boat would become so noisy, every American in the Pacific could have heard it. Now, you have given me time to fix it. Thank you."

Travis swore bitterly under his breath.

Bertanelli pushed his way past the cordon of off-duty seamen waiting outside of sonar to catch a glimpse of the woman manning the equipment.

"Haven't you something better to do?" the captain asked in annoyance as he passed into the sonar room. Taking the hint, the men dispersed rapidly.

Bertanelli stopped beside Maggie. She smiled up at him. Bertanelli shot a quick glance toward Caldwell, who shrugged. Ralston simply shook his head. "What is it, Miss O'Brien?" the captain demanded.

"Without going into a long, detailed, and highly technical explanation, Captain," Maggie explained calmly, "I know where the Russian is going."

"It seems obvious, even to this non-technical layman," the captain replied shortly.

Maggie frowned. "You needn't get snippy," she said.

"I was merely pointing out the obvious. He is heading for the Soviet sub pens at Sumsu."

Maggie smiled. "That's what I'd expect you to

think. I would think that too . . . except for this."
She pointed to a track laid down on her equipment
over the western Pacific. It showed a gradual course
outline heading toward the southern end of the
Kuril Islands. She pointed to a change on the track.
"He changed course a while back."

"How do you know that?"

"With my equipment I can monitor traces of
nuclear waste in the ocean. As you know, Soviet subs
are not well shielded."

Bertanelli stared at her silently.

"That lead-bismuth reactor of his," Maggie went
on, "has left a trail a blind man could follow."

"Nuclear submarines, even Soviet ones, do not
irradiate the water around them," Bertanelli stated
flatly, beginning to doubt his decision to entrust his
boat to her. "If they did," he added, "we wouldn't be
allowed in any port."

Again she smiled. Bertanelli was suddenly reminded of his third grade teacher patiently instructing him.

"All reactors, Captain," Maggie explained, "even
ones using liquid metal as a coolant, must pipe sea
water around the steam condensers and generators to
keep them from overheating. When running all out
that sea water is either changed constantly, or it
becomes hot and the condensers overheat."

Bertanelli thought for a moment. A nuclear reactor
had to be kept at sixteen hundred degrees. Cooling
sea water was circulated constantly to keep the
reactor from overheating and scamming. But even so,
he knew, she was talking about a minute amount of
radiation. "What you suggest would be impossible to
measure," he said doggedly.

"When my equipment was installed aboard *Pocatello*, the bow was fitted with a special type of

175

scintillation counter, Captain. Using a new type of trans-stilbene crystal, we can pick up neutrino and pi-meson light bursts, though only billionths of a second long, and amplify them through the electron-emitting surface of the dome. That, in turn, sends an impulse to the photomultiplier tube in this equipment."

"I thought you weren't going to get technical," Bertanelli grunted.

A disarming smile spread across Maggie's face, displaying two rows of even white teeth. "Particles irradiated by the exchange of sea water through a Soviet sub are picked up here electronically," she explained, indicating her special equipment.

"Why didn't you say so!" Bertanelli boomed, returning her smile. "But even if you can do that, whatever trailing radiation there is would be spread over miles of ocean."

"True, Captain, but it remains hottest at the center, or point of origin for about an hour. That's what this track shows. The trail of a Soviet nuclear sub, headed for the Friza Straits."

Bertanelli stared at the curving track.

"But why turn away from Sumsu?" he wondered out loud. "He is obviously carrying something vital to the Kremlin. Sumsu is a major submarine port with direct high-impact, direct communication capability to Moscow. Preznev is just a repair dock."

"What if he has a cracked shaft?"

Bertanelli spun around suddenly to face her. He knew that Soviet subs carried no spare parts nor backup machinery. A cracked shaft would eventually break under the strain, especially at flank speed. And if that happened, the Russian would be dead in the water, a sitting duck for any American vessel within shooting distance. "He'll want to get to the nearest

176

repair yard!" Bertanelli exclaimed happily.

"And where is that?" Maggie prompted.

"At Preznev on Urup, of course!"

Maggie's grin broadened. "Through the Friza Straits," she said, "six hundred miles closer than Sumsu."

Suddenly Bertanelli turned serious. He eyed the young woman warily. "How do you know he has a cracked shaft?"

"I don't. But something is making more noise. If it wasn't for the mask, we could readily identify it on the sonar."

Bertanelli frowned. "You're sure about all this?"

"I know something is terribly wrong for him to have stopped for repairs knowing we're on his tail."

"How could he know that?"

"He hasn't been running full with damaged machinery for nothing."

"But how do you know he has something damaged?"

"Why else would he stop?" she asked, annoyance creeping into her voice. "He's been running at flank speed for ten hours. Why stop now?"

Bertanelli glanced at Caldwell. The sonarman shrugged again. "She has a point, Captain," he said.

Bertanelli nodded. "All we need is a miracle to slow him down until we can reach him," he muttered. "Once through the straits he's out of our reach."

"Well, at least now we have a chance," Maggie pointed out enthusiastically.

Bertanelli nodded. "Carry on," he said simply, and left the sonar room.

"I take it that means a job well done?" she asked of Caldwell.

"He expects excellent work."

Maggie frowned. "I see. To get a compliment from that man, I've got to perform a miracle. Maybe I should walk on water and overtake the Russian myself!"

Caldwell grinned. "He'd like that," the sonarman said.

Maggie shook her head. "A hard man, your captain."

"Tell us about it," Zimmer muttered from across the room.

CHAPTER SIXTEEN

2:05 a.m. Honolulu/1205 Hours Zulu

Yakunin was wrong in believing the top speed of the *Los Angeles* class boat that followed him was only thirty knots. The originally planned S6G General Electric reactor had been updated for the last fiscal year programming. Finished ahead of schedule, *Pocatello* received the first of the new S7G reactors built by Westinghouse. No longer a mere update of the D2G power plant, the new reactor could generate forty-five thousand ship's horsepower. This added another five knots to *Pocatello*'s speed.

That put the pursuing boat less than eighty minutes behind *Suslov*.

Had the Soviet captain known this, he might have made different plans. As it was, he sat now in his cabin, a cramped box distinctly lacking in comfort, and stared at the American pilot who was sitting on his bunk. Yakunin shook his head sadly. "What am I going to do with you?" he asked. "I thought I was being considerate by not locking you up and look how you repay me."

Travis eyed the chief engineer standing directly behind the captain.

"I told him we ought to give him a medal," Ternovsky said.

"For saving one of the Motherland's most important boats?" Yakunin's lips thinned in a rare smile. "Perhaps we should." He paused, eyeing Travis up and down speculatively. "Do you know what this is all about?" the captain asked finally. "What was in the plane you shot down?"

Travis shrugged, inwardly surprised to learn that the Russian knew as little as he did.

"Surely you don't go around shooting down civilian planes for nothing," Yakunin suggested to the American judiciously. "Come, Captain, what could possibly be on that plane that was so important?" *And is putting my boat and crew at such risk,* he thought but did not say.

Travis began to squirm slightly, feeling somewhat uncomfortable in the cramped cabin. "I don't have to talk to you," he said defensively, "or answer any questions."

Yakunin clicked his tongue against the roof of his mouth. "You Americans," he scoffed. "You think the rest of the world should play by the rules you create." He stood up abruptly and stepped toward the door. "When you get to Moscow, I'm sure you'll find people who do not adhere to your rules." Opening the door, he motioned to an armed guard standing outside. "See that he can't get into trouble again," the captain ordered.

The guard nodded and led Travis, hobbling down the corridor on his walking stick, aft.

When the men were gone, Yakunin closed the door and turned to his nuclear officer. "Are you sure the shaft will hold up until we reach Urup?" he asked.

Ternovsky nodded. "Luckily it was close enough

to a bearing to have gained support until we located it," he replied. "For the time being, we have packed and strapped it." They had been running on battery power at a very slow speed for nearly an hour in order to study the effect. Other than a tendency to vibrate at higher speeds, the shaft had been working perfectly. "On any other boat, Comrade Captain, the crack would have worsened and shaken apart. But the packing around the shaft and the hydraulics of *Suslov*'s quiet construction have kept the fracture localized."

The captain frowned. "Still, I'll bet American submariners are not faced with such poor workmanship."

"I recommend we not run at more than thirty knots with it," Ternovsky said. "Actually, I'd feel safer at twenty."

Yakunin shook his head. "We are being followed, Veli. A devil of an American submarine captain is on our heels and I do not wish to be overtaken."

"But Mezhova has been reporting nothing on our sonar."

Yakunin stared at his nuclear officer intently. "He's out there. I can feel it."

"Once we reach the Zenkevich Rise, we will have an escort."

The captain shook his head sadly. "I don't know, Veli. I have a bad premonition about this one."

"We are ready to come to full power whenever you say, Comrade Captain. No American boat can catch *Suslov*!"

Yakunin nodded absently. He knew Ternovsky was right. Still, he could not ignore the sharp pain in his chest and the awful premonition he felt.

*   *   *

Maggie had her fingers crossed. She had been hoping to reacquire neutron emissions from the Soviet submarine for quite some time. Her intuition and deductive reasoning had told her the boat was heading for Urup. But nothing on her instruments supported that assumption. And if they did not pick something up soon, she would have to be the one to explain to Bertanelli that her guess was wrong. Maggie shuddered at the thought.

Caldwell had been watching her every move. He was enamored with the entire SUBDACS system and was hungry to learn all its mysteries. "How far can you reach with it?" he asked.

"We're tracking about thirty thousand yards at this speed," Maggie replied, only too happy to get her mind off her troubles. "Without bowshock at slower speeds, the scintillator can reach twice that distance. Probably about thirty-five miles."

It was a far cry from the thousand-mile range of the towed array. But it worked at flank speed—something sonar could not do. When *Pocatello* was running full out, the TBS array was reeled in. The boat had to be below twenty knots and either running in an S pattern or in a large, continuing arc, in order for the towed array to "hear" forward. "Does it register speed?" Caldwell asked.

"Not exactly," Maggie said, smiling like a proud parent. "But the neutron traces give off a different rate of decay when the reactor is running at higher efficiency levels. So by comparing the decay rate, we can come close to knowing the speed the boat was traveling at that point in the water."

"And you created this all by yourself?"

Maggie blushed. "Well, I did have help, Mr. Caldwell."

"If we're going to get married, you'd better start

calling me Jason."

Maggie giggled girlishly. "To a guy who's got a girl in every port? Never."

They shared a friendly laugh for several seconds. Then Maggie sighed dreamily. "Some day we'll be plotting and tracking Soviet submarine emissions with my equipment from aerial reconnaissance or satellite monitors," she said. "We'll have all their subs zeroed in and targeted. We won't have to rely on SOSUS or chance encounters by our own boats. We'll know exactly where every sub they have is located. We'd be able to shoot them out of the water if the need ever arose."

Caldwell got suddenly serious. "You expecting a war?" he asked, frowning.

"With equipment like this and others that we're working on, there won't be a war," Maggie said with assurance. "We'll be so far ahead of the Russians they won't dare think about attacking."

Caldwell shook his head skeptically. "You don't believe the Soviets are also developing new technology?"

"Most of their technology is purchased or stolen. We have seen very little inventive genius from them so far." She spun a few dials and worked the keyboard as she spoke, continually feeding the changing readings into the BC-10 computer. "Oh, they come up with something unique once in a while, like the titanium hull of the *Alfa*. A technology, by the way, that is not beyond our capability. The problem lies in our not having much titanium and the Russians sitting on the largest deposits anywhere in the world. But Soviet industrial technology is far behind ours. They can't refine and tool to the specifications needed to duplicate much of what we do, even when they steal the plans."

183

Caldwell nodded. "I read somewhere that they're still using vacuum tubes in their electronics."

"Perhaps. The point is that we're working on quantum leaps the Soviets will have great difficulty duplicating, Our next generation reactor will be using its own coolants and not require pumps. Talk about quiet submarines, they'll be undetectable."

Caldwell grinned. "That's why we should get married, Miss O'Brien," he said. "With your brains and my ability, we'd be unstoppable."

Across the room, Zimmer looked up from his sonar controls. "That'd be like uniting Einstein and Dr. Seuss," he said.

In his situation room, Adm. Feliks Gugin was handed a brief message by the board supervisor. He read it, then did so twice again, excitement coursing through his veins like a narcotic.

ADM. GUGIN
SEND OUT PRAVDA BATTLE GROUP.
F. ISTOMIN.

We're on our way, he told himself incredulously. *We're actually going out!* Containing his enthusiasm, he turned to his floor supervisor. "Radio Admiral Stirlitz," he said calmly. "Tell him to proceed through the passage."

The supervisor looked up, stunned. "Very well, Admiral," she replied stoically.

The news was received in the center with quiet awe. The celebration was already over. Now was the time for action. After long years, they were finally going out to secure the Pacific for the Motherland. It was a proud moment for all and all heads turned to

Admiral Gugin.

He acknowledged their silent praise and nodded.

"Congratulations," his aide said quietly.

"To all of us," the admiral said. Then, turning suddenly grim, he added, "We've got a foothold, now let's hope we can keep it." Gugin was no fool. To enter the Pacific was one thing, he knew. To stay there would be something else entirely.

Colonel Turbin roamed *Suslov* restlessly. Despite his earlier exhausting ordeal, he had been unable to sleep. If there was one thing he had learned in his years in the secret police, it was that he could trust no one, not even those inside the KGB. *Especially* those in the KGB. Everyone was his enemy. And certainly Captain Yakunin was no exception. In his earlier years, Turbin had run afoul of a KGB colonel who pictured himself the next chairman. It had nearly cost Turbin his life and had meant exile to Hungary for seven years. Eventually, he had worked his way back into the good graces of his bosses, but not until he had successfully carried out a brutal mass assassination of twenty Hungarian rebels who had plotted a takeover of the government.

Entering the officers' mess, Turbin saw the executive officer, Lev Savitsky, sitting alone at a table, nursing a *Kvass*—a non-alcoholic beer. It was one of the few excesses he allowed himself when at sea. Turbin sauntered in, dished up a plate of *pel'myeni,* and sat down across from Savitsky. "Very tasty," he said, pointing at the stuffed dumplings.

The executive officer nodded. Neither spoke as Turbin greedily dug into his meal.

After several seconds, Turbin belched loudly. "Sailed with the captain before?" he asked, not looking up from his food.

"Once or twice," Savitsky replied guardedly.

"What kind of a man is he?"

Savitsky eyed the KGB man suspiciously. He slowly raised the bottle to his lips and took a long pull. "Why do you ask?" he said, wiping his moustache with the back of his hand.

Turbin struggled to keep his anger in check. There was nothing he hated more than being questioned by inferiors that he himself was interrogating. "Just making conversation," he said, stuffing a cabbage-filled dumpling into his mouth. He slowly savored the delicious flavor, allowing his rage to subside. It would not do to lose control of the situation.

"Besides," he continued after several seconds, "I like to know something about the man who is safeguarding my life at any given moment. Call it being overly cautious if you will." That, of course, was a lie. Col. Vladimir Turbin entrusted his life to no one.

Lev Savitsky regarded Turbin coldly before answering. He was not about to reveal his true feelings about the captain to anyone from State Security. One of his most steadfast rules was *never tell the Komitet anything.*

"Captain Yakunin is considered the best submarine commander in the Far Eastern Red Banner Fleet," Savitsky replied without emotion.

Turbin nodded, devouring another dumpling. "Then I am in safe hands?" he asked.

"The safest."

"That is good to know." Turbin belched once more. A steward came over to him with a cup and a pot of steaming black coffee, poured the colonel a serving and left without a word. Turbin took a sip of the rich, dark liquid. "You submariners live well," he observed.

"One of the perks granted men who are at risk every minute of every day at sea."

"Does it bother you that an American submarine is following you?"

Savitsky's eyes narrowed sharply. "Should it?"

"I understand they already fired on you once."

"It was the other way around. We accidentally fired on them. You were there, Colonel. Do you not remember?" He stared unflinchingly into Turbin's eyes. "Yet, they still follow. Now why is that, Colonel?"

The KGB officer met his gaze coldly. "I was about to ask you the same question," he said.

"It must be because of you, or what you brought aboard." Savitsky stood up abruptly. "You have put this boat and its entire crew at greater risk than normal. I certainly hope it is worth it, Colonel." He turned quickly on his heels and left the mess.

Turbin sat back, sipping the hot coffee. There were a few people on board he intended to take care of permanently once they reached port. The captain was first. And then came his executive officer. Vladimir Turbin did not take kindly to insubordination. He would relish their punishment. For an instant he allowed himself to indulge in pleasant visions of revenge. The images before him shifted quickly from Yakunin and Savitsky to a myriad of faces in a dozen different countries—men and women he had stalked, tortured, and finally killed. A smile crept across his features as he recalled those glorious, euphoric moments when he could feel lives slipping away beneath his fingers. Death by bare hands was always the most gratifying. To Turbin, the feeling was more satisfying than being with any woman he had ever known.

In the small galley adjacent to the officers' mess, the steward, Igor Melnik, stood just behind a curtain waiting anxiously for Turbin to leave. He watched the KGB colonel with abject fear. Such men, he had found, were to be avoided at all costs. And until the man left, he was not setting foot back into the mess. But Turbin was in no hurry to leave. He sat sipping the coffee, reliving his blissful moments of terror and intrigue. To such men, drugs and sex were often unnecessary.

In *Pocatello*'s control room, the reactor was chopped to fifteen percent as Bertanelli ordered a reduction of speed. The boat came nose up as the bow wave swept over them.

"Control to sonar," the captain called over the intercom. "Let's take a look and see what's out there."

The TBS array was reeled out and *Pocatello* began running an S pattern. As the noise reduced to normal and the computer began filtering out typical sea sounds, Zimmer sat up straight in his chair. "Holy shit!" he shouted.

Caldwell swung around to the repeater.

"Sonar to control," Zimmer yelled. "Cut power! All stop! Target sub fifteen thousand yards dead ahead!"

Maggie shifted from emission search to reglar sonar. "Damn!" she swore. "He's running turbo-electric. No wonder we couldn't find any emission trail."

"All ahead stop!" Bertanelli ordered. "Repeat, all ahead stop!" He picked up the intercom mike. "Are you sure it's the same boat?"

"Positive ID," Zimmer affirmed excitedly.

Bertanelli turned to the officer of the deck. "Sound General Quarters. Battle stations, nuclear."

The order was repeated throughout the boat as the crew rushed to their preassigned positions. Some donned asbestos suits and took up their fire control assignments while others raced to action stations.

Aboard the seventy-five thousand ton nuclear-powered CTOL aircraft carrier *Pravda*, Adm. Gely Stirlitz received his sailing orders calmly. He had been steaming toward the channel for several hours and was only minutes away from entering the Pacific. He had naturally assumed that would be his final destination and now that it was an accomplished fact, he was not in the least bit surprised.

Passing the orders along to Capt. Konstantin Gorokhov, commander of the *Pravda*, Stirlitz settled back in his flight chair on the command bridge, six stories above the 984-foot flight deck, and folded his hands across his rock-hard stomach. Contentedly, he surveyed his battle group—a battle-cruiser, two helicopter cruisers of the *Moskva* class, three CG cruisers, and five destroyers, three of the *Udaloy* class, and nine antisubmarine combatants. It was a formidable group, larger than anything the Soviets had ever put together in the Pacific before. Stirlitz smiled, imagining the surprise and concern his excursion into the Pacific would cause the Americans.

In the sonar room of the *Pocatello*, Maggie was staring intently at the screen. She now realized the Soviet submarine would have been shut down for nearly two hours for her to have no indication whatsoever of neutron emission readings.

Beside her, Caldwell fed continuous information to the control room. "Soviet *Mike* at fourteen thousand five hundred yards. Bearing two zero four degrees. Speed four knots. Elevation/deflection, two degrees positive."

The *Suslov* was running two hundred feet above *Pocatello*'s track, just under a thermocline layer.

"You are positive it is the same boat?" Bertanelli insisted. "There can be no mistake, Jason."

Caldwell once again checked the signature with the one they had previously recorded. "It's the same one, Captain," he confirmed. "You can bet the farm on that."

Bertanelli's face darkened. He reached for the intercom mike. "Control to weapons," he said. "I want a firing solution on the target. *Now!*"

"Aye aye, sir," came the reply.

"Sonar, feed your readings into the one-seventeen."

"Feeding now," Caldwell responded. He plugged in the data and sent it along to the Mark 117 Mod 3 firing solution computer. In the control room, the UYK-7 computer was primed and readied for relaying communications between command and the torpedo room.

"Weapons, load tubes two and four with Mark forty-eights," Bertanelli ordered. "Put a Tomahawk in VLS-one."

Across the room, Admiral Sward's face went white with shock. He leapt from his chair and raced over to Bertanelli. "What the hell are you trying to do?" he shouted frantically, his eyes blazing. "That's a nuclear warhead! You don't have the authority to launch a nuclear missile!"

Bertanelli's body tensed with anger. "I have the authority to do anything I choose on *my* boat!"

Sward opened his mouth to reply when a voice over the intercom interrupted him. "Weapons to control," the voice said. "Tubes two and four loaded with Mark forty-eights. VLS-one loaded with a Tomahawk."

Bertanelli abruptly turned from the seething admiral and spoke into the mike. "Control to weapons," he said, his voice firm and commanding. "Arm them!"

Sward grabbed Bertanelli by the arm and swung the captain around roughly. "You can't do this!" he shouted. "You could start a war!"

Bertanelli glared at the admiral. "Need I remind you," he said, his voice low but intense, "that this is *my* bridge, Admiral?" He jerked his arm from Sward's grasp and turned to study the weapons panel.

Sward's body shook with rage and more than a little fear. This was more than simple distaste for the captain's boyish pranks, more than anger at watching the flamboyant young officer who had made a fool out of him at the Academy rise meteorically through the ranks. This man was threatening the lives of every man, woman, and child on the face of the earth!

"I could relieve you of your command," Sward said, his voice thin and shaking.

Bertanelli turned to stare at the little man at his elbow. "You could," he admitted, "but you won't."

"Weapons armed and ready," a voice announced over the intercom.

Bertanelli kept his eyes locked on Sward's. "Flood the tubes," he ordered.

"Flooding tubes, aye."

Sward suddenly felt weak. He knew he should act, but could not bring himself to do so. It had been just

191

too long. And personal feelings aside, the younger man was a hell of a commander, much stronger and more capable than he himself had ever been. And deep inside, Sward knew this to be true.

"Sonar to control!" Caldwell's voice over the speakers shattered the tension in the room. "Multiple screws. Surface ships, one bearing zero niner five degrees. Heading two three eight degrees. Eight thousand yards. He's going to pass right over us!"

CHAPTER SEVENTEEN

3:00 a.m. Honolulu/1300 Hours Zulu

Six hundred feet above the *Pocatello*, the storm was raging full force. Black clouds hung low over the ocean as eighty-mile-an-hour winds kicked up fifteen-foot waves, pushing the water in sheets across the Pacific.

A thousand miles from its home port, the 155-meter-long *Toyota Maru #10* churned through the rough seas making her top speed of twenty knots. She rode high, her side ramps bolted closed, her nine decks clear of the 2,080 export cars delivered to pier 94 in San Francisco fifteen days earlier.

Her captain, Akira Shinjyo, stood on his bridge, looking out through the glass windows, watching the storm build. A twenty-one-year veteran of Pacific crossings, his first command—delivering export cars for Toyota—had been back in the days when Japanese imports were the laughingstock of the world. In those days, four crossings a year were considered adequate. This year, he was already on his sixth run with four months left to go.

Shinjyo stood stoically, watching the rain batter the glass. His experience had taught him just how nasty the weather could be out here and he wished fervently to soon catch a glimpse of his vaunted homeland. *The children of the rising sun,* he thought simply. Shinjyo had long believed himself to be one of the last of the Japanese *samurai,* a warrior caste that came into existence during the Kamakura period. In good weather, he often stood on his flying bridge, dressed in battle gear—with his two *samurai* swords tucked in his waist sash—practicing *zazen* meditation. He considered himself *bushido*— fearless in the face of death, loyal to the warrior's lord, contemptuous toward money and possessions —though he seldom practiced this tenet personally— and resolute in defending his own honor and that of his family.

He was so dressed today, having planned to take a turn around the flying bridge. But the inclement weather had kept him inside. Though he looked like a throwback to an earlier century, no one on the bridge would have dared to snicker or scoff, as they would have on an American vessel. Shinjyo's crew believed in their captain's *karma,* and trusted in it for a safe crossing.

But no one on board realized that they were running interference for an unwelcome visitor who was riding directly beneath him. Or that, on their present course, they would cross directly over the *Pocatello* five minutes later.

Caldwell's tensed muscles relaxed. "Sonar to control," he radioed. "Surface vessel is a merchant, probably a Japanese freighter on its way home."

In the control room, a collective sigh of relief was breathed. "Do you still have the target sub?" Bertanelli radioed back.

"Aye, Captain. No change."

194

Bertanelli was in a quandary. His orders had been to keep the Soviet submarine from reaching any port at all costs. The Tomahawk was the only sure method of achieving that goal, but he could not fire it with a friendly surface vessel nearby. Reports and incriminations would flow across the Pacific and there would certainly be hell to pay.

"We have firing solutions on tubes two and four, Captain," a seaman reported. "And on the VLS."

Bertanelli spoke into the mike. "Control to weapons. Cancel the Tomahawk."

"Disarming the Tomahawk, aye."

Relief flooded through the boat. Admiral Sward allowed himself his first free breath in many minutes. He had been gripping the edge of his chair so tightly, his fingers hurt.

In the sonar room, Maggie wiped away the perspiration on her forehead. Like everyone aboard *Pocatello*, she knew full well what was in the warhead of the missile. "He wouldn't really have fired the thing, would he?" she asked.

Caldwell shot her a puzzled look. "What do you think all this is, a game?"

"That's what you said earlier. And, as a matter of fact, yes. I thought that's what you people did out here. Play war games." She glanced at her instruments. What she saw made her nearly jump out of her chair. Somehow the instruments were registering neutron emissions. "Could that freighter up there be nuclear powered?" she asked.

"Of course not," Caldwell said.

"Then we have a visitor."

Caldwell rocketed out of his seat and over to her side. "Where?"

Maggie pointed to her instruments. "I'm picking up emissions. There's a nuclear power plant in

195

the water."

"The target sub?"

She shook her head. "No. He's not using his reactor."

"Then, what?"

"Search along zero niner five degrees," Maggie suggested.

Caldwell raced back to his own panel and worked feverishly to lock the towed array onto the bearing. "A salt water pump!" he exclaimed suddenly. He adjusted his gain and enhancer controls. Across the room, Zimmer switched on the overhead speaker. The unmistakable sound of seawater circulating around a steam condenser came over the loud-speaker.

"Sonar to control," Caldwell announced over the intercom. "We have another contact. Same bearing and distance as the surface vessel, but it is submerged. I repeat. It is submerged."

"Control to maneuvering," Bertanelli's voice whispered back. "Switch to electric. I repeat, switch to electric power. Ultra quiet in the boat."

The steam was immediately throttled back and the main pumps fell almost silent. Barely enough steam was moving through the side system now to power the turbogenerators and turn a small electric motor coupled directly to the propeller shaft.

The abrupt drop in noise seemed eerie. In sonar Caldwell manipulated his controls, studying the CRT screen intently. As the blips appeared down the waterfalls, a target solidified. The information was fed into the BC-10 and the computer identified the signature.

"Sonar to control," Caldwell reported quietly. "It's a Viktor III. Seventh in the class. He's running under the Japanese freighter, about seventy-five feet submerged."

In the control room, Jamison turned to Bertanelli. "He'll be operating on his Brick Spit and Pulp passive arrays."

"Probably hasn't picked us up yet," Bertanelli said, his eyes glued to his monitoring screen.

Suddenly another streak appeared on the sonar, quickly solidifying into a blip.

"Sonar to control," Caldwell whispered, the excitement in his voice apparent. "We have still another contact. This one is on the surface. Repeat, on the surface. Bearing three four three degrees. Speed three two knots. Range six miles."

"I have him," Bertanelli replied.

Below the image on Bertanelli's screen, the information from the ID computer began to assemble:

Modified *Petya II* Class Frigate.
268 foot, 950 tons
2 Gas Turbines, 1 Diesel, 3 Shafts, 30,000 hp
Radar: One Slim Net
Fire Control: One Hawk Screech
Navigation: One Don 2
IFF: One High Pole B
Sonar: One hull-mounted MF active; towed
    array
Armament: Four 76mm Guns, twin mounted
ASW/ Four RBU 6000, Two DC Racks
    Three 21" Torpedo Tubes
Range: 4870 Miles at 10 Knots
       450 Miles at 29 Knots

"Sonar to control." It was Caldwell again. "The frigate is actively searching on his MF."

Jamison glanced over Bertanelli's shoulder. "He

keeps up that speed, he won't be around here for very long."

"Exactly. He knows what he's after."

"You think it's us?"

The two men exchanged concerned glances.

"I think we're about to find out," Bertanelli said.

On board the *storozhevoy korabl* escort ship, the *N.V. Yezhov*, Captain Second Rank Safar Epishev looked out the forward bridge windows. It was dark and stormy, the water rough and unsure. He would have much preferred to turning for port, but his orders were to find the disabled *Suslov* so it could surface and transfer over important papers. These, in turn, were to be rushed to Korsakov where a waiting Illuysin 62 would fly them to Moscow. Epishev knew that a large flotilla had left the Okhotsk Sea to support any activity necessary to ensure the safety of *Suslov* and, more importantly, the special cargo it carried. These papers must be of utmost importance, the captain realized. And that thought made him uneasy.

His orders were to run full out until he reached the disabled submarine. Yet at this speed, he was burning up all his bunker oil. He would have to make contact with the *Aleksei Kosygin*, the nuclear-powered 74 LASH-type barge that plied the western Pacific supporting and resupplying Soviet vessels. He did not look forward to making a fuel transfer in such rough seas.

"Any response?" he asked his communications officer.

"None, Comrade Captain. Recommend we slow to fifteen knots so we can sound more accurately."

"Navigation," he said, still staring out the window. "Where are we?"

"Five minutes to the specified coordinates, Comrade Captain."

"In five minutes, then, Yevgeniy."

The communications officer nodded.

Seconds before *Pocatello* chopped power and then went to turboelectric, *Suslov*'s sonar officer, Aleksei Mezhova, thought he noticed something. While his RD1 sonar computer continued to analyze the passive arrays, Mezhova played back the tape recording of the event that had triggered his interest.

"Comrade Captain," he said, looking up. "I believe I have picked up an American submarine."

Yakunin swung around from the instrument panel. "What?" he demanded. "Where is he?"

"Bearing one eight eight degrees. Range, fourteen thousand meters, two degree depression track. Speed, six knots."

A tightness began to form in Yakunin's stomach. This American was a devil! "Is it the same boat?" the captain asked wearily. He glanced across to Savitsky. His friend returned the look but said nothing. Yakunin was obviously worried. He had an American bulldog on his heels and was not sure how to shake him.

"It is the same boat, Comrade Captain," the sonar officer confirmed. "There is no question about it. It is the same signature."

Yakunin had known it would be. "Do you have an ID?" he asked.

At that very moment, Colonel Turbin entered the control room wearing a heavy parka common to arctic submariners and carrying the cherished briefcase tightly in one hand. "I am ready," he announced.

Mikola Govskaya glanced at the bulkhead clock

199

across the control room. "It is nearly time for the rendezvous, Captain."

Ignoring both men, Yakunin watched as Mezhova typed information into the computer. "I have it, Comrade Captain," the sonar officer reported. *"Los Angeles* class, forty-third in the line, named *Pocatello.*

The captain turned to Felix Stelest. *"Michman,* what do you have on *Pocatello*?"

The quartermaster punched information into the USV computer. The boat guide flashed on the screen. "This is strange, Comrade Captain. We have it listed in Honolulu drydock at Mid-Loch."

"So it has completed its refitting."

"But the boat was launched just this past March."

"Refitted after only four months?"

"Yes, Comrade Captain."

"That is strange." Yakunin considered the information. Had the American boat been damaged? Had something gone wrong? He doubted it. The Americans, imperialists though they were, built excellent submarines. They did not have a history of breaking down like Soviet boats. Then what? It could only be the installation of some new type of equipment. The Americans loved to update their boats. They were always coming up with something new. What could it be this time?

"Who do you have as captain of the boat?" he asked reflectively.

Stelest punched a button. A picture of Anthony Bertanelli appeared on the screen. Yakunin looked at it and froze. "The devil be damned," he muttered.

"You know this American captain?" the warrant officer asked. Yakunin simply nodded, staring at the image.

Govskaya crossed over to the screen and peered at

the information below Bertanelli's picture. There was a black diagonal border across the bottom left-hand corner of the picture. "It's yellow-flagged!" he exclaimed.

Yakunin nodded. The tightness he had felt earlier was growing, spreading up through his chest and into his left shoulder. Every Soviet captain was on orders to sink any submarine that Anthony Bertanelli was known to be occupying.

Savitsky moved beside Yakunin. Staring at the image on the computer screen, he placed his hand lightly on the captain's shoulder. "He *is* a devil, Emelyan."

Stelest glanced at his captain. "I didn't think yellow flags were still operational."

Yakunin nodded gravely. They were not only operational, they were mandatory.

"Then we must sink the American boat!" Govskaya bellowed loudly.

"Later," Turbin snapped. "The *Yezhov* will be above us at any moment. We must surface so I can go aboard."

"We can't surface with the American nearby," Yakunin said matter-of-factly.

"You have your orders, Captain!" Turbin demanded, clutching the briefcase closer to his body. "These documents must reach Moscow immediately."

Yakunin turned away from the Colonel. "Have you located the exact position of the American sub yet, Aleksei?" he inquired.

The sonar officer shook his head. "Nothing since that one registration."

"Perhaps your officer misread his instruments," Turbin suggested forcefully. "Perhaps there is no American submarine."

"Of course there is an American boat!" Mezhova replied, on the defensive. "And he's very close!"

"Then we must sink him!" Govskaya cried.

"Just how do you propose we do that?" Stelest asked. "We do not know exactly where he is."

Govskaya glanced at the *michman* with hatred in his eyes. "Shoot a spread of torpedoes and home them in on the American's signature. Let the torpedoes do the finding!"

Savitsky looked at Yakunin. While neither had any love for the political officer, both men knew his suggestion was workable.

"He *is* yellow flagged," Savitsky reminded him quietly.

Yakunin nodded. He turned to Stelest. "Have weapons load up all tubes and prepare to fire."

CHAPTER EIGHTEEN

Jamison watched the approaching surface blips on the ancillary screen in *Pocatello*'s control room with growing concern. "They're running convergent courses," he reported. It seemed the Japanese freighter and the Russian frigate were on a collision course.

Bertanelli could imagine the smaller frigate bearing down on the Japanese, trying to intimidate the merchant seaman. "A hell of a spot," he noted with some irritation. "We've caught up with the Soviet submarine, but have a *Viktor* under the freighter heading right over us. On the other hand, if the Japanese alters course, we've got a frigate going to cross over us. And he's hard sounding."

"And somebody said it was a big ocean," Jamison muttered.

"One mistake," Sward interjected from across the room, "and you're going to be in a shooting war against three Soviet vessels. Are you prepared to handle that, Captain?"

Bertanelli glared at the admiral, but said nothing. He turned back to the weapons station. "Ash, keep our bow tubes targeted on the Russian sub we've been following." He picked up the intercom mike. "Harmon, load up both stern tubes with Mark forty-eights." Turning back to Ashton, he added, "I want the stern fish targeted on the *Viktor*. And be prepared to launch everything we have when I give the word."

Akira Shinjyo watched the rapidly approaching Soviet frigate with mounting annoyance. "Bear off!" he shouted, shaking his fist at the Russian. "Get out of my way!" He turned to the officer on deck. "Signal him to bear off!" he ordered.

The communications officer quickly relayed the message to the radio room. It went out over international morse code as well as over the merchant EBS side band. But even after Shinjyo had ordered the first mate to send the message over the light blinker from the flying bridge, there was still no response from the Russian gunboat.

Stepping outside into the swirling storm, Shinjyo glared at the Russian. "Get out of my way!" he yelled, dancing along the deck in agitation. But the Russian still would not alter his course. *"Baka!"* Shinjyo roared. "Crazy fool!"

"He is Russian," the mate said at the door. "What do you expect?"

The Japanese stood with feet apart, both hands on his swords. He glared across the stormy sea at the approaching Soviet vessel, ready to do battle with the Russian pig. In his years on the ocean, he had run across several Soviet vessels. He knew they would never fire on him, and he felt no compunction to give them any quarter.

"Move over!" he screamed wildly. Shinjyo drew his sword and raised it over his head level to the deck, in *jodan no kamae*, the second position in "The Way of the Long Sword." Shinjyo was an adamant follower of Miyamoto Musashi, the fifteenth-century *ronin* and developer of the *Bushido Way*. And, Shinjyo knew, according to Musashi, a *samurai* could win under all circumstances.

"He is not turning away," the communications officer said warily. "Perhaps we should . . ."

"He will!" Shinjyo replied with confidence. He jumped up and down, shaking a fist at the Russian, the rain soaking him to the skin. He sliced at the air with his sword as the mate watched dubiously. But Shinjyo's resolve was as solid as a rock as the distance between the two vessels narrowed.

Suddenly, a cloud of white smoke erupted from the forward gun turret of the frigate.

"They're firing on us!" the mate shrieked.

The incoming 76mm shells screamed through the air, crossed over the bow of *Toyota Maru* and slammed into the ocean beyond.

The captain—a descendant of *bushi,* a follower of the path of *Heiho,* and a self-styled *zen samurai*— stared at the geysers in wide-eyed astonishment, then ran inside yelling, "Left full rudder!"

The Japanese cargo ship swung to port, buffeted heavily as she turned into the howling wind. Beneath her, the Soviet *Viktor* submarine was caught off guard, suddenly running unprotected. His noisy reactor was no longer covered by the throb of Japanese diesels. He was naked to enemy sonar.

The long- and close-range sonar aboard the *Pocatello* were feeding information into the computer which was simultaneously tracking four different vessels. In the control room, Bertanelli watched the ancillary screen tensely, mentally debating whether to engage or not. He had ordered the torpedo room to flood the tubes and open the outer doors just moments earlier. He now had immediate launch capability of both the bow and stern torpedoes. The nuclear Tomahawk in the VLS tube had been rearmed.

"Sonar to control," Caldwell reported. "The frigate is still actively sounding."

Ping, ping, ping, ping.

They could hear the noise through the hull. Bertanelli was growing edgy. He wanted to turn, but if he did so, both Soviet subs would be able to hear him. There was no choice but to wait it out.

Suddenly the atmosphere was shattered by a new sound.

Pong!

The frigate's sonar had struck the *Viktor.*

"The surface vessel is slowing," Caldwell announced, broadcasting the action to the rest of the sub play by play. "He's making a wide turn. He's circling the *Viktor.*"

Above them, the *Toyota Maru* came back on course. Captain Shinjyo stood outside on the flying bridge, shaking a fist and waving his sword over his head, paying no attention to the sheets of spray the wind was blowing into his face. He was furious. He had not been fearless in the face of the enemy, losing face in front of his crew. He shouted and gestured crudely at the Russian frigate.

Six hundred feet below him, Bertanelli asked for an update. "Where's the *Mike?*" He could well imagine the consternation aboard the *Viktor,* but that was none of his concern. Not knowing who was sounding on him, the Soviet captain would dive deep and high-tail it out of the area. At least temporarily, that boat was out of the picture. Bertanelli hoped he would take the frigate with him. His immediate concern was the boat he had been following.

In the sonar room, the staccato beat of hull popping noises confirmed the *Viktor*'s sudden descent. Zimmer followed the boat as it turned north and tried to dust off the tail of the Russian frigate. It seemed one Russian was trying to outfox another. The thought made Zimmer smile.

Aboard *Suslov*, several pairs of eyes watched the weapons console as the torpedoes were armed and readied. Yakunin was about to order weapons to activate the arming wires when suddenly the sonar officer cried out, "Two surface ships, bearing—the devil be damned! Surface explosions, hard sounding, high-speed props! What the hell is going on up there?"

Yakunin swung around to look at the sonar screen. The ocean was momentarily alive with activity. The captain smiled and turned to Savitsky. "I think it is time to leave," he suggested.

"A wise thought, Emelyan," his friend agreed soberly.

Caldwell flipped on the intercom. "The *Mike* is right where we left him," he reported to the control room. "He's—"

There was a sudden movement as the *Suslov* blip darted across his screen. "He's moving, and *fast!* He's making a run for it, skipper. He's digging big holes in the water." Caldwell stared at the blip as it disappeared off his screen.

Bertanelli picked up the mike. How in hell did the Russian find out *Pocatello* was near? "Control to sonar," he called. "Get a course on him. Fast!"

Caldwell worked frantically at his keyboard. But it

was to no avail. "He went into a thermal, Captain," he reported. "There's so much noise right now, I've lost him."

"With him so close?" Bertanelli asked in astonishment.

"He used a mask," Maggie said. Caldwell nodded and repeated it over the intercom.

A sudden burst of light on her photomultiplier caused Maggie to boost power on the SUBDACS. A streak slipped across it, solidified, then steadied. "Tell him he's at twenty-one thousand yards!" she called to Caldwell without looking up. "Bearing one eight two degrees. Speed, over twenty-five knots and increasing rapidly!"

Caldwell relayed the information over the line.

"I have nothing on the monitor," Bertanelli insisted.

"He's out there, masking our long-range suites. Miss O'Brien has him."

Jamison raised his eyebrows skeptically. Bertanelli wanted to give chase, but knew he dare not disclose his presence to the frigate still circling the area.

"Track him, Miss O'Brien," Bertanelli ordered over the intercom. "And don't lose him!"

Gen. Harris Shriner watched the huge situation board in the basement war room of the Pentagon. Red lights, representing Soviet combatants, were ablaze all over the western Pacific, from Kamchatka to the Honshu Ridge.

"What in the holy hell is going on?" he bellowed, having just returned to the center from the White House.

"You won't believe it, General," Col. Chip Haggarty said, turning away from the board, his eyes wide with incredulity. "They've sent a battle group into the Pacific from Okhotsk. *Pravda* is leading the flotilla."

Shriner stared at the lights moving south toward Hokkaido. He shook his head in disbelief. "I've never seen anything like it in that part of the Pacific before."

"Looks like a strike force. The Japanese are screaming their heads off. They want to know what we're going to do about it."

Shriner fought down a rush of anger. The Japanese suddenly becoming concerned about safeguarding the Pacific was, typically, like shutting the barn door after the cows had escaped. "Serves them right," he muttered. The United States had been trying to get the Japanese to pay their fair share of the Pacific rim budget for years, but they had only been interested in investing in American property and importing cars and electronics to capture world markets. They had just naturally assumed that the United States would take care of providing the protective umbrella. "Has the president been notified?" Shriner asked.

"Yes, sir," Haggarty informed him. "The minute *Pravda* entered the Pacific."

Shriner surveyed the blue lights that represented American combatants. "Order the *Nimitz* carrier group north toward Hokkaido," he ordered.

"Admiral Olsen has already issued that order, sir."

Shriner nodded. "What about the mid-Pacific submarine picket line? Has ComSubPac sent any toward Kuril?"

"Less than ten minutes ago. The only two six-eighty-eights near enough to possibly intervene are the *Helena* and the *Phoenix*. They will be on station within five hours."

209

Shriner's eyes were riveted to the board. The red and blue lights racing toward each other seemed almost like two football teams converging on the line of scrimmage for the next down. But there was a lot more at stake in this game than simply a playoff spot.

Stepan Krylov, *Suslov*'s engineering officer, second rank, stepped into the nuclear compartment where Veli Ternovsky was studying his instruments intently. "How goes it?" Krylov asked, prepared for the worst.

Ternovsky did not take his eyes off the readouts. "It is doing fine, Comrade Engineer," he said.

"It seems noisier."

"The hydraulic platform had shifted because of the vibration from the cracked shaft," Ternovsky explained. "I bolted everything down for our run to Preznev."

"Did you get permission from the captain?."

"Of course."

Technically, Ternovsky realized, this was not completely true. He had told Yakunin he was making repairs, and that the repairs would result in the sub making more noise. But he had not specifically explained what it was he was about to do. Nor did he think it mattered. The hydraulic system of platforms on *Suslov* which made the boat quieter was susceptible to heavy vibration. If the crack in the shaft worsened, the platforms would be the first affected. Ternovsky had chosen to eliminate that problem. The end result was a noisier boat, but one less likely to shake apart.

Turbin stormed over to Yakunin, the KGB man's

face a bright crimson highlighted by the circle of fur rimming the parka's hood. "You had specific orders, Captain," he said angrily, "and you disobeyed them. I wish to know why!"

Yakunin regarded the stocky man calmly. "There was far too much unexplained activity, above us and below," the captain answered. "The risk was too great."

"It was a risk that should have been taken!"

"Relax, Comrade Colonel," Yakunin said, a hint of bitterness coloring his words. "You can rest assured that there is nothing I wish more than to have you and your precious briefcase removed from my boat as soon as possible. The opportunity will come again, I promise you. Besides," he said, mischievously, "patience is a very great virtue." He turned to Savitsky. "Is that not so, Lev?" he said, winking. His friend merely grunted in response.

"Just remember how important time *is*, Captain Yakunin," Turbin hissed. "Remember. Because yours is rapidly running out!"

With that, the shorter man spun around and barreled out of the room. Yakunin raised his eyebrows slightly. "I believe I have just been threatened," he observed. Seated across the room, the *zampolit* glared at him irritably.

"Why did you not fire on the American?" Govskaya demanded. "You had the chance and you did nothing!"

Yakunin rolled his eyes heavenward. "Yet another!" he cried, then glared at his accuser. "I had no desire to begin another World War unless it was completely unavoidable," the captain said. "Besides, there were other vessels involved and I—"

"You should have fired and instead you ran away!" Govskaya bellowed. "You are going to wish you *had* fired when my report to the Committee lists you as a coward!"

"To the devil with your report!" Yakunin shouted. In a flash he was across the room, towering over the surprised and trembling political officer. "And *my* report will show you to be a fool, incapable of decisions at sea!" the captain said, spitting his words out angrily. He leaned down closer until his face was nearly touching Govskaya's. "Listen to me, *zampolit*," Yakunin growled, menacingly. "There were other vessels involved. The Motherland's vessels. If one of them had been damaged or destroyed in the action, who would have accepted the responsibility? *You?*" The captain stood up and turned away in disgust. The political officer sat there shaking violently, too shocked by the normally controlled Yakunin's outburst to speak.

The *Suslov*'s commander crossed back to Lev Savitsky, shaking his head. "It's this American," he said sadly, "this Bertanelli. That is why I am so . . ." He sighed heavily. "I do not understand. How does he keep finding us?"

Savitsky shrugged. "It is as you say. He is a devil."

"Perhaps," Yakunin replied distractedly. "Perhaps."

The helm officer looked up at the captain. "Do you want to continue on our present course, Comrade Captain?" he asked.

Yakunin considered for a moment. "Yes," he said finally. "We will continue for, say, an hour and a half, then come back to course two zero five."

"Very well, Comrade Captain," the officer replied. Across the room, the boat's *zampolit* glared at the captain with undisguised hatred.

*　　　*　　　*

Travis Romney sat on the bed working slowly at his restraining handcuffs with a small piece of wire that he had taken from the bunk's under ribbing. For hours, nothing but the thought of escape had occupied his mind. Earlier, the boat's doctor had looked in and given him a strong sedative. But the pills had never been swallowed. And now, though the pain in his arm and leg seemed to be increasing, Travis was alert and scheming.

Conscious of the increased noise and vibration in the boat, Travis did not know what the problem could be. But the increased sound could turn out to be a blessing in disguise, covering his attempt to carry out the plan he had finally formulated. Its success depended on the inexperience of the young guard posted outside—and a great deal of luck.

With a final twist, the lock *clicked* and the cuff came free from his left wrist. Gritting his teeth in pain, he turned his attention to the right cuff.

In *Pocatello*'s sonar room, Zimmer was listening to the reduction gears and coolant pumps of the *Viktor* as it faded into the distance. Caldwell had tracked the *Petya* class frigate as it tried to make contact once again. Maggie kept track of the neutron emissions of the *Suslov*. The BC-10 logged the tracks of all three.

Bertanelli avidly followed the three contacts on the ancillary screen. He was waiting for the ideal moment to quit the area, but none presented itself. The frigate kept sounding all around him. Finally, anxious and frustrated, he stepped into the sonar room.

"Miss O'Brien," Bertanelli began hesitantly, "do you think you can work one of those masks of yours for us?"

Maggie beamed with pride. "Certainly, Captain," she said gleefully, not even attempting to conceal her happiness. "What would you like? A *Viktor*, an *Alfa*, whales, dolphins?"

"I don't care. Whatever it is, I want it to sound a long way off. I don't want that frigate to know we're anywhere near him."

Maggie pondered for a moment. "I'll use one of the four-layer masks," she said, finally deciding on a course of action. "By the time they figure it out, we'll be long gone."

Bertanelli nodded. "Do it."

Maggie grinned. "Aye, aye," she said, as the captain ducked out of the sonar station on his way back to the control room.

Maggie whistled softly as she looked over her assortment of compact discs. She was about to choose a pack of dolphins when Zimmer caught her eye.

"Caldwell loves whales," Zimmer suggested.

"Yeah, Miss O'Brien," Caldwell chimed in. "Make it whales."

She smiled. "Whales it is," she said, and reached for the appropriate disk.

In the control room, Bertanelli checked the banks of instruments, then wandered over to Jamison. "Let's hope this little ruse works," he said.

"If it doesn't," Jamison pointed out unnecessarily, "we're going to have a *Viktor* and a frigate breathing down our necks."

In the sonar room, Maggie inserted the disc and activated the laser tracking. Within seconds, the sound of bowhead whales echoed about them. Moments later, *Pocatello* started her reactor and once again came to life.

CHAPTER NINETEEN

4:30 a.m. Honolulu/1430 Hours Zulu

Capt. Safar Epishev leaned over the shoulder of his sonar officer. The commander could not understand why the *Suslov* had darted away as soon as the boat had been located. Epishev had been trying to reestablish contact for the past twenty minutes. The submarine was down there somewhere. Why didn't the captain simply surface so the documents could be transferred?

"Perhaps it is not the *Suslov*," the sonar officer suggested.

Epishev nodded. He had been considering that very fact for the past five minutes. There could be no other explanation. But if that were so, it merely compounded his problem. *Suslov* had been ordered not to surface in the sight of any western vessel.

Epishev sighed, totally perplexed. "Helm, steer one eight five degrees," he ordered.

"Very well, Comrade Captain," came the response.

The ocean was getting choppier as the storm worsened. Though mid-day, he could see no more than a mile in front of him. Epishev had no desire to stay out here any longer than absolutely necessary.

Suddenly the sonar screen erupted in a bright

green clutter.

"What is it?" Epishev asked.

"Whales, Comrade Captain," the sonar operator responded, spinning dials and pushing buttons to filter through the mess, as heartbeats, hoots and whistles came through the speaker. "Sounds like bowheads."

Epishev had started to nod his head when it struck him. *Bowheads?* "That is not the *Suslov*," he shouted. "Helm, hard right rudder. Take us over that noise!" He stepped out onto the flying bridge. "Weapons," he ordered, "ready the RB six-thousands. Both racks!"

"Holy shit!" Caldwell shouted. "He's turning right into us!" He flipped on the mike. "Sonar to Control," he shouted. "The frigate's turning, bearing one three seven! Six thousand yards! I'm picking up internal racks being activated! He's hard sounding!"

In the control room, Bertanelli swore loudly as he swung into action. "Left full rudder!" he yelled. "Take us down!" He spun around on the diving officer. "Straight down! Flood all tanks!"

Pocatello dropped like a rock as vents opened to the sea. She fell quickly toward her maximum tested depth of four hundred and fifty meters—fourteen hundred and seventy-five feet.

In the sonar room, Caldwell heard the first of the mortars shooting out from the frigate's racks. He spun the gain and enhancer dials down, then glanced at Maggie. Still searching for neutron emissions from the *Suslov*, she had not bothered to remove the earphones she used to cross-check her findings with sonar. Oblivious to the pending explosions, she had left the gain controls on high.

Caldwell reached over, ripping the earphones from her head just as the first depth charge ignited, sending a reverberating explosion through the hydrophones. Then the second charge exploded. The twin concussions, still hundreds of feet away, rocked the boat as *Pocatello* continued to fall.

"There's nothing to do now, but hold on," Caldwell warned her.

Maggie nodded, the color draining from her face as beads of sweat broke out across her forehead. She gripped the console counter tightly, keeping her eyes locked on the emission readings on her instruments.

In the control room, Jamison was watching the fathometer with growing concern. "Four hundred meters," he warned. "We're getting awfully low."

If the helm lost control, *Pocatello* could slide down, stern first, into the depths below and implode.

"Four hundred twenty-five meters," the diving officer called, his voice shaking perceptibly.

They were falling too fast.

In dazed exasperation, Sward stared at the depth indicator. "Mother of Heaven, Captain! Do something!" he yelled. "You're putting this boat in jeopardy!"

The next detonations were much closer than the first two. "No more than those," Bertanelli said, his voice surprisingly calm.

"They're not trying to sink us!" the admiral insisted. "They only want to force us up to the surface."

Bertanelli glared at him. "How the hell do you know that?" he asked bluntly.

"Because they don't want to start a war any more than we do!"

All other eyes in the control room were glued on

the fathometer. "Four hundred fifty meters," the diving officer announced.

"You're going to kill everyone aboard!" Sward yelled angrily.

"The *Thresher* imploded at two thousand feet," Bertanelli shot back with equal intensity. "*Poco* is a hell of a lot stronger than any *Permit* class boat."

"Five hundred meters."

They were at sixteen hundred and fifty feet and still falling. The sweat poured from the crew in buckets. Shirts and jumpsuits became damp, then soaked.

"I demand you stop this descent *now!*" Sward screamed.

"Or what?"

"Or I'll relieve you of command."

"Five hundred and twenty-five meters."

"Do it, or get out of my control room!" Bertanelli demanded, his face hard and impassive. Their eyes locked in a supreme test of wills.

Sward felt his body trembling with rage. He had reached the end of his rope. "Captain," he declared loudly, "you are relieved of your command!"

There was an audible gasp. Those in the control room stared in disbelief. Bertanelli glared at Sward but said nothing. "Five hundred and fifty meters," the diving officer announced.

Sward glanced at the fathometer. They were plunging into depths far beyond *Pocatello*'s safety zone. His face drained of blood, leaving it ghostly white. He was trembling, aware that everyone in the room was looking at him.

"What are your orders, Admiral?" the diving officer asked nervously.

Sward opened his mouth to speak and then froze. It had been a long time since he had commanded a submarine. Too long. And he had never commanded one quite like the *Pocatello*.

The crew stared at the admiral apprehensively. Sweat cascaded down faces and arms. Each knew in his heart that he was about to die.

"Five hundred seventy meters!"

Panic rose up inside Sward's body. He could feel the bile collecting in his throat. *These men are depending on me*, he thought, the realization making him lightheaded. Suddenly all knowledge of modern war technology seemed to fly from his brain. In one terrifying instant, Sward felt as unschooled as a three-year-old. What exactly were the capabilities of a nuclear sub? How far could she be pushed? What would happen if . . . ?

"Admiral, please!" the diving officer pleaded. "Your orders!"

"Damn it, Admiral!" Jamison swore. *"Do* something!"

Sward swung around to face Bertanelli. In that instant, he hated the captain more than ever. Because, deep in his heart, he knew only Bertanelli could save them all. Sward realized that he had no idea how deep the boat could plunge, nor how to stop the descent. The wrong order could result in the *Pocatello* bobbing back to the surface and cracking in two. Or they could slide over and fall, stern first, into the ocean's depths. And then there was the Russian frigate . . .

"I rescind my original order, Captain," Sward muttered, his voice low and defeated. "The bridge is yours."

Bertanelli turned to his anxious crew. "Blow all tanks," he ordered. Instantly the control room came alive as the crew leapt into action.

Sward shook with impotent rage. "Damn you, Captain," he muttered softly. "Damn you!" Without another word, he turned and stormed out of the control room.

Pocatello shuddered as her descent slowed. Buoyancy tanks between the twin hulls all along the boat pumped water back into the sea. The sudden change in air pressure popped the ears of the skittish crew as neutral buoyancy was achieved.

"All ahead slow," Bertanelli said.

In maneuvering, Chief Engineer Paul Hargrove was on a tear, issuing orders as fast as his crew could carry them out. Only once before in all his years had he known a captain to order a straight drop down by flooding all tanks at once. And never had he known a boat to drop so far. It was the most dangerous maneuver a submarine could employ.

"Steady, gentlemen," he said, forcing calm into his voice. "Keep the trim."

Control was the most important thing, for both him and *Pocatello*. If the boat lost it, they would shoot upward or down and most probably implode. He stared at the instruments, trying desperately to read everything at once.

Sweat poured from the crew as they struggled to maintain the trim. "We do not have enough steerage, sir," one reported nervously.

The bow was starting to dip from lack of momentum. Hargrove reached for the telephone. "Maneuvering to control. I need more steerage, Captain."

Compressed air expelled sea water in some tanks as others took on ballast to maintain both the desired buoyancy and trim. But without more power, they were in danger of losing that precious balance.

"All ahead standard," Bertanelli ordered.

Slowly *Pocatello*'s propeller began to bite into the water, pushing her forward. Sea water was adjusted

220

in trim tanks to keep her level. Soon she began to make headway.

In sonar, Caldwell shook his head in wonder. "Damn, but Crazy Tony's done it again," he said admiringly.

Zimmer, sweating profusely, was able to manage a weak grin. "We must be at two thousand feet," he guessed.

Caldwell nodded. "At least the Russians won't be looking for us this deep."

Ralston sat speechless, his hands shaking uncontrollably. Not far away, Maggie sat back in her own chair staring straight ahead, her face drained chalk-white, her hair limp and soaking. She had been convinced they were all going to die. And now her mind was just beginning to realize that life was, in fact, continuing.

Five hundred feet above them, the depth charges continued to explode. But at that distance, the sound was barely discernible through the *Pocatello*'s hull.

General Shriner put one shaking hand on the red phone in the Pentagon's Situation Room. As soon as he lifted the receiver, similar telephones would automatically buzz in the Oval Office, the White House basement War Room, and on Air Force One. During his long tenure in Washington, there had never been a reason for advancing beyond the standard defense condition. But he was now about to recommend to the President of the United States that they go to DefCon Two.

Advancing the condition would force the Soviets to respond in kind and the world would move one step closer to nuclear war. Suddenly, images of his wife and three daughters flashed through Shriner's

221

mind. The girls were married now, each had children of their own. Little Jeffrey, he thought, would have his first birthday on Saturday.

His hand paused over the instrument momentarily. With an iron will he fought to control his trembling, then picked up the phone.

"Mr. President?" he said, hearing a voice on the other end. "This is Shriner. I am recommending we go to Defense Condition Two." There was a long pause, then Shriner answered, "Yes, sir." He hung up the line and turned to Colonel Haggarty. "Order us up to DefCon Two," he said, his voice suddenly icy calm.

"Yes, sir," Haggarty responded. He turned and signaled to two officers standing in front of computers situated at opposite ends of the room. Each officer inserted a key into an appropriate slot in each control computer. Immediately a loud buzzer sounded and the number on the call board on the wall changed from a large white One, to a yellow Two.

Immediately throughout the world, Air Force ready rooms were buzzed and hundreds of pilots went racing for their airplanes. Combatant ships at sea were ordered onto prearranged courses, while ships at port recalled their liberty crews.

Within minutes, Moscow was apprised of the change in American readiness, and ordered up a change in their own defensive posture. Thousands of men and women who, moments earlier had been relaxed and even lethargic, were now arming to the teeth. Should the next step, DefCon Three, be ordered, planes would become airborne, missile silos would be opened, submarine launch platforms would be dialing in their targets—and the world would be one heartbeat closer to destruction.

*　　　*　　　*

Yakunin hovered over the shoulders of his sonar officer, Aleksei Mezhova. "Anything?" the captain asked.

Mezhova shook his head. "There has been nothing since the depth charges. Perhaps the American was destroyed."

"Perhaps," Yakunin said, not at all convinced.

"Do you wish to change course, Comrade Captain?" Felix Stelest asked.

The mysterious pain was still bothering Yakunin. Somehow he felt the American had escaped again and was still on his tail. "No, *michman*," he ordered. "We will stay on this heading for an hour and a half, then come back to two zero five."

"But the shaft, Comrade Captain."

Yakunin angrily spun on his warrant officer. "I have given you orders, *michman!*" he snapped. "Carry them out!"

Stelest snapped to attention and turned on his heels, hurrying to obey. Savitsky placed a hand on Yakunin's shoulder. "Our enemy is the American," he reminded the captain. "Not our own seamen."

"I know, old friend," Yakunin said at length. He smiled apologetically at Stelest, who nodded back with understanding. The nerves of everyone on board were badly frayed.

"He's out there, Lev," Yakunin confided quietly to Savitsky. "I know it." He glanced at the sonar screen. There was no indication of any pursuing vessel. "And he's coming after us."

Bertanelli stuck his head in the sonar room. They had been eluding the Russian frigate by staying at two thousand feet for ten miles. Then, coming up to one hundred twenty-five meters, they had found a thermal layer to hide in.

"What the hell happened?" the captain asked angrily.

"Nothing, sir," Caldwell replied.

"That's not true, Captain." Bertanelli turned to the speaker, Maggie O'Brien. "I used bowheads when I should have inserted fins, or humpbacks."

Bertanelli looked puzzled. "Would you mind telling me what the hell you're talking about?"

Maggie met his accusing eyes without flinching. "Bowheads stay around drifting ice, Captain," she replied stoically. "They don't come this far south. It was all my fault." Her eyes wavered, dropping down to his chest. "I'm sorry," she said softly.

"Bowheads?"

"Whales, Captain," Caldwell explained.

Bertanelli's eyes widened. "Whales?" he exclaimed incredulously. "This is about whales?"

Maggie nodded. Her lower lip began to quiver. She had failed. And for the first time all day, she was on the verge of losing her composure.

Bertanelli shook his head in amazement. "I'll be damned!" He looked at Maggie, regarding her thoughtfully. "Hell," he said finally. "That could have happened to anyone." And without another word, he turned and left the room, leaving Maggie standing there open-mouthed.

Maggie watched him leave, dumbfounded. She had expected him to be raving mad, to stomp around the room, reaming her out with a torrent of off-color Navy vernacular. Wasn't that the way men were supposed to act when they got mad? Maggie cursed under her breath.

"What's wrong now?" Caldwell asked. He himself had been shocked by the captain's lack of pique.

"He didn't scream at me."

"And that upsets you?"

"Yes . . . no! I don't know!" She turned away from the door to see Caldwell, Ralston and Zimmer staring at her strangely. "I thought I had him pegged," she explained. "Now I'll have to revise my opinion. And I don't like to do that!"

Caldwell shook his head. "You're a hard lady," he admitted.

"You're damn right I am!"

Soviet Premier Oleg Ognev paced back and forth across the polished wooden floor of his third-story office at Dzerzhinsky Square in Moscow. On the far side of the room, Field Marshall Nikolai Istomin stood ramrod straight, struggling to keep his impatience from showing. *The world is coming apart,* he thought to himself, *and all this fool can do is pace.*

Istomin cleared his throat finally. "Excuse me, Comrade Chairman," he began, trying to sound as diplomatic as possible, "but the military must have your answer. What do we do if the Americans go to their DefCon Three?"

The premier stopped walking and turned to face his questioner. Ognev's pig-like face was squeezed into a look of great perplexity. Then his features relaxed. He waved his hand in a gesture of carefree dismissal. "They will not," he said with assurance. "They have this new president. He will do nothing."

Istomin felt his cheeks burning with anger and frustration, but managed to keep his face impassive. "He has already moved them to Defense Condition Two," the field marshall reminded Ognev gently.

Ognev crossed to the window and stared down into the courtyard. Below was Lubyanka Prison. Ognev reminded himself that two former premiers had already been executed there. He had no wish to be the third.

The Russian leader sighed. How could he have misjudged the American so badly? Who would have thought that an inexperienced nobody like Colin Freeman would have responded as quickly and decisively as he had? Perhaps, if pushed too far, he would even . . .

Ognev dismissed the thought. "They would be crazy," he said out loud. "If they escalated then we would escalate. Then their only move left would be to fire their missiles, as would we. It would be suicide!"

Fool! Istomin screamed inside his head. But his outward self was calm and respectful. "Of course it would be suicide, Comrade Chairman," he agreed. "But we cannot allow them to move from one strike condition to another without increasing our own state of readiness. And to do that past our present condition, we must have your approval."

Ognev grunted and started pacing once again, making a wide circuit around the office, from the window to his desk, to the large, intricately carved oak chest in which he kept his liquor. As he passed, he considered pouring himself a tall glass of vodka but resisted. Perhaps after the field marshall left. But now his head must be clear. It was his duty to try and figure out what the American president would do next. Did the man even realize the storm he was unleashing? *Ahhh!* he thought angrily. *It is foolishness trying to read the mind of a madman!*

Ognev stopped abruptly and turned toward the officer. "All right, Field Marshall," he said decisively. "You have my permission to escalate one more condition. But only if the Americans do so first. Is that clear!"

The already tall Istomin seemed to grow five inches in height. *"Da,* Comrade Chairman," he answered quietly.

President Freeman stared out of the French doors of the Oval Office, looking out onto the rose garden beyond. It was hot and sticky in Washington this time of year and Freeman fervently wished he were elsewhere. After all, Reagan had his Western White House on his Santa Barbara ranch, Carter had his peanut farm in Georgia, and Nixon had his beach house in San Clemente. None of them stayed in Washington when it got this hot and muggy. Only him. If only he was . . .

"Mr. President?" Charlie Carmody's voice seemed to come from another dimension. "I believe a decision has to be made."

"Hmmm?" Freeman turned back into the room. "A decision?"

"On our defense condition, sir." Richard Rifkin, the secretary of defense, picked up the ball. He was sitting on a couch in front of the fireplace, across from Bruce Falk of State, who lounged carelessly on another couch.

"Oh, yes," Freeman said, brought abruptly back down to earth. He walked to his desk and sat down. "Tell me again, Dick, what would prompt us to go to DefCon Three."

Rifkin cleared his throat noisily. "Both the Soviets and ourselves are now at DefCon Two," he began. "We are in a state of alert. If the documents stolen from Honolulu reach Soviet shores, we must go to DefCon Three to show the Russians we will not just stand by and let them take over the Pacific Ocean."

The president frowned. "And you are absolutely sure that is their intention?" he asked.

Rifkin nodded. "They have already moved the *Pravda* battle group into the Pacific," he said. "At the moment, they could already be in control west of Midway and north of Japan."

"But what about our submarines?" Freeman asked. "You have been telling me since I took office that our submarines control that area."

Rifkin slid forward onto the edge of the couch, glancing around the room uncomfortably. He and Freeman had been together a long time—first when Freeman was in the Iowa legislature, then when he ran for governor, and most recently in the presidential race. No one knew Colin Freeman better. And Rifkin knew, when the stakes were high, the Iowa farm boy with the winsome smile and the razor-sharp, calculating mind tended to slow down a bit. Freeman was a man who would never be accused of acting overly hastily. Rifkin cleared his throat once more, causing Bruce Falk to wince slightly. "With those documents, sir, the Russians can nullify our submarines. We'd either have to withdraw them, or take the chance of losing them."

"All right, Dick. Let's concede that. But why DefCon Three?"

"They have to know we will not stand by while they take over the Pacific."

"Right now, they could cut us off from Shemya and the Cobra Dane network," Falk interjected. "And cut our sea lanes to Alaska."

"We must be ready to act," Rifkin continued. "The moment that submarine reaches the Kuril chain, we've got to send a message that Moscow could not possibly misunderstand. We'll have to use the

DefCon Three threat so they will know we're serious!"

Freeman looked from man to man to man. To escalate up to one step short of nuclear war was something Freeman dearly did not want. For a fleeting moment, in his mind, he was back home on his Iowa farm with his wife and children. He was playing with the twins, running in and out among the cornstalks, with no concerns past the weather conditions. The children were squealing happily as acres and acres of ripening corn as far as the eye could see rustled gently in the breeze.

"Mr. President?" Rifkin said tentatively.

Freeman came crashing abruptly back to reality. He looked at his secretary of state, then glanced around the room at the others, who stared at him expectantly. The president frowned. It was time for some hard choices and Colin Freeman had never ducked an issue in his life. "All right," he said firmly. "If the Soviets continue their mad plot to get those documents to Moscow, we will go to DefCon Three!"

In the control room of the *Pocatello*, Bertanelli considered his options. The neutron emission readings showed the Soviet sub to be too far ahead to catch. And unless the mechanical trouble on the faster boat worsened, slowing the Russian down, there was no way *Pocatello* could close the distance. The *Mike* boat had too great a head start.

Bertanelli leaned into the mike. "Control to sonar," he radioed. "What's the last heading you had on the *Mike*?"

"One eight five degrees," was Caldwell's response.

"How long has he been on that course?"

"Since he ran away to hide."

Bertanelli turned to the watch supervisor. "Come to course two zero five."

Jamison stepped up to Bertanelli's side. "If he's heading south, why are we going west?"

"He'll have to come back to two zero five if he's going to make the straits."

"And if he doesn't?"

"Then that cracked shaft will tear apart on him."

CHAPTER TWENTY

6:10 a.m. Honolulu/1610 Hours Zulu

Colonel Turbin walked down the corridor, stopping in front of the cabin where Travis was being kept under guard. He nodded to the young seaman guarding the door and offered him a cigarette.

"Da," the young sailor replied readily. *"Spasibo."*

Turbin removed a pack of Marlboros from his jacket pocket, The young seaman's eyes lit up. *"Amerikantze,"* he said, grinning. The KGB man smiled back.

Turbin flipped the pack open and held it out to the young sailor. The boy removed a cigarette, glanced nervously up and down the corridor and then placed the smoke between his lips, his youthful features lit up in anticipation. Slipping the pack back into his pocket, Turbin removed an engraved gold lighter. He flipped the top up with his thumb and spun the small wheel several times until a bright orange flame flared up. *"Pozvol'tye,"* he said, smiling at the sailor. "Permit me."

As the young man leaned over and placed the tip of his cigarette into the flame, Turbin's free hand slipped into the waistband of his trousers. In one swift movement, the colonel pulled a knife from his

231

belt and rammed it into the sailor's stomach. The seaman grunted in shocked surprise, the lit cigarette falling from his lips as his mouth fell open in a silent scream. His eyes widened as Turbin jerked the weapon upward, slicing through the young man's entrails. The seaman exhaled one final time and slumped against the KGB man, his face contorted into a death mask of shock and pain.

As silently as possible, Turbin let the sailor's lifeless body slide to the floor. He then closed the lid of his lighter, extinguishing the flame, and slid it back into his pants pocket. Then he crushed out the lit cigarette with the sole of his shoe.

Stepping over the corpse, Turbin opened the door to the cabin. He grabbed the young man's blouse and dragged him through the passageway, then quickly shut the door behind them.

Inside, Travis looked up in surprise, dropping the wire that he had been using to open the last handcuff beneath his leg. The blood drained from his face as he noticed the young seaman's blood-soaked body. Appalled, Travis stared open-mouthed at the KGB colonel panting heavily by the door, a bloodied knife clutched in his left hand.

"So, my American friend," Turbin said, grinning maniacally. "We meet once more."

Travis did not reply. He could only stare at the knife in Turbin's hand.

"I promised you that you would regret your act of aggression," Turbin added, not waiting for a response. He chuckled insidiously, the sound of his laughter sending chills down Travis's spine. "You'll be dead long before you reach Soviet shores."

Turbin tossed the bloodied knife onto the floor and then pulled a *Tokarev* service revolver from

232

inside his blouse. He pointed the gun at Travis. "You are going to be shot while attempting to escape after stabbing your guard to death," Turbin informed him coldly.

Travis swallowed with great difficulty. "Why?" he whispered.

Turbin stared at the American as if confused by the question. "It is the principle of the thing," he replied. The Russian swung the gun around suddenly and slammed it into Travis's jaw. The airman was knocked off the bunk and onto the deck. He shook his head groggily, dazed but still conscious.

"Pick up the knife!" Turbin hissed.

Travis looked up at the killer, trying to bring him into focus through the dense fog that filled the airman's head. "I . . . I'm handcuffed," he protested.

Turbin grunted in annoyance. Keeping the revolver trained on the American, Turbin leaned over and started rifling through the pockets of the dead seaman until he came up with a set of keys. He crossed over to Travis, bent down and unlocked his leg irons. He then reached up to free the pilot from his wrist shackles, unaware that the American had already undone one cuff. As the KGB man bent over, Travis grabbed the knife from the floor in front of him and quickly swung it up, catching Turbin in his upper thigh. The Russian shrieked and stumbled back a step.

Travis tried to roll away, but Turbin unleashed a savage kick, slamming the airman in the face and knocking him backward into a bulkhead. Searing pain shot through Travis's entire body as he landed heavily on his injured leg. The momentum of Turbin's kick sent the Russian crashing to the floor.

Through the agonizing haze of impending unconsciousness, Travis noticed his attacker struggling to get to his feet, blood soaking his trouser leg. *Stay alert!* he screamed inside his brain. Through the fog, the American saw Turbin, his face contorted with agony and rage, slowly lift the gun and aim it at Travis. *Now!* his brain screamed. *Now!*

His hand moving almost by reflex, Travis flipped the knife out in front of him just as he saw Turbin's finger begin to close around the trigger of the *Tokarev.* The blade sailed across the room, burying itself in the Russian's upper chest. The gun dropped from Turbin's hand as the stocky man was thrown backward into the wall. He slumped heavily to the floor, sitting motionless with his back up against the wall.

For what seemed an eternity, Travis didn't move, the sound of his own ragged breathing deafening inside his head. Dazed, he glanced around at the bloody carnage surrounding him. Noticing his cane leaning against the wall about a foot way, Travis reached over and grabbed it. Then slowly, using the walking stick to support his weight, the pilot worked his way to his feet. Once standing, it was all Travis could do to remain upright. Wobbling violently, fighting back a feeling of nausea, Travis waited patiently until his equilibrium returned. Then, slowly and painfully, he worked his way to the door of the cabin. Drenched with sweat and shaking like a leaf, he leaned against the door jamb. He closed his eyes, then inhaled and exhaled deeply for several seconds.

Feeling somewhat more in control, Travis opened his eyes again. Summoning all of his remaining strength, he pushed his body away from the door frame and reached down for the handle. He slowly opened the door and peered out into the hallway.

"Where are we, Barker?" Bertanelli asked of his navigation officer.

Lt. Cmdr. Barker Higgins punched some keys on his precision strapdown SINS—Submarine Inertial Navigation System—computer, and a plot track appeared on the screen. He pointed to a spot on the overlay. "Right here, Skip."

"I need a course plot."

"No problem." The high-accuracy ring laser gyros, with the advanced plasma design and polished laser gyro mirror, could plot *Pocatello*'s whereabouts to within a few feet of her exact position. And the ASPJ—Advanced Self-Protection Jamming system —kept enemy electronics from interfering with its operation. "From where to where?" Higgins asked.

"Starting with where we lost the *Mike*, take him along a course of one eight zero for . . ." Bertanelli thought for a moment. How long would the Russian continue on a course away from his destination with a cracked shaft? "Say for two hours at thirty-nine knots. No, make that an hour and a half at thirty-nine knots. Then, from that point bring him back to a heading for the Friza Straits."

The navigation officer typed information into the terminal. He brought up the track of the Soviet sub and traced it back to the point where it had been identified by sonar just before the Japanese freighter and Russian frigate interfered. Lines formed on the TV screen as he plotted in the course and time.

Bertanelli nodded his head. "Good," he said. "Now, with *Poco* traveling at thirty-five knots, plot us a course from our present position to intercept the

235

Russian this side of the Straits."

Again Higgins punched information into the computer. He corrected for the built-in error factor of the SINS—the gravity anomalies that were too great for the accelerometers and often threw off the system's vertical reading. He projected the intercept track onto the chart table and waited for the computer to respond. Finally he had what he wanted and turned to Bertanelli. "You need to come to course two three one. Interception will take place in ten hours, twelve minutes."

Bertanelli turned back to the helm. "Come to course two three one."

"Course two three one, aye," the helmsman responded.

Bertanelli picked up the intercom mike. "Control to sonar. What do you have out there?"

"Sonar to control," Caldwell answered. "The Kuril SOSUS line is clear, sir. We have two *Viktors* six hundred miles to the north, a picket line of three *Yankees* between Ketoj and Siaskotan, there's an *Alfa* making a hell of a lot of noise coming down Red Route Two, still four hundred miles to the north, and two SSBN *Typhoons* off southern Honshu. Scattered blips to the south too far to identify. But nothing close."

Bertanelli nodded to the helm. "Flank speed."

"Flank speed, aye," came the response.

Travis glanced up and down the corridor, then slipped back inside the cabin to retrieve the guard's AK-74 rifle. With what seemed like every single muscle in his body aching, he picked up Turbin's *Tokarev* from where it lay at the KGB man's feet. He slung the automatic weapon over his shoulder and stuffed the *Tokarev* inside his blouse. Then, using the cane for support, he hobbled out into the hallway, shutting the door behind him.

Travis was uncertain exactly where he was, but knew his destination was forward of the reactor. This time, he decided, he was going to stop the boat by going straight to its leadership—in the control room.

Seeing the passageway empty, Travis started slowly and shakily down the corridor.

The pain in his chest and shoulders still bothered Yakunin. He knew the American sub was out there somewhere, not very far behind him. "He is closing in," the captain said to Savitsky.

His friend clicked his tongue against the roof of his mouth in disbelief. "How is that possible?" he said to his friend. "How could he find us?"

"He must have been refitted with something new, Lev. Something so advanced, it can find us anywhere in the Pacific."

Savitsky shook his head. "The Americans are not magicians."

"It's their toys, my friend. They are never satisfied. They are always creating new ones. This time, I think, they have come up with something far beyond our understanding."

"Perhaps this briefcase we carry will offset this new invention," Lev suggested. The captain said nothing.

But Yakunin knew it was more than toys. This American, he thought, this Bertanelli was a devil. Somehow he had survived the depth charges. Somehow he had survived the earlier torpedo.

Somehow he was still on *Suslov*'s trail. How he had done it no longer mattered to Yakunin. The pain had increased to such a degree that he now knew he would not survive this voyage. He told his friend that he believed this would be his last passage.

"You cannot retire, Emelyan," Savitsky said quietly. "The Motherland cannot lose you."

"It is not retirement I am thinking about, Lev." He rubbed his shoulder vigorously. "It is the American. He will dog us until we have nowhere left to run."

"Screws, diesel," Mezhova announced.

Yakunin turned to the sonar screen.

"Surface vessel," Mezhova elaborated. "Bearing two four two degrees. Ten thousand meters. Speed eight knots."

"If it's American, it could be searching for us," Savitsky suggested.

"Go to slow speed," Yakunin ordered. "Aleksei, I need an identification quickly."

On the surface, tossed about by the building storm, the British tanker *Dart* was making little headway. With a ten thousand ton load of benzine and diesel fuel, she was on the last leg of her 12,405-mile journey from London, through the Panama Canal, and on to Yokohama.

A small ship of just under twenty-six thousand tons, and only one hundred eighty meters long, she gave the initial appearance on *Suslov*'s sonar of a missile cruiser. And with the storm forcing her to make only half her speed, to Aleksei Mezhova she appeared to be searching with ASW gear for a submarine.

*   *   *

Blanchard, Cummings, and Vice Adm. Edwin Rowden, Commander Submarine Pacific, clustered around the desk in the office of the Commander in Chief of the Pacific Fleet. Cobra Judy had just reported through Kapalama that a large Russian naval force was moving south along longitude one-fifty, two hundred miles northwest of Hokkaido. The newly commissioned *Pravda* was being escorted by the thirty-thousand-ton nuclear-powered surface combatant *Voronez*, a *Kirov* class battle cruiser, two helicopter cruisers, the *Volgograd* and *Novgorod*, and the *Ponoi*, a *Slava* class cruiser with eight Side Globe and four Rum Tub surveillance bells which were the eyes and ears of the group.

"Moscow claims they're just on an exercise," Cummings said skeptically.

"Hell, they know what's out there and what's at stake in this," Blanchard replied angrily, his cheeks burning with rage.

"From the hardware they've assembled, they're loading up for bear," Rowden added. "*Nimitz* will not get there in time, but Seven-twenty-five and Seven-fifty-one might."

Cummings shook his head. "*Lexington* is closest."

"She's just a training CVN," Rowden said. "Nothing aboard that could do much damage. A few Vought 8s, but not a single F-eighteen."

There was an uncomfortable silence in the room. They all knew it would take a larger force than they could muster in such a short time in order to offset the Soviet presence along *Pocatello*'s intercept path. The Russians had out-guessed them.

"They could locate and kill *Pocatello* and claim it was an accident," Blanchard said angrily.

Rowden stiffened. "My boats are not that easily detected," he replied icily. "And *Pocatello* is the

239

quietest in the fleet."

"Still, they'll have enough ASW equipment in the area to keep your boat from sinking the Russian sub. It's all the same."

Rowden smiled. "I'll put my money on Crazy Tony."

"He's one boat against fifteen ships!"

"Then I'd say the odds were in *Pocatello*'s favor."

Maggie sat wearily in the officers' mess. Now that *Pocatello* had turned onto the intercept course, there was nothing much for her to do. Jamison had noticed her exhaustion and ordered Maggie to take a break. She had accepted gladly, having been in sonar for twelve straight hours.

The cook placed a plate of sandwiches in front of Maggie and a bowl of New England clam chowder left over from lunch. She dug into both with gusto.

"These are mid rats," Jamison said, watching her with amusement from across the table as she greedily devoured the rations. "The midnight snack or fourth meal served."

"You've got to be the best-fed men in the Navy," Maggie said as she wolfed down a roast beef sandwich in about three monster bites. "Pancakes and eggs for breakfast, Veal Parmesan for lunch, and lobster and steak for dinner. How am I supposed to keep my girlish figure on this cruise?"

Jamison smiled. "Everyone gains weight on patrol," he informed her.

The cook set mugs of coffee before them on the small table. He lingered for a moment, staring down at the lovely, if disheveled, young woman who was busy scarfing down every bit of food he set in front of her. Every man on board had been taken with Maggie's pleasant and engaging personality. "Hamburgers are the favorite meal on board," the cook told her, smiling. "I can spend hours concocting a special dish, but the crew would prefer hamburger. They'd eat it two, maybe even three times a week without complaint."

"You must be well equipped." Maggie took another bite of roast beef.

"We come on patrol with over eight tons of food, six hundred dozen eggs, and five thousand gallons of milk. The Navy wants to keep its crews well fed." He smiled warmly and left.

Maggie finished her sandwich and soup, then toyed with the coffee cup. It was the first time she had been able to relax since coming on board at Pearl early that morning. She watched the XO sip his soup, then glanced at the other officers scattered around the mess.

"You may not appreciate this, Miss O'Brien," Jamison said, looking over the rim of his coffee mug. "But a woman on board a submarine is not only uncommon, it has always been considered extremely unlucky. Yet scuttlebutt has it that you've made a big hit with the crew."

"Why thank you, Commander!" Her mischievous smile sent a pleasant tingle up Jamison's spine. "And what kind of hit have I made with your captain?"

Jamison cleared his throat and looked around the mess uncomfortably. "I think the jury is still out on that one."

"Hmmmm. I'll bet." Maggie sipped her coffee slowly. "Is he always so uncommunicative?" she asked.

"The skipper has a lot on his mind."

"You sound like a politician, Mr. Jamison."

Jamison smiled. "I'm third-generation Navy," he said, the pride in his voice apparent. "I guess it just comes with the territory."

The cook stopped by again to refill their mugs. "Anything else you'd like, Miss O'Brien?"

"If you have any of that chocolate cream pie left over from today, I'd love a piece. It was delicious."

The cook smiled brightly. "I'll see what I can do."

He hurried off to the galley as Maggie studied Jamison closely. "Is your captain married?"

Jamison blinked. "Married? Of course he is."

Maggie's face fell. "Oh," she said quietly.

"This boat's his wife."

"Oh?" She brightened. "So he isn't married."

Jamison noticed the look in her eyes. He had seen it before when she was bringing her equipment on board at Pearl and the chief was trying to keep her off his boat. She'd let him have it just like an old salt, brushing past him and stalking to the sonar room with Grady on her heels, bellowing like a wounded bull. She had been out to achieve something and nothing was going to stand in her way.

"If the Navy wanted a man to have a wife, Miss O'Brien," Jamison said pointedly, "they would issue him one."

"I see," Maggie said, frowning. "And is that how the captain feels?"

"Tony has two lovely daughters on the beach," Jamison replied, choosing his words with care. "He loves them dearly. But he spends most of his life at sea."

"Daughters? Then there is, or was, a wife?"

"Was. She died in a car crash three years after they were married."

242

"Oh, I'm sorry."

"It was not a happy life for her, Miss O'Brien. Tony loves to be at sea."

She started to reply when a voice over the intercom shattered the serenity of the boat. "General quarters, general quarters! All hands man battle stations!"

CHAPTER TWENTY-ONE

Bertanelli had ordered power chopped immediately. In maneuvering, the watch reduced steam demand, increasing the temperature in the reactor. This allowed neutrons to escape out of the pile, rapidly slowing the fission reaction and slowing the boat. *Pocatello* wobbled like a wounded whale as she was caught up in her own wake.

"Sonar to control," Ralston reported. "The whole freakin' Russian navy is above us!"

"Diving planes down twelve degrees," Bertanelli ordered.

Pocatello was gliding at four hundred and fifty feet, protectively hidden in a thermal layer of warm water, beyond passive sonar reach of the surface ships.

"Sonar to control." Caldwell's voice was calm in comparison with Ralston's just moments before. "I count twelve surface combatants. It's a CVN battle force."

Jamison stared at the monitoring screen. The ID computer was listing the ships as it identified their signatures. "We don't have a listing on this baby," he said, "but it looks like their new CTOL." Jamison shook his head in awed amazement. "Geeze, will you look at the size of her!"

Pravda was more than twice the size of the biggest ship Russia had built previously. Constructed at Nikolayev East, a top-secret yard heavily camouflaged from satellite surveillance at Tukur in Akademii Bay, it far outstripped the *Kiev* class carriers in both size and capability. The existence of the super carrier had not been known until it was launched three months earlier, and it had never been seen outside the Sea of Okhotsk. It had taken the western powers completely by surprise.

"It's a hell of a flotilla," Jamison said breathlessly. "If I didn't know better, I'd say war's been declared."

A stunned silence overtook the control room. Every man knew that, in a few short minutes, the biggest Soviet battle group ever seen in the Pacific would be directly above them.

Admiral Sward stood in the aft hatchway, his left eyelid twitching nervously. "You can outrun them," he suggested quietly, trying to keep the fear in his voice from showing.

Bertanelli's thoughts raced madly. He knew each surface ship could make thirty-two knots. True, if they could slip away undetected, *Pocatello* could no doubt outrun them. But the *Udaloys* alone were each capable of firing eight torpedoes as well as two RB-6000 twelve-barreled rocket launchers at them. If the *Pocatello* was heard, all three ships could blanket the area, making escape impossible. And even on the off-chance that was unsuccessful, there were always their SS-N-14 submarine killer missiles. The question, as always, was would the unpredictable Russians fire? They had demonstrated their willingness to do so earlier. And even if they didn't, they could still effectively cordon off the route to Friza, making it impossible for *Pocatello* to catch the Russian *Mike*. No, Bertanelli's only option was to lie low.

"My orders are to prevent that *Mike* from reaching a port," he said evenly. "I intend to carry them out." He turned to the helm. "Steady as she goes," he ordered.

Despite the downward angle on the planes, *Pocatello* began to rise due to her lack of momentum. Her reactor was down to four percent of rating, barely enough to work the necessary internal machinery. Suddenly the *Udaloys* switched from passive listening on their VDS larged towed body sonars to active search on their bow-mounted LF suites.

"Captain, we need some steerage," the diving officer said. "We're losing neutral buoyancy."

Bertanelli knew it was essential to stay in the thermocline. The warm water was causing the Soviets' search frequencies to bounce back up to the surface. "Control to maneuvering," Bertanelli said quietly into the intercom. "Switch to battery power and run electric. I want to maintain two knots."

Onboard *Pravda*, Admiral Stirlitz stared out from the command bridge above the twin decks. The water was rising, breaking fifteen-foot waves across his bow. The sky was black and winds whipped sheets of water across the ships, driving sailors to cover.

On the bridge, Captain Gohrokov approached the admiral. "Comrade Admiral," he said, saluting smartly. "We are entering the area where *Suslov* should be." Gohrokov glanced briefly out through the windows. Rain and spray blew against the glass, making visibility nearly impossible. "We have switched to hard sounding to locate the boat and let him know we are here."

246

"Very well, Captain. You may continue."

"Thank you, Admiral." Gohrokov saluted once more, turned and retraced his steps.

Stirlitz returned his attention to the rough seas. On some downward plunges, waves crashed across the flight deck, making it impossible for any planes to be launched. Stirlitz knew they would be into a squall soon. But his orders had been specific: find *Suslov* and effectively arrange a transfer of Colonel Turbin and his cargo.

When the orders had been received, Stirlitz had sent the *Admiral Tributs* steaming ahead at flank speed with a helicopter ready. In this weather, it was the only conceivable way any type of transfer could take place.

As Maggie rushed through the boat, she was accidentally jostled—and sometimes not so accidentally touched—by the seamen rushing to their own stations. By the time she reached sonar, Caldwell was glued to his CRT screen and logging in targets. Zimmer was running information through the ID computer as Ralston watched, immobile, from his chair behind them. It was a sight that would intimidate a veteran, let alone a new, inexperienced sonar officer.

"We've got a battle group directly above us!" Zimmer told her, his voice shaking with fear and excitement.

The sound of propellers increased. Caldwell muted the speaker noise. "Computer identification lists the ship passing directly over us as the *Admiral Tributs*," he reported.

Maggie looked upward. "Sounds like an earthquake," she observed.

"They don't call them babies *bolshoy protivolod-ochny korabls* for nothing." When Maggie looked at him blankly, he amended, "Large antisubmarine ships."

Zimmer stiffened. "I hear rotors."

Through the racket, the faint but distinct whine of helicopter rotors could be discerned.

Caldwell nodded. "He's probably launching one of his Helix A choppers. They'll be looking for us in earnest any minute."

As Caldwell called the information to the control room, Maggie sat down heavily behind her SUB-DACS station, dazed and frightened. Then she shook herself violently and got to work, plugging into the sonar computer.

Caldwell was not totally correct. The helicopter warming up on the stern platform of the *Admiral Tributs* was a Helix C, the Kamov Ka-27, equipped for search and rescue missions. While it contained IFF, two radar warning antennae above the tail-plane, and two ESM radomes above the rear fuselage, it carried no torpedoes in the ventral weapons bay, nor sonobuoys in the rectangular containers on each side of the fuselage.

Anastas Tsvigun, pilot second grade, had watched earlier as the Helix was wheeled out of the port hangar, the twin, three-bladed coaxial rotors unfolded and the chopper moved into launch position. He had then climbed on board and moved forward to the chopper's large, air-conditioned flight deck. He and Navigator Semyon Agayan went over the pre-flight check, then warmed up the twin turbines that began moving the carbon- and fiber-glass rotors. As the contra-rotating blades started to spin in earnest, vibration dampers on the lower section kicked in, and Tsvigun lifted off the pitching deck and turned to the south.

On the starboard side, behind Agayan, sat Sasha Osipova, the rescue hoist operator. Behind him was the rearward sliding, jettisonable door with blister windows on each side, separating the flight deck from a cabin that could hold sixteen passengers. Osipova absent-mindedly rubbed his gloved hand up and down the hoist cable as they hurtled over the fifteen-foot waves. Within minutes the 537-foot destroyer diminished in size until they could barely make her out.

"This is foolhardy," Agayan muttered irritably. "What do they expect us to see in this weather?"

"The *Suslov*," Tsvigun replied, his eyes scanning the rough waters beneath them.

"We can't see a foot below the surface!"

"We have a frequency transponder. When *Suslov* hears it, she will surface and we will pick up our cargo."

Agayan glanced at Osipova, then down at the rough seas. Before long the waves would be cresting thirty feet. "Who's going to surface in that?" he said, dejectedly.

Lev Savitsky glanced at Yakunin and shook his head with concern. What he was hearing was madness.

"We are to surface once the transponder registers, Lev," Yakunin told him. "Colonel Turbin is to be hoisted up with his briefcase."

"It's building up to a squall up there," Savitsky protested. "What they ask us to do is—"

"Ours is not to reason why," Yakunin interrupted,

249

his voice toneless.

Savitsky shook his head once more. "Has Turbin been notified?" he asked.

"I've sent a runner for him."

"This is crazy!" Savitsky shouted. He was a Party member, having joined the Little Octobrists when he was seven, the *Komsomol* in his teens, receiving full Party membership at the age of twenty-one. Because of his devotion, he had earned himself an appointment to VVMUPP, the principal higher naval school for underwater navigation. But five years at the school had weaned him from the Party, making him, instead, a loyal naval officer. And in his thinking, the boat came first. Politics be damned.

"What the devil is so important as to risk the entire boat?" the *michman*, Stelest, asked, his voice quivering with annoyance as he stepped up beside the two.

"An interesting question, Felix," Yakunin replied. "But it must be important. They've brought the *Pravda* down to intimidate the Americans and keep them off our back."

"*Pravda* is in these waters?" Savitsky asked, his eyes widening in awe.

Yakunin nodded. "And he's got a formidable battle group with him."

Savitsky's frown was replaced by a mischievous grin. "Well now," he said happily, "I wonder what the Americans think of that!"

"I've got neutron emissions," Maggie announced. "Bearing zero niner eight. Eighteen thousand yards."

They looked at the waterfalls on the CRT screens. That was on the same course as the aircraft carrier.

"*Pravda* is nuclear," Zimmer offered.

Maggie shook her head. "This is something else," she said, the concern evident in her voice. "It's submerged."

"A picket sub." Caldwell turned up his gains to the top of the scale. "I've been wondering where their escort was."

In the control room, Bertanelli saw the submarine at the same instant Caldwell notified him of its existence. Quickly he brought up the outside course track display on the monitoring station screen. *Pocatello* was running eighty degrees to the east of the submarine's course, and fifteen to the west of the nearest surface ship, the ·*Vitse-Admiral Kulakov*, another *Udaloy*-class ASW destroyer.

"Helm," Bertanelli ordered, "come left fifteen degrees."

"Fifteen degrees port, aye."

"Bring us up to one hundred feet."

The helm officer gasped audibly. "One hundred feet, aye," he replied.

Admiral Sward heard the announcement and started, but said nothing.

Bertanelli picked up the intercom telephone. "Engineering," he said, "I want you to be ready to answer bells in five minutes. I'm going to need twenty knots very fast."

"Engineering, aye."

Both Jamison and Higgins eyed the captain curiously. He was going to bring *Pocatello* right up under the approaching destroyer, then match her speed.

Bertanelli noticed his officers' concern. "She isn't sounding," he said by way of explanation. "And with her bow-mounted LF, we can ride along beneath with no one the wiser."

Jamison and Higgins exchanged grave looks.

Sailing with Bertanelli was always an experience. One that, at times, they would rather have done without.

In the sonar room, Zimmer looked at the changing tracks with disbelief. They had all heard the captain's commands.

"Crazy Tony's at it again," Caldwell said, his voice a mixture of respect and disbelief.

"What's he doing?" Maggie asked.

"Using the destroyer as a shield," he explained. "We're going to play piggy-back."

Ralston's face turned chalk-white. It was only his first cruise and already he was becoming an old man. "He wouldn't!" the young officer exclaimed.

Caldwell grinned. "You have a lot to learn about our skipper, sir."

Ralston closed his eyes and felt a tremor passing through his body. Shadowing any surface ship was chancy enough. But coming right up under one of Russia's largest battle groups was pure folly.

The sound of the *Vitse-Admiral Kulakov*'s propellers increased as it closed the distance. *Pocatello* drifted upward, the deck making popping noises against the struts as the outside temperature changed.

In the control room, the diving officer's eyes were glued to the depth indicator. "One hundred fifty feet, and rising," he announced.

Specialists manned their equipment, all sweating profusely despite the high-level air conditioning. Fire control technicians followed their targets on monitoring screens. Electronic tracking vectors pointed to blips as firing solutions were determined.

The sound of twin screws above the *Pocatello* grew louder. Those not staring at gauges or screens involuntarily glanced upward.

"One hundred twenty feet, and rising," the helm

officer reported.

"Control to sonar," Bertanelli radioed. "How much longer?"

"Forty-five seconds, sir," Caldwell reported, "and we'll be right beneath him."

"Speed?"

"Still constant at eighteen knots."

Bertanelli picked up the telephone and dialed engineering. "Get ready, Stan. I want eighteen knots with as little noise as possible."

"Aye."

"One hundred feet," said the helmsman.

Bertanelli nodded. "Neutral buoyance, helm," he said. "Do it quietly."

Outside, the Soviet destroyer closed in, then passed over the *Pocatello*. Only thirty feet separated the two as the propeller noise washed out all readings on Caldwell's CRT screen.

"Sonar to control," Caldwell reported. "He's moving ahead. We're under his baffles."

Bertanelli picked up the telephone. *"Now*, Stan," he ordered. "Eighteen knots."

"Eighteen knots, Captain."

"All ahead standard. Maintain this speed."

"All ahead standard, aye. Maintain eighteen knots, aye."

Bertanelli spoke into the intercom mike. "Control to sonar. If that ship up there so much as even thinks about moving off this course track, I want to know about it!"

"Aye," Caldwell answered.

The noise above them was deafening. Jamison moved over to stand beside Bertanelli. "What do you have in mind?" the XO asked quietly.

"I don't think this battle force is out here because of us," Bertanelli replied. "I think they came to pick up whatever that Russian *Mike* is carrying."

Jamison looked doubtful. "Isn't that overkill?"

Bertanelli shook his head. "I don't think so," he said. "It obviously has to be of critical importance. We wouldn't have been asked to sink a Soviet sub unless whatever it carried could tip the balance of power out here. And if it's that important, the Russians won't want to trust it to a submarine." He motioned toward the surface. "Up there, it would be safe. Nobody is going to attack that flotilla."

Jamison's eyes narrowed. "You're going to let them lead you to the *Mike*," he said, his tone accusing.

Bertanelli grinned. "Exactly."

"What then?"

"Then we sink us a Russian submarine."

Jamison groaned involuntarily. "And just how do you plan to do that with all this ASW stuff around?" he asked.

"I figure we'll have one shot."

"And then?"

"And then we run like hell."

Jamison stared at his captain in disbelief. "That's the craziest plan I've ever heard!"

"It is, isn't it?" Bertanelli's smile spread from ear to ear. "That's why the Russians won't think of it."

CHAPTER TWENTY-TWO

Twenty-six miles to the south, the *Suslov* was narrowing the gap between itself and the approaching carrier force. Yakunin did not relish surfacing in this weather. He seriously doubted that any helicopter could maneuver in the fierce winds above, let alone pick someone off a rolling, pitching sail. But he was merely a sea captain and trained to follow orders.

A seaman entered the control room and stopped a few feet from Yakunin, shifting his weight nervously from one leg to the other.

"Yes? What is it?" Yakunin asked with impatience, not bothering to take his eyes off the monitor that would inform him when the helicopter had arrived.

The young seaman cleared his throat. "We . . . we cannot find Colonel Turbin anywhere, Comrade Captain."

Yakunin swung around and stared at the sailor in disbelief. "What do you mean you cannot find him?" he demanded angrily.

"He is nowhere on the boat."

"What do you mean he is not on the boat!"

Yakunin exploded. "Where the devil could he have gone? We're in the middle of the Pacific, eight hundred feet below the surface!"

The seaman looked down, unable to meet his captain's accusing glare. "He is not in his cabin, sir," he replied meekly. "He does not respond to calls, and is in neither the heads nor the mess."

"Well look again!" Yakunin ordered forcefully.

"Yes, sir." The seaman hesitated.

Yakunin's eyes narrowed. "Well? Something else?" he asked menacingly.

The sailor swallowed. "Comrade Captain, we . . . found his briefcase."

Yakunin spun his head around to look at Savitsky. The executive officer shrugged. Yakunin turned back to the young sailor. "Where is it?" he asked.

"It's . . . It's in his cabin."

"Get it up here," Yakunin ordered. "On the double!"

"Yes, Comrade Captain!"

The seaman turned and hurried from the control room. Yakunin glanced at Savitsky. "Perhaps we can tie it to the hoist of the helicopter."

Across the room, Govskaya's face lit up with excitement. If Turbin could not be found, and he, himself, could take the documents to Moscow, then that would certainly nullify his earlier mistake. He could present his case any way he saw fit. And by the time *Suslov* docked and Yakunin was summoned to a hearing, Govskaya would be a hero—not only with the Party, but with the Politburo and the High Command as well!

"I will carry them," Govskaya announced, stepping forward.

Savitsky eyed the *zampolit* with distaste. "You would vacate your post?" he asked.

"This is obviously the most important assignment I could take," Govskaya said, puffing out his chest with pride.

"It will be dangerous," Yakunin offered, secretly thrilled with the *zampolit's* suggestion. "The sail will be pitching several degrees."

"I can do it."

"I think you can," Yakunin replied, looking past the political officer and winking at Savitsky.

"Then it is settled. I will go and get ready."

"Better hurry," Savitsky prompted. "The rendezvous will be very soon."

The *zampolit* turned and left the room. Yakunin smiled broadly. With his boat free of the political officer, he would not have the Party looking over his shoulder the rest of the voyage. Yakunin knew there had to be at least one—probably more—KGB plants among the crew, keeping an eye on everyone and reporting back to Party Central. But none had the authority to penetrate his command and question his decisions. He would be running his ship without political interference.

Savitsky edged closer to Yakunin. "Be careful," he whispered. "He will have much time in Moscow to turn everyone's mind against you."

Yakunin looked at his friend soberly. "As I said, this is my last voyage."

A look of genuine love and concern passed between them. Then Yakunin turned and moved to the sonar station. Mezhova, sensing his captain's presence, looked up. "Still nothing, Comrade Captain," he reported.

Yakunin nodded. "I can still feel him out there somewhere, Aleksei."

"I've dropped SB-ones and -twos, Comrade Captain, over the past hundred kilometers. He is not behind us."

The Soviets were far behind in sonobuoy development. The SB-1 and -2 carried subservice electronics that had a tendency to short out at deep levels, and the sea water batteries had a very short life. And even if they picked up something over their omni-directional hydrophones, there was a thirty-degree error factor involved. But despite all this, Yakunin accepted the report that the American submarine was not behind him. At least that's what he wanted to believe.

"Let us hope you are right, Aleksei," Yakunin said softly.

Bertanelli picked up the telephone and dialed in the torpedo room. "Control to weapons. Very quietly, load tubes two and four with Mark forty-eights."

"Loading two and four with forty-eights, aye," came the response.

"Control to sonar," Bertanelli said. "Somewhere out in front of us should be that Soviet submarine. The minute you pick up his signature, I want to know. And when you do, plug the input into the Mark one-seventeen."

Bertanelli turned to Lieutenant Ashton. "Marv, we're only going to have one shot. It has to be a good one."

Ashton nodded. "It will be, Captain," he said.

The Helix helicopter wobbled dangerously above the rough seas, the wind tossing the twenty-four thousand-pound craft about like a cork in breakwater. Her two Isotov TV3-117V turboshaft engines were laboring to keep it on course. The dual hydraulically powered flight controls were sluggish under Tsvigun's gloved hands. The ASW bays beneath had been filled with extra fuel cells, but against the strong seventy-knot headwind, reserves were quickly being depleted.

"See anything?" Osipova, the hoist operator asked nervously.

Tsvigun shook his head, staring into the darkness through his infrared face plate.

"We should be about over it," Agayan said impatiently. He had checked and double-checked his instruments. The HSI air data computer informed him that they had reached the coordinates. "We're here," he said.

Tsvigun turned back to Brodsky. "Send the signal," he ordered.

Brodsky pushed the impulse button. A blue-green limited-depth laser shot downward into the darkness.

Swells broke over the bow of the *Vitse-Admiral Kulakov* destroyer. Her LF sonar was being defracted by the tumultuous water activity, sudden temperature changes, and the salinity differences brought about by the sea's upheaval.

Beneath him, *Pocatello* was being hammered by the same waves, pitching and rolling as she struggled to maintain a speed consistent with that of the destroyer. In the sonar room, Zimmer was beginning to turn an interesting shade of green. "I thought submarines weren't supposed to be affected by the surface weather," he groaned.

"At this depth," Caldwell informed him, "we might as well be on the surface."

"That's why I volunteered for submarines," Zimmer replied dejectedly. "To get beneath all this topsy-turvy surf. Now look at me."

Caldwell grinned. "Green becomes you," he said.

"That's what I like about you," Zimmer replied. "You are sympathetic to the core."

"I'm picking up something," Maggie announced suddenly. "It's nuclear. And it's dead ahead."

In *Suslov*'s control room, a red light indicating the helicopter's arrival blinked on and off, casting an eerie shadow across the faces of the officers and crew. Yakunin glanced at Stelest. "Where's Govskaya?"

As if on cue, the political officer entered, dressed in heavy sea gear and a life vest. "I am ready, Comrade Captain," he announced proudly.

Yakunin handed him Turbin's briefcase. "See that you take good care of this," the captain ordered. "It seems to be the source of all our current troubles."

Govskaya clutched the case tightly. "You can count on me, Comrade Captain."

Yakunin nodded absently. He could not have put into words the elation he felt at having the political officer leaving his boat. "Better get above," he suggested.

Govskaya nodded and climbed the ladder to the conning tower.

"All ahead slow," the captain ordered. He turned to sonar. "Anything, Aleksei?"

"All clear, Comrade Captain."

Yakunin took a deep breath. Surfacing in this kind of weather was always a little chancy, and even more so, considering their present purpose. "Blow forward tanks," he ordered.

"Blowing forward tanks," came the response.

"Take us up to periscope depth."

Suslov began to rise. The creaking and popping noises of the hull were indistinguishable from the water swirling outside the boat. As *Suslov* neared the surface, it began to pitch and roll from the wave action.

"Periscope depth, Comrade Captain."

Yakunin nodded. "Bring up the EMS mast and the aft periscope," he said. "And switch to red battle lights."

The white lights were immediately replaced with red to accustom the eyes to the outside night.

Those seated at their stations strapped themselves into their chairs. The others tried to hang on as the boat was tossed about roughly by the angry waves. Yakunin moved to the periscope, holding on to the rail around the pedestal.

"Radar emissions directly above us, Comrade Captain," Savitsky informed him.

Yakunin nodded. "That'll be the helicopter. Anything else?"

Savitsky shook his head.

Yakunin looked into the periscope, turning it quickly in a wide sweep, then slowly began to search the horizon. He could see little other than the high waves swirling all around them. *Suslov* was temporarily sitting in a deep trough. Yakunin waited patiently until the wave action brought them up and visibility improved. Through the infrared lens he could see only the dark, angry ocean assaulting his boat. He turned and glanced at his sonar officer inquisitively. Mezhova shook his head sadly.

"Take us up," the captain ordered.

The periscope and mast were retracted and the ballast tanks blown dry. *Suslov* buoyed slowly toward the surface.

Across the Potomac from Washington, the Pentagon was just settling down after the noon break. Traffic on the George Washington Memorial Parkway was crowded with employees rushing to get back to work after a long lunch hour. The temperature was pushing a hundred and the humidity was ninety percent. The vast parking lot around the vast five-sided military complex was jammed, with officers and civilians making their hurried way inside.

In the war room on the third basement level, overlooking the situation board, several men and women had been laboring through the lunch hour. Cups of coffee were everywhere, and the remains of take-out meals, hastily devoured, had been pushed aside. Among these devoted workers, tempers were beginning to rise, bodies saturated with perspiration were starting to smell, and worst fear scenarios were developing in active minds.

"Give me an update," General Shriner bellowed.

The board flashed, lights changed, then everything stabilized. "Current on satellite feed," a voice on the floor reported.

"Look at that!" Shriner said, slamming the table in annoyance. "That damn battle group is right over the spot where we've placed *Pocatello* and the Russian sub!"

"If they can take the Russian in tow, or transfer the documents, we're beaten," Admiral Olsen complained bitterly.

They had been at it all night and nerves were totally frayed. *Nimitz* was still hours away, and only the two 688 boats, *Helena* and *Phoenix* were within DefCon Two readiness. General Shriner felt his heart start beating faster. Unless *Pocatello* radioed a successful kill of the Russian sub before any possible transfer could have taken place, he would have no choice but to recommend to the president they go to DefCon Three!

* * *

In Honolulu, however, high command had a much different perspective.

"That weather out there is mounting to a force-three gale," Cummings said, checking the latest weather report.

Vice-Adm. Edwin Rowden nodded thoughtfully. "A sub on the surface in that sea," he said, would find it very difficult to effect any transfer of personnel or material."

"We can't count on luck!" Blanchard shouted out suddenly. "We can only hope that *Poco* will attack the Russian before any attempt is even made."

Rowden frowned. "And if Tony fails?" he asked.

Blanchard looked across at the situation board monitoring the combatants in the Pacific. "Then we wait until *Nimitz* can make contact," he said, "and we *attack* in force!"

All eyes locked on Blanchard. There hadn't been a Naval engagement since the Second World War. And everyone believed one now would mark the beginning of World War Three.

CHAPTER TWENTY-THREE

9:13 a.m. Honolulu/1913 Hours Zulu

The Helix was suddenly blown sideways by a ninety-knot gust of wind, nearly standing it on its port side. Tsvigun looked out of his side window, staring straight down into the tossing sea. Frantically he struggled to level his craft. It was by far the worst weather he had ever flown in. He had radioed the ship earlier to request the mission be aborted, but the *zampolit* on board would not even hear of it.

He was about to turn back and take his chances with command when bubbling white foam erupted on the surface of the water below him. The dark sail of *Suslov* broke through the dark, swirling ocean and poked above a swell.

"There he is," Osipova shouted.

Tsvigun nodded, studying the pitching, rolling sail. His worst fears had been realized. The boat was rolling nearly thirty feet from side to side. "Get ready, Sasha," trying to keep his voice calm.

The hoist operator slid open the window and released the pin on the RBT-2000 hoist. Electrically driven and electronically controlled, it was an exact duplicate of the Western Gear lift used on all U.S. Army search and rescue helicopters. He attached the lift collar to the cable, then began lowering it toward the rolling submarine. He shook his head. "This will never work," he muttered.

Two hundred feet below, in the control room of *Suslov*, Yakunin was issuing orders rapid-fire in an attempt to keep the boat steady. "Lookouts to the bridge. All ahead standard. Helm, minimize that roll!"

As his orders were repeated, two seamen in heavy gear and vests scrambled up the ladder and cracked open the hatch. Water poured in and down to the conning station. In seconds they were out in the night and looking over the raging surface of the water with specially designed infrared binoculars.

Savitsky joined Yakunin at the foot of the ladder. "I hope he drowns," the XO said softly.

Yakunin sighed. "Better go on up, Lev, and see that he gets strapped into the collar. Let's not have anyone saying we didn't do our duty."

A seaman handed Savitsky a life jacket and vest. The officer eagerly accepted the rain gear but shook off the proffered inflatable vest. In this rough sea, it would be totally useless.

Govskaya crawled through the hatch and onto the bridge. With the sail pitching so violently, he was forced to hang onto the coaming to keep from being tossed overboard.

Above them the Helix hovered, slowly lowering the hoist which was being blown nearly horizontal by the wind.

"You are sure you want to do this?" Savitsky asked tentatively, coming up beside the political officer.

"Of course!" Govskaya shouted into the howling wind. "It is for *Rodina!*"

Savitsky shook his head with disgust. It was true he felt nothing for the political officer but a deep, emotional hatred. But this was suicide! "Of course," Savitsky said dryly. "For the Motherland."

The lookouts were strapped into the foul-weather mast harness, diligently searching the darkness for intruders. One worked the FLIR pod on the starboard side of the bridge, the other used his binoculars.

In the helicopter above, Tsvigun was struggling valiantly to hold the craft steady in the sweeping, gusting winds. He had tried using the electro-mechanical flight director off the Doppler radar altimeter, but the autopilot could not operate fast enough to make necessary adjustments in the rough weather. Plus he knew it was particularly susceptible to wind shear, that unique downward thrust of wind that can drive a plane into the ground—or in this case, the water—without warning.

Tsvigun watched the men standing on the submarine's sail. He moved his helicopter further into the wind in an attempt to maneuver into a position where the collar would be blown toward those waiting below. Though the copter was but fifty feet above the water, over a hundred feet of cable had already been played out.

"Hold it steady!" Osipova shouted. The collar was swinging back and forth wildly across the pitching sail.

"I am trying, damnit!" Tsvigun yelled in frustration. Still the heavy winds buffeted the craft to and fro.

Below, Govskaya reached for the collar as it swung past. But the boat pitched and he frantically grabbed for the coaming to keep from falling into the raging waters. Savitsky watched the *zampolit's* ineptness with disgust. "Use both hands!" the executive officer shouted.

Govskaya shook his head vigorously. "The briefcase!" he screamed into the roaring wind.

"It will be safe on the deck! It's not going anywhere."

Again the political officer shook his head. Savitsky shrugged and pushed Govskaya aside roughly. "Here, I will get it for you!"

The political officer nodded his thanks, holding on tighter to the coaming. Savitsky moved against the sail and braced his legs while waiting for the collar to swing past once again. As it came racing back toward him, he reached for it, just barely getting his fingers around the leather harness.

Field Marshall Istomin could hardly contain himself as he picked up the direct line to Ognev's office. Within seconds the premier answered. "Comrade Chairman," Istomin said excitedly, "the convoy has made contact with *Suslov*. A helicopter has been dispatched to pick up Colonel Turbin and the documents."

On the other end of the line, Ognev felt suddenly light-headed. All his planning was about to pay off. There was nothing the Americans could do now that would make a difference. Within hours every U.S. submarine in the Pacific would be exposed, targeted, no longer a threat to the Motherland. "That is good news, Nikolai," the premier said, grinning from ear to ear. "Let me know the minute they reach Moscow."

The helicopter ride from the Pentagon in Arlington to the White House had taken only ten minutes. Another five and General Shriner had been escorted through the west wing and into the Oval Office. It was a calculated risk, Shriner knew, to leave the Situation Room at such a crucial moment, but as Chairman of the Joint Chiefs, it was his responsibility to counsel the president on the defense condition of the country. And right now, a change in that status was due.

"We cannot wait, Mr. President," he said, once Freeman had shut the door of the Oval Office and the two of them were alone. "The Soviets will have the documents within minutes. And there will be no way for us to counter their advantage."

Freeman sighed heavily. He had been hoping against hope that this moment would never arrive. He leaned back into the soft cushion of his chair and clasped his hands tightly across his stomach. "And what do you suggest, General?" he asked, his voice barely a whisper.

Shriner sat ramrod stiff on the edge of his chair. "We go to DefCon Three immediately!" he said without hesitation.

Once again Freeman sighed. He had known what the general's answer would be before it was even spoken. Still, he had hoped cooler heads might have prevailed at the Pentagon. He picked up a pencil and chewed absently on the eraser for a moment. He wanted alternatives, but none seemed available. "Is there no other way?" he asked sadly.

Shriner eased back slightly in the chair, suddenly aware of Freeman's eyes on him. His historically oriented mind knew this was a moment of great decision. Whatever happened in the next few hours could well determine history for the next twenty years. Perhaps longer. "Well," he started, "I talked to Blanchard in Honolulu."

"And?"

Shriner hesitated. He leaned forward, meeting the

president's stare with equal intensity. "He wants permission to attack the *Pravda* fleet with his *Nimitz* carrier group."

Freeman was silent. He stood suddenly and crossed to a sideboard. He poured himself a cup of coffee from an urn and glanced inquiringly toward Shriner. The general shook his head. "And what do you think of that?" Freeman finally asked, adding sugar and cream to his coffee.

Shriner coughed once and cleared his throat. "The up side is that such an action would not automatically result in a missile launch."

The president crossed back to his desk, stirring his coffee slowly. "What chance would we have to accomplish our goal?" he asked thoughtfully, setting his cup down gently to the middle of the desk's ink blotter.

"Blanchard thinks we can bottle them up so they couldn't get anything to shore."

Freeman placed both elbows on the desk in front of him and rested his chin on his interlocking fingers. He stared off in silence for what seemed an eternity. "And then what?" he said finally.

"We could bring an entire fleet on station long before they could reinforce their position. With any luck—a lot of luck, actually—we could force them east toward Hawaii. If we put enough pressure on, they might return the documents."

Freeman smiled sadly. "Of course," he said. "And how many copies would they retain?"

Shriner cleared his throat once more. "That's the downside. There's no way we could be insured they wouldn't have the information they seek anyway." Shriner shifted his weight, trying to find a more comfortable position. He liked Freeman, but the man had an uncanny way of staring right through a person. "Hell," Shriner added, "they could be faxing it ashore as we were fighting them."

"So much for a direct confrontation."

Shriner nodded. "My point exactly, sir. We must go to DefCon Three. That'll send a message loud and clear to Moscow that if they persist in moving into the Pacific, we will strike!"

The light glinting off the rows of campaign ribbons that Shriner wore proudly on his chest caught Freeman in the eyes briefly. The president turned toward the window. He recognized the general's bravery and trusted his judgment—but DefCon Three was a major step to take. "If we move to the third condition, General," the president said quietly, still staring out over the rose garden, "the law demands that I call Ognev on the hot line." The president turned back to face Shriner. "Just what would you suggest I tell him?"

"Tell him to stay the hell out of the Pacific, sir."

Freeman's lips tightened. "Or what?" he asked.

"Or we launch our missiles!"

Because of his injuries, it had taken Travis the better part of a half hour to work his way forward. He had had to duck into several corners in order to avoid detection, but now stood just outside the control room. The boat was being tossed from side to side and the motion set sharp, shooting stabs of intense pain through his leg. He gritted his teeth and, using his cane to steady himself, he unslung the AK-74 and took a deep breath.

He burst into the control room with the weapon held at the ready. The crew, occupied with trying to keep the boat trim in the pitching sea, paid no attention to the American. The deck officers monitoring the vast complex of instruments were shouting rapid-fire instructions to the seamen. Only Yakunin noticed Travis's dramatic entrance. The captain turned to the American standing just inside the hatch.

"The devil be damned!" Yakunin muttered. Switching to English, he ordered, "Put down the weapon, Captain. There is nothing you can do here!"

Travis pulled the bolt back and shoved the gun forward threateningly. "I'm now in control of this sub!"

For one of the few times in his adult life, Yakunin laughed outright. "Right now, Captain," he roared with amusement, "I'm not sure any of us are in control of this boat!"

Travis glanced around the control room. Still no one but Yakunin seemed aware of his presence. All hands were at their stations frantically working controls and shouting orders back and forth.

Yakunin motioned toward the bustle of activity. "As you can see, we are experiencing a little difficulty." As if on cue, a heavy roll of the boat emphasized his words, sending Travis crashing into a nearby wall. The American grimaced in agony but managed to keep the gun trained on the Russian captain.

"Order them to take us up!" Travis shouted, tears of intense pain burning his eyes. He figured if he could keep the sub on the surface long enough, an American boat would, no doubt, show up eventually. "*Now*, Captain!" Travis ordered, brandishing the gun wildly. "Take us up *now!*"

Yakunin stared at the insane American and shook his head. "But we *are* up," he said quietly.

Travis glanced around the room cautiously. For

the first time, he noticed the water that was occasionally sloshing down from the conning station. As he edged toward the conning ladder, he passed directly behind Mezhova. The sonar officer looked up and started at the sight of the armed American intruder.

On Caldwell's CRT, the waterfall was registering a blip racing through the rough seas. "Target straight ahead," he announced. "Five miles. Elevation angle, ten degrees positive."

He glanced over at Maggie. "You were right," he said. "He's right where you said he was." Maggie looked up at him and smiled.

Seconds later, Bertanelli burst into the sonar room. "O'Brien," he said, "we're going to need a counterfeit signature to get out of here. Make it a *Sierra*."

Maggie nodded. "Aye, aye," she replied and immediately got to work on it as Bertanelli stormed out as abruptly as he had entered.

Caldwell grinned. "I see you've just been promoted to O'Brien," he said.

"It's about time," Maggie responded without looking up from her equipment.

Back in the control room, Bertanelli shouted orders to the active crewmen. "Let's look lively! We're only going to have one shot!" He picked up the telephone and dialed the torpedo room. "Control to weapons. Arm the warheads."

"Arming, aye," came the response.

"And flood the tubes."

"Flooding, aye."

Pocatello dipped nose-down as the extra weight was added. Computers automatically activated trim tanks to keep the boat level.

"Ashton," Bertanelli called out. The fire control officer glanced up quizzically. "Do we have a firing solution?"

"Negative."

"Get on it!"

"Aye." Ashton turned to two technicians working the electronic controls at his side. "Bring 'em up," he ordered. "Now!"

Bertanelli appeared to be everywhere at once. He seemed to possess an uncanny awareness of every single thing that was happening on his boat at any given time. When someone gave or repeated an inaccurate order, Bertanelli was right there to immediately correct him.

"Firing solution acquired, Captain," Ashton reported.

"Stand by," Bertanelli said to him. "We'll fire at twelve thousand yards."

The collar was ripped out of Savitsky's hands as *Suslov* rolled to the port side and the chopper was simultaneously blown to starboard. Savitsky just barely managed to grab the coaming to keep from being washed overboard.

In the control room, Yakunin turned his back on Travis and strode to the foot of the conning ladder. "What's happening up there?" he called up.

Above, the deck was awash with water flowing in from the open sail hatch. Slipping and sliding, the officer of the deck made his way to the hatch opening and poked his head down the ladder. "They can't grab the hoist collar," he yelled down.

Yakunin turned back into the control room. "Helm, hold us steady!" he ordered.

The helm officer's eyes remained glued to his

273

instruments. "We're pitching almost eighteen degrees, Comrade Captain," he reported.

"Bring us up five knots," Yakunin ordered. "Perhaps with more speed we can cut down on the roll."

"Very well, Comrade Captain."

Travis could not believe it. There he stood, an intruder with an automatic weapon, and no one was paying him the least bit of attention. He hadn't noticed the sonar officer near him, crouched and ready to spring.

"Why are you on the surface?" Travis demanded, jamming the weapon into Yakunin's ribs.

"We are effecting repairs," Yakunin lied, pushing the muzzle of the AK-74 aside and striding back toward the helm.

It was at that moment that Mezhova attacked.

"Target increasing speed," Caldwell called over the intercom.

"Control to weapons," Bertanelli ordered. "Open outer doors on two and four."

"Open outer doors, aye."

Jamison glanced up at Bertanelli. "He's on the surface, running with decks awash," he said.

Bertanelli frowned, his forehead creasing with concern. "The transfer must be taking place."

Jamison shook his head. "In this weather it'll be impossible."

"Let's hope so." Bertanelli flipped on the intercom mike. "Control to sonar. Distance to target."

"Sixteen thousand yards," Caldwell replied.

They were at the optimum range for the Mark 48 wire-guided torpedo.

"We can't wait much longer," Jamison said. "If

274

they make that transfer, we've lost."

Bertanelli nodded. "Control to weapons," he ordered. "Fire tube two!"

In the torpedo room, Lieutenant Crippin released the fire lever. A loud gushing sound enveloped the room as compressed air shot the thirty-four-hundred-pound torpedo into the sea. "Tube two, away!" he announced excitedly.

"Fire tube four!"

Again Crippen released the fire lever.

The green Mark 48 torpedo angled out from the cantered tube, passed the fiberglass nose of *Pocatello* and knifed through the water at sixty-three miles per hour. The single-strand guiding wire played out from the dispenser in the torpedo's stern, receiving messages multiplexed from the fire-control computer. In seconds, the other torpedo joined the path of the first.

In the control room, Ashton followed the torpedoes' paths on his monitoring screen. "Running time eight minutes, thirty seconds," he announced.

CHAPTER TWENTY-FOUR

9:20 a.m. Honolulu/1920 Hours Zulu

In the sonar room of the destroyer directly above *Pocatello*, the chief officer sat bolt upright, seeing the wake of two torpedoes running out from beneath his ship. "Torpedoes in the water," he screamed into the intercom. "Torpedoes in the water."

"Direction! Bearing!" the bridge radioed back.

"On our course, moving away from us."

"What?"

Captain Second Rank Vladimir Klepikova turned toward the window and stared into the blackness before him. He could see nothing. His ship carried eight twenty-one-inch torpedo tubes, but they were not even supposed to have been loaded. He spun angrily on his first officer standing at the helm. "Find out who the devil gave permission to fire those torpedoes!" the captain snapped.

The officer saluted and quickly quit the bridge.

"I'll string him up by the *m'acha'*," Klepikova muttered angrily. He knew the *Tributs* was ahead of him to his left, and *Marshall Sudeikin* was to his right. And out there somewhere in front was the *Suslov*. An errant torpedo could hit any one of them.

"And after that," he added, "I'll skin him alive!"

Savitsky grabbed for the collar once again and missed. "Damn this weather!" he yelled in frustration. He looked up and shook his fist at the helicopter, then immediately felt guilty. No one in his right mind would have chosen to attempt this foolishness. The pilot was under the same stupid orders as the *Suslov*.

Savitsky yanked a mike from under the coaming. "Captain, this is not possible," he yelled, battling the roaring winds and crashing waves.

"Come back inside," Yakunin called up. "We can try it later when the weather calms down."

"Very well." Savitsky replaced the mike and motioned for the lookouts to get below. As they scrambled into the hatch, he grabbed Govskaya. "Get below!" he yelled in the *zampolit's* ear. "We will try it later!"

The political officer shook his head violently. "I must go *now!*" he demanded. If they waited any longer, Turbin might be found and Govskaya would lose his chance at vindication and revenge. He grabbed desperately for the collar as it passed overhead once again.

Mezhova struck Travis hard, barreling into him from behind. His momentum carried them both across the control room and sent them crashing into one of the planesmen. The helm officer, unaware that one was an American, shouted frantically in Russian for them to stop.

Two Russian seamen leapt into the fray, grabbing

at Travis's weapon, trying to wrest it from his grasp. The rest of the sailors in the control room turned away from their instruments to observe the commotion. "Man your stations!" Yakunin ordered. "Keep this boat trim!" He grabbed a secure phone and called for security guards.

Travis whirled and kicked one seaman in the groin with his good leg. He yanked the weapon free from the many hands that tried to grab it, and slammed the butt end into one man's jaw and the muzzle into the stomach of another.

"Keep this boat trim!" Yakunin yelled.

Four seamen, answering their captain's call, rushed into the control room. They ran over to subdue Travis, and within moments the American was grappled to the deck and pinned there. Yakunin charged across the room and glared down at the captured flyer.

"Just what is it you hoped to accomplish?" Yakunin shouted, his face flushed with rage. Though it was not usually within his nature to kill a prisoner, this time he was sorely tempted.

Waves of intense pain washed over Travis. His injured leg felt as if it had been ripped violently from his body. "I wanted to stop this boat!" he gasped.

"We *are* stopped!" Yakunin roared with frustration.

"And to gain control."

Yakunin snapped his head back, his eyes widening in disbelief. "One man capturing a hundred and fifty?" he shouted, pointing to the small AK-74. "And with a toy? You Americans. You watch too many cowboy movies!" He glanced at the instruments. "Keep us trim, I said!" he snapped. The crew hurried back to work.

The captain glared at Travis. "I ought to lock you up in a torpedo tube," he threatened. He turned to the seamen holding Travis down. "Take him back to the officers' mess," he ordered. "I want you four guarding him at all times!"

One of the seamen nodded. "Very well, Comrade Captain," he said. He motioned to the other three. Together they grabbed Travis's arms and dragged him out of the control room, the American screaming in agony.

Yakunin glared after the airman, then turned to his warrant officer. "Where's Savitsky?" he asked. "He should be down by now."

Mezhova sighed heavily as he climbed back onto his chair and automatically glanced at his sonar screen. What he saw caused him to stiffen in terror. "Comrade Captain," he shouted. "Torpedoes!"

Yakunin swung away from Stelest before the warrant officer could answer his question and hurried over to Mezhova's side. "What did you say?" the captain demanded.

"Torpedoes in the water," Mezhova repeated, his voice high and strained. "They're heading one nine eight degrees. Range, six kilometers. Deflection angle, zero. Speed, one zero seven kilometers an hour." He gulped, staring at the screen. "They're coming right at us!"

"Full left rudder!" Yakunin shouted. "Prepare to dive!" He grabbed the sail phone. "Clear the bridge. Incoming torpedoes! Repeat, clear the bridge!"

Above, the two lookouts raced to clamber down the ladder inside the sail. On the flying bridge, Govskaya successfully grabbed hold of the collar. He tried to steady himself but lost his balance, dropping the briefcase as he reached for the coaming with his other hand. Savitsky clutched the political officer's arm.

"Get below!" the XO shouted. "Incoming torpedoes!"

Govskaya shook his head. "I've got it!" he yelled back, shrugging out of Savitsky's grasp. "I've got it! Hand me the briefcase!"

Savitsky could hear the two short blasts of the klaxon horns sounding below. *Suslov* was about to dive. "There's no time!" he shouted. "Let go!"

"*Nyet!*" the *zampolit* insisted stubbornly. "The briefcase!" Govskaya's eyes were inflamed, his mind a clutter of chaotic thought.

Savitsky reached for the case as Govskaya tried to pull the collar closer to work himself inside. To do so, it was necessary to let go of the coaming. Shutting his eyes, the political officer released his hold and reached for the collar with his other hand.

Another heavy gust of wind struck the Helix, knocking it sideways fifty feet. The cable jerked tight, yanking the collar from Govskaya's grip. The *zampolit* fell forward as the sail dipped fifteen degrees to starboard. Flying over the coaming, Govskaya started to drop toward the swirling waters. Seeing Govskaya going over the sail, Savitsky dropped the case, and dove for him, grabbing the *zampolit's* hand just as the man was disappearing over the side.

Below, Yakunin looked at the watertight integrity lights and saw the sail hatch still glowing red. "Lev!" he yelled up to the bridge station. "Get below! We're diving!"

The first officer of the *Kulakov* ran into the destroyer's fire control center. One glance at the panel informed him that no torpedoes had been fired, and he reported this information over the secure radio to the captain.

Valdimir Klepikova shook his head in amazement. Torpedoes had apparently been fired from his ship, but all twenty-two were still in their housing racks. Suddenly the answer hit him like a bolt of lightning.

"Left full rudder," he yelled. "Battle stations!"

The call to general quarters went out over the public address system and three hundred seamen ran for their positions.

"Fire up the RBU computers," Klepikova ordered. "Sonar, get me a bearing on that submarine beneath us!"

In the sonar room, Technician Third Rank Alla Kendrashin stared at the green clutter on his CRT screen. Running in such weather, the towed array had long ago been reeled in. Dependent on the LF in the bow, he was picking up so much ambient noise that the computer was unable to filter it out. He worked frantically at the terminal keyboard. As *Kulakov* left its course track, he noticed a flitting shadow.

Caldwell saw the destroyer above them turn left and instantly called the heading change to the control room.

"Left full rudder!" Bertanelli ordered. "Stay with that damned ship!"

Outside, the three miles of wire coiling out from the two torpedoes, snapped from the sudden course change. Immediately, the small sonar computers inside the missiles switched to acoustic and began searching for the target noise.

* * *

281

On *Suslov*'s bridge, Savitsky was unable to hear Yakunin's last command, fighting the wind and pitching bridge as he was to haul Govskaya back over the coaming. Vaguely aware that the hull was completely under and the sea was moving rapidly up the sail, he dragged the political officer over the side. They fell together amid the rushing water onto the bridge deck.

"Below!" Savitsky shouted, pushing Govskaya toward the hatch. "We're diving!"

Govskaya jerked free. Using the coaming for support, he climbed to his feet. All his plans were dependent on successfully catching the collar and being hoisted aloft. As he saw the collar swing past once again, he made a leap for it, circling one arm through the harness. Savitsky grabbed the *zampolit*'s leg and tried to drag him below. Govskaya screamed in rage, kicking wildly at the executive officer with his free foot. He slammed a heel into the man's jaw and Savitsky went down hard, a wave washing him into the metal coaming. His temple struck a flange and bright lights exploded inside his head.

Below, Yakunin could wait no longer. "Get that hatch closed!" he shouted.

A seaman started up the ladder inside the sail when the briefcase, washed inside by a rush of water, struck him, knocking him heavily to the conning deck below. Another seaman stepped over him and the briefcase, and started up the ladder. But the ocean, starting to pour through the hatch full force, washed him off the ladder before he got halfway up.

On the deck above, blood gushed from the wound in Savitsky's head. Only dimly aware of his surroundings, he could see the ocean flooding in over the coaming. He could vaguely hear Govskaya swearing as the political officer struggled to slip the collar around him, unaware that the briefcase had been washed below. Realizing the hatch was still open, Savitsky tried to stand, but discovered he could not move. He tried to yell for Govskaya to throw the electric circuit that would close the hatch from the bridge, but no words came out.

Another wave washed over the wounded executive officer, pinning him between the mast and periscope housing. The amount of water pouring through the hatch was increasing. If the boat stayed on the surface, it would be blown apart by the torpedoes. If it submerged with the hatch open to the sea, the entire crew would drown in minutes. Savitsky had to act.

Unable to move, his vision obscured by the stinging mixture of rain, salt water and blood running down his face, Savitsky managed to locate the hatch release control just inches from his foot. But try as he might, he could not extend his leg far enough to reach it. His entire body shuddered as he stretched in vain, his foot falling short by millimeters. He felt an inner fog overtaking him as he grunted and struggled, but to no avail. *I have failed you, Emelyan,* Savitsky thought bitterly as consciousness began to escape him.

Just then a wave struck him heavily, knocking him free of the mast and washing him across the deck. As he slid past, almost by reflex, Savitsky's left foot kicked out, hitting the hatch control lever. The electronics slowly forced the hatch down, fighting the pressure of the onrushing ocean which was cascading through the opening. But technology finally triumphed over nature, and the hatch opening was sealed.

Once again the sea swept over the coaming. It picked up the body of the *Suslov*'s executive officer and slammed him further into the mast webbing. Then a final darkness overtook Lev Savitsky.

When Captain Yakunin saw the hatch light change from red to green, his heart stopped in his chest. Intuitively he knew what had just transpired on the bridge and that his closest friend was no more. Ice formed in his veins as he felt a dizziness threatening to overcome him. *Not now!* his mind screamed. *This is not the time! Your boat is in danger! First things first!*

Yakunin turned to his officers. "Steep angle," he ordered. "Take us down *fast!*"

As *Suslov* dived below the surface, Govskaya was suddenly washed up and deposited into the collar. He swung wildly, trying to force both arms through the loop. The water carried him past, then swirled him around the masts. The cable snarled on a flange, and held.

Above him, Tsvigun saw *Suslov* disappear and swore. He pulled back on the collective and the Helix started to ascend. Suddenly it was jerked downward, red lights flashing all across Tsvigun's control panel.

"We're caught!" Osipova yelled.

"Reverse the cable!" Tsvigun ordered frantically.

Seeing Govskaya grab the collar, Osipova had begun to reel him in. Now, he worked desperately to reverse the control. He pushed the release with one hand and yanked at the lever with the other, trying to wedge it up out of the lock position. But the rod would not budge. "It's stuck!" he screamed in terror.

That was not quite true. In his panic, he had

forgotten to trip the safety stud. As a result, the electrical impulse to the hoist motor was bypassed, thus causing the motor to continue to reel in the cable. With the *Suslov* descending, the Helix was being dragged down toward the roiling sea. Not understanding the problem, Tsvigun continued to pull up while boosting power. Suddenly a powerful gust of wind struck the craft, knocking it sideways. One of the blades on the lower rotor platform collided with a rising wave, sending the copter into a somersault and plummeting into the water.

The Mark 48 torpedoes, running on acoustic homing, had not yet picked up the submarine's signature, when the Helix slammed into the ocean and broke up. The acoustic transducers registered the fallen copter's noise, the torpedoes turned, and sped toward the wreckage.

Marvin Ashton monitored his fire control board intently, ignoring the constant course changes that passed between sonar and control. "Fifteen seconds to target," he announced.

Bertanelli heard the timing call and glanced up at the bulkhead clock. A faint explosion, followed swiftly by a second, could be heard through *Pocatello*'s hull. Bertanelli spun around to look at Ashton, who shook his head. "Too soon," the officer said gravely. "They hit something else."

"Out here?" Bertanelli asked incredulously.

Ashton merely shrugged. Bertanelli was not convinced. He crossed to the intercom mike and radioed sonar. "Caldwell," he said. "What did we hit?"

"I thought it was the *Mike*," came the reply.

"O'Brien," Bertanelli shot back. "Do you have any

of those emissions of yours?"

"Checking now," Maggie said.

"Shit!" the captain swore. "What next?"

"Depth charges in the water!" Caldwell's voice shouted over the intercom. "I repeat, depth charges in the water!"

CHAPTER TWENTY-FIVE

9:32 a.m. Honolulu/1932 Hours Zulu

"Bring us up to sixty feet," Bertanelli ordered.

The diving officer's throat went instantly dry. "Sixty feet, aye," he croaked. Sixty feet would place them directly underneath the destroyer with no room left for maneuvering. And in an ocean tossing as badly as this, that could be almost certain suicide.

Pocatello came right up under the *Kulakov*. The sound of the destroyer's propellers was loud and distinct through the sub's hull.

"Why the hell is he depth charging?" Jamison asked nervously. "He hasn't the slightest idea where we are."

Bertanelli shook his head. "Another trigger-happy Ivan," he opined.

Caldwell's voice blasted loudly over the intercom. "Sonar to control. O'Brien reports neutron emissions beyond the ensonified zone."

"The bastard got away again!" Jamison stormed angrily. "Maybe we're snake-bitten."

Bertanelli stared at his executive officer with unwavering intensity. "The third time's the charm," he said with assurance.

Outside, far off to the rear, depth charges exploded

noisily. Then suddenly all was quiet.

"Control to sonar," Bertanelli said. "O'Brien, get ready to use the *Sierra* signature."

"Aye," Maggie replied.

Bertanelli turned to the helm. "All ahead slow," he ordered. "Slide us back into her baffles."

With the soaking wet briefcase clutched in his hand, the officer of the deck climbed down the ladder into the control room.

"Condition," Yakunin asked quietly of the helm.

"We are at flank speed, Comrade Captain. We are still diving. Now at one two five meters."

"Level off at one five zero meters," he ordered. "Maintain flank speed." Yakunin turned to Mezhova. "And the American?"

Mezhova shook his head. "I'm picking up too much surface noise. The fleet is screening out the submarine."

The captain turned to the deck officer. "Report!"

"The lookouts are below." The seaman paused. He cleared his throat self-consciously before continuing. "Comrade Savitsky and the *zampolit* did not make it off the bridge, Comrade Captain."

Yakunin did not blink an eye. "Damage?" he asked.

"The EMS mast is out of commission, but the explosions did not affect our water-tight integrity. We are fully operational."

Yakunin turned back to the helm. "Maintain this course." To Mezhova he added, "Keep a look out. I know that American will be after us."

"Maybe he will think the torpedoes hit us."

"Maybe." But Yakunin's voice betrayed his skepticism. He knew the American would not rest until

288

absolutely certain *Suslov* was lying dead at the bottom of the Pacific.

The *michman* crossed slowly to his captain. "I am sorry about Comrade Savitsky," Stelest said quietly.

Yakunin shook his head, a wave of irreconcilable grief washing over him. "Somehow I knew that American submarine was back there. I should have listened to myself and not the orders."

"We must obey orders, Comrade Captain."

Yakunin looked at the warrant officer. The captain sighed. "Of course, Felix," he said sadly. "Of course."

Yakunin took the water-logged case from the deck officer and shoved it into Stelest's hands. "Take care of this," he said bitterly. "If there were some way to do it, I'd give it back to the Americans myself."

Stelest frowned. "It would not bring Savitsky back, Comrade Captain."

The sonar officer on board the *Kulakov* tried desperately to relocate the fleeting shadow he had caught a glimpse of. But try as he might, his screens remained blank. The raging sea was easily screening out any plant and steam noises *Pocatello* was making, and her silent propeller was so quiet, it would have been hard to detect even if there had been no ocean turbulence.

For the moment, *Pocatello* was well hidden.

"Secure frm bombing," the sonar officer suggested with a sigh. "I have no target."

"Secure the RBUs," Klepikova ordered. On the deck, seamen replaced the safety pins in their depth charge racks and secured from general quarters, returning inside the tossing, rain-pelted ship. Had it been an American vessel, the racks would have been cleaned, oiled, and readied for the next use, with the empty rocket cannisters reloaded. It would take *Kulakov* longer, next time, to respond to a fire order.

Bertanelli watched the CRT tracks as *Pocatello* slid back slowly into the noisy wake of the destroyer. Within seconds they would be picked up by the ship's sonar.

"O'Brien, switch us over to your *Sierra*," Bertanelli radioed.

"Switching now."

On sonar sets throughout the battle force, a *Sierra* submarine suddenly appeared on their screens. Though it had not been there before, no one paid much attention. They were looking for an enemy boat.

"What now?" Sward asked. They were the first words he had spoken in some time. "Do we turn home?" he asked hopefully.

Bertanelli shook his head. "We still have battle orders, Admiral."

"But—"

"We know where the *Mike* is going," Bertanelli went on, "and we know how long it will take him to get there."

Sward's face reddened. "And just how do you propose to catch him before he reaches the Straits?"

"Right now, Admiral, I'd say he's had a bad scare. He won't be in a hurry to head for Friza."

Sward felt the familiar dislike welling up inside of himself. "You haven't forgotten that we're surrounded by a carrier battle group, have you?"

Bertanelli grinned ear to ear. "The *Pocatello* is surrounded, sir," he said with an impish twinkle in his eyes. "But we're a *Sierra* boat now. And we can go

290

anywhere we damn well please!" He winked and turned to the navigation officer. "Barker, plot a course for Friza and plug it into the computer. We're going hunting again."

Everyone in the control room knew his words were crazy. But Bertanelli's optimism, as always, was contagious. Any other boat would have turned tail for Pearl, glad to have escaped the largest ASW force the Soviets had ever assembled in the Pacific. But not Crazy Tony. *Pocatello* was going hunting! And right under the noses of the Russian battle group!

In the sonar room, Caldwell took the news with cheerful good humor. If anyone could get them out of this predicament without getting their butts burned, Crazy Tony could. He smiled as he saw targets automatically registering on his sonar. With the towed array out, he could call up anything within 360 degrees. He was ready, if called upon, to begin feeding firing solutions into the Mark 117.

Maggie, on the other hand, was not quite so cheerful. "I don't know what you're grinning about," she said, busily tracking the neutron emissions coming from the *Suslov*. "He's getting away!"

"There's no way we can catch him now," Caldwell replied calmly, as he worked at his terminal to wash out the outside ambient noise. "He's faster than we are, plus he has a twenty-mile headstart. Besides, we try to dust out of here and the Russkies are going to get mighty suspicious." Caldwell looked up at Maggie and smiled. "So you might as well just relax. You might live longer."

Maggie simply grunted and turned back to her instruments.

The nuclear carrier *Pravda* steamed ahead, making

twenty-eight knots in the turbulent ocean. Thirty-foot waves broke over the forward ski jump of the flight deck. The center-line lift was in place, but both side lifts were secured below decks. The usual standby squadrons of Flanker, Frogfoot and Fulcrums had all been taken below, and only two Helix-A helicopters were left topside, both tied down securely.

In the radar room—a large, darkened cabin near the top of the stack with banks of electronics lining three walls—five technicians monitored the entire fleet. At one end of the room, separated by a short partition, two sonar operators watched as their CRT screens indicated a *Sierra* submarine was changing course and turning west—a course that would take it directly beneath the carrier.

The first technician studied his screen in confusion. "That *Sierra* is not listed on my call board," he said.

"Nor on mine," the other agreed. "We had better report it."

On the command bridge, both Captain Gohrokov and Admiral Stirlitz felt somewhat uneasy. Neither officer had had any experience on a carrier so large. More than twice the size of previous Soviet carriers of the *Kiev* class, and the first nuclear carrier the Russians had constructed, the *Pravda* would have been difficult to operate under normal conditions. And in this squall, both men had their hands full.

"Comrade Admiral?" the radio officer reported. "Sonar informs us that a *Sierra*-class submarine is passing beneath us. It is not one of our picket boats."

Admiral Stirlitz waved his hand before his face in annoyance. "Who in the hell cares?" he replied impatiently. "Do not bother me about our own submarines. Have we found that American boat yet?"

The radio officer shook his head. "No word yet,

Comrade Admiral."

In sonar, the operators logged *Pocatello* on their charts as *Sierra*-17, the *K.E. Solovyov*. Under more normal circumstances, the log might have been checked against computer verification, and the operators would have found that the real *Solovyov* had reported in earlier that day sixteen hundred miles north off Point Navarin just south of the arctic circle.

The operators watched as *Pocatello* passed beneath them at two hundred feet. The isobars became blurred, and part of the image broke down, but the operators merely chalked that up to fast-moving undercurrents caused by the bad weather. In reality, it was their new ABD-7 bow-mounted sonar, which replaced the MF active and VDS suites of its predecessor, the non-nuclear *Kiev*-class CV. Working in conjunction with the BABD towed array, *Pravda* had the most advanced sonar capability in the Soviet Navy. Fortunately for *Pocatello*, the sonar operators were still trying to figure out their new equipment. This was their initial voyage with it, and its first test in such poor weather conditions.

Later, when the tapes were reviewed under less trying circumstances, flag officers would note that they had passed over an American boat using some type of acoustic cover. But for now, *Pocatello* passed on unobserved by all—except for one *Akula*-class Soviet submarine, four miles to the northeast.

The White House Situation Room was located fifty feet beneath the main structure, buried beneath a hundred tons of concrete. It had been constructed back in the late '50s, and had been done with so little fanfare, few members of the media had even known of its existence.

The room housed a large oval conference table, capable of seating eighteen dignitaries at one time. The president's command chair was on one side of the oval. A wealth of electronic gadgets had been added over the years, giving him direct contact with every necessary station around the globe. On the wall opposite from the president's chair, a large rear-mounted projection screen stood, capable of tracking fifteen different images simultaneously, including a duplication of the NORAD ready board, the Pentagon Situation Board, and Omaha's SAC Big Board.

Now seated around the table were several members of the National Security Council, the vice-president, Generals Shriner and Robert Dadow of the Air Force, the president's favorite translator, Hilde Galbraith— a woman nearing seventy and a long-time Kremlin watcher from Georgetown—both defense and state cabinet members, and the president's personal advisor on Russian affairs, Tanner Washington.

When Freeman entered the room, everyone stood. The president motioned for them to be seated as he moved around to his chair and sat. General Shriner checked the open line to the Pentagon Situation Room, the vice-president held the receiver on an open line to the Security Committee of both houses of Congress, and General Dadow checked his open line to Andrews where Air Force One was being warmed up as a precaution.

Freeman glanced at the pad and pencil neatly arranged in front of him. His hands were steady and his forehead dry. It was important, he knew, to show confidence at such a momentous occasion—a confidence he did not completely feel. DefCon Three had only been invoked thrice in the past thirty years. The first time had been during the Cuban missile crisis, the second when the *USS Pueblo* was captured by the North Koreans, and the last time was when the Soviets invaded Afghanistan. It was not an action to be taken lightly. Freeman had been struggling with the decision for hours. When running for the office, he had never seriously considered that one day he might find himself at a meeting such as this.

He took a deep breath and glanced around the table, staring grimly at each person for a moment before turning to the next. "Gentlemen," he began, then nodded toward Hilde Galbraith, "and lady. I am about to authorize our defense condition to be brought to level three."

Several around the table looked up at the president in surprise. The rest did not.

"Each of you has been apprised of what is at stake here," Freeman continued. "If the Soviet Union succeeds in acquiring the documents stolen from Kapalama yesterday morning—and it appears they may very well have accomplished that—then the entire Pacific Ocean is at risk. We cannot, and I believe all of you here would agree with this, we cannot allow that to happen."

The others glanced around the table at one another uncomfortably. No words needed to be spoken. DefCon Three was one step short of nuclear war.

"I have children," Freeman added quietly. "Six of them including a set of twins I love dearly. Three of them live here in Washington. It is not my desire or intention to start a war that will end their lives." He paused, pushing from his thoughts the image of nuclear missiles raining down upon his family. "Yet, it would be just as unthinkable," he continued, "to let the Soviets take the Pacific Ocean away from us and nullify our western defenses. If that were to happen, America's underbelly would be exposed and unprotected. That, too, would jeopardize the lives of my children."

There was no sound in the conference room. All eyes were glued on the president. Many had thoughts of their own families.

"The Joint Chiefs of Staff and I have been discussing all possible alternatives," Freeman said. "So far, no feasible plan has been presented." He looked around the room slowly. "Before I give General Shriner the order, does anyone have any suggestions?"

The people around the table glanced expectantly at one another. None spoke.

Freeman took a deep breath. He knew now there was no one to save him from the agony of his decision. "General," he said softly. Shriner turned to look at the president. "Tell your people to go to DefCon Three."

The Chairman of the Joint Chiefs of Staff passed the word along over the open line to the Pentagon. His voice was the only sound heard in the solemn chamber. When he was done, he looked up at the president and nodded. "We are at DefCon Three, Mr. President."

Freeman sighed once more and stared down at the blank pad in front of him. *My God*, Shriner thought, *he looks ten years older than he did this morning!* The people seated around the table stared at the president expectantly, worriedly.

Finally Freeman looked up. He glanced at the other occupants of the Situation Room. "Well, we've settled that," he said. "Now let's discuss our options before I call Premier Ognev."

At the headquarters for Strategic Air Command in

Omaha, Nebraska, Air Force Lt. General Jack Rickman, the highest ranking black officer in the military, ordered all of his reserve SAC bombers on the ground into the air.

In the bunkers at Black Mountain, Colorado, Maj. Gen. Sy Wordstein inserted his key on the missile readiness board. At the same instant his second in command, Brig. Gen. Marcus O'Reilly, did the same. Together they turned the switch that sent the ready codes along to the three hundred missile silos across North America. At these hard sites, officers and crews prepared for launch, their firing orders already beginning to be encoded and acted upon. All that remained now was the final-stage order.

In Brussels, the top U.S. NATO official, Gen. Curtis Chance, reported to the organization's secretary-general, Serpa Salazar of Portugal, informing him of the changing American defense condition. Salazar shook his head sadly. "It is madness," he declared. "Madness." But he immediately issued orders to the Military Council for all NATO forces to come to a heightened state of readiness.

At sea, carrier task forces turned into the wind in preparation for launching attack and protection flights. Men and women of American, NATO, and allied armed forces all over the world were gearing up for war. The signal was not lost on the Kremlin bosses in Moscow.

At Thule on the northwestern coast of Greenland, on the edge of Melville Bugt off Baffin Bay, two sections of Bomber Group 6 taxied out onto the runway and revved up their engines. Within seconds they were racing down the runway and lifting off into the air.

Inside the lead B-1b bomber, Capt. Richard Franks tore open his readiness orders. He checked the encoded instructions against his Day Code. Reading their instructions he let out a low whistle.

"What is it?" co-pilot 1st Lt. Pedro Gomez asked.

Franks looked Gomez square in the eye. "Our target is Leningrad," he said.

CHAPTER TWENTY-SIX

Not subject to ocean noise or biologics, Maggie O'Brien's SUBDACS screen was free of confusing images. But she could make out every nuclear vessel in the area clearly—including the one that was now turning directly toward them. "I'm picking up a submersible," she announced breathlessly. "He's changing course to the east of us!"

Caldwell had been too busy washing out conflicting images and registering course tracks for more than twenty vessels to have noticed it first. "Which one?" he asked, squinting at his CRT screen.

"He is coming onto our heading!"

There it was. "I see him," Caldwell confirmed.

Zimmer ran the input through the ID computer. "It's an *Akula*," he said excitedly.

Caldwell leaned in to the intercom mike. "Sonar to control. We have a curious *Akula* sniffing on our heels. Range four miles. Speed, eighteen knots. Just turned onto our heading."

"We're never going to get out of here alive," Ralston said, almost to himself, a cold shudder running through his body.

Caldwell shrugged. "Nobody lives forever," he

said calmly. Caldwell was not concerned. In fact, he was excited. His talents and energies had not been tested like this since they had run those two Soviet subs aground up near Alaska. And that had been over two years ago. Since then there had been nothing but one test exercise after another. It was all boring as hell. But now all that was changed. Now their lives were actually on the line. And nothing in the world could have made Jason Caldwell happier.

On CVN 68, Adm. Matthew Graham sat in command of the *U.S.S. Nimitz* and the battle group that made up the rest of his flotilla. His orders had been non-specific, but he was close enough to the Soviet task force west of Hokkaido to expect the next forty-eight hours to turn into a real shooting war. For that reason, he had put his group on battle alert.

Cmdre. Shelby Thames was the actual captain of *Nimitz*, and was personally responsible for the 5,684 officers and men aboard, including the 2,480 that were assigned to the air wing. But Graham commanded the group and was in charge of overall strategy. Each man had a cadre of officers to assist him, and in the captain's conference room below decks, ten of these men were meeting as representatives of *Nimitz*'s Management Team.

"Status report," Commodore Thames demanded.

Each man around the table had a folder in front of him listing all information on battle status and ship's readiness.

"We're doing thirty-two knots, five hours away from station," reported Capt. Jerry McFerson, the ship's executive officer.

"Four Hornets on catapult, four Tomcats on standby," Lt. Sam Teich, the air officer, added.

"Three sections of A-six Intruders on ready reserve on the swing deck." Teich was incredibly excited, as were all the junior officers below decks. This was their first real engagement and everyone eagerly awaited the word to go.

The more senior officers in the room glanced at the lieutenant somberly but said nothing. Each was remembering his first taste of battle. It had been both exciting and terrifying at the same time. None had slept well in anticipation, nor would many sleep easily this night.

"We have two Vikings in the air, flying loops to the north and south, two EA-six-Bs to the east and west," Lt. Tom Chasin, the air security officer, reported. It was his job to make sure the group was protected from above and from below the sea. "We have a KA-six tanker up, another on standby, and two Sea Kings in the air."

Thames looked out across the table, staring into the faces of the officers who would lead *Nimitz* if the battle call came. He knew each man intimately, and trusted their judgment. He was filled with pride knowing each would carry out his individual responsibility with the highest degree of professionalism. He glanced over at Lt. Leonard Sylk, the onboard security officer.

"Sonar shows we're clear at the present time," Sylk said, quickly picking up the ball. "We've logged several long-distance SWs, but nothing close enough to concern us. We have feeds both from our pickets and from an E-two Hawkeye."

A brimming coffee cup and a danish roll sat before each man, but no one seemed aware of them. Each officer's complete attention was riveted on either his folder or his captain.

When the information was completed, Thames

nodded to his men in thanks and cleared his throat. "When we reach station," he began slowly, "we may be asked to engage a superior force of Soviet combatants, including their new CTOL, the *Pravda*." He waited, observing their surprised reactions. Then he continued. "At the present time, there is no war, but we have been informed by Pearl that we are now at DefCon Three." There were a number of audible gasps around the table. Thames let that information sink in before going on. "As this meeting breaks up, we will go to full alert with all crews at battle stations."

The officers glanced around nervously at one another. "Does that mean we are operating under rules of engagement?" Tom Chasin asked finally.

"Yes!" Admiral Graham interjected firmly. "Definitely yes."

Adm. Gely Stirlitz looked out through the windows from his position on the command bridge of *Pravda*. He was directly below the radar station near the top of the stack and would have had an excellent view were it not for the storm conditions. He scowled as he listened to the chatter coming over the secured band from the battle group he managed.

This had only been intended as an exercise, he thought. *A show of force to prove to the West that the Motherland had the capability to control the Pacific*. For years the Americans had roamed the ocean like it was their own private lake. But now all that was changing. With the new shipyards along the Okhotsk, icebreakers that could keep the lanes open year 'round clear to the Chukchi Sea, and such power as *Pravda* now led, the Pacific would soon be Soviet domain.

"Comrade Admiral?"

Stirlitz looked up to see a young officer waiting patiently to be acknowledged. "Yes?"

"Captain sends his compliments, Comrade Admiral," the officer said respectfully, handing his superior a message. "There is an American battle group five hours to the south. They are steaming at flank speed in our general direction."

A smile crept slowly across Stirlitz's face. "How many surface combatants?" he asked.

"Seven, Comrade Admiral."

Seven. The admiral was doubly pleased. "Tell the captain I am bringing the group to full alert status."

"Yes, Comrade Admiral." The young officer turned and left.

Stirlitz motioned for an aide. "Radio the group to prepare for engagement."

"Very well, Comrade Admiral."

"Wouldn't it be nice, Feliks," Stirlitz added with obvious delight, "if the Americans force us into an open confrontation?"

"They would be no match for you, Comrade Admiral."

"How I'd love to give them a bloody nose!" Stirlitz had brought his battle group into the Pacific as part of what he believed to be a political statement. Not knowing the rationale behind the decision, he could only conclude that Moscow had finally decided to test America's claim to the Pacific—a claim most naval officers of the Far Eastern Red Banner Fleet found to be insulting.

The admiral turned to his aide. "Any word on the pickup?" he asked.

"None, Comrade Admiral."

Stirlitz nodded. "Gather my battle team together. We have plans to make."

*   *   *

Pocatello continued west, out from under the battle group steaming at flank speed to the south. Bertanelli, the eternal optimist, had faith that the mask would hold up and cover their escape. Now, as *Pocatello* ran toward the Friza Straits, only one thing concerned the captain—the *Akula* that dogged his tail.

"Helm," Bertanelli ordered, "increase speed to twenty-five knots."

"Twenty-five knots, aye."

Behind them the *Akula* was picking up speed.

"Helm. Slow to twenty knots."

"Twenty knots, aye."

The *Akula* did not slow down, but continued rapidly closing the gap between them.

The XO turned to face Bertanelli. "Our tubes are empty," Jamison reminded him grimly.

Bertanelli nodded. If he loaded torpedoes now, the noise might be detected on the Soviet submarine.

"Steady as you go," he ordered the helm.

The air in the boat seemed to thicken. The officer of the deck checked the life-support systems, but the electrolysis generators, distillers, and air-conditioners were all functioning normally. Still, the crew squirmed uncomfortably, their jumpers and tans becoming soaked with perspiration. All eyes and ears were attuned to sonar's constant updating of the *Akula*'s position.

"Three miles and closing," Caldwell announced over the intercom.

Bertanelli ducked into the sonar room. He glanced at Ralston who was biting his lip, and shaking with white-faced fear. "Take it easy son," the captain told him gently. Had there been time, Bertanelli might very well have relieved him of duty. He turned to Maggie. "O'Brien," he asked, "just how good is this

304

counterfeit signature of yours?''

"I think we're about to find out, Captain," she whispered.

"How close has it been tested?"

Maggie shook her head. "Not this close," she replied.

Bertanelli frowned. The *Akula* had narrowed the gap to under five thousand yards. It would no doubt be listening on its passive arrays and there would be little interference at this depth. If the counterfeit signature did not hold, the Russian could put a fish up *Pocatello*'s tail in a matter of minutes. And there wouldn't be a damn thing Bertanelli could do about it.

He stared intently at Maggie. "Opinion," he said.

Maggie squirmed uncomfortably in her chair. "I . . . I don't know, Captain."

Bertanelli's glare intensified. "Well, you'd better know," he said menacingly, impaling her with his cold blue eyes. "You designed it."

Maggie glanced nervously around the room, desperately searching for support from the others. But the looks on their faces told her she was on her own. "It should fool anyone at a distance," she muttered, staring at the desktop. For one of the few times in her life, Maggie realized, she was actually being successfully intimidated. "At least it was designed to. We are broadcasting the signature over a normal Soviet frequency." She hesitated.

"But?"

Maggie looked up, her eyes seeking and holding the captain's. "Our concern is whether or not the *Akula* is familiar with the boat we're faking."

For the briefest instant, an unfamiliar expression flashed across Bertanelli's face. Concern. Doubt? Fear? But then it was gone.

Maggie continued. "Maybe they know something about it that we don't. Maybe it had an overhaul since we taped this sound. Perhaps the *Akula* knows it is supposed to be in Oktohsk, or the Berings, or the Atlantic Ocean right now." She turned back to her instruments and shook her head. "For all we know, this boat could be listed on their records as being in dry dock, or even at the bottom of the ocean."

Bertanelli stared without speaking for a moment. "I can see where your system has a few flaws," he said finally.

Maggie felt a rush of anger passing through her. "SUBDACS, working in concert with other onboard systems, is merely meant to help an SSN on its mission," she replied defensively. "Nobody spoke about total dependency."

Bertanelli's expression softened. "That's the trouble with new systems," he said, only half aloud. "Sometimes you put too much faith in them."

"We are certainly committed now," Maggie snapped.

A sly smile crept across Bertanelli's face. "What the hell," he said optimistically. "It got us this far." He picked up the intercom mike. "Helm, steady as she goes," he transmitted.

"Helm, aye."

Caldwell looked up from his instruments. "Two miles," he said, "and closing."

In the Situation Room, the atmosphere around the conference table was charged. It had been a lively discussion, with strong positions being stated, both for and against any further show of force. Freeman had listened patiently, though few valuable suggestions had been offered.

"I've been sitting here patiently listening," the vice president, Kenneth Girard, interjected during a lull in the discussion. "And there is one thing I still don't understand." Freeman sighed, expecting the worst. The vice president had en forced on Freeman as a running mate in order for him to carry the East. Since being elected, they seldom spoke except for meetings of state where the presence of both was either expected or demanded, and they absolutely never conversed socially. Girard had said too many negative things about Freeman during the primaries for the presidency to easily forgive. It was just one of those situations where politics, indeed, do make strange bedfellows.

"What's that, Girard?" Freeman asked.

"Just why is it we're so concerned about the Russians moving into the Pacific?" he replied, standing up as if making a speech. "After all, we share the Atlantic, Mediterranean, and Indian oceans with them. They're even in the Persian Gulf, though we'd wish they weren't. What's so sacred about the Pacific?"

"The Pacific has always been an American ocean," Shriner responded quickly.

"And that's reason enough to go to war?" Girard asked. He turned to the others around the table, silently seeking their support.

"In the other oceans," Freeman said calmly, though underneath, his patience was wearing paper-thin, "there are several countries with military power that have a vested interest in the sea lanes. But in the Pacific, we stand alone. While the Pacific Rim countries have a vested interest, they do not have any real military or naval power. They could do little to help us maintain the sea lanes, or reacquire them if they were lost."

The vice president grunted and sat down. He would neither vote for escalation nor against it. He would play his agreed role and would not oppose the president publicly.

Freeman glanced around the room. "Anyone else?" he asked. When no one responded, he continued. "By now, Moscow will be well aware of our preparations." The president of the United States spoke quietly but firmly. "Their big boards will be lighting up, showing hundreds of our planes moving toward their air space. They will have confirmation that our ships, subs, and missiles are all gearing up for battle. It is time we called their hand."

The room suddenly fell deathly silent. This was the moment of truth. Freeman glanced over at Shriner inquisitively.

"We still have no word on *Pocatello*," the general replied without having to be asked the president's all-important question.

Freeman sighed and nodded to Hilde Galbraith. She immediately picked up the red phone between herself and the president and placed the instrument in a modem. She punched in a code and a computerized program activated the scramble circuits that would mask the call. "Ready, sir," she answered.

The president flipped a switch on a speaker box. "Mr. Chairman?" he began when a voice came on at the other end.

CHAPTER TWENTY-SEVEN

11:05 a.m. Honolulu/2105 Hours Zulu

The vibration aboard the *Suslov* had been getting steadily worse. Several items on the shelves in Yakunin's cabin were rattling and the small writing desk had already been shaken loose from the bulkhead. But through it all, Yakunin barely noticed. His mind was filled with thoughts of his dead friend Lev Savitsky, and of the useless orders which had cost him his life.

He had been conjuring up thoughts of brighter times when the two of them had sailed together on happier missions. Savitsky had been *tovarishchi*. It meant *Comrade*, friend—a Russian word of endearment long before the Communists had come to power and cannibalized it. A loyal friend was something hard to find in Russia these days. And Yakunin figured he had just lost the only one he would ever have.

For nearly a half hour, Yakunin had been lying on his bunk, staring at the ceiling while considering aborting the mission and returning home. He had been at sea most of his life. Perhaps now was the time to give it up.

"Lev, why didn't you just push the idiot overboard

and save yourself?" he cried out loud, slamming the wall next to the bunk with his fist. Yet, Yakunin knew his friend would never have even considered that possibility. Lev had been ordered to see the *zampolit* safely aboard the helicopter, and to Savitsky, responsiblity was everything.

The curtains to Yakunin's cabin were gently pushed aside. The captain looked up to see Felix Stelest poking his head in.

"Comrade Captain?" Stelest said tentatively.

"Yes *michman?*"

"We have been on this course for nearly an hour."

Yakunin sighed. He swung his legs off the side of the bunk and stood. He knew he had the lives of a hundred men in his hands and could no longer afford the time mourning his dead friend. He walked past Stelest and out into the narrow corridor, the *michman* following on his heels. As Yakunin entered the control room, Stelest announced that the captain was back on the bridge. All eyes turned to him, curious and concerned.

"Steady as she goes, helm," Yakunin ordered in a firm, confident voice. Several of the crew members smiled. Everyone on the bridge relaxed. Their captain was back in charge.

Yakunin turned to Aleksei Mezhova. "Anything on sonar?" he asked.

The officer shook his head. "I show no register of the American, Comrade Captain. But on this course, there are many submarines and surface vessels ahead. We are nearing the main Japanese Island of Honshu."

Yakunin nodded. He glanced around the control room. Most of the crew watched him eagerly, waiting for the order to change course. They knew their destination was Preznev, beyond the Friza Straits.

310

"If we wait much longer, Comrade Captain," Stelest volunteered, "the shaft will grow worse and the vibration noise will be heard for miles."

Yakunin returned Stelest's look with an icy stare of his own. The warrant officer looked away uncomfortably. Yakunin moved closer to his sonar officer. "Where is the American, Aleksei?" he asked. "I can feel him in my bones nearby."

Mezhova shrugged. "I show nothing."

"You have said that before," Yakunin snapped, "and each time he has shown up exactly where he was not supposed to be!"

Mezhova squirmed with discomfort. "Perhaps he knows our destination," he suggested.

"But how does he get ahead of us? His six-eighty-eight is slower than *Suslov*, he must slow occasionally to search for targets, and he is sailing nearer our home waters!" Yakunin's voice rose with frustration. "We should be opening a gap, not allowing him to close it!"

Mezhova cleared his throat. "If we make a run for Friza, Comrade Captain," he suggested carefully, "we will beat him there."

"He would have an hour headstart on us!"

"Only if he knew where we were headed," the sonar man said. "Besides, he was buried in the battle group. He could not have possibly escaped so easily. In fact, I'd be surprised if he escaped at all."

Yakunin shook his head. "Oh, he escaped all right," the captain responded bitterly. "Crazy Tony isn't yellow-flagged for nothing." He slammed his fist down on the pedestal, causing several crew members to jump. "Perhaps Govskaya was right. We should have sunk the devil when we had the chance!"

The sonar officer shook his head. "He is only a man, Comrade Captain," Mezhova replied, choosing

311

his words carefully. "He is no match for you. His boat is inferior and his luck is nil. He had two chances at us and missed both times. Why not forget him and take us home?"

"I see the daily political meetings are having their effect on you, Aleksei," Yakunin said with bitter sarcasm. He turned to the warrant officer. "And you too, Felix. Our technology is nowhere near that of the Americans. Their boats are quieter, their sonar better, and their training superior. I've even heard they have double shields around their reactors, which exposes them to less radiation in their submarines than they would get walking down the street on a normal sunny day!" Yakunin leaned back wearily against the pedestal. "It is no secret that all our lives are shortened by the radiation we receive on *Suslov*."

The two officers were shocked. While most submariners knew of the danger, no one ever talked about it. Radiation was something you just ignored. Stelest glanced at the seamen in the control room. From their stunned expressions he could see that each had overheard. "Perhaps we should talk of something else, Comrade Captain," Stelest suggested warily.

Yakunin looked around the room at the faces of his crew. The captain sighed. "Perhaps so, Felix." He turned to the helm. "Come right full rudder. Navigation, plot me a course through the Jakatirny Straits."

Stelest glanced at Mezhova in alarm, then turned back to Yakunin. "We have been ordered to stay away from those Japanese waters," he protested.

"I know, my dear Felix. But I believe the American is lying in wait for us outside Friza. We will simply change the game plan and outflank him." He rubbed his arm. The pain was still there, but now it had

312

lessened considerably. Yakunin smiled slightly. "How I'd like to see the look on the American's face when we don't show up this time."

Bertanelli stuck his head into the sonar room.

"One mile and closing," Caldwell said, aware of the captain's presence.

"He'll be abeam of us in five minutes," Zimmer added, looking up. He could feel the sweat running down his arms.

"He'll veer off," Ralston said with false assurance, but his chalk-white complexion betrayed his true feelings. "There's no reason for him to come close in."

A chilling thought stopped Bertanelli in his tracks. "Unless," he suggested, his voice suddenly dry as the Sahara, "he thinks we're disabled."

Everyone in the room swung around to face their captain.

Understanding dawned on Caldwell first. His eyes opened wide. "Do they have gertrudes?" he asked.

"That or something like them," Bertanelli said as he ducked quickly out of sonar and hurried down to control. He knew he had no time to lose. "Willie!" he shouted, racing into the control room. "Check the files and see who on board can speak Russian. And make it *fast!*"

In the *Pocatello*'s torpedo room, Seaman Second Class Mavery Ellis lay in his bunk among the torpedo racks, studying the centerfold of a *Playboy* magazine intently. Few on board would choose to sleep here, preferring the three-tier curtained bunks forward. But for everyone to have his own individual bed,

313

some would have to put up with the torpedo room. A tall, gangling kid of twenty-two, Ellis was the only one on board who did not mind. In fact, he preferred the greater privacy. And his fellow crew members, believing Ellis to be an unpredictable flake, were perfectly happy with any arrangement that kept him out of the mainstream population. Ellis's bunk opened into a locker below, so there were few interruptions. And if general quarters was sounded, Mavery was only five feet from his duty station.

The communications telephone buzzed and Chief Petty Officer Crippin sauntered over to answer it. Listening to the command on the other end, the CPO turned slowly and stared at Ellis. "Are you sure?" Crippin asked, scratching his head in astonishment. He nodded once at the answer, then placed the instrument back in its wall cradle. He exhaled, shaking his head in disbelief. "Ellis!" Crippin called.

The seaman peered up over the edge of the magazine.

"The captain wants to see you in the control room, on the double!"

"Hey, Mave," one of his buddies yelled. "Now's your chance to tell the captain what he's doing wrong."

"Yeah, Mave," called another. "You been telling us for days that this boat can't get along without you. Now's your chance."

Ellis smiled. He saluted and carefully refolded the pull-out page.

"He wants you *now*, Ellis!" Crippin yelled.

"All right, all right! Hold your water, Chief." Mavery swung his legs over the bunk and dropped down heavily to the deck. "I'm coming."

"Make it fast. The XO said the captain needs

someone who can speak Russian."

"Mavery? Speak Russian?" a nearby seaman scoffed, looking up from the solitaire game spread out in front of him across his bunk. "Hell, I didn't know he could speak English!"

"Funny," Ellis said. "Hardy har har." He started for the hatch and then turned back. "And don't anyone touch my *Playboys*," he ordered. "Every time one of you goofoffs takes a gander, I find saliva all over the pictures."

A seaman tossed his pillow at Ellis as he passed by. In less than a minute, the torpedoman was entering the control room for only the second time ever in his short career aboard *Pocatello*. Ellis performed a rough imitation of standing at attention and saluted. "Seaman Second Cl—" he began, only to be immediately interrupted by Capt. Tony Bertanelli.

"The files say you speak Russian," the captain said gruffly.

The seaman eyed Bertanelli warily. "Well, yes, sir, I do."

"How well?"

Ellis shrugged. "Well enough, I suppose."

"Enough to fool the Soviet sub coming alongside us?"

Ellis's eyes became two saucers. "You mean . . ." He gulped hard. "You mean you want me to speak to a *real* Russian?"

Bertanelli glared at the young seaman. "Well?"

Ellis shuffled his feet nervously. "No."

"No?" Bertanelli bellowed. "You mean you won't do it?"

"I mean I *can't* do it!" Ellis croaked. "I couldn't fool a real Russian."

Bertanelli's glare seemed to burn itself into Mavery Ellis's brain. "Well, son, you're going to have to."

"But I've never studied Russian, sir!" Ellis whined, beads of sweat breaking out across his forehead. "My mother's parents were Russian. They taught me when I was a boy. But I haven't spoken Russian in years!"

The sound of an approaching propeller could be heard distinctly through the hull. Ellis glanced up nervously and listened.

Bertanelli placed his hand paternally on the young man's shoulder. "I could tell you it'll be a piece of cake, Ellis," he said, his voice softening. "But I'm not going to bullshit you. The survival of everyone on this boat depends on your carrying this off."

"I'll never get away with it, sir!" Mavery insisted, his voice shaking.

"Yes, you will, son," the captain assured him. "Because I say you will." Bertanelli turned to Jamison. "Get ready to lower a gertrude."

"Aye."

Caldwell's voice burst through on the intercom. "Sonar to control. He's right next door."

The sound of the Russian boat was almost deafening through the *Pocatello*'s hull. A microphone was shoved in Mavery's trembling hands.

"I've heard tell you're quite a character, Ellis," Bertanelli said, seating him in front of the transmission equipment. "Just consider this a practical joke. Surely you've pulled a few in your day?"

The young seaman smiled faintly. His complexion had turned an interesting shade of green.

"Sonar to control. They've lowered a gertrude."

"Control to sonar," Bertanelli radioed back. "Pipe it in, Jason."

Suddenly a Russian voice filled the room, coming in over the speaker mounted in the bulkhaed. Involuntarily, all eyes swung upward.

316

Bertanelli leaned down to Ellis. "What's he saying, son?"

"I, uh, I think he's, uh . . ." The terrified seaman turned from the speaker and looked at his commanding officer, his eyes wide and frantic. "Geeze, Captain! What if I'm wrong?"

"You won't be, son," Bertanelli assured him firmly. "Now what'd he say?"

Ellis took a deep breath. "He says he's the *Pronin*, and I think he wants to know if anything is wrong."

Bertanelli glanced at Jamison who sighed heavily. The captain turned back to the young torpedoman. "Tell him our electronics is breaking down, that we're having trouble with internal communication. Tell him our inertial navigation system is not functioning accurately. Tell him—"

"Hell, I don't know those kinds of words!" Ellis blurted out. Then, remembering who he was talking to, he added quietly, "Sir."

Bertanelli's words were gentle and slow. "Then tell him what you do know, son. Just make him believe we're fine and he can go on about his business."

Ellis slowly brought the microphone up to his mouth and began nervously, *"V.N. Pronin, u nas—"*

"The button!" Jamison hissed. "Press the goddamned button!"

Flustered, the young seaman looked down at the microphone. Bertanelli put his hand on Ellis's shoulder and squeezed reassuringly. "Everything'll be fine," he whispered.

Ellis nodded. He cleared his throat, depressed the button and began to speak.

In the Soviet War Room, on the floor beneath

317

Ognev's office, the Russian premier and several of the U.S.S.R.'s highest-ranking officers and Politburo officials sat behind a long table. In front of Ognev was an awkward-looking electronic device with a telephone on top.

Ognev had gathered the others as witnesses before calling the American president. He wanted them to see how he had Freeman on the run. It never hurt, Ognev knew, to strengthen one's own position. The lesson of Khrushchev's failure in Cuba had not been lost on him.

"Mr. President." Ognev spoke firmly into the mouthpiece of the telephone. "You must turn back your bombers that are presently headed for Russia. Otherwise we will be forced to shoot them down."

Halfway across the world, in the White House Situation Room, President Colin Freeman glanced at those seated around the table with him. "Mr. Chairman," he replied soberly. "As you must already know, the United States is at DefCon Three." He paused. Though Freeman did not want to be the one to start a nuclear war, he knew he could not lose this test of will to the Soviets. The fate of the free world hung in the balance. "The next step, if you continue to up the ante, will be nothing short of World War Three. Is that what you wish?"

"No one wishes nuclear war, Mr. President." Ognev's voice was harsh and demanding. "But your actions have left me no choice except to dispatch my own bombers toward America. I warn you now, turn back or the result will be total destruction!"

Freeman glanced at Shriner. The general sat ramrod straight, his ear glued to his own telephone. "Mr. Chairman," Freeman responded, his own voice firm but reasonable—it could be fatal giving in to anger at this all-important juncture. "Need I remind you that this present crisis is your doing? It was one of your people who stole top-secret files that we cannot possibly allow to reach the hands of your military."

"I believe it was your own officer who stole your documents, Mr. President," the premier corrected.

Freeman's blood began to boil but he kept his fury in check. "An officer recruited and paid by your people, Mr. Chairman. Not only that, but you've sent a carrier battle group into the Pacific to threaten our shipping."

"Your *Nimitz* carrier group is only a few hundred miles from our shores, Mr. President. How do you feel the *Pravda*, thousands of miles from America, is a threat?" Ognev looked at those around him, smiling confidently. "If you would like to avert this nuclear war you are building toward, you could start to show good faith by turning your *Nimitz* carrier away from our shores."

"We will turn the *Nimitz* around only when you send *Pravda* back into the Okhostk Sea!"

Angered, Ognev yelled into the receiver. "We will withdraw *Pravda* when you turn your planes around!"

"And we will turn our planes around when you return those documents to us . . . *unopened!*"

General Shriner was delighted, feeling tremendous pride that his commander-in-chief displayed the inner and outer strength necessary for true greatness. It frightened the general, however, that the Russians were not caving in over the threat implied by DefCon Three.

"You are threatening the peace and safety of the entire world with your stubbornness!" Ognev screamed.

Freeman forced himself to be calm. He had learned a long time ago that when your opponent started to yell, the most successful tactic was to lower your own voice. "It is you, not me, Mr. Chairman, that has upset the balance of power in the world," he replied softly. "When you stole the documents and sent your battle group into the Pacific, you tipped the scales. It is obvious we cannot, under any circumstances, allow that to happen."

Ognev was livid. He had gathered his supporters and detractors with the single purpose of showing his strength and solidifying his position. Now the American was undermining that effort. He slammed his fist on the table in anger. "I'm giving you fair warning, Mr. President," he threatened ominously. "If your planes continue on their present course, I will consider it an act of war and shoot them down!"

"And I will give *you* fair warning, Mr. Chairman," Freeman replied, his voice hard as steel. "Unless that submarine carrying the stolen documents surfaces and turns the papers over to us immediately, I will order more planes into the sky and send battle orders to our nuclear missile submarines. We will not stand by and let you take over any more of this globe!"

For a moment Ognev was unable to speak. His entire strategy had been based on the assumption that Freeman was too inexperienced, too vulnerable to respond quickly and with strength. The man had caught him off guard—and in front of Ognev's own people. He knew he could not allow himself to lose control of his emotions, something that had hastened Khrushchev's downfall. "Mr. President," the premier responded after a slight pause, forcing a false note of calm confidence into his voice. "It would not be wise for you to escalate the present condition any further. Your submarines in the Pacific are exposed, your planes are targeted, and the Soviet Union has three times the missiles you possess. Any confrontation would leave America in ashes while we, though devastated, would survive."

Freeman saw an opening. It was not much, but the premier was sending a signal. War must be avoided. He thought quickly, trying to determine how far he could go, how much he could get, how much he had to forfeit. Everything, he knew, depended on the success, or failure, of the U.S.S. *Pocatello*.

CHAPTER TWENTY-EIGHT

11:20 a.m. Honolulu/2120 Hours Zulu

"*V.N. Pronin, u nas prudnosti komunikatzy,*"
Mavery Ellis began. "*Vse' drugi'e khorosho.*"

The silence in *Pocatello*'s control room was
deafening.

"What did you tell him?" Bertanelli asked.

"That we are having communication problems."

Every man in the control room held his breath,
waiting for the Russian to reply. Several seamen
crossed their fingers. Bertanelli clutched the telephone in his hand. He already had the torpedo room
on standby and Crippin was awaiting his instructions.

"*Pon'atno,*" a deep baritone voice boomed over the
loudspeaker. "*Kakaya probl'ema u vas?*"

"He wants to know the nature of our problem."
Ellis's eyes seemed to be pleading with Bertanelli for
salvation. "How'm I supposed to answer that?"

Relief broke out on seamen and officers' faces
alike. "By damn!" Jamison said, grinning broadly.
"He thinks he's talking to a Soviet submarine!"

Bertanelli leaned over and whispered in Ellis's ear.
"Fake it," he said, then turned to Lieutenant
Lamonica. "Fade the signal in and out. Make it

sound like it's breaking up." Bertanelli patted Ellis affectionately on the shoulder. "Just nod to him when you need help."

The communications officer adjusted his controls as Ellis took another deep breath and continued. *"Probl'ema kotoraya u nas . . ."* Ellis nodded to Lamonica. The officer spun the dials causing static on the line. Ellis put out a hand, then said, *". . . i eto d'el'ayet shto . . ."* Again he motioned to Lamonica once more. The longer Ellis spoke, the more confident he became. Soon he was babbling on happily, with a big smile on his face. *". . . nam nado . . ."* More static. *"s posl'ednevo raza my . . . somals'a i nam nado b'ylo . . ."*

"Don't overplay your hand," Bertanelli whispered. "That should do."

Ellis nodded. He motioned for Lamonica to clear the line once again. *". . . znachit', my vplyv'om za r'emontom."* He lifted his finger off the button and grinned at Bertanelli. "Damn if this isn't fun, Captain."

"Let's not make a command performance out of it, Ellis," Bertanelli said. "The object is to get rid of him."

"I told him we were going in for repairs."

Suddenly the Russian's voice boomed over the speaker once again, requesting to talk to the boat's captain.

Ellis did not even hesitate for a second. *"Kapitan zabol'el v'en'ericheskim bol'eznyu,"* he said.

The Russian chuckled. *"Posadit' v galoshu."*

Ellis glanced at Bertanelli. *"Da,"* he said, smiling.

"Khorosho," the voice replied. *"Pozvolim vam vkhodit'."*

Ellis nodded. *"Do svidoniya,"* he said, then released the button. *"Kogda rak svisn'et,"* Ellis mumbled half aloud. Bertanelli looked at the sailor quizzically. "I said when crayfish whistle," he explained. Realizing he was using a Russian idiom, Mavery grinned and added, "He thinks he'll meet us in Preznev. I said when pigs fly."

"Sonar to control," Caldwell's voice announced over the intercom. "He's reeling in his gertrude."

The unmistakable sounds of poppet valves, vents, and steam buildup could be heard through the *Pocatello*'s hull. The propeller sounds became louder as the *Pronin* picked up speed. Everyone in the control burst into spontaneous cheering. Ellis gloried in the applause. He took a deep bow in all four directions. "It was nothing, really," he said, with feigned modesty. And in his best Yogi Bear voice he added, "The American seaman is smmarrrter than the average Russian."

The applause turned to laughter.

Admiral Sward, standing next to Jamison, shook his head. "I don't know how he does it, but that captain of yours is the luckiest man alive."

The XO grinned. "He does it with mirrors, sir."

Sward glanced at Jamison and smiled for the first time since the *Pocatello* had been "sunk" by the *Batfish*. Maggie O'Brien appeared in the doorway, drawn to the control room by the raucous sounds of celebration.

"And now, for my encore act," Ellis was saying. He launched into a zany soft-shoe routine, then did a few Groucho Marx one-liners, finally segueing into Charlie Chaplin's famous penguin walk. The crew roared their approval.

"It's amazing," Sward said to Jamison

"What is, sir?"

"How this boat seems to attract all the weirdos."

Ellis finished his routine, dipped low, and motioned for approval. The crew roared and hooted.

"All right, men," the officer of the deck called above the din. "Back to work. We're still at risk out here."

Bertanelli stepped up beside Ellis and patted him on the back. "That was a fine job, seaman. You saved our hide."

Mavery grinned. "A piece of cake, Skipper."

"What was all the chatter about?"

"They wanted to speak to the captain."

"And?"

The seaman shrugged. "I told them you were sick in bed with a severe case of the clap."

The crew chuckled. Maggie smiled from the hatchway. Bertanelli squinted, frowned, and finally smiled. He roared with laughter and the crew happily joined in. "And what did he say to that?" Bertanelli asked, clasping Ellis on the shoulder.

"He said you were in the galoshes. Uh, that means that you must be embarrassed."

"I get the drift." Bertanelli smiled. "Better get back to your duty station, now."

"One last thing, sir," Ellis said, turning back from the hatchway. "He thought this boat was the *K.E. Solovyov*." Ellis disappeared into the corridor. Bertanelli turned back to see Maggie staring at him. He flashed her a winning smile.

"How about joining me for a cup of coffee, O'Brien?"

She smiled, then shook her head. "I can't. I'm still on duty."

"I'll talk to the captain."

"It won't do any good. I've heard he's a hard man. A stickler for protocol." She met his eyes squarely. "Besides, how would it look if he relieved just one person from a watch?"

"I see your point." He turned to Jamison. "Willie, relieve the Gold Team from their sonar watch. We're going to have some down time 'till we reach Friza."

"Aye, Captain."

"And Willie? Have Jason start work on that little job I asked him about."

"Aye."

Three minutes later Maggie was sitting across from Bertanelli in the wardroom. She had tried, with little success, to straighten her hair, shoving errant strands up under the baseball cap she had donned to hide her goo-ruined hairdo.

"You might have warned me about my appearance," she said self-consciously, referring to her initiation at Caldwell's hands.

Bertanelli laughed. "It was too good to interfere with," he said.

"Might as well have gone in there stark naked," Maggie smirked good-naturedly. "Couldn't have been any worse."

"Every new recruit is initiated on *Poco*."

Maggie leaned forward. "And what was your initiation?" she asked, her voice low and conspiratorial.

Bertanelli sat up as if stung. "Me?" he exclaimed. "Don't be silly. I'm the captain."

Maggie peered at him over the rim of her coffee cup. "I see," she said impishly. She took a sip of the steaming liquid and smiled.

Bertanelli stared at her across the table. As he did so, Maggie became suddenly self-conscious. She knew, after more than thirty hours, her makeup had to be a shambles. And her hair, whatever wasn't pushed up under the baseball cap, was hanging down limp and straight. I would kill for some lipstick, she thought. Out loud, she stammered,

"I . . . I must be an absolute mess," unconsciously tucking another strand under the cap.

Bertanelli smiled at her reassuringly. "Actually," he said softly, "you look quite beautiful."

Maggie blushed. "Careful, Captain," she said, her voice hushed. "Your ship might get jealous."

"Yes, she's a hard taskmaster," he said, sipping his coffee. For a moment there was an awkward silence. "Miss O'Brien," Bertanelli began again, "I asked you to join me because I wanted to compliment you on the fine job you did for—"

"For being a woman?"

He stared at her intently. "For your first time on the screens."

Maggie looked down at the tabletop. "Oh," she said, embarrassed.

"Tell me, O'Brien, are you stoop-shouldered?"

Maggie snapped her head back up and blinked. "Am I what?"

"The weight of that chip you carry around has got to affect your posture."

Despite herself, Maggie smiled. "I guess I had that coming," she said.

"You certainly did." He eyed her speculatively for a moment. "Has it really been that difficult for you?" he asked.

Maggie sighed. "It has been an uphill climb all the way," she said. "At MIT I was told I had to be better than the four hundred male engineers to even get a consideration. I finished second in my class, and still didn't get one of the first ten job offers. At Consolidated Dynamics, I had to outperform every man in my classification. In three years I had secured five patents for them, and yet was passed over twice for management promotions. By the time I got to Rockwell, I had learned to play the game. Now, no one takes advantage of me."

Bertanelli regarded her evenly. "I'll bet they don't," he said.

She smiled self-consciously. "You must think I'm hard as nails."

Bertanelli stared at her for several seconds without speaking. "We play hardball out here, O'Brien," he said firmly. "One wrong move and a lot of people could die. No one wants a softie."

"That sounds like one of your left-handed compliments."

Bertanelli smiled. His tone softened. "What I mean is, out here no one cares whether you're a man or a woman, black or white, Jew or gentile. All that matters is that you do your job."

"You said this was a man's world down here."

"And so it is. At least, it certainly cannot be a co-ed world."

"Why is that?"

Bertanelli sipped his coffee before continuing. "We're at sea for sixty to seventy days at a time," he said. "We live in cramped quarters. The crew spends one third of their day off duty. Despite the fact the Navy has gone to great lengths to provide amusements, such as libraries, television, VCRs, movies, stereo, and the like, seamen usually get pretty bored on these two-month voyages." Bertanelli paused for emphasis. "One more form of entertainment would not be wise."

Maggie felt the hair on the back of her neck bristle. "I wasn't thinking of prostitutes," she said sharply.

"Neither was I, O'Brien," he continued. "In the space of this small world, with male egos being what they are, and male-female attraction being what it is, it wouldn't take much for boy and girl to get together."

Maggie shook her head emphatically. "I think you're being a little overly dramatic," she insisted. "Men and women can work together without becoming emotionally involved."

"On the beach, maybe, but not down here. Hell, O'Brien, half my crew is probably already in love with you. And most haven't even seen you yet!"

Maggie threw her hands up in frustration. "Now you're exaggerating!" she exclaimed.

The cook stopped by with a plate of sandwiches. Bertanelli glanced up at him and, as if on cue, they both smiled. "A pool was started in maneuvering," the captain said, reaching for a sandwich. "It pays off to the first man who lays a claim on you. At last report, ninety of the crew had put up twenty bucks apiece to enter."

Maggie stared at him in disbelief.

Bertanelli took a bite of his sandwich. After swallowing, he went on. "Another pool was begun in engineering. It pays off to the first man who kisses you. Or vice-versa. That one's only five bucks. The crew figures that should be a piece of cake."

Maggie's eyes opened wide. "You can't be serious!" she said.

"That's not the latest one," the cook interjected, a coffeepot poised over Maggie's mug. "Maintenance has a pool on who will be the first to corner Miss O'Brien in the, uh, head."

Maggie shook her head. "You . . . You're making this all up!" she sputtered.

The cook grinned. "Not at all, Miss. I put ten dollars on it myself."

Bertanelli laughed out loud as the cook turned and left the mess.

Maggie's face turned as red as a beet. "You put him up to that!" she accused.

Bertanelli picked up his napkin and wiped the tears from the corners of his eyes. "Face it, O'Brien. Six thousand years of recorded history is against you."

Maggie's eyes narrowed. "Tell me, Captain," she challenged, "are you in any of the pools?"

"Me?" Bertanelli struggled to keep his merriment in check. He feigned a frown. "How would it look if the captain was competing with the enlisted men?"

"Are you in the twenty-dollar pool, or the five-buck one?" she asked defiantly, her lips pursed and pouting.

Bertanelli's eyes were drawn to her lips. He suddenly wondered what it would be like to kiss Maggie O'Brien. "It's a long time 'til payday," he said.

A Russian seaman heading down the corridor in front of the cabin where Travis had previously been kept in detention walked a few steps past the door, then halted abruptly. *Was there not a crewman standing guard at that door earlier?* he thought to himself. Curiously, he placed his hand on the knob and slowly opened the door.

A moment later in the control room, Felix Stelest replaced the telephone on its cradle. "Captain," he said to Yakunin breathlessly, "your presence is urgently requested in the aft crew's quarters."

Within minutes, Yakunin was standing in the doorway to the small cabin where Colonel Turbin lay in a pool of blood, and a young crewman lay dead. Maj. Ivan Dorofeev, the boat's surgeon, was kneeling over the colonel. Behind Yakunin several seamen craned their necks to get a better look at the carnage within.

"Back to your duty stations," the captain ordered sternly.

The seamen reluctantly drifted off.

"How is he?" Yakunin asked the doctor. "What happened in here?"

Dorofeev glanced over his shoulder and sighed. "Utemov there is dead," he said, indicating the seaman. "He was stabbed. The colonel here is alive, but only barely. Also stabbed, once in the leg and once in the chest. With this." He handed the captain the knife.

Yakunin said nothing as he inspected the weapon.

Dorofeev shook his head. "I must get this man to sick bay immediately."

Yakunin nodded. He stepped aside as two corpsmen hurried in and placed Turbin on a stretcher. After they had left, he turned the knife over in his hands. It was not a Soviet weapon.

CHAPTER TWENTY-NINE

11:37 a.m. Honolulu/2137 Hours Zulu

Premier Ognev looked up from the telephone as an officer entered the room and strode over to Istomin and handed the field marshall a note. As Istomin read silently, from thousands of miles away, the American president began speaking once more.

"Mr. Chairman," Freeman said, "we cannot continue to play a game like two spoiled little children. A mistake here could reduce the world to ashes."

Ognev grunted. "There need be no mistake, Mr. President," he replied. "You have considered the Pacific Ocean an American lake for years. But now you must realize that is no longer the case. The Pacific is open to whoever sails in it . . . and can hold it! I would advise you—"

Istomin signaled the premier, shaking his head.

Ognev glared at the officer. "Excuse me a moment, Mr. President," the premier said, and hurriedly broke the connection. He turned to Istomin. "Well?" he asked impatiently. "What is it, Field Marshall?"

Istomin's expression was grim. "The pickup of the documents was aborted," he said.

"What?" Ognev's face became twisted with anger,

his pig-like eyes blazing. "You mean to tell me we do not have those documents?"

Istomin shook his head. "Not yet. But they are still aboard the *Suslov*."

The Politburo members sitting around the table turned to each other and began murmuring among themselves. A high-ranking official turned to the premier. "Comrade Chairman," he asked, "is there a problem?"

Ognev felt the control he had been attempting to master all throughout his conversation with the American president beginning to crumble. He turned to the minister, forcing what he hoped was a confident smile. "No problem, Comrade," Ognev assured him. "Just a slight setback."

The Russian premier swung around and glared at Istomin, his pig-eyes red with rage. "And just where is the *Suslov*?" he hissed.

The field marshall felt all attention in the room focused in his direction. "We lost contact with her after the explosion," he explained, his voice firm and even.

Ognev's face burned a fiery crimson. "What explosion, damnit?" he demanded.

"An American submarine attacked *Suslov*, but we believe our boat escaped."

Ognev slammed his fist down on the table so heavily that those sitting around it jumped. "Damn the devil, Istomin! I told you I had to have those documents before I talked with the American president. You said they were aboard our fleet. Now you're telling me we don't have them!"

Istomin felt the sweat beading up on his forehead. Still he remained calm. "It is only a matter of time, Comrade Chairman," he assured the Russian leader.

Ognev's eyes flamed and his nostrils flared. "You

have been saying that for hours!" he screamed. "But we still do not have the documents!"

Istomin glanced around the table and noticed the head of the KGB staring at him intently—a look that warned the field marshall that it would not be wise to remind the premier that it was a KGB foul-up that had caused the problem, not Istomin's own. The field marshall nodded slightly and turned away. "I promise you that we will have the documents very shortly, Comrade Chairman," he said.

Ognev glared at the officer, holding his tongue as he fought down his murderous anger. When he had finally gotten control, he picked up the telephone and re-established the connection with Washington. "Mr. President," he said flatly, his voice toneless. "I will have to call you back. Something has come up." And without waiting for a response, Ognev once again broke the connection.

In Washington, Colin Freeman carefully placed the telephone back in its cradle. He looked around the table, thoughtfully. "Opinions?" he asked.

"It sounds like he might have gotten some news he wasn't expecting," Rifkin said.

"Perhaps that explosion picked up by satellite was the Russian submarine," Shriner suggested. "Maybe Ognev was just informed that they don't have the stolen documents after all."

"Perhaps," Freeman said quietly. "Perhaps."

Colonel Turbin lay on a flat bunk in the *Suslov*'s medical bay. Blood bags hooked to a metal tree were attached to his body by clear plastic lines conducting the life-saving liquid into his veins. His face was chalk-white and there were dark circles under his eyes, but he was breathing. Dorofeev was inspecting the patched-up wound in the patient's chest as Yakunin entered.

"How is he?" the captain asked.

Dorofeev looked up from his work. His gloved hands were stained with blood, as was the apron covering his uniform. "The knife entered the pectoralis minor, just below the subclavian artery. He is very lucky to be alive."

Yakunin stared down at the prostrate figure. "Can he talk?"

The doctor frowned. "Is it necessary?" he asked.

Yakunin nodded. "I want to know what happened."

"Don't you have enough to worry about right now, Comrade Captain? Can't port authority take care of this?"

"I want to know who is running loose on my boat knifing my crew."

"Perhaps they knifed each other."

"Perhaps. Can he talk?"

The doctor sighed. "Just for a minute," he insisted. "The colonel has lost a lot of blood. Only the devil knows how long he lay in that cabin."

Yakunin looked up in surprise. "You mean this didn't just recently happen?"

Dorofeev shook his head. "As far as I can determine," he said, "Utemov has been dead for two or three hours."

Yakunin's eyes widened with understanding. "Can you wake him?" he asked the doctor.

"I believe he is awake, Comrade Captain," Dorofeev replied. "Or at least partially. He should respond to his name."

Yakunin bent close to Turbin's ear. "Colonel?" he

335

whispered. When there was no response, the captain spoke again. "Colonel Turbin?"

The patient's eyes fluttered open.

"This is Captain Yakunin, Colonel. Tell me what happened to you?"

Turbin opened his mouth, but no words came out. His eyelids closed again.

Yakunin put his hand on Turbin's good arm and pressed slightly. "Who did this to you?" he asked forcefully.

Turbin's words were barely a whisper. "The . . . American . . ." the KGB man said.

Yakunin jerked upright. *The American?* he thought. He had been so certain it was Govskaya. He had hoped for a confirmation so he could close the log on the matter. But the American!

Angrily Yakunin turned and stormed out of sick bay.

Bertanelli showed Maggie to his cabin. "You can catch some sleep here," he suggested.

She nodded her thanks and leaned against the door jamb, nearly dead on her feet. "What about you?" she asked.

Bertanelli smiled warmly. "I'll catch a few winks elsewhere. This is the only single cabin on the boat."

"But—"

"Go on," he insisted. "The sleep will do you good. Besides, I'll need you well rested when we get to the Straits."

"I'll expect you to write a glowing report on my SUBDACS when we get back to Pearl," Maggie said, as she crossed to the bunk and lay down on top of the covers.

"Of course," he replied.

For several seconds neither spoke. Each knew there was a strong possibility they might never see Pearl Harbor again.

"It performed well?" Maggie asked groggily.

Bertanelli smiled. "It performed better than well."

"Then you would want it permanently installed?"

"I can't imagine sailing without it."

Maggie sat up and looked at the captain. "We are talking about my equipment, aren't we?" she asked softly.

"Of course," he replied. Their eyes met and held. Seconds passed.

"Well, I'll be going," Bertanelli finally said. But he didn't move. Something about this woman was stirring up old, long-dead feelings. Feelings he thought he had buried long ago.

Maggie stood up and crossed to Bertanelli. "I'd better turn in," she said. She reached up and touched his arm. Bertanelli felt an electric charge course through him. "Thank you for your cabin," Maggie said, her voice as gentle as a summer breeze.

"It'll be ten hours before we reach the Straits." The captain could think of nothing else to say.

Their eyes held for a long moment. Then Maggie turned and crossed once again to the bunk. Bertanelli watched her for a second, then stepped outside and shut the door quietly. He shook his head. *She's growing on you,* he warned himself.

Freeman turned to Hilde Galbraith, the interpreter. "Did you pick up anything?" he asked her.

She looked around the table at the officers and presidential advisors. Ognev's sudden departure had left them all in a state of shock.

"Well, sir," Hilde Galbraith said, "I noted a

hesitancy, almost an irritation in his tone before he disconnected."

"Uncertain?" Tanner Washington asked.

Hilde shook her head. "More like frustration," she replied.

"Maybe he's having second thoughts about tangling with our Navy," Admiral Olsen suggested.

"More likely," Rifkin said, "he does not yet have the documents. I think we can safely assume *Pocatello* has kept the transfer from occurring."

"But for how long?" Freeman asked. "How long before we have a go-no-go decision on our bombers, General?"

Shriner glanced at the clock. "Ten, maybe eleven hours," he responded.

The entire room fell silent.

High over eastern Greenland, Group 6 out of Thule raced across the skies at forty-two thousand feet making sixteen hundred kilometers per hour. Its maximum weight of two hundred forty-nine tons included twenty-four internal and fourteen external SRAM, eight internal and fourteen external ALCM missiles. It also included eight guided nuclear bombs in the aft ejection rack.

"Where are we, Pete?" Capt. Richard Franks asked.

"Thirty minutes till we clear land," Pedro Gomez replied. They had flown a circuitous route up over the ice cap to confuse Russian radar, then turned east back over Greenland.

With a refueling over Scotland, Franks knew they could hold a pattern for maybe another five to six hours tops. But that would make them vulnerable if they got the go-ahead toward the end of that time. By then Soviet radar would know exactly who they were, where they were, plus have a very good idea what their target was.

Franks turned to the man seated directly behind him. "What have you got, Al?" the pilot asked.

Lt. Albert Cody of Parowan, Utah, stared at his offensive computer, a device able to track and list the offensive capabilities of all aircraft, seagoing vessels, and land-based platforms coming within range of the plane. "All clear, Cap," Cody responded.

"Ben?"

Lt. Benjamin Mitchell of Lander, Wyoming, sat opposite Cody looking at the screen of his defensive computer, capable of constantly updating distances to targets, weapons availability, speeds, and approaches, while continually listing alternatives for the pilot's consideration. It also held the program destination for the nuclear bombs aboard but could not arm them without the proper presidential encrypted codes. "We're tracking clear across the Baltic," Mitchell replied. "We're ready for the run any time you are."

Admiral Cummings looked at the message he had just been handed. It stated that a Russian submarine had been spotted off the coast of Japan.

"There's no question it is the same boat?" he asked.

Keith Terry nodded. "It's the same configuration. The satellite imagery is conclusive."

Cummings swore under his breath. "That can only mean *Poco* was the vessel destroyed in the explosion," he said grimly.

Admiral Rowden turned from the operational map on Cummings's wall. "Don't mark *Poco* off so quickly," he said.

Cummings shook his head in disgust. "What other explanation could there be?"

"I don't know, Admiral," Rowden said firmly. "But nobody's going to kill Crazy Tony that easily."

Vice Adm. Kendall Brighton sat back in his chair across the room and sighed. "He's only a man, Ed," he suggested softly. "You put a fish up his butt and he dies, just like anyone else."

Rowden stormed over to Cummings's desk. "*Poco*'s not sunk, sir," he insisted. "I can feel it in my bones!"

Cummings shook his head sadly. "I'm afraid I've got to go with the obvious, Ed." His voice was low and tired. "I'm going to tell T-Bone that we lost *Poco*."

Yakunin stormed into the officers' mess where Travis sat, leaning up against a bulkhead, his broken leg elevated on an adjoining chair. Four armed seamen surrounded him, watching the American intently. Had it not been for the guards, Yakunin might very well have struck the pilot, incensed over his apparent lack of regret for having killed one man and having severely wounded another.

Yakunin slammed the bulkhead behind Travis's head with his fist, causing the American to sit up, startled. "And just what had you hoped to gain?" the Russian commander demanded angrily.

Travis glanced up at the captain. He had been on the brink of dozing, sleepy from the painkillers the boat's doctor had injected in him earlier. But now he was wide awake. "I wanted to slow you down," Travis answered, misinterpreting Yakunin's question.

"And how would killing one of my men and wounding another accomplish that?"

Travis sighed. He had been wondering when the murder would be uncovered, thoroughly convinced that he would be the one accused. "Your man stabbed the guard," Travis said evenly. "He came in intending to kill me and make it look like it was me who killed the sailor."

Yakunin was taken aback. Whatever it was that he had expected the American to say, this was certainly not it. "Turbin killed Utemov?" he asked incredulously.

"The one built like a fireplug, yeah," Travis replied. "He stabbed the younger one. And he was trying to kill me when I stabbed him."

"Why would he do that?" Yakunin asked.

Travis shrugged. "I believe he was angry over my shooting down his plane."

Yakunin stared, his eyes wide with disbelief. Travis added, "Your man seems to enjoy holding a grudge."

Yakunin shook his head skeptically. Not even Turbin could be that bloodthirsty. "Who murdered whom will be decided back in Moscow," he grunted and turned toward the door.

"I have heard of Soviet justice," Travis called to the Russian's back.

Yakunin spun around angrily. "Even if Turbin wanted to kill you, he would have no reason to kill Utemov. He was just a boy, barely eighteen!" The look of pain crossed Yakunin's face.

"I'm sorry about your seaman," Travis said sincerely. "But I did not kill him. Twice I've managed to escape without injuring anyone."

"But Turbin could have ordered Utemov away!" Yakunin insisted. "He is a colonel, damnit!"

Travis's look didn't waver. "He needed a reason to kill me," he said. "With your seaman dead and the blame placed on me, he had his reason."

Yakunin shook his head emphatically. "I find that hard to believe."

"When I was brought aboard, your colonel was angry enough to threaten me," Travis insisted. "He said I would never get off this boat alive!"

Yakunin considered this. He found himself in the uncomfortable position of having to defend the KGB. "I do not want to discuss this," he said finally. "I will leave it up to Moscow." And with that he turned and stormed out the door.

"Then your colonel was right in one thing," Travis yelled after him. "I will not live in the hands of the Soviets!"

Outside in the corridor, Yakunin stopped and leaned heavily against the bulkhead. Could it be true? Was it possible that it was Turbin who had killed the boy? Could he believe an American? The enemy?"

CHAPTER THIRTY

5:28 p.m. Honolulu/0328 Hours Zulu

After a long, uneventful run, *Pocatello* entered the twenty-mile-wide, three thousand-feet-deep Friza Straits. After the *Pronin* had taken in the gertrude and continued on, *Poco* had followed the Russian's course track across the American SOSUS line, over the thirty-five-hundred-feet-deep Kuril Trench, and into the narrow canyon knifing through the island chain.

"We have to go *into* the Straits?" Jamison asked warily, seeing Soviet combatants registering all about them.

"Why not?" Bertanelli said. "We're just another Soviet submarine to them."

"You could stay outside and wait for the Russian *Mike*," Sward suggested nervously. His concern was not unfounded. No American submarine had ever penetrated the Straits before.

Bertanelli shook his head. "We're facing a mighty smart and skittish Russian captain," he answered. "Outside, he might be looking for us. But inside? Never."

"I can understand why," Jamison said, staring at the multitude of blips appearing on the ancillary screen.

"There's a reason why no U.S. boat has ever gone through here before," Sward insisted. "Pearl considers it impossible!"

A mischievous smile spread across Bertanelli's face. "I hope the Russians know that," he said.

In the sonar room, Ralston was staring at the sonar screen with his mouth open. At Submarine School he had learned about these Straits. They were known as the best-protected channel in the world.

"I think he's going to need a new pair of shorts," Caldwell said sotto voce to Zimmer while glancing at Ralston.

Zimmer chuckled nervously. Maggie, well rested from her earlier nap, smiled despite the fear that was gnawing at her insides.

Following the directional beacons mounted on the canyon walls meant to guide submerged traffic through the channel between Iturup and Urup Islands, the *Pocatello* passed two *Yankee* submarines, a *Sierra*, and an old *Echo* on picket duty. Several patrol boats of the *Purga* class roamed the surface and a radar picket of the *T 58/PGR* class was on constant surveillance with its Big Net and Knife Rest radars in continuous operation. All of them, no doubt, knew of *Pocatello*'s passage. But hearing a *Sierra* signature, they allowed the boat unmolested passage.

Caldwell whistled sharply as the screens registered a mine net across the narrowest point of the channel.

"What now?" Zimmer asked, his voice trembling slightly.

Caldwell switched on the intercom. "Sonar to control," he reported. "Mine net straight ahead. One thousand yards."

"All ahead standard." Bertanelli's voice was calm and collected.

Ralston turned an interesting shade of green.

Maggie stared transfixed at the approaching configuration. Zimmer groaned and crossed himself.

"I didn't know you were religious," Caldwell said, puzzled.

Zimmer looked up. "I'm not," he said. "But I figure it couldn't hurt."

Suddenly the net began to move, pulling back to create a small hole just wide enough for *Poco* to pass through.

Zimmer breathed in sharply and turned his eyes heavenward. "Thank you!" he whispered.

They waited, nervously watching the screen. The entire boat seemed to be holding its breath. They all knew that somewhere electronics and sonar waves were monitoring their every move. Would the mask hold up? Maggie hid her hands in her lap and crossed all her fingers.

Finally, they slid quietly past the net and into the inner channel. Five minutes later they broke out into the Okhotsk Sea.

"We're through, Captain," Caldwell announced happily, the relief evident in his voice.

"Control to weapons," Bertanelli ordered. "Ready the MOSS Caldwell worked on."

In the torpedo room, Chief Petty Officer Crippin ordered his men to slide a white MOSS torpedo into tube four. With rachets they slid it along the rack and positioned it just right for the electrical arm to lift and ram into the opened tube. A big black X had been taped to it by Caldwell to distinguish it from the other remaining white decoy nestled between the green sub-killers.

Maggie looked quizzically at Caldwell. "The MOSS has our signature," she said apprehensively. "If he fires it, the recording will expose *Pocatello*'s presence."

Caldwell smiled. "The captain asked me to fake

345

the *Sierra* signature on the MOSS recorder."

Maggie's eyes widened with admiration. "You know how to do that?"

The MOSS was a very expensive piece of equipment. Housed in a twenty-foot-long decoy torpedo, the special electronics sent out a recorded message of the submarine's signature to fool incoming torpedoes and rockets, leading them away from the boat under attack. It had also been used to fool a tracking submarine on occasion.

"There isn't a piece of electronics on this boat I haven't taken apart a time or two," Caldwell said, beaming proudly. "The MOSS wasn't that difficult. I just recorded a *Sierra* off our signature tapes and reprogrammed the MOSS electronics with it."

"It won't be the same *Sierra* they've been picking up," Maggie protested.

Caldwell chuckled. "I'm not as dumb as I look. I took a match print off your equipment and ran it through our computer. The Russian *K.E. Solovyov* is our *Sierra-17*. It'll be the same."

Maggie grinned. "You're right," she said.

"About what?"

"You're not as dumb as you look."

Zimmer laughed so hard he nearly fell off his chair.

"Weapons to control," Harmon Crippin's voice came over the intercom. "MOSS-X ready."

"Control to weapons. Arm it and flood the tube."

"Aye."

There were more nuclear plant readings than Maggie had ever seen registering on her screen. "I didn't realize this place was so busy," Maggie said quietly, in frightened awe. "There must be twenty nukes within ten miles of us."

Ralston cleared his throat. "It's the southernmost route the Russkies take out of Okhotsk," he explained from his perch behind them. The terrified shaking of his voice seemed somewhat under control, now no more than a nervous tremor. "Any further south and they run afoul of the Japanese who aren't too fond of the Soviets." He took a deep breath, his voice getting calmer the more he spoke. "Moscow has never complied with the 1945 peace treaty that ceded back to Japan everything south of us in the Kuril chain. As a result, the Nips lie in wait for violations."

"You mean Iturup was once Japanese?" Maggie asked.

Ralston nodded. "The Japanese call it Etorofu."

A mile beyond the signal beacon signifying Urup's most southern tip, Bertanelli ordered the outer door opened on tube four and the MOSS launched. *Pocatello* lurched as the decoy cleared the tube, clanking noisily.

"Activate the MOSS, Marv," the captain ordered.

Ashton pushed a button on his weapons console. "MOSS activated," he announced.

"All ahead stop. Left full rudder."

"All stop, aye. Left full rudder, aye."

"Helm, slowly fill our ballast tanks. I want negative buoyancy."

"Negative buoyancy, aye."

Pocatello glided silently away from the MOSS track, dropping quietly in a downward spiral.

Bertanelli watched the instrument readings intently. "Steer the MOSS onto course zero five five," he ordered.

"Zero five five, aye."

"How much bottom do we have?"

"Two thousand eighty-five feet."

Pocatello turned between two of the four major seamounts that curved south, just west of Urup's shelf. To the south was the Kuril Basin and to the north, the Okhotsk Abyssal Plain. It was a perfect place to hide. In low by the seamounts, the three-hundred-sixty-foot submarine would be hard to distinguish from the clutter echoes of the mountains.

"MOSS-X running true," Ashton announced.

Bertanelli nodded. "That ought to fool whoever is tracking incoming boats," he said with a smile. "They'll think *Pronin* is continuing on course for Preznev. By the time they figure it all out, our mission here will be finished. One way or the other."

Jamison groaned. "Did you have to add that last part?" he asked.

CHAPTER THIRTY-ONE

9:53 p.m. Honolulu/0753 Hours Zulu

Suslov slid quickly along the Japan Trench at just over two thousand feet, far below any monitoring devices in the area. But five hours earlier, it had passed over the American SOSUS—sonar surveillance system—line that runs from Japan north to Kamchatka, around Mednyj Island to Saint Lawrence Island, then north through the Bering Strait. Anchored along the ocean floor, the array of interconnected hydrophone sensors with their own signal processors to presort data, continually fed Kapalama with the movement of Soviet submarines in and out of the Okhotsk Sea.

The *Mike* boat was the only one of its class to cross over the SOSUS in the past three days. Because of this, the information was passed on to Vice Adm. Edwin Rowden who, in turn, brought it to the attention of Adm. Bryan Cummings who alerted Adm. William T. Blanchard. An emergency meeting was called with Vice Adm. Jenkins Brawley, Commander, Naval Air Force, U.S. Pacific Fleet. He, in turn, put in a call to NAF Tactical Air at Guam, and Rear Adm. Austin McGuyver, Commander, Rapid Deployment Naval Force, who coordinated the land

and air deployment in the western Pacific.

By the time *Suslov* was passing to the east of Hokkaido Island, two Orion PC-3s were dropping three-foot-long, five-and-a-half-inch-wide sonobuoys into the water. As each cannister hit the air, wind flaps caught and pulled off its top, and a small parachute emerged. Upon splashdown, the electronics separated from the housing and descended into the ocean. Powered by sealed sea batteries, the RF transmitter gathered data from directional and omnidirectional hydrophones, sorted it through its own microprocessor, and sent the radio signals aloft to the Orions's linked computers.

Within thirty minutes, the Orions were joined by two LAMPS Mark III helicopters from *Nimitz*, now off the northeastern coast of Hokkaido. Dipping cable-dragging active sonar suites into the ocean, the ASW helicopters flew in crisscrossing patterns searching for the *Suslov*. An hour later, two surface ships, the *Knox*-class frigate *Kirk*, and the *Brooke*-class guided missile frigate, *Talbot*, from the *Nimitz* battle group joined the hunt, trolling with hydrophone arrays.

It was only a matter of time before *Suslov* would be located.

The war room at Pearl was ablaze with activity. Nearly the entire register of Honolulu's top-ranking naval officers were present. Junior officers felt intimidated by all the brass, and non-coms on the monitors and electronic equipment could hardly wait to be relieved so they could spread the news to those outside. Within twenty-four hours, all of Honolulu would be aware that something very important was taking place in the Pacific.

"When we find it," Vice Admiral Brawley said gruffly, staring at the probable locations of the combatants on the big board, "just what are we planning to do with it?"

Blanchard glanced at Cummings, then looked at Brawley. "We're going to sink the bastard!" he announced.

Brawley snapped his head back, stunned. "Sink him?" he asked incredulously. "Sink him? Just like that?"

Blanchard nodded.

"But the whole world will know!" Brawley protested.

Blanchard stared at the admiral, his features rock-hard. "We have two six-eight-eight boats on their way," he said. "All you need to do is tie up the *Mike* until *Helena* and *Phoenix* reach the scene."

"What's so almighty important about this one boat?" Brawley sputtered, regarding the others with obvious skepticism.

"If it reaches a Soviet port," Cummings cut in, "we could lose the entire Pacific."

Brawley laughed. "Oh, yeah, right," he roared.

The others looked at him seriously. Brawley's laughter abruptly died in his throat when he realized they were not just pulling his leg.

Aboard the *Nimitz*, Commodore Thames and his XO, Carlton Payne were standing in the situation room below decks. Radar and sonar feeds lit up several electronic panels, tracking combatants across a large glass wall, with updates every fifteen seconds. Messages were continually passing between the carrier and the intercept mission on the lookout for *Suslov*.

"We'll have *Phoenix* and *Helena* in the area shortly," Thames said quietly, glancing at the indicators on the wall.

"When we find it, what?" the executive officer inquired.

Thames glanced at a wadded paper in his hand. He gave it to Payne, who read it over quickly, then looked at his commanding officer. "This verified?" he asked.

Thames nodded. "We find him, we sink him."

At Pearl, Admiral Rowden rushed into the war room, nearly out of breath. "Bill," he said, panting, "I think you ought to see this." With a trembling hand he passed Blanchard an encrypted message.

The admiral read over the brief report, then glanced up at Rowden quizzically. "So? *Sierra-seventeen* passed over the SOSUS heading toward the Friza Straits four hours ago? That's supposed to be earth-shattering news?"

"*Sierra-seventeen* was identified nineteen hours ago off Point Navarin!" Rowden said excitedly.

"But that's sixteen hundred miles to the north."

"Exactly."

Blanchard narrowed his eyes, studying the younger man. Finally he shook his head. "I'm not following you, Ed."

"*Sierra-seventeen* can't be in two places at the same time!"

Blanchard clicked his tongue against the roof of his mouth in annoyance. "Obviously somebody's signature ID is off. Probably the one on the SOSUS line. Those hydrophones don't last forever."

"What if both IDs are correct?" Rowden suggested.

Blanchard hesitated. "That would mean—"

"That the *Pocatello* has reached the mouth of Friza!" Rowden gleefully finished Blanchard's thought.

"But what about the satellite photos of the explosion just south of that carrier battle group," Cummings asked. "I thought we'd agreed it had to be *Pocatello* when the *Mike* showed up off Hokkaido."

Rowden shook his head enthusiastically. "I told you that *Poco* couldn't have been destroyed that easily. I believed then that she was still alive. I know it now!" Rowden grinned happily. Cummings nodded. But the look on Blanchard's face still indicated disbelief. "It's got to be her," Rowden insisted, "heading into Friza."

"Hell, Ed," Brawley snorted from behind them, causing the others to turn suddenly. "That'd be suicide, even if it could be done. Nobody in his right mind would make that attempt. A million tons of Soviet shipping pass through there each year, not to mention the hundreds of surface combatants and submarines."

"But Tony Bertanelli is driving *Pocatello*," Cummings explained quietly.

Brawley's entire face lit up. "Oh," he said. Brawley knew all about Crazy Tony. Nothing more needed to be said to convince him.

Rowden slapped his thigh and hooted. "Damn if he didn't pull it off! That freakin' fool will try anything! Imagine, sitting in the mouth of Friza waiting for that *Mike* to pass within shooting range. I'll bet Sward needs a change of underwear about now."

Despite the seriousness of the situation, the admirals laughed. Blanchard was the first to regain control. "This changes everything," he said. "Call off the LAMPS with their active sonar. We'll dog the

353

Mike's tail until he leaves Japanese waters. That way nobody can say we did anything to him when we had the chance. When Tony gets him at Friza, everyone'll believe it was a natural disaster. After all, who'd believe an American boat was inside Friza?"

The admirals grinned, all except Brawley. His face had become a mask of concern. "All right, Bill," he said quietly. "But I don't believe even Bertanelli is going to be able to get out of this one alive."

Emelyan Yakunin had been listening to the surface ships for more than three hours. He knew they were searching for him, the dropping of sonobuoys having been monitored on his instruments. By now he believed the Americans knew where he was. He had no idea why they didn't attack, but he was sure they would eventually. And with the noise from the broken shaft bleeding through *Suslov*'s masks, hiding from the Americans was out of the question.

He sat back in his bunk and breathed deeply, feeling older than ever before, and more exhausted than he believed possible. He had been awake for more than thirty-five hours now. And though it was not the first time he had been forced to go without sleep, somehow this time was different. The pain in his chest and shoulder refused to go away, telling him the American was out there somewhere, waiting. Even if he could escape the anticipated surface assault, he would still have to elude Crazy Tony.

How can he keep finding me? Yakunin asked himself. *What do the Americans have that we don't know about?*

Yakunin had originally blamed Bertanelli for Lev Savitsky's death. But that feeling had quickly passed.

It was the briefcase that had killed his executive officer, he knew. The briefcase, a KGB colonel and a crazed *zampolit*. And, of course, a set of ridiculous orders—orders that were responsible for this no-win situation in the first place.

Thoughts of Turbin brought a tight frown to Yakunin's lips. Years of belief in the infallibility of State Security—the *Komitet Gosudarstvennoy Bezopasnosti*—had led Yakunin, like most Russians, to fear such men. And, indeed, Turbin was a man to fear. But seeing him seriously wounded had brought to Yakunin's mind an awareness of the man's mortality.

Yakunin stood and made his way aft to sick bay. As he entered, Dorofeev was changing the bandage on Turbin's shoulder wound—an ugly purplish welt, the skin surrounding it browned and blackened, with a cross-hatch of catgut suture that would, no doubt, leave an irregular scar. Dorofeev, Yakunin knew, was not the best of surgeons. Like so many doctors in the Soviet Union, he had his history of wrongful deaths usually, as in Dorofeev's case, caused by a combination of too much vodka, too little training, and inadequate equipment. Yet Yakunin knew *Suslov* was lucky to have a surgeon on board. Most boats carried only a corpsman who could do little else besides dispensing a few pills.

The oscillation of the shaft had grown progressively worse, and here in sick bay the vibration was shaking and rattling everything in sight. Bottles of pills danced along the shelves, seemingly on the verge of leaping off to their shattering deaths on the floor below.

Yakunin crossed to the patient. "How is he?" he asked.

The surgeon grunted. "He will live," he replied,

checking the KGB man's pulse.

Yakunin stared down at Turbin, who appeared to be floating somewhere between consciousness and sleep. The captain leaned down until his face was just inches from Turbin's ear. "Can you hear me, Colonel?" he said gently.

The patient's eyes fluttered open and he turned his glassy stare toward the captain. Turbin nodded very slightly, and his face contorted with pain. Soviet boats carried few medicines, especially anesthetics, and almost no post-operative painkillers. The Kremlin did not want its sailors developing a taste for drugs.

Yakunin wondered if American submarines were as ill-equipped to handle such operations as he studied the man lying before him. He shook his head in disgust.

"Tell me, Colonel," Yakunin asked. "What was it you brought aboard my boat that is so important?"

Turbin opened up his mouth to speak, but no sound escaped. Yakunin leaned over until his ear was almost touching the KGB man's lips.

"The . . . briefcase . . . Where?" Turbin's voice was a rasping, pained whisper.

Yakunin stared into the colonel's eyes. The sub commander had opened the case in his cabin. But though he spoke flawless English, reading it was not one of his talents. "It is safe," he said.

"Bring . . . it . . ." Turbin whispered.

Yakunin turned to the doctor, who shook his head grimly. "He is not strong," Dorofeev said.

Yakunin turned back to the immobile secret policeman. "I must know what is in that briefcase," he demanded, his eyes burning with intensity. "It has already killed two men!"

"Top . . . secret . . ." Turbin rasped.

"It is placing my boat in jeopardy!" Yakunin insisted. "Tell me!"

Turbin's eyes closed, as if the effort to talk had exhausted him.

Images of Lev Savitsky danced inside Yakunin's head. He saw his friend struggling to close the hatch, being washed away into the raging Pacific, being blown to pieces by the torpedo explosions. His blood boiling with rage, Yakunin reached down and shook the colonel roughly. "Wake up!" he yelled. "How did Utemov die?"

The KGB man grimaced in agony. "Comrade Captain!" Dorofeev protested.

"Be quiet!" Yakunin snapped. He shook the patient again. "Tell me, Colonel! How did Utemov die?"

Turbin opened his eyes. His mouth moved slowly, with great effort. "The . . . American . . ." he whispered hoarsely.

"Where did he get the knife?" Yakunin demanded. "He was thoroughly searched. He had nothing. Where did he get the knife?"

Turbin grimaced. "From . . . seaman . . ."

"It was not a Russian knife!" Yakunin shouted angrily.

"Comrade Captain," the doctor insisted, pulling the commander away. "Please!"

It suddenly occurred to the captain that the American had been telling the truth. Turbin had brought the knife aboard. It had been Turbin all along.

Yakunin stood up ramrod straight. He glared at the wounded KGB man with undisguised hatred. "It was you who killed Utemov," the captain said quietly. "Was it not, Colonel?"

Turbin was silent.

Yakunin leaned down once more, his face just above Turbin's own. "And then you tried to kill the American," the captain whispered accusingly. "You tried . . . but you failed!"

The colonel's eyelids shot open and he glared at Yakunin. The captain felt his blood chill as Turbin's hate-filled stare bored its way into his brain. "He will die!" the wounded man hissed with surprising strength. His menacing look intensified. "And you will die too . . . Captain!"

Yakunin took a stunned step backward. He started to reply, but no words came. The commander felt himself riveted to the spot. Several seconds passed. Then Yakunin spun around and stormed out of sick bay.

When the captain was gone, Col. Vladimir Turbin closed his eyes once more. Despite the pain, his entire face relaxed. The corners of his mouth curved upward with the hint of a smile.

In a warehouse-sized cement bunker about half-way between Malka and Petropavlovsk in Kamchatka, an encrypting technician glanced at a satellite photo coming in over the AMSAS line. The IRAT satellite, measuring magnetic anomalies, had registered a disturbance in the Kuril Basin. Normally, this would not be any cause for concern, except the "disturbance" had not moved for several passes of the satellite. At first the technician believed it to be an old, sunken vessel, perhaps left over from the Russo-Japanese war earlier in the century.

With the unbounded curiosity of a new recruit—which is what he was—the technician ran the information through the computer, calling up grid patterns over the past several days. When the fourth overlay fell into place, he realized he had found something important. Without delay, he called for his section chief.

Halfway around the world, a specialist at Fort Meade was studying the same input feed from an American surveillance satellite monitoring the Okhotsk Sea. Picked up on the Cobra Dane network and funneled to Kapalama, and from there to Maryland, the magnetic disturbance had escaped detection until a standard computer check kicked out the image.

An hour later the information was in the hands of Admiral Blanchard.

"It can't be," the admiral said, staring at the photo with its overlay tracks printed at time intervals. "Not even Crazy Tony would dare go *through* the Straits."

Admiral Rowden, who had also been summoned, looked at the photo in Blanchard's hands and smiled. "Damned if he didn't," he said. "There's no other explanation."

"There'd be no reason for the Soviets to position a sub there," Blanchard agreed. "But if it is Bertanelli, he can't remain hidden forever. The Soviets have satellite images, too."

CHAPTER THIRTY-TWO

10:35 p.m. Honolulu/0835 Hours Zulu

"Mr. President," Premier Ognev said angrily into the telephone. "Your planes are just minutes away from violating Soviet air space! If you do not recall them, we will consider it an act of war!"

Hilde Galbraith covered the mouthpiece of her extension with her palm. "He sounds more confident, sir," she reported to the president. "Whatever was bothering him earlier seems to have been settled."

Freeman nodded. He glanced around the room, frowning. Then he spoke firmly into his own telephone. "Your planes are heading into American air space as well, Mr. Chairman. You withdraw yours and I will withdraw mine."

"You sent your planes up first!" Ognev reminded him. "You should withdraw first!"

"One moment please, Mr. Chairman," Freeman said, breaking the connection. He looked across at General Shriner.

"Well?" the president asked.

The general shook his head. "We have not been able to contact *Pocatello*, sir," he answered. "But we are certain the Russian *Mike* we are tracking is the same one Bertanelli was after."

Freeman raised his eyebrows. "The one that has the documents?" he said.

Shriner nodded. The president turned to General Dadow. "Where are our planes?" he asked.

Dadow looked at the screen behind them that was tracking the American flights directly from the Situation Board in the Pentagon. "The closest ones are already circling just outside the target runs, sir," he reported. "The farthest are two hours away from Point Alpha."

Colin Freeman glanced around the table. The tension in the room was electric. He felt the sweat rolling down his back, between his shoulder blades. It had been a very long day, and it was far from over. The president knew that everything might depend on what was said in the next minute. He re-established the telephone connection. "Mr. Chairman," he began softly, "I will authorize the recall of our bombers, provided you do so as well."

There was a lengthy pause as Ognev conferred with his advisors. Finally, the premier came back on the line. "What about your *Nimitz* battle group?" he demanded.

Freeman glanced at Shriner. "As long as you keep *Pravda* in the Pacific," the president insisted, "*Nimitz* will dog its heels."

Ognev grunted. "That hardly seems fair, Mr. President."

"Fair is for ball games, Mr. Chairman. We are not playing a game here."

In Moscow, Ognev's mind was working furiously. He would not lose anything by turning back his bombers. Not even if he sent *Pravda* back into the

Oktoshk Sea. The victory would come when he had the documents, in his hands, and that, he was assured, would happen momentarily. The *Suslov* had been spotted nearing Preznev. "All right, Mr. President," the chairman said finally. "You recall your bombers. And when we see them turning back, we will recall ours as well. But *Pravda* remains at sea."

Freeman frowned. "As you wish, Mr. Chairman," he replied, then added firmly, "But understand this. As long as *Pravda* is in the Pacific, the United States will remain at DefCon Three!"

At thirty-nine thousand feet over the North Sea, flying the third leg of a holding pattern that took Group 6 over the coasts of Denmark, Finland, the U.K., and Netherlands, Captain Richard Franks cruised at six hundred and twenty miles per hour. He glanced at his gauges, glad the B-1b had been redesigned to carry more fuel. It now had a seven-thousand-mile range, and Group 6 had already refueled once in the air. Franks knew that he could remain aloft for several more hours if need be. What worried him now was the Soviet radar zeroing in on his plane. The more time spent in the air, the greater the chance enemy radar could identify even the low-flying configuration of the B-1b.

"Message coming in over Tact One," Navigator Willie Busby announced. "Code word *Adam*."

Franks looked up the word in his Day Orders. "Well, I'll be damned!" he exclaimed. "We're being recalled!"

"All right!" Gomez hooted gleefully, raising his left hand to Franks. The pilot smiled, raised his right hand and slapped Gomez's palm.

"Just another milk run," Franks said, grinning.

Gomez rolled his eyes. "Any more like this," he said, "and I'm putting in for early retirement!"

The shaft on the *Suslov* was beginning to whip dangerously out of alignment, the noise becoming almost deafening. If this continued, it would dislodge, or perhaps rip apart a bulkhead. The mounting vibration was felt throughout the boat, and was beginning to seriously fray everyone's nerves on board.

As Yakunin hurried down the corridor, still smarting from his encounter with Turbin, he passed the officers' mess. On a sudden whim he turned around and entered, crossing directly to the table where Travis still dozed, surrounded by his quartet of guards, a cup of cold coffee sitting at his elbow. Yakunin shook him gently. "Captain?" he said. "Captain?"

Travis slowly opened his eyes and looked up, surprised to see the Russian commander standing above him.

"I must know, Captain," Yakunin said quietly but firmly. "Why did you shoot down a civilian plane?"

Travis stared at him quizzically. "Orders," the American replied groggily.

"You have no idea what it carried?"

Travis shrugged. "Probably spies and traitors," he said.

"And for that you shot it down?" Yakunin asked. "A civilian plane?"

Travis glared at the Russian. "At the moment I fired," he said, "I considered it part of the Soviet Air

363

Force. I follow orders, Captain. The same as you.

"Ah yes, orders." Yakunin sighed. He motioned toward the seat opposite the American flyer. "Do you mind?" Yakunin asked. Travis nodded. The Russian sat down.

"Orders," the Russian repeated sadly. "It is the fate of officers like ourselves to be forced to carry out orders we neither understand nor agree with."

Travis straightened, shifting his elevated leg slightly. "Nobody forced me to fire, Captain," he replied defensively. "In my country, an officer does not have to carry out an order that he feels is unlawful."

Yakunin said nothing, just eyed the American meditatively, his unwavering gaze making Travis considerably uncomfortable.

"I am not here to condemn you, Captain," Yakunin said finally, breaking the silence. "Others, no doubt, with less judgment and concern, will do that after we reach port. I merely want to know what the plane carried that made you feel compelled to shoot it down. And also makes your Navy want to try and sink this boat."

Travis laughed. "If the U.S. Navy is trying to sink you, mister," he said happily, "you don't stand a chance."

"Perhaps." Yakunin stood. He crossed around the table and bent over the airman, his face just inches from Travis. "Are you not concerned about dying along with us?"

Travis's laughter caught in his throat. Thoughts of his wife, Jan, and their son, Tyson, whom they had named after the heavyweight boxer filled his brain. Shaking off the painful images, he spoke. "I am a fighter pilot, Captain," Travis said, grimly, "because

I believe in trying to keep the peace on this globe so my son can grow up in a free world. If that means I have to die to insure those freedoms for him, then so be it."

Yakunin stared at the pilot. "You are a principled man, Captain," he said.

"It is an American trait."

"I see." Despite himself, Yakunin was starting to like the man. He reminded the Russian of how his own son had been before he was contaminated by Party ideology.

Yakunin straightened. "You have a son, Captain," he said. "So do I. When I first went to sea, I did so with the belief that I could help make his world a better place to live. We are not too different at that."

"Perhaps," Travis said quietly. Slowly, unbeknown to the captain and the guards lounging lazily around the table, Travis slipped his hand into his blouse and touched the protruding butt of Turbin's *Tokarev*. In their haste to disarm him of the AK-74, it had never occurred to the Russian seamen to further search the American for other concealed weapons. Through the slight, drug-induced haze enveloping his thoughts, Travis realized that this might be his last chance to stop the *Suslov* from reaching Russia. The boat carried something vital to United States security. Travis had to act.

The American pilot suddenly cried out in pain. Yakunin moved closer to him, concerned. "Captain, are you—?"

Instantly, Travis whipped the *Tokarev* from the waistband of his trousers and aimed it at Yakunin, the barrel just inches from the Russian's face. Immediately the four guards leapt to their feet and scrambled for their weapons. "Don't move!" Travis shouted. The seamen froze.

Yakunin started to straighten up. "Don't you move either, Captain!" Travis ordered. "I mean business!"

The Russian stopped, staring intently at the American. "What do you hope to accomplish?" he asked calmly, disgusted with himself and his men for being so careless.

Travis waved his gun threateningly in Yakunin's direction. "Tell these men to get out of here!" he ordered. "Tell them! Now!"

The submarine commander shook his head sadly. He turned to the guards and spoke quietly in Russian. The seamen looked at each other, then glanced back at their captain nervously. Yakunin nodded. Slowly, reluctantly, the sailors started for the door, looking over their shoulders apprehensively at the armed American. Then they exited into the corridor.

Yakunin stared at Travis. "You are a very foolish man," he said.

"Shut up!" Travis snapped. He felt queasy. Two captains stood before him. The American blinked to bring Yakunin into better focus. "The briefcase!" the pilot shouted gruffly, beads of sweat breaking out across his forehead. "Where is it?"

"In my cabin," Yakunin lied.

"Take me to it! Now!"

The Russian looked down at Travis's damaged leg elevated on the chair in front of him. "Your leg is broken," he observed quietly. "You can hardly walk."

"I'll manage," Travis grumbled. He grasped the edge of the table with his free hand and tried to pull himself up. Despite the megadose of numbing drug that had been injected into his bloodstream, the pain was excruciating. Travis winced in agony, the gun shaking wildly in his hand. As his body began to lift up off the seat, waves of nausea swept over him. Travis felt the room spinning. He glanced down to see if the floor was still beneath him.

Yakunin saw his chance. He quickly brought his right foot up and kicked over the chair supporting Travis's broken leg. The damaged limb crashed to the floor, jarring the smashed bone ends together roughly. Travis screamed, involuntarily dropping his gun hand to his side, and sprawled across the mess table.

Yakunin charged, grabbing the American pilot by the shirt, lifting him up and throwing him roughly to the ground. Travis clung to consciousness by a thread. Every nerve-ending in his brain screamed in agony. But still he clutched Turbin's revolver.

Suddenly Felix Stelest burst into the mess accompanied by two heavily armed guards. Seeing the American lying on the floor, they raced over to him. One of the guards leaned down and wrested the weapon from Travis's grasp.

Stelest crossed to Yakunin, who stood panting over his fallen assailant. "Comrade Captain," the *michman* asked. "Are you all right?"

"Yes, Felix," he said, glaring at the pilot who lay groaning on the floor.

The guard kneeling beside Travis looked up. "Comrade Captain," he said. "This man is hurt. Shall we bring him to sick bay?"

Yakunin shook his head. "No," he replied. "We must keep him and Colonel Turbin apart." He pointed to the tabletop. "Put him here."

The second guard knelt by Travis's head and

slipped his hands under the American's arms. The first gingerly grabbed the pilot's legs near the knees. Together they lifted him slowly. Travis shrieked as the two Russian sailors carried him to the mess table and laid him across it.

"Now go get the doctor," Yakunin ordered. The first guard nodded and hurried out of the room.

The Russian commander looked down at the airman. Travis's eyes were closed and his breath was coming in short, ragged gasps. "You are a foolish, foolish man, Captain," Yakunin said sternly. "And a dangerous one as well." He turned toward the remaining guard. "Keep an eye on him," Yakunin ordered. "If he tries anything else, shoot him!" With that the Russian captain spun around and stormed out of the officers' mess, Stelest following close on his heels.

Entering the control room, Yakunin immediately crossed to the sonar screen. He could hardly believe his eyes. The two American frigates were apparently reeling in their sensors and turning away to the south.

Mezhova looked up. "The sounding has stopped, Captain," he said unnecessarily.

Yakunin just stared in amazement. He had fully expected the American vessels to begin shooting, or at least to try forcing *Suslov* to the surface. This retreat made no sense at all.

"Why are they doing that?" Mezhova asked, as if reading his captain's thoughts.

Yakunin shook his head. "I don't know, Aleksei," he replied softly. He wished Savitsky was with him. Sometimes his friend offered fresh ideas that had helped Yakunin to understand better the American mind.

Yakunin hurried over to the chart table. He ordered up charts of the southern Kuril chain. "We will turn south of Shibotsu and west into the Nemurdo Straits," he said.

Felix Stelest gasped at Yakunin's pronouncement. "But we are not supposed to use Nemurdo," he reminded the captain.

"I know, Felix," Yakunin replied. "But that American is out there. And I think he has been reading my mind. Once through the Straits, we will turn north into Okhotsk. No American would dare follow us in there!"

Stelest shook his head. He knew that if they were discovered by the Japanese, High Command would jerk their papers and send them all off to do menial labor in Magadan. The *michman* did not relish spending the rest of his life surrounded by slant-eyed Siberian women.

Yakunin glanced past Stelest to the soaked briefcase still lying on the command counter next to the aft perisocope where he had originally tossed it. He had a sudden urge to throw the damned thing overboard. In that way, he might be able to save the lives of his crew and his boat. But it would also mean his own court-martial and execution. Was he as willing to die for his convictions as the American pilot had been? Yakunin sighed. He knew he was not.

In Pen-7 at the Preznev repair yards, Captain First Rank Ilyin Kuzmich hurried to get his boat under way. The *Alfa*-class attack submarine, *Osadchy*, had just completed repairs on a new turbine. Kuzmich had originally been under orders to take his boat out to sea on what the Americans called Red Route Two, and what the Russians referred to as the Chernenko Railroad—a series of razor-sharp mountains making up a portion of the Emporer Seamount chain running between Kamchatka and Hawaii.

But just as he was casting off lines, emergency orders had been received to investigate a possible enemy submarine about ninety kilometers to the south. Traveling at over sixty kilometers per hour, *Osadchy* could be there in less than two hours.

In *Pocatello*'s sonar room, Caldwell and Maggie were busy recording a wealth of information about the Soviet Far Eastern Red Banner Fleet.

"By the time we get out of here," Caldwell observed excitedly, "we'll have every boat and ship in the Russian Navy recorded and catalogued!"

"I'm picking up something to the south," Zimmer announced.

Caldwell shook his head. "It's not our *Mike*," he said. "He'll be coming through the Straits to the east."

"I think you better take a look at this one anyway," Zimmer insisted.

Caldwell adjusted his callup. A new blip appeared, moving very slowly, its image mingling with the shelf's bottom echoes. "It's pretty fuzzy," he observed, turning up the gains to their maximum. "Can't get a tracker on it yet."

"I'm on elevation three," Zimmer said. "I think it's a *Mike* and it's making a lot more noise than it should."

Caldwell flipped to the new elevation angle. As the data fell along the waterfall of his CRT screen, the third level solidified. Caldwell let out a low whistle.

"*Mike* she is," he concurred.

The question was, which one?

At the Bekkai tracking station along the northern coast of Hokkaido, fifty kilometers north of the Nemuro Peninsula, the Japanese Third Home Guard monitored the Straits between the northern island and Russian-held Kunashiri. The station was manned twenty-four hours a day for the sole purpose of looking for Soviet infractions of the 1945 treaty.

Kota Kamiya, station supervisor, was on duty when *Suslov* began moving up the straits, hugging the ocean's bottom. Had it not been for its damaged shaft, the sub might have passed right by Kamiya unnoticed. But as it was, the submarine was easily identified, and alarms went off all over northern Hokkaido and as far away as Tokyo.

"Notify the Americans at Misawa," Kamiya told his communications operator excitedly.

The information was relayed to Misawa Air Base on the northern tip of Japan's main island of Honshu, and from there to the 6920th Electronic Security Group at Wakkanai located on Hokkaido, across the Le Parouse Straits from the Russian island of Sakhalin.

Within minutes, a CRITIC—Critical Communications System—message was sent via satellite through the Special Intelligence Communications network to Kapalama. From there the message made its way to Fort Meade, Maryland, and was dispersed immediately to National Command Authorities. The president, defense secretary, and Joint Chiefs of Staff all received the data within minutes.

General Shriner also received confirmation of the *Mike*'s passage over "Wimex's"—World Wide Military Command and Control Systems'—Honeywell 6000-series central computers. Shriner immediately understood the grave significance of the information. The Soviet submarine would *not* be passing through the Friza Straits where Bertanelli and the *Pocatello* lay in wait.

CHAPTER THIRTY-THREE

August 29-12:20 a.m. Honolulu/1020 Hours Zulu

Suslov was rapidly being shaken apart. The vibration noise was deafening as it echoed along the interior bulkheads. By now, most of the crew had stuffed cotton in their ears, and those not on duty moved as far forward as possible to try to get away from the racket.

Veli Ternovsky watched the shaft rotating at slow speed. All the rust had worked its way out, and the crack was more than halfway through the shaft. The clamp he had applied earlier was being stretched to the breaking point. If that went, the shaft would undoubtedly split. Even now the fourteen-inch solid metal tube was whipping around like a drunken sailor.

"Too damn far from the bearings," Ternovsky muttered to himself.

Had the crack appeared within a foot of the bearing housing, it would have been manageable. But three feet away was just too far for the beating it had been taking. Shaking his head, Ternovsky walked over to the engineering station and picked up a telephone.

"Yes?" Yakunin said on the other end of the line.

Ternovsky swallowed nervously. "Comrade Captain," he said, "if we don't surface and find a tow right away, the shaft will snap. And if it does, it will take a bulkhead or two with it."

"Yes. Thank you," the captain said distractedly and hung up the telephone. He knew sonar had been tracking a tug heading into the Kurils for the past twenty minutes. Perhaps they could surface and signal it with the blinker. Of course, that would mean the merchant would have to have someone on board who knew the code. And Yakunin doubted that such would be the case.

The captain started to consider the alternatives and found there were none. To be towed into Preznev would be hard to live down. Unfortunately, *Suslov* could limp no farther on her own. He turned to the helm. "Blow tanks," Yakunin ordered. "Take us up."

Bertanelli stared down at the sonar screen. "Are you sure?" he asked.

Caldwell nodded. "The signature matches, Captain."

"But coming from the south, up the Kuril Channel? What the hell is he doing *there?*"

Caldwell shrugged. "I don't know," he replied. "But that's where he is."

Bertanelli ran that fact through his mind. *Of course,* he thought suddenly. *That wily old skipper knew I'd be waiting!* "Pipe him over the speaker," the captain ordered.

Caldwell flipped a switch. Immediately the room was filled with the racket from *Suslov*'s vibrating shaft. With nothing in the water to diffuse the sound traveling at thirty-two hundred miles an hour, the noise of the shaft was being amplified nearly ten-fold by the time it reached the *Pocatello*.

"I think that cracked shaft of his is about to break," Maggie volunteered, almost shouting to be heard over the noise.

Bertanelli shook his head. "How can they stand it?" he wondered aloud. "It must be shaking them apart."

"He's going up, Captain," Zimmer announced suddenly.

The hull-popping sounds came over the speaker loud and clear.

Bertanelli smirked. "Confident, isn't he?" he asked.

Caldwell just shrugged his shoulders. "These are his waters," the sonar man replied. "He thinks he's home free."

"Well, he's in for a big surprise." Bertanelli ducked quickly back into the control room and picked up the intercom mike. "Maneuvering," he said. "I want you to bring us up to ten percent, very slowly, and as quietly as you can." He turned to the diving officer. "Right full rudder," he ordered. "Bring us on to a course of two four three degrees. Maintain this depth."

Left alone in *Suslov*'s sick bay when Major Dorofeev rushed out to tend to Travis in the officers' mess, Col. Vladimir Turbin turned to look at the door. Though still very weak, the flow of adrenaline in his body was pumping him up. He had much to do before the *Suslov* reached port.

Captain First Rank Ilyin Kuzmich watched the

minutes drag by on the bulkhead clock. He was still an hour away from station and had been fantasizing since leaving Presnev that the target sub was an American boat that he was about to destroy. But that was impossible. No American could have found his way into Okhotsk, let along through the Friza Straits.

He sighed. It was a good fantasy and helped to pass the time, but when he arrived on station, he knew he would find some old diesel boat with a broken radio and transponder.

"Comrade Captain," the sonar officer called. "The target is no longer at the designated coordinates."

In his mind's eye, Kuzmich imagined his fanciful American submarine sneaking out from the protection of the seamounts, off on some special rendezvous. Since he was south of the Straits, and not likely to run back toward all the combatants in and around Friza, that left south the only direction for him to go. His mind made up, Kuzmich ordered his boat to maintain a southerly course and wished he could get more power out of his twin liquid metal cooled reactors.

"Weapons Officer," he called forward over the intercom. "Load up all bow tubes." *After all,* he thought, *anything could happen.*

Suslov broke the surface five miles off the coast of northern Iturup, just beyond the Itu Peninsula. Lookouts scrambled up the ladder and broke the hatch. Yakunin himself climbed up to the bridge.

Less than a mile away, heading toward the island, he could see the running lights of the small tug.

A seaman carrying a light blinker climbed onto the bridge.

"Get ready," Yakunin said.

The sailor nodded obediently. "Very well, Comrade Captain."

The seaman braced himself against the coaming and positioned the blinker on the ledge.

Caldwell called into the control room. "He's on the surface!" he said excitedly. "Bearing two four two, range twenty thousand yards! Speed, two knots!"

Bertanelli studied the sonar monitor. The *Suslov* was a sitting duck. "Control to weapons," he ordered. "Load all four tubes with forty-eights."

"Aye."

Bertanelli moved to the chart table and motioned Jamison and Higgins to join him. "Opinions?" he asked.

"We hit him on the run and don't stop to look back," Higgins suggested, perspiring heavily.

Jamison shook his head vigorously. "We'd have to haul ass to Hokkaido, then hug the bottom through to the Pacific," he protested. "It'd be touch and go all the way."

Bertanelli nodded. He had been thinking the same thing. The captain glanced over to Admiral Sward who had just entered the control room. He motioned for the admiral to join them at the navigation station.

"Admiral," Bertanelli said, his tone friendly and surprisingly respectful, "I understand you spent some time out here a few years back. What are we likely to run into around Hokkaido?"

Sward's entire face lit up. Here was Bertanelli asking *him* for his opinion! *Maybe*, the admiral thought, *the man has some redeeming qualities after all!* "The Russkies have a net from Sakhalin to

377

Wakkanai," Sward told them. "No sub could get through there at any speed. And Friza and Jekatiriny can be sealed off in a moment. Your best bet would be to move east through the Nemuro Straits and into the Pacific."

Bertanelli nodded. "I figure it would take the Soviets an hour or two to know what had happened, another hour to make a decision, and one more to locate us," the captain said, offering his thoughts out loud. "By then, we could be less than an hour from Nemura." He looked at Sward. "What do you think, Admiral?"

Sward nodded. "It'll be tight."

The others glanced at the computer projected chart table. "Our biggest worry will be the shipping at Kunasir," Higgins said. "They're bound to have ASW capability there."

"If you hit the *Mike* at night and they don't get off a radio alert," Sward suggested, "it might buy you enough time."

Bertanelli had also arrived at that thought earlier. He looked around at the others. Jamison and Higgins nodded. "Then that's how we'll play it," Bertanelli said with finality. He smiled at Sward, then moved over to the ancillary screen.

"I may have been mistaken about your captain," Sward acknowledged quietly to Jamison

The XO grinned. "Tony's an enigma, Admiral," he offered by way of explanation. "He scares the hell out of me most of the time, but I'd rather sail with him than any man alive."

Sward nodded. "I am beginning to understand that a little more."

Bertanelli checked the boat's functions on the screens, then turned away. An idea was beginning to germinate in his mind. It was an idea wild even for

Crazy Tony. But the more it whirled around in his head, the more appealing it became.

"Willie, keep us on course," he ordered. "And maintain ultra quiet. I don't want that *Mike* to know we're even on the same planet with him." He started to leave the control room but then stopped. "Oh, and Willie," he said, almost as an afterthought, "ask Mr. Hamilton to step into my quarters."

The pain in Yakunin's chest and shoulder was becoming much worse. Though he rubbed at it vigorously, it refused to disappear. There was simply no way the American could have gotten into Okhotsk. But still the pain persisted.

"There is no answer, Comrade Captain," the seaman holding the blinker replied, awaiting further orders.

Yakunin watched the tug continue on its course, disgusted at the government for stupidly keeping radios off Soviet merchant ships. The same demented thinking that put limited fuel on board ships at sea had also decided radios might tempt someone to defect. He shook his head. "Try again," he ordered wearily.

Aboard the merchant tug *Vladivastok*, a smallish man in his sixties stood on the bridge. Rudolf Vasilevich Lvov had been a sea captain for thirty of his fifty-two years on the water. And he had learned that it was more prudent to mind his own business than to interfere in matters that did not include him.

He had been moving merchant ships in and out of *Kuril'sk* harbor for more years than he could remember. He knew every reef, shoal, and tide current swirling around the point and into the bay. It was a tricky business, but one he enjoyed and hoped to continue until he was no longer able to draw breath. This was the reason he ignored all matters around him but business at hand. The military, he well knew, did not like merchants getting in their way.

"What is that, Captain?" a deck hand asked, pointing seaward.

"It is nothing," the tugboat captain grumbled.

"But—"

"It is nothing!"

He had seen the blinking light five miles earlier. Only military vessels signaled like that, he knew. Usually, only military vessels knew such codes. Lvov knew them but simply did not bother to read them. It was military and he wanted no part of it. Refusing to even acknowledge the signal's existence, the old man continued to guide his tug in toward the harbor.

Lt. (j.g.) Gene Hamilton, a tall, good-looking young man with blond hair and boyish features, stopped in front of the captain's closed cabin door. This was his first voyage with Crazy Tony and, in the engineering officer's opinion, the mad captain had well lived up to his nickname. But despite the nervous fear that kept crowding in around Hamilton due to pressures from outside the hull, the young officer was beginning to find he liked submarines. Transferred from the Marines, Hamilton had decided to try submarines just for the hell of it. He had excelled in Naval engineering school and had always been a reckless adventurous soul, and therefore had immediately felt a kinship with Bertanelli.

He rapped soundly on the cabin door.

"Come," a voice called from the other side.

Hamilton opened the door and stepped through. The cabin was smaller than he had thought, with hardly any personal touches. A photograph of two small girls seemed to be the only thing not Navy issue. "Lieutenant Hamilton reporting as ordered, sir," he said, saluting.

Bertanelli motioned the young officer to be seated. "I have a special assignment for you," he began, folding his hands on the desk in front of him. As Bertanelli outlined what it was he had in mind, Hamilton's eyes grew wider and wider. At first the young man could not believe what he was being asked to do. But as Crazy Tony went on, Hamilton decided that the assignment was very much to his liking.

Yakunin was furious as he watched the tug disappear behind the outcropping of hills marking the end of the Peninsula. He angrily ordered the lookouts and the seaman below, and climbed down after them. "Maneuvering," he said into the intercom, "take us down."

The klaxon horns sounded and seamen turned to their assigned tasks as orders flew back and forth across the control room.

The secured line buzzed and Yakunin picked up the telephone. "Comrade Captain, I do not think it wise to submerge," Ternovsky reported on the other end. "If the shaft breaks, which I am certain it will, we would lose steerage and maneuverability. We will be better off on the surface."

And let the Americans know we are disabled? Yakunin thought disgustedly. Satellite pictures of his crippled boat would doubtlessly be beamed back to Washington. He considered that fact for a moment, then shook his head. The safety of his crew was far more important than any political statements in Moscow or Washington. "Very well, Veli," he said softly. "We will stay on the surface."

"Should I call Preznev?" Stelest asked after Yakunin had cancelled the order to dive. "They could have a tug out to us in a few hours."

Yakunin sighed. His career was down the tubes anyway, what would it matter if he brought in the *Rodina's* newest and most modern attack submarine under tow for all the world to see?

"Yes, Felix," he said. "Put in the call."

Turning away, Yakunin noticed the briefcase sitting on the counter. In a rush of anger, he seriously considered throwing it overboard.

Adm. Feliks Gugin swung away from the situation board he had been monitoring for more than thirty hours and rubbed his eyes. He had caught an occasional catnap, but most of the time he had been observing the approaching confrontation between *Pravda* and *Nimitz* as they raced toward one another. Now, however, there was a new wrinkle.

Suslov had been spotted!

And he was not in the Pacific. He had come through the Nemuro Strait. Under normal circumstances Gugin would have automatically ordered severe punishment for the captain for breaking standing orders. But the *Suslov* was safely in Okhotsk. And that was all that mattered.

Suslov's documents would be in the hands of High Command within a few short hours. Gugin could hardly contain his elation. *The Navy has come through again*, he told himself.

But what to do about *Pravda*? Gugin considered the possibilities. If left on its present course, the battle group would come abreast of the American flotilla within hours. And, until the documents were decoded and understood, American submarines still held the power in the Pacific. But not for long! He decided to recommend that *Pravda* be slowed, and its course altered, so that no confrontation with *Nimitz* would occur until they were absolutely ready. And that would be very, very soon.

Flight Commander Albert Locasta stood in the ready room looking out at the pilots of the entire Air Wing aboard *Nimitz*.

"Gentlemen," he said sternly, "first of all I would like you to know this is no drill. We are two hundred miles from a formidable Soviet carrier group that is sailing in our direction. Every indication is that they are hostile, though no air approaches have yet been instigated." He paused to let the information sink in. He knew that most of the pilots in the room were unseasoned youngsters, many with fewer than fifty hours in the air.

"We have been given the green light to mount a deterrent run on the Soviet carrier *Pravda*," Locasta continued. "It is nuclear powered, about the same size and configuration as *Nimitz*. We're going in with four sections of F-eighteens. All sections will fly at fifty feet, and each will come in from a different compass point. The approach will be timed so all eight aircraft will come over the target at five second intervals."

The pilots glanced apprehensively at one another. They all knew that the fourth section would be exposed for fifteen seconds longer than the rest—

plenty of time for enemy computer tracking to pinpoint and line up their missile platforms.

"Sir?" Capt. Manny Mercado raised his hand. Mercado was the lead pilot in the wing's number two section. He glanced at his wingman, Tony Scott. "We'd be willing to fly the fourth leg."

Locasta nodded. He had fully expected Mercado and Scott to volunteer.

"What are our orders regarding ordnance?" another pilot asked.

"You'll carry two Sparrows," the flight commander replied, "just in case you are engaged by Soviet planes. But there will be no bombing ordnance aboard. This is not an attack, but a run at the heart of their ships. We want to show them that we could sink every last one of them if we were a mind to."

The pilots looked at each other. Many smiled. Others simply nodded. It was about time, they all believed.

CHAPTER THIRTY-FOUR

1:47 a.m. Honolulu/1147 Hours Zulu

"Steady as she goes," Bertanelli commanded, keeping his eyes glued to the sonar monitor.

"Sonar to control," Caldwell reported over the intercom. "Sixteen thousand yards. Target depression/elevation, positive four degrees."

Pocatello was at the optimum shooting range.

"Take us in closer," the captain ordered. All eyes in the room focused on their commander.

"The tubes have not been flooded," Jamison reminded him quietly.

Bertanelli nodded.

"Sonar to control. Target has switched off his engines. He's dead in the water."

Bertanelli smiled. It looked as if everything was going his way. "Get Seaman Ellis up here on the double," he ordered.

Bertanelli turned and strode forcefully into the sonar room. "O'Brien," he said as soon as he cleared the doorway. Maggie looked up. "Is it possible for you to give me an *Akula* signature altered just enough so it would not register as any known submarine on the Russian's computer?"

Maggie thought for a quick moment, then nodded.

385

"Sure," she said. "I can run two parallel *Akula*s. The result would be an overlapping signature. I doubt the Russian operator would think to try and separate them."

"Put it on now," Bertanelli ordered.

"Aye."

Hurrying back into the control room, Bertanelli picked up the phone and dialed maneuvering. "Paul," he said, "I want you ready to answer bells with full power when I give the word."

"Aye," came the response.

Bertanelli turned to look at Jamison who was up on the periscope pedestal. The captain's face split into that mischievous ear-to-ear grin that Bertanelli was famous for. The executive office took one look and swore under his breath. *Damn!* he said to himself. *He's at it again!*

"Sonar to control," Caldwell radioed into the room. "Target at eight thousand yards."

Jamison was beginning to get the picture. And he did not like it. "You can't be serious," he said with exasperation.

Bertanelli's smile only widened. "Steady as she goes," he ordered.

Lt. Lyle Jefferson was as excited as he had ever been in his life. He was also scared half to death. He was flying his F/A-18C Hornet fifty feet above the ocean, at nine hundred ninety miles per hour. He was screaming over the waves below so fast, they appeared no more than a blur. He felt if he stuck out his feet, he'd be able to touch the water. Adjusting his night-vision goggles, Jefferson checked his instruments once again.

The single-seat, all-weather night attack plane was

the most modern in the Navy's arsenal. And Jefferson was the Number One pilot aboard *Nimitz*. He led Gold Section, with Lt. (j.g.) Bryan Leon as his wingman. But at this altitude, he dared not take his eyes off his instruments even for a second. Jefferson just had to take for granted that Leon was keeping up.

The Hornet's airborne self-protection jammers were operating, and Jefferson was flying well beneath the Soviets' normal radar net. If all went as planned, he and Leon would be the first to arrive over the target, buzzing the Soviet carrier from their western approach at less than one hundred feet. Within five seconds, Blue Section would arrive from the east. Five seconds later, Green Section from the north, and five seconds after that, Manny Mercado leading Red Section in from the south. In the space of fifteen seconds, eight F-18s would converge on the *Pravda*.

Aboard the *Suslov*, Aleksei Mezhova had been dozing at his sonar station. It had been a long, sleepless run and, since entering Okhotsk, there had seemed no reason to remain vigilant. The *Suslov* was home.

Suddenly a soft noise in his earphones awoke him from his half-slumber. Mezhova glanced at the screen as a large, fuzzy image suddenly appeared. The sonar officer sat bolt upright. "The devil be damned!" he said, breathing heavily. A submarine was surfacing right next to them. "Captain!" he called frantically.

"Are we broadcasting the *Akula*, O'Brien?" Bertanelli asked softly over the intercom.

"Aye," Maggie replied.

Bertanelli smiled and turned to Mavery Ellis. "All right, son," he said, clasping the young man on the shoulder. "You know what I want you to do."

The seaman looked confused. "Won't they wonder why we're not using our radio?" he asked.

"Tell them it's malfunctioning."

The lights danced in Ellis's eyes mischievously. "I'll think of something," he said, grinning.

Bertanelli grinned back. "I'm sure you will, son."

Ellis's earlier nervousness had vanished completely. It was all a game to him now. He started up the ladder, hesitated and glanced back at Bertanelli and grinned once more. Then he disappeared into the conning station.

Pocatello's sail broke the surface amid the gurgling of displaced air and water. Decks awash, the American sub slid slowly in beside the *Suslov* as the Russian bridge lookouts watched in open-mouthed amazement.

Ellis, dressed in a black turtleneck and dark pants, climbed out of the hatch and looked across at the Soviet boat. *"Izvinit'e tovarishca, u vas yest' b'eda,"* Ellis shouted confidently. "What's your trouble?"

"I don't believe it, but it . . . just . . . surfaced beside us!" Mezhova was sweating nervously. If the captain asked him how he had let anyone get past his guard . . .

Yakunin yanked the telephone off the hook. He quickly dialed up to the bridge. "What the hell is out there?"

"A submarine, Comrade Captain," a young officer answered.

"I can see that!" Yakunin bellowed angrily.

"What's it doing there?"

"They want to know if we need help, Comrade Captain. They say they're the *Lavut*, a new experimental boat."

"What does he look like?" Yakunin demanded.

"Like nothing I've ever seen."

Mezhova read the signature verification. There was no question it was a new boat. An *Akula*. "That's why I didn't hear him," he said quietly, breathing a sigh of relief. "He must be ultra quiet, or using jamming measures." He silently prayed that the captain would accept his answer.

Col. Valdimir Turbin rolled weakly off his sickbay bunk, every movement sending sharp stabs of pain through his entire body. The doctor had not yet returned from tending to the American in the officer's mess, so the stocky KGB man was alone. Though dressed from the waist down, his upper torso swathed in bandages, without a weapon, Turbin felt naked. He had passed the aft stores bin during one of his earlier investigative tours of the boat, so he knew where to get his hands on one.

Shakily, he exited from the sickbay. Shuffling along in excruciating pain, having to stop every few seconds to rest against the bulkheads, it took him fifteen minutes to maneuver the short distance to the store room. His hands shaking badly, he just managed to pick the lock with a scalpel he had pocketed.

Entering the room, Turbin's vision cleared momentarily when he saw what was inside. Rows of AK-47 submachine guns, shelves of *Tokarev* handguns and miscellaneous other weapons lined the walls.

Despite the intense pain, Turbin smiled as he reached for one of the handguns. Armed once again, he felt better, despite the fact that his movements through the boat had reopened the wound in his chest. A bright crimson stain was rapidly spreading across the bandages. But if he was fated to die on this submarine, Col. Vladimir Turbin was going to take the meddling American with him.

The second that *Pocatello* rose out of the water, Lieutenant Hamilton was already undogging the hatch at the base of the sail. He had twelve men standing behind him, all wearing dark wet suits. Each was carrying an M-16 rifle in a watertight container strapped to his back.

The door opened and sea water flooded in. When it had reached its level, about chest-high, the thirteen men waded out. As quietly as they could, they swam around the sail and to the deck of *Suslov*. Silently they started up the outside sail ladder of the Soviet boat.

On the bridge, the two lookouts were joined by the officer of the deck. "Where is he?" the officer asked.

The lookouts pointed to port. The deck officer moved to the coaming and across the short distance to *Pocatello*. Unlike earlier, the seas were now quiet and the officer was able to get a clear view of the mystery sub. "Doesn't look like anything I've ever seen," the officer said, shaking his head in awe.

"He said it's experimental," one of the lookouts informed him.

"Do you need a tow?" Ellis called in Russian across the short distance separating the subs.

"Yes," the Russian officer called back. "Can you throw us a line?"

Ellis nodded. "Stand by."

"He's tossing us a line," the deck officer called down to the control room. "It looks like our luck is holding out, Comrade Captain!"

He had no sooner replaced the microphone beneath the coaming when an arm covered by black rubber snaked around his neck and yanked him backward off the sail. The startled lookouts could only watch helplessly as four men from *Pocatello* leveled their automatic weapons at the Russians. One by one the rest of the American assault team climbed over the side and onto the bridge of the *Suslov*.

Below, Yakunin heard the noise coming from topside and looked up in time to see three men wearing glistening black wet suits drop from the ladder into the conning station. Before the captain could react, he was staring into the barrels of three M-16s. The intruders pushed their way roughly into the control room.

"N'e shevelit'e ili my strel'n'om!" one of the Americans yelled, repeating the command Ellis had taught him. "Don't move or we'll shoot!"

Four more of *Pocatello*'s sailors climbed past the others and dropped into the control room. They moved quickly to the exit hatches and sealed them. Within seconds, the control room had been cut off from the rest of the boat. By the time Yakunin realized what was happening, he was being covered by half-a-dozen automatic weapons.

A soaking wet Mavery Ellis climbed down the ladder and sauntered over to the surprised Yakunin. *"Priv'et kapitan!"* he said, smiling broadly. "You're probably wondering who we are."

Yakunin stared in disbelief at the Americans holding his boat hostage.

Ellis grinned. "Let me introduce to you some of the crew of the *U.S.S. Pocatello*," he said, still speaking Russian, his eyes sparkling. Ellis was having the time of his life. "In case you haven't noticed," he went on, "you are now prisoners of the United States Navy."

Yakunin was speechless.

Ellis laughed. "Cat got your tongue, Captain?" he asked.

Somehow Yakunin found his voice. "You are . . . Crazy Tony?" he asked tentatively.

Ellis blinked in surprise. "You know our captain?"

Yakunin just stared as Ellis translated for his crew. "You mean even the Russkies know old Tony?" Seaman Second Class Sam McAdams asked. "I'll bet they're scared spitless of him! I know I sure as hell am!"

"*Ya mastros* Mavery Archibald Ellis," Mavery said, turning back to the Russian captain.

"*Ya mastros?*" Yakunin felt his head swimming. He could not believe he had been captured by a common seaman.

"Get on with it, Ellis," Hamilton ordered irritably. "We haven't got all day!"

But Ellis was enjoying himself too much to stop now. He glanced around the control room, staring at the Russian officers and seamen. "I guess you've all been wondering why I called this little meeting," he said in Russian with a straight face. Then he burst out laughing, slapping his leg with a free hand.

"Ellis!" Hamilton hissed.

Mavery looked around at the quizzical expressions on the Russian faces. "I guess it loses something in the translation," he added.

"Ellis, will you get on with it?"

"All right, all right." He turned to Yakunin. "I believe you have something that belongs to the United States Government, Captain," Ellis said, switching back to Russian.

Yakunin involuntarily glanced at the briefcase on the command counter. Following his glance, one of the Americans picked it up and tossed it to Hamilton. The young lieutenant broke the lock and peered inside. "Holy shit!" he exclaimed, thumbing through the pages. "No wonder Pearl wanted this back!"

"Yest' kakoy-nibud' shtoby vy khot'et'e?" Yakunin asked suddenly. "What else do you want?"

"Nada kapitan," Ellis replied, smiling pleasantly. He turned to Hamilton. "That it?" he asked.

The officer nodded. He stuffed the papers back in the briefcase. "Take care of their radios," he ordered.

Yakunin watched stoically as two sailors smashed the communications gear with the butts of their M-16s. Felix Stelest moved to intervene, but the captain restrained him. Within seconds, the radio and the sonar were a shambles. Yakunin noted that none of the steering, navigating, or life-support systems had been touched. The boat's intercom was also still operable.

Yakunin looked past Ellis to Hamilton. "We have an injured American pilot on board," he said to the lieutenant in perfect English.

It took a moment for the shift in languages to register with Ellis. Then the hitherto unflappable seaman's mouth fell open.

"An American?" Hamilton asked skeptically.

Yakunin nodded. "We picked him up when we took that aboard." He motioned to the briefcase.

"Well, get him up here!"

Yakunin looked at the smashed equipment. "Perhaps I can send someone?"

Hamilton hesitated.

"Maybe it's a trap, sir," one of the sailors volunteered.

"Let's go. We've got what we came for."

Yakunin shook his head. "He is aboard," the captain insisted. "His name is Travis Romney. A captain in your air force."

Hamilton was not sure why he should believe the man. For several moments he just stared suspiciously at the Russian. Finally he nodded. "O.K., send someone," he agreed. "But don't try anything or we'll blast you all to hell!" He turned to Ellis. "Listen carefully to every word he says. I don't trust any Russian!"

Adm. Gely Stirlitz sat staring out into the night aboard *Pravda*. He had just been awakened and returned to his command bridge chair. The group, he had been informed, was now two hundred miles from *Nimitz*.

He picked up the command phone. "Captain Gohrokov," he said, "I would like to recommend we send a flight of—"

Suddenly, from out of nowhere, two dark silhouettes flashed across the bow of *Pravda*, their nearness and speed causing the admiral to jump up out of his seat. "Who the devil is buzzing us?" he yelled.

In the radar room, the operators had been slow in reacting to the blips that had appeared out of thin air on their Top Steer radar screens. Then, without warning, two more planes materialized as the first pair shot upward, kicking in their afterburners and passing through the ship's Top Knot radar net. The radar room was reduced to chaos.

On the flight bridge, Captain Gohrokov dropped

the phone. He rushed to the windows just as the second two planes streaked across the deck from the east. His voice caught in his throat. He turned to the communications officer on the bridge and croaked, "What the hell is happening?"

Ten thousand feet above *Pravda*, Lyle Jefferson was laughing so hard, the tears were impairing his ability to see the images on his radar scope. Turning the plane over and rolling, he came back on a heading toward *Nimitz*, knowing the other sections were now flashing across *Pravda*'s deck just as he had done.

In the command center, the fire direction supervisor was screaming into the phone to the bridge as Captain Gohrokov fought hard to remain under control. "Two more planes approaching from the south," the FDS yelled excitedly. "Do we fire?"

"Do you have a lock on?"

"*Nyet.*"

"Then what are you going to hit?"

"I . . . I don't know," the supervisor sputtered.

"Do not fire!" Gohrokov shouted at his sadly inexperienced crew. Obviously the Americans were only sending a message. And a damned embarrassing one at that.

In *Pravda*'s flight center, the flight director, Boris Koselov's face was turning a blazing fire-engine red as he screamed to his pilots to get their fighters airborne. Just then the last of the F-18s buzzed the aft deck, turning up into a steep climb as soon as it was done. It was the only flight *Pravda*'s Owl Screen or Bass Tilt fire control radars had been able to lock on to. But no fire order was given. Had it been a real attack, it was doubtful the super carrier's 96 SA-N-3, or 60 SA-N-4 SAM missiles, or the six twin 76mm guns or twelve 30mm Gatling mounts would have still been operative after six direct hits from the previous three sections. Nor would *Pravda* have been able to launch any of its Flanker VSTOL aircraft because of the extensive damage that would have been done the decks.

On the command bridge, Admiral Stirlitz understood that fact all too well. He had effectively been put out of commission by the Americans—albeit hypothetically—and he was fit to be tied. He picked up the phone again and screamed into the receiver. He wanted answers, and he wanted them fast.

Maggie watched her monitoring screen intently. Something was moving very fast in their general direction. "I'm picking up submerged emissions," she said nervously.

"Nothing strange about that around here," Caldwell remarked.

Zimmer's mouth dropped and his throat suddenly went dry. "Holy shit, Jason," he croaked. "She's right!"

Caldwell adjusted his callup and swore fiercely. He flipped the switch on his intercom. "Sonar to control," he yelled. "We have an *Alfa* coming at us like a bat out of hell! Bearing two four one degrees! Range, fifteen miles! Speed, forty-two knots! He's making a helluva racket and doesn't care who knows it!"

In the control room Bertanelli swung around to face Jamison. "Get those men back here," he ordered. *"Now!"*

Jamison dialed in the frequency on the small docking radio.

* * *

Hamilton switched off the small radio attached to his utility belt. "You heard him, men," the young lieutenant said. "Let's move it!"

Sonarman Second Class Pedro Jaime, one of the black-garbed crew members who had taken over *Suslov*'s control room, glanced at the Russian sonar screen and was able to pick out the approaching *Alfa*. "Hell, man, we'll never make it," he announced nervously. "That sucker will be here in no time at all!"

CHAPTER THIRTY-FIVE

2:10 a.m. Honolulu/1210 Hours Zulu

"Sir?" Ellis said to Hamilton excitedly. "Tell the skipper to hold on. I've got an idea."

Hamilton hesitated, then radioed the message across to *Pocatello*. Ellis turned to Yakunin. "Tell your torpedo room to slide a couple of their fish into the tubes," the American ordered.

Yakunin bristled. *"Nyet!"* he said, shaking his head violently.

"Can it, Captain." Ellis shoved the muzzle of his M-16 into Yakunin's face and slid back the bolt. "Tell them!"

"What with? You've ruined our communications equipment.

"There's nothing wrong with your intercom system," Ellis demanded.

"Do it!"

The captain reluctantly crossed to the mike, with Mavery and his M-16 following closely behind. As Yakunin reached over to switch the speaker on, Ellis shoved the muzzle hard into the Russian's temple. "You sure that's the torpedo room?" Ellis hissed.

Yakunin's finger stopped, then moved to a different button. He glanced at Ellis, then pushed it.

"Viktor, zar'adit'e torp'edy v truby odin i tri."

"Och'en khorosho tovarishch kapitan," a voice replied over the line.

Ellis covered the instrument. "Tell him to arm them!"

"Vooruzhit'e ikh."

Aleksei Mezhova, still sitting at his sonar station, slowly edged his hand toward the impulse button in order to send a warning by bouncing a hard contact off the approaching *Alfa*. As he unobtrusively flipped the switch that powered up the active sonar and reached quickly for the button, a hand shot over his shoulder, pinning his wrist to the set.

"No, you don't!" Jaime said. He slammed his rifle butt into Mezhova's temple, knocking him onto the deck.

Ellis whirled around to see the sonar operator sprawled unconscious at his feet. "Damnit, Pedro!" he shouted. "Now who's going to home in the torpedoes?"

"I will!" Jaime replied.

"You know how to operate that?"

"I'm a sonarman, ain't I?"

By now Hamilton had a pretty good idea what Ellis had in mind. The lieutenant turned to McAdams. "Sam, you're a weapons technician," he said. "Can you operate their firing console?"

McAdams had been studying the weapons electronics ever since securing the control room. Like any technician, he was curious as to the Russians' capability in the area of his expertise. "Hell, yes!" he exclaimed confidently. "Looks like child's play."

"Get on it."

"Tovarishch kapitan," Viktor called forward. "Tubes one and three loaded and armed."

Ellis leaned down and whispered in Yakunin's ear.

"Tell him to flood the tubes and open the outer doors," the seaman ordered. "And by the way, captain, I'm the chief petty officer over torpedoes on my boat. So don't try anything funny!"

If Yakunin realized Ellis had just promoted himself, he showed no sign of it. *"Navodn'ayt'e truby i tri gotov'ats'a str'el'at',"* he said into the intercom. *"Och'en' khorosho."*

Ellis turned to Hamilton and nodded. "Okay, Pedro," the lieutenant ordered. "Do your stuff."

Jaime sat at the sonar controls and began manipulating the instruments. "Geeze, is this thing ancient," he swore under his breath. "They're probably still using transistors."

Bertanelli was in a serious quandary. Fourteen of his crew were aboard the Russian *Mike*. An *Alfa* was under full steam heading straight for them. The *Pocatello* was facing south, preparing to make a quick dash for Hokkaido, with its torpedo tubes turned away from the approaching enemy. Bertanelli knew he dared not make the slightest threatening move, or the Russian might launch his torpedos. The American boat was a tiny U.S. island in the middle of the entire Soviet Far Eastern Red Banner Fleet. They did not have a prayer.

Despite the hopelessness of the situation, Bertanelli turned to Jamison and grinned. "I love it when a plan comes together," the captain said cheerfully.

The executive officer shook his head. Sailing with Tony Bertanelli was an experience, unequaled by any other life had to offer. He only hoped they would live long enough to be able to tell his grandchildren about it.

Bertanelli picked up the intercom mike. "Control

to weapons. Load two VLS tubes."

"You planning to start World War Three?" Sward asked without rancor.

Bertanelli shrugged. "I'm open to suggestions, Admiral."

"Sonar to control," Caldwell reported. "The *Alfa* is still closing. Range ten miles. Speed, forty-four knots."

Bertanelli turned to Jamison. "Willie," he said, "get the men back on board. Tell Gene to forget everything and get back here."

Hamilton dropped the docking mike into his pocket and turned to the rest of his assault team. "Captain wants us back, *now!*"

"We've almost got it," Jaime insisted. "You ready, Sam?"

McAdams nodded.

"He said now!" Hamilton yelled.

Suddenly the aft hatchway was undogged. As the metal door started to swing open, ten M-16s turned to level on it. Captain Travis Romney was half carried into the control room by the surgeon, Fikrat Dorofeev and the Russian seaman who had been dispatched earlier. Travis looked around and saw his American rescuers. "Well, I'll be damned!" he said weakly, his face beaming.

"We *all* will be," Hamilton said, "unless we get off this tub." The lieutenant waved his weapon toward the ladder. "Can you make it?"

Travis's leg was a mess. Even with the support of the cast, it still hurt like hell to stand up. That coupled with the painkillers they had given him earlier, and the recent beating his leg had sustained, left the American shaky, to say the least. He looked like death warmed over, but his smile was genuine, and his eagerness contagious. "I'll do it," he said happily, "even if I have to crawl!"

In the aft corridor outside the control room, Colonel Turbin moved slowly along the wall. His leg wound had reopened and his chest was throbbing with every step, but he doggedly continued. Unobserved, he had watched the seaman and the doctor carry the American from the officers' mess to the control room. Though his mind was hazy and his body racked with pain, Turbin was sure of one thing: the American was going to die!

In the control room, Hamilton turned to two of his men. "Dean, Brad, give the Air Force a hand." The sailors rushed over and each grabbed one of Travis's arms, relieving the two Russians.

"Wait a minute," Travis said weakly. "This boat is carrying something that . . . that . . ."

Hamilton held up the briefcase. "You mean this?" he asked.

Travis smiled and nearly collapsed onto the strong arms that held him.

"Okay, lads, let's be on our way," Hamilton ordered.

"Wait a minute, Lieutenant," Ellis insisted. "We can't leave until we dust that *Alfa*."

"The captain said—"

"The only thing *Poco* can fire from her position is a nuke. You want that?"

Hamilton hesitated.

"We're ready, Lieutenant," McAdams called excitedly. "The sonar track is plugged in and we have a solution."

"Range, eighteen thousand yards," Jaime said. "Give or take a little. This equipment is far from accurate."

Hamilton hesitated briefly. Then he nodded. "Fire 'em and let's get the hell out of here!" he ordered, then turned to the two sailors supporting Travis. "Get him across and into sick bay. Let Pritchard take a look at him."

The two men lifted Travis and carried him over to the ladder.

Turbin struggled up the corridor. One hand rested on the heel of the handgun, the other clutched at the bandages around his chest where the blood continued to seep through. His face was masked in pain, but his eyes were sharp and clear.

In the control room, Jaime looked up and smiled. "The fish are on acoustic," he reported.

Hamilton nodded. "Okay, Ellis. Do your stuff."

Ellis turned to Yakunin. "You have a choice, Captain," he said. "You either give the order to dust that *Alfa*, or we sink your boat. Which will it be?"

Yakunin's shoulders sagged. He had lost the documents and his captive. He had been taken prisoner aboard his own submarine. High command would not even bother to ask questions. They would simply shoot him. Unless, of course, the crew could be sworn to secrecy. It would certainly be in all their best interests. But the thought of Colonel Turbin entered his mind and he knew there was no chance.

Outside the aft hatch, Turbin slid slowly along the wall. His bandages had been completely soaked through with his blood, but he paid it little mind. Limping to the undogged hatch, he peered inside, startled to see the room filled with wetsuit-clad American sailors, two of whom were starting to help his adversary up the ladder. Instinctively, Turbin understood what was happening. He pulled the handgun from his waistband and pushed his way into the control room.

Yakunin was the first to notice Turbin's entrance. The captain noted the glowering look the colonel was giving Travis. Then he saw the gun come up.

"*Nyet!*" Yakunin shouted, leaping between Turbin's gun and the American pilot just as the KGB man pulled the trigger.

At the sound of the explosion, three American sailors whirled around and brought up their M-16s.

Turbin's bullet struck Yakunin square in the chest. The impact knocked him back into the periscope pedestal. He slumped slowly to the floor as the American sailors opened fire with their M-16s.

Turbin was slammed back into the corridor bulkhead and splattered with fifty bullets before he hit the deck. One sailor poked his head into the corridor and waved the M-16 as Russian seamen ducked for cover.

"Seal off that hatch!" Hamilton ordered.

Ellis knelt beside Yakunin. Blood was streaming from the captain's chest wound. Ellis tore the white turtleneck away and pressed his hand over Yakunin's wound to stop the flow of blood. Yakunin stirred slightly. He looked up and past Ellis to Travis halfway up the ladder. "*Tovarishchi,*" he mumbled. Then his face went slack.

The surgeon dropped beside his captain and pushed Ellis's hand away. Dorofeev took one look at the wound and shook his head sadly.

"Target at six miles," Jaime announced.

"We'll never get them fired now," yelled Hamilton. "Everyone out of here!"

As the Americans moved quickly to the ladder, Ellis ran over to the intercom mike and pushed the torpedo room button. "The captain is wounded," he shouted in Russian, "and the American is closing on us. We've got to fire!"

"But—"

"*S'eychas! Prokl'anit'e vas! Str'elayt'e!*" Ellis yelled. "Now, damnit! Shoot!"

Suslov lurched backward in the water as both tubes were fired simultaneously. Ellis glanced at Hamilton and grinned. "Time to go, Lieutenant."

Hamilton nodded to the two remaining American seamen. "Up the ladder, laddies."

Ellis looked at Felix Stelest. The warrant officer was bent over Yakunin's lifeless body, tears in his eyes. He knew he would never sail for a finer man.

Ellis turned and started up the ladder. Just before disappearing into the conning station above, he looked back down at *Suslov*'s crew, a devil-may-care expression on his face. "Well, I can't say it's been great . . ." he said in fluent Russian. Then, mimicking Porky Pig, he waved slowly and added, "Th—that—that's all f-folks." He disappeared into the conning station, then flew up the sail ladder.

CHAPTER THIRTY-SIX

2:23 a.m. Honolulu/1223 Hours Zulu

"What the hell?" Caldwell's mouth dropped open in astonishment. He flipped the intercom switch. "Sonar to control," he reported. "Captain, the *Mike* just fired two acoustic torpedoes at the *Alfa*!"

Bertanelli grabbed the microphone. "What? You sure?"

"Positive ID."

Bertanelli glanced at the sonar monitor. "I'll be damned!" He swung around to Jamison. "Those men back, yet?"

The executive officer had the docking radio to his ear. "They're coming across now," he said.

"Get someone up there to help them on board." Bertanelli immediately dialed maneuvering. "Paul, I want full power the second I ask for it."

"Ready now, Skipper."

"Helm, stand by to dive."

The klaxon sounded twice as Pedro Jaime led the sailors into the aft hatch. Within seconds the Christmas Tree lights were green. "Dive the boat," Bertanelli ordered when all his crew members were aboard and his unexpected guest, the American Air Force pilot, was taken down to sickbay. "All ahead full.''

"Captain!" It was Caldwell's voice. "Torpedoes in the water! Say again, torpedoes in the water!"

Bertanelli grabbed the mike. "Where?"

"Aft. Range, six miles. Wire-guided. Speed, fifty knots."

"Helm, flank speed!" the captain shouted.

Pocatello darted forward, leaving a wake that rocked *Suslov* like a cork.

"Sonar to control," Caldwell radioed. "The outgoing torpedoes running hot and normal. Running time, six minutes, nineteen seconds."

"The hell with those!" Bertanelli yelled impatiently. "What about the incoming?"

"The *Alfa* is turning away to starboard. The wires on his fish have broken. Incoming torpedoes now acoustic. Running time seven minutes and closing."

Bertanelli dialed up weapons. "Harmon," he said, "get that last MOSS in the water, *now!*"

In the torpedo room, Crippin lent a hand himself as they slung the last MOSS into place. He flooded tube four, opened the outer door, and fired the decoy torpedo.

"Weapons to control. MOSS away."

"Ash, turn it back on our track," Bertanelli ordered.

"Turning now."

Outside, the MOSS flashed past *Pocatello*'s nose, turned to starboard, and curved back toward the incoming torpedoes.

Bertanelli watched the incoming torpedoes' progress on the screen grimly. "Activate the MOSS," he said.

Ashton pushed the arming button and the MOSS began telegraphing *Pocatello*'s noise signature.

In sonar, Caldwell turned down the gain controls

on his terminal. "Intercept time four minutes," he reported.

Maggie stared, transfixed with fear, at her CRT screen. In a mere four minutes, their ultimate fate would be determined.

Behind her, Ralston had turned chalk-white. "We fired too late," he mumbled, shaking like a leaf in a windstorm. "The incomings were already locked on. The MOSS won't do any good." His eyes, bloodshot from fear and lack of sleep, seemed to have shrunk, almost disappearing into his puffy face. "We have four minutes to live!"

Caldwell turned around with a big smile on his face. "Hell, Lieutenant. It's really not necesary to try and cheer us up."

Three miles away the incoming torpedoes followed the acoustic lock on the Alfa's computer while, five miles beyond that, the Russian boat was turning forty-five knots trying to outrun the two torpedoes dogging it.

Aboard the *Alfa*, Ilyin Kuzmich knew that his only hope was to dive deep into the Kuril Basin. If he could get the boat below the depth limit of the torpedoes, they might survive.

As soon as he passed over the basin lip, he ordered a steep-angle dive. The two Russian Mark C torpedoes followed the boat down into the stygian depths.

At thirty-two hundred feet the Mark Cs imploded from the heavy pressure, one hundred yards behind the *Alfa*. The shock wave swept the Russian boat downward, slamming it into a bottom shelf. The *Alfa*'s titanium hull took the impact just aft of the sail, caving in three feet, then bouncing back. But the hydraulic wires to the stern planes were snapped, and several trim tanks were ruptured in the process. The boat would live, but it would take a deep-sea rescue vehicle to save the crew.

Bertanelli entered the sonar room quietly. He watched as the CRT screen showed the torpedoes closing rapidly. "How about another of those famous masks of yours, O'Brien?" he asked.

Everyone turned to stare at Bertanelli. "Hell, we're not going to need a mask!" Ralston shouted, his voice pinched and shaking with fear. "In two minutes, those fish—"

The distant explosions of two torpedoes came over the bulkhead speaker.

"Outgoing," Caldwell said.

"One minute, twenty seconds on incoming," Zimmer announced.

Bertanelli glanced at O'Brien. "When the incoming explodes with the MOSS, insert another mask." His voice was firm with a confidence that somehow soothed Maggie's jangled nerves. "I want Soviet detection to think we're an old diesel, say a *Whiskey*- or *Foxtrot*-class boat."

She looked at him blankly.

"Get it ready, O'Brien," he said firmly.

"Aye, aye," she mumbled. She reached hesitantly for the masks in her disc file.

"One minute to—"

An explosion roared through the overhead speaker. Then, almost immediately, a second explosion followed. All eyes except Bertanelli's turned upward. The torpedoes had hit the MOSS only five hundred yards away.

"Now, O'Brien. The mask!"

The shock wave following the explosions rocked the boat, as a cheer went up throughout the *Pocatello*.

Maggie glanced at the captain. She inserted the mask and flipped on the acoustics.

"Make us disappear," Bertanelli ordered.

She smiled. "Aye, aye," she said loudly and saluted.

As he observed her deftly manipulating the keys in front of her terminal, Bertanelli grinned.

"Damned if I'm not beginning to change my mind about you down here."

Maggie looked up in shock. "You mean I'm becoming just one of the guys?" she asked.

Bertanelli's grin widened. "Something like that."

She beckoned him closer with her finger. When Bertanelli was beside her, Maggie motioned for him to bend down toward the screen. "What is it, O'Brien?" he asked, puzzled.

Maggie arched her neck and kissed him lightly on the lips.

Surprised, Bertanelli straightened quickly, banging his head on the console overhang. "What was that for?" he sputtered.

Maggie grinned. "I just didn't want you to forget that I'm a woman."

"Who the hell could ever forget that?"

Maggie giggled girlishly. "Now go collect your winnings," she said, then leaned back and devoted her attention to the screen in front of her.

For perhaps the first time in his entire life, Anthony Bertanelli blushed.

2:55 a.m. Honolulu/1255 Hours Zulu

Lyle Jefferson's F-18 hit the deck of *Nimitz*, was captured by the hook and slowed immediately to a stop. He was thrown heavily against his shoulder harness. The blood rushed into his eyes and for a split second the pilot nearly blacked out. Then the canopy was opened and his crew chief was staring up at him.

"Damned if we didn't do it, Chief!" Jefferson shouted happily. "Hell, we would've sunk him on the first pass!"

The chief grinned. Deck crews lived and died with their pilots. They were a team. And their team had just hypothetically knocked out the biggest Soviet aircraft carrier ever built.

4:10 a.m. Honolulu/1410 Hours Zulu

Soviet Premier Oleg Ognev was so angry froth was forming at the side of his mouth. He banged his fist repeatedly on the desk while listening to Admiral Gugin's voice on the phone.

"They claim they never had it, Comrade Chairman," Gugin insisted, having just come from direct contact with the *Suslov's michman*, Felix Stelest, now in nominal command. "Turbin came aboard, and said he had stolen documents, but in fact they learned he did not." Gugin paused, allowing Ognev's renewed ravings to peak and then subside. "Seems the KGB colonel was responsible for firing two torpedoes on a brother submarine," the admiral continued. "And when they tried to restrain him, he murdered Captain Yakunin and a seaman in a fit of rage. He, in turn, was killed by security."

Ognev could hardly speak. His mouth fell open but nothing came out for several seconds. "What am I going to tell the Americans," he croaked finally.

There was a long pause. "I don't know, Comrade Chairman," Gugin said.

Ognev slammed the phone down onto its receiver. His hands were clammy and shaking, and for the first time he truly felt his age. He reached into a drawer

and yanked out a bottle of Ulusell, a Russian copy of
the American ulcer drug. He downed half a bottle
before sitting back, wondering what he would give to
the American president as his rationale for ordering
the *Pravda* back to the Okhotsk Sea. It was a task he
seriously dreaded.

5:23 a.m. Honolulu/1523 Hours Zulu

As the *Suslov* was being towed by *Purga*—a radar
surveillance ship that had been ordered to make
contact with the disabled boat—Felix Stelest glanced
around at the faces in the control room. The crew and
officers exchanged looks. The plans, the American
submarine, the true manner of the KGB colonel's
death, all this would go with each man to his grave.
They had agreed to it in memory of their captain,
who had the respect of every crew member aboard.

Besides, each man secretly enjoyed putting something over on the KGB. And it was something the
Komitet could never discover. It was a secret worth
telling—but only to their great grandchildren. And
only on their deathbeds.

11:05 a.m. Honolulu/2105 Hours Zulu

Admiral Blanchard received the news with great
aplomb. The report had come over the SSIX naval
satellite from Bertanelli once he had reached the
Nemura Straits. The high-impact message had been
bounced off the parabolic dish and down to Pearl
receiving stations where it was played back at slow
speed and decoded. A runner had hand-delivered it to
Blanchard's office.

But while the Commander-in-Chief of Pacific received the news of Bertanelli's escape in typical stoic fashion, Cummings and Rowden whooped and hollered like fans at a college football game.

"Damn that Crazy Tony!" Cummings exclaimed. "There isn't anything he wouldn't try."

"Boarded a Soviet sub in the Okhotsk Sea," Rowden added gleefully. "And got away unscathed."

"Hell," Cummings said. "No one over there is going to admit that an American boat found its way in and out of their backyard. I'll bet they didn't even try looking for him."

"I'd love to know how they're going to explain everything away," Cummings laughed.

"Sward is going to have a hell of a time living with Tony's unprecedented victory," Blanchard added with a chuckle.

5:33 p.m. Honolulu/0333 Hours Zulu

When *Pocatello* reached the Pacific, they found *Nimitz* and her battle group waiting for them. Bertanelli was ordered to surface his boat, and amid an unusual twenty-one-gun salute, with sailors ringing every deck, *Poco* was cheered wildly for several minutes.

Bertanelli ordered everyone he could spare topside, and with Jamison and Admiral Sward representing command on the sail, *Pocatello* reveled in the applause. As the cheering continued, Bertanelli stepped into the nearly deserted sonar room.

"Hell," he said to Maggie, the room's sole occupant besides himself, "we ought to send you topside. You did as much as anyone."

She laughed, her voice pleasant and friendly. "As

413

the saying goes, captain, 'you've come a long way, baby.' But I don't think the U.S. Navy is quite ready for a woman to show up on the deck of an attack submarine at sea."

Bertanelli joined her in laughter. "I think you're right." Then the laughter subsided and their eyes locked together.

She stood and crossed over to stand beside him. Their eyes met and held for a long moment. Slowly he bent and their lips came together. The touch was electric and for a heartbeat they forgot where they were.

Just then Zimmer entered the sonar room. Seeing the two, he blushed, turned and hurried out.

Maggie looked up. "Hell of a place for romance," she said, grinning.

"On the beach," Bertanelli promised and smiled. He turned and walked out of the sonar room. Entering the control room, he began whistling loudly. Startled, the skeleton crew turned to look at their captain. No one had seen him in such a good mood in a long, long time.

ACTION ADVENTURE

SILENT WARRIORS   (1675, $3.95)
by Richard P. Henrick
The Red Star, Russia's newest, most technologically advanced submarine, outclasses anything in the U.S. fleet. But when the captain opens his sealed orders 24 hours early, he's staggered to read that he's to spearhead a massive nuclear first strike against the Americans!

THE PHOENIX ODYSSEY   (1789, $3.95)
by Richard P. Henrick
All communications to the USS *Phoenix* suddenly and mysteriously vanish. Even the urgent message from the president cancelling the War Alert is not received. In six short hours the *Phoenix* will unleash its nuclear arsenal against the Russian mainland.

COUNTERFORCE   (2013, $3.95)
Richard P. Henrick
In the silent deep, the chase is on to save a world from destruction. A single Russian Sub moves on a silent and sinister course for American shores. The men aboard the U.S.S. *Triton* must search for and destroy the Soviet killer Sub as an unsuspecting world races for the apocalypse.

EAGLE DOWN   (1644, $3.75)
by William Mason
To western eyes, the Russian Bear appears to be in hibernation — but half a world away, a plot is unfolding that will unleash its awesome, deadly power. When the Russian Bear rises up, God help the Eagle.

DAGGER   (1399, $3.50)
by William Mason
The President needs his help, but the CIA wants him dead. And for Dagger — war hero, survival expert, ladies man and mercenary extraordinaire — it will be a game played for keeps.

Available wherever paperbacks are sold, or order direct from the Publisher. Send cover price plus 50¢ per copy for mailing and handling to Zebra Books, Dept. 098 , 475 Park Avenue South, New York, N.Y. 10016. Residents of New York, New Jersey and Pennsylvania must include sales tax. DO NOT SEND CASH.